A
Dysfunctional
Legacy

An Unfulfilled Promise

LEONARD SMITH

iUniverse, Inc.
New York   Bloomington

A Dysfunctional Legacy
An Unfulfilled Promise

This is a work of fiction. All of the characters, names, incidents, organizations, and dialogue in this novel are either the products of the author's imagination or are used fictitiously.

iUniverse books may be ordered through booksellers or by contacting:

iUniverse
1663 Liberty Drive
Bloomington, IN 47403
www.iuniverse.com
1-800-Authors (1-800-288-4677)

Because of the dynamic nature of the Internet, any Web addresses or links contained in this book may have changed since publication and may no longer be valid. The views expressed in this work are solely those of the author and do not necessarily reflect the views of the publisher, and the publisher hereby disclaims any responsibility for them.

ISBN: 978-1-4502-5731-2 (sc)
ISBN: 978-1-4502-5734-3 (dj)
ISBN: 978-1-4502-5733-6 (ebook)

Printed in the United States of America

iUniverse rev. date: 09/14/2010

ESTRANGEMENT
AND ARRANGEMENT

WHILE VIEWING THE MORNING activities of his herders, Abraham felt pangs of guilt over his recent conduct. His despair and remorse over having to expel his concubine, Hagar, and son Ishmael were understandable, but he couldn't let his despondency continue his neglect of the community. The dry season had scarcely begun, but the verdant plains of the Negev near Beersheba had turned to dry stubble, which the flocks were rapidly consuming. The previous rainy season had produced abundant rainfall, which filled the wells and water basins to the brim and restored the springs of the hill country to the northwest to an abundant flow. Nevertheless, Abraham knew that conservation and irrigation procedures must start now to ensure adequate water and grazing for his abundant flocks during the remainder of the dry season. This season had also begun with above normal heat. Should this heat persist, more wells would need to be dug.

Before he could reach a conclusion on how to assign future work, he noticed a rare, animated discussion between his chief administrator, Eliezer, and lead shepherd, Salah. Work communication between the two was usually brief and quiet, enabled by knowing each other's methods of animal husbandry after years of working together.

As Abraham arose to walk toward the two men, Eliezer made a departure gesture and started to walk toward Abraham. Showing a renewed interest in the affairs of the community, Abraham exclaimed loudly, "Eliezer, what's wrong?"

"I have just finished talking with Salah about our recent losses of cattle through theft—and, surprisingly to me, through attacks by wild animals. I have discovered that these losses were caused by improper assignment of shepherds. Only a certain amount of luck and outstanding diligence by our shepherds have prevented our losses from being greater. I know that life has been trying and boring of late, but you must take greater care with the herding assignments if our community is to thrive. As it is, our financial coffers will have to be reduced noticeably to replace some of our prized breeding stock that has been stolen."

"Do you think I should give my supervisor job to someone else?" Abraham asked. "It is only vanity for me to think that I can still manage the large herds that we maintain, considering how despondent I have been."

Eliezer agreed that Abraham should relinquish his duties to Eliezer's assistant and take on a role as a general overseer. Also, Eliezer opined, he should start having more talks with the leaders of the communities. Indeed, it had probably been Abraham's infrequent contacts with his people that had led to his mismanagement of assignments.

Eliezer started to leave, but Abraham called to him, "I must talk to you about some other matters."

"What are they, my lord?"

"I hate to mention it again, but Sarah's attitudes and moods are making me miserable … so miserable that, ashamedly, I have failed to act properly as a leader. I thought my taking on more chores would make me more cheerful. But if anything, the work reminded me of happier days, which led to further despondency and neglect by me."

"Sire, may I speak frankly?"

"Yes. Please do. I doubt that there is anything you would say that would offend me, however hurtful the statement might be."

"The problem with Sarah results from dealing with her in a way that makes you a superior person overall, but unfortunately that way doesn't work well with her. We know that she has never been a strong individual when it comes to controlling her emotions. She needs someone who is both compassionate and strict at the same time. You were strong on compassion, but you let that compassion fail to guide her properly. She has slowly grown throughout her life to distrust you. For years, her awe and respect for you counteracted her distrust—a distrust that she may still not realize she has. She is probably confused over her feelings for you, as some of her reactions toward you have indicated."

"Eliezer, you have gotten to the core of my main problem in life. I have never been comfortable with reprimanding her. Actually, I don't think I know how to reprimand her. I mostly thought it best to let her tantrums go unchallenged. The few times that I challenged her tantrums in some way brought forth rather extended pouting or avoidance periods from her."

"Sire, in retrospect, your forbearance was a mistake. It would have been better to have tried and said the wrong things than just be quiet. After each tantrum that you ignored, she came to feel that you really didn't think that she was important, except possibly as a business assistant. She felt she was too insignificant to merit your guidance."

"How would you suggest that I deal with this problem now?"

"Sadly, any advice I can give you is unlikely to work. Your problem can only be solved if you recount your lack of guidance to her and ask forgiveness. Whether such an act will work, even if she says that she forgives you, is doubtful. I would suggest that you get the advice of several of the men in camp who have successful marriages. Many know of your problem—it won't be news to them."

"Eliezer, I want to give you my deepest thanks. Maybe this advice will turn my life for the better. Before you go, would you give me the latest news about Ishmael and Lot?"

For the first time, Eliezer admitted that he had instructed spies to bring regular reports on the activities of Abraham's oldest son and nephew. Both relatives continued to prosper, but were showing growing animosity toward Abraham, although Hagar always directed her hatred toward Sarah and not him.

"I suppose that I should thank you for seeking out Ishmael and Lot," Abraham said. "You should understand, nevertheless, that my lack of action to seek them out wasn't caused by my unconcern for them. I had seemingly exhausted all ruses to get Lot to return. I trusted God to spare his life. But if the horrors he must have experienced didn't turn him toward us, there was nothing I could do to change his attitude. It was clear from the direct instructions from God that I was to stay out of Ishmael's life. I took one long last look at him and Hagar before I left them in the desert, because I knew it could be the last time that I would ever see either one."

"Sire, do you mean that I should cease having others keep me informed of their actions?"

"No. Please continue what you are doing, if you like. I now realize it would be good to see where their belligerence toward me or others in our community is going."

The resumed meetings with the community leaders helped not only to lift Abraham's spirits but seemed to make the animals more content also. Their appreciation of the increased care and attention was obvious. Nonetheless, Sarah's growing aloofness didn't allow Abraham to be really happy. Surprisingly, she seemed upset when Abraham suggested that Salah teach Isaac some herding skills. Her reaction to the idea of this necessary education for someone who was to inherit his wealth was so exasperating that Abraham couldn't hold back a sharp retort.

"Sarah, how can you be so obstinate by refusing to let your son learn skills needed for his livelihood?"

"I am not rejecting the training of Isaac, except by your herders. I don't trust them to see that he is properly protected at all times."

"Sarah, that is absurd! I plan to have Salah do all of the overseeing. I have never seen a more competent shepherd in all of my life. His skills exceed any that I or Eliezer ever acquired. Isaac would be taught the simple things first and then the more difficult things as his learning progressed."

When Sarah seemed unconvinced by his argument, Abraham decided once again not to counteract her. He would let the subject of Isaac's training rest for a while. He had finally come to feel comfortable with the idea of apologizing to her for his past actions. He would wait a couple of moons and then bring up training again after his formal apology.

About two weeks later, Abraham was forced into an apology. One morning, Eliezer approached Abraham's tent in a state of agitation. "Sire, I have a request from Sarah to move her and Isaac to Hebron. She says that Isaac needs to be taught a livelihood, and she doesn't feel comfortable with the personnel or surroundings here. There are tutors more to her liking in Hebron. She also told me that she doesn't want you to accompany them to Hebron. She feels that your, hers, and Isaac's interests would be better served if she and Isaac separated from you."

Abraham stood still at the door of his tent, looking off into the distance, while not speaking a word. From the way he shifted his weight from foot to foot, Eliezer clearly felt uncomfortable with the awkward silence, but waited patiently to give Abraham ample time to recover from this shocking news—yet another tragedy in his life.

"Eliezer, what have I done with my life? Even after you warned me to apologize to her, I never found the words or the right time to utter such an apology. Despite the mercy and blessings bestowed upon me by God, it seems that my life has never been peaceful for any great length of time. And now the woman that I love is deserting me. This really hurts, because I know that at one time, she loved me."

"A thousand pardons, but her estrangement probably happened some time ago. This upset over Isaac's training is just an excuse for her leaving. And as I told you in the past, an apology probably wouldn't have worked anyway."

"Well, I feel that I must send her away with an apology—futile as it must be. There is one good thing about this dire news: she is staying with our people by choosing Hebron as her residence. Unlike Lot, she isn't headed for a place of shame and degradation."

Abraham refused Eliezer's offer to accompany him to see Sarah, asserting that he had to deliver his now vain apology alone. Sarah accepted his entrance politely, but firmly insisted that her resolve to leave was final, although she was happy that he saw fit to apologize. She readily accepted a request from him to be able to visit Isaac often—even to give him fatherly advice. Nevertheless, he was not to countermand any instructions made by Isaac's tutors.

Just as Abraham was reconciling to her terms, she launched into a tirade about how he had favored Ishmael over Isaac. Also, Sarah complained, even though Abraham had sent Ishmael away, he still showed more interest in news about Ishmael than he did about Isaac, who was dwelling with him. Abraham explained that it had been the sole idea of Eliezer to keep track of Ishmael's activities and that his primary interest in Ishmael was to learn how his belligerence toward their community was progressing. Abraham's appeal did little to assure her as she continued to list neglect after neglect by Abraham toward Isaac. Abraham finally began to wonder how he had had enough time since Isaac's birth to commit all of these neglects. He clearly saw that the rift could never be repaired and asked what he could do to help with the move and what supplies should be provided to make them comfortable in Hebron.

Diplomatically, the community stayed out of the dispute, offering no advice or pleas for reconciliation. The countenances of Sarah and Abraham were enough to tell them that any entreaties would be useless. Only Eliezer was with Abraham to say good-bye to her entourage as it left for Hebron. Affectionately, the two embraced one last time before departure. Abraham had rarely been known to cry; this time he wept almost like a child who was experiencing some great trauma in his life.

"I know that it may seem improper for your leader to weep so much," Abraham managed, "but losing the love of my life through my own fault has caused a grief that I can barely endure. I feel that I will never get another chance to kiss her."

"Sire," Eliezer offered, "may I suggest that we travel back to Bethel? There you can offer petitions and sacrifices from God's chosen spot. Not only would it help with your spiritual recovery, but the change of scenery would do you good."

"Eliezer, you may be right. I feel that I have neglected worship there ever since our move to Hebron, and now we have distanced ourselves even more by our long sojourn in the land of the Philistines."

Abraham took two other aides besides Eliezer on the trip to Bethel. As the group approached Hebron, one of the aides went ahead to tell the community that they would be passing through and weren't to be acknowledged unless necessary. If possible, the camp was to ensure that Sarah and Isaac didn't notice their passage.

*   *   *   *   *

As Abraham stood by the offering, Eliezer noticed for the first time that Abraham was starting to take on the look and movements of an old man. He had seemingly aged many years in the past few moons. The chief administrator couldn't help seeing how unique and tragic this man Abraham was. No other man he knew had such respect and admiration from those with whom he had interpersonal relations. Yet, when it came to the closest of blood relatives, Abraham seemed thoroughly incompetent in personal interaction. Almost from the beginning of his marriage to Sarah, she had been a problem to him. His first child, Ishmael, while quite talented, had led a life of disrespect to all but his parents, along with barely controlled mayhem, in the more than thirteen years that he was with the community—and this disrespect had appeared before the child could have really understood the unsure status in the community of his mother, Hagar. Then, when Abraham was blessed with the promised heir, Isaac, he clearly demonstrated that he favored Ishmael. His unabashed delight over any news about Ishmael definitely showed that Ishmael was still his favorite. While some commendation could be extended for Abraham's obedience to God through acceptance of Isaac as heir, this literal act did nothing to avoid the psychological blow Sarah endured every time she observed his attitude toward her child, the heir chosen by God.

*   *   *   *   *

The next day, after the sacrifices were finished, Abraham approached Eliezer. "I want to return to Beersheba tomorrow. I sense this tragedy will not be healed in my lifetime. Therefore, I will cease complaining about it. I understand that my complacency toward Sarah led to this estrangement. I have enjoyed so many blessings in my life that I always assumed she would be there, regardless of my actions. Such conceit obviously didn't work in this case. Nevertheless, I still have a duty to many people, and I mustn't let remorse over one neglect cause me to neglect the many. Hence, we need to get back home and ensure the safety and nurture of our communities."

"My lord, I am well pleased that you have reacted thus. I don't often express my gratitude for the gracious benefits that you bestow upon your subjects. Of course, I understand that you are able to do this because of God's blessings, which are extended to us also. Given all of the blessings, his lack of intervention with Sarah is perplexing. God must have a reason, and I believe that you have told me that you don't always understand some aspects of his way. Nonetheless, I am happy that you accept the reality of this matter, although there are no words of remorse to express properly my feeling of concern for you. Now, to practical matters: Are there any jobs to perform before we prepare for departure? Also, do you want to contact anyone in Hebron on this return trip?"

*   *   *   *   *

Abraham had hardly had time to get accustomed to the absence of Sarah before the local chieftain Abimelech arrived with several aides and servants, asking for a chance to speak with him. One of those servants was an attractive and rather young woman by the name of Keturah, whose husband had recently been slain in a border skirmish near Egypt. The camp gossip immediately declared this visit a matchmaking endeavor by Abimelech. A few gossipers had even dared to assert that the attention paid to her by Abraham on previous visits had been the last effrontery to Sarah, causing her to decide to leave Abraham.

Nonetheless, Abimelech made few casual comments to Abraham before he started to recount the growing turmoil caused by Egypt.

"My Lord Abraham, I have some disturbing news to report. The leadership within Egypt has stopped most of their internal squabbling and is starting to look outward. I am expecting an armed campaign to capture all or part of the land east of the Great Sea."

"Chief Abimelech, Egypt isn't the only area of concern, either. The Assurites are gaining strength in Shinar, and you know their desire for power and control is legendary. When we defeated the four kings during Lot's rescue, I thought that tyranny wouldn't appear again in the world around us in my lifetime. I should have known that our world has grown so large that some tyrant will always see an opportunity to grab some power and territory somewhere. Greed controls the mind of most men."

Abimelech replied with an elaborate plan to unite all of the tribes in Canaan, even to Aram, and follow up the assembling of forces with some retaliatory raids against the border areas of Egypt.

"Chief Abimelech, I don't believe that plan would be wise. We should, however, increase our training of our warriors and servants. Some years ago, when part of our community moved to Haran, we conducted extensive military exercises, but the defeat of the four kings gave us a false sense of security, resulting in a lax attitude toward conflict preparation."

Abimelech thought about the suggestion only briefly before he offered another long-winded set of reasons why some show of force was necessary to scare Egypt into refraining from attacks. Abraham suspected that his peer wasn't so much interested in intimidating Egypt as he was in acquiring more booty from there.

"Chief Abimelech, I have lived or traveled over much of the country between Shinar and Egypt—even sojourned in Egypt for a season. In all of my wanderings and encounters with rulers from those areas, I have never met with an attacking force that I couldn't overcome. Only on one occasion have I had to exert strong force to protect my family and property."

Abimelech interrupted to verify that this one occasion had been Abraham's war with the four kings.

Abraham nodded assent and continued, "I have never been directed by God to conduct an aggressive attack not connected with defense of my family. I know that many of my more distant relatives have engaged in action to thwart a prospective enemy from gaining in strength to conquer or rule. Nevertheless, that has never been my philosophy, and I am sure that my God approves of my conduct in this matter of choosing when to fight."

Abimelech seemed upset but became quiet. Abraham sensed that the proper time had arrived for the suggestion of a rest before a night of festivities. In fact, his suggestion was strong enough to convey that the subject of offensive warfare would no longer be discussed.

The attitudes of everyone attending the evening entertainment were jovial and happy. The generous supply of wines and other beverages helped to lower everyone's inhibitions. None seemed shocked by a suggestion from Keturah to dance with Abraham. More sober minds would have shown disbelief over such familiarity.

"Keturah, I don't think I can dance to your liking," Abraham said. "I believe that you should select a younger partner. I know this from the way that Eliezer has started to treat me. His actions indicate that I am feeble."

Keturah, enabled by wine, wouldn't take such a reply for granted. She asked Eliezer if that statement were true.

"Keturah, I suppose that I may be guilty as he says. Recent events seemed to have aged my lord rapidly within a few months, but a recent resolve to accept past adversities and live for the present and future has enlivened him. If you were willing to accept a less agile dancer as a partner, I believe the dance would do him good."

Keturah agreed that she could dance with a partner of any competence, adding that she was sure he still had enough agility and skill left to make the dance enjoyable. The dancing abilities of his youth would be good until he could no longer walk.

After a week of festivities to lift Abraham's spirits, Abimelech prepared to leave. As he was saying good-bye, he offered his servant Keturah to Abraham.

An awkward pause in conversation followed before Abraham replied, "I would be pleased to have her as part of our community. She is a happy and respectful woman. I am sure she will brighten my day. If she can improve my mood, my associates should have a much more pleasant place to live."

The anticipated happiness expected from her presence didn't occur immediately. While none showed open coolness toward her or Abraham, a subtle aloofness was evident from nearly all of the servants. Abraham again approached Eliezer for help with this problem.

"Sire, you tend to create complex problems with some of your personal interactions. This time, however, I believe that the solution is obvious. Keeping Keturah as a close personal servant will continue to cause resentment by those who have been your longtime helpers. The only status that will ease the resentment would be for her to be your wife. I know that you have an aversion to taking another wife as long as Sarah is alive. Am I wrong in stating that there is no specific directive from God against your marrying her, even while Sarah lives?"

"Not directly, but my affair with Hagar displeased him. However, much of that displeasure resulted from my acting on my own in trying to fulfill his promise. Nevertheless, several of my forefathers were adamant in their resolve to have only one wife."

"May I respectfully remind you that Sarah has ceased to observe most or all of the duties of a wife? I would suspect that those ancestors, confronted with a situation as this, would take another wife."

"Eliezer, I agree with you, despite my reluctance to marry Keturah. If I don't marry her, my only choice is to send her away, possibly to Hebron."

"Sire, I would advise that you act one way or the other soon. You should also consider the likelihood that Abimelech was hoping to provide you with a wife when he gave her to you. He could be offended if you assigned her a low status within the community."

Abraham's decision became evident soon after the talk with Eliezer when the two informed the community of their intent to marry. A close former servant of Sarah was dispatched to Hebron to tell her about the marriage. Because there was no likely way to keep the marriage secret from Sarah, it would be best to let her know immediately. Abraham also requested that the servant not convey any of Sarah's comments to him. He had resolved to finish out his life without her.

Shortly after their marriage, Keturah discovered that she was pregnant with her first child. All jesting remarks about his youthful virility were politely accepted. Only a few were surprised when she became pregnant with a second child soon after the weaning of the first one.

The marriage also helped to unite the forces of Abraham and Abimelech, easing some tensions about the prospects of warfare with Egypt. In fact, the border raids stopped once the united front presented a formidable challenge to the attacking Egyptian forces.

T W O

ISAAC COMES OF AGE

ONCE AGAIN ABRAHAM SETTLED into a pleasant routine, fully expecting to live out the rest of his life in peace. Only a slight tinge of regret remained in his mind over what might have been. No explicit directives from God occurred to disrupt his life until one so shocking came that he momentarily couldn't believe it. Nevertheless, his long familiarity with Melchizedek caused no doubt as to the source of the message.

"My Lord God, are you telling me that I must sacrifice my son, Isaac?"

When the reply was yes, Abraham shook to the point that he thought he would lose his balance. A host of thoughts went racing through his head. It was beyond belief that he, who had been a role model to surrounding tribes who did engage in child sacrifice, would himself engage in such practice. This act would be the ultimate in hypocrisy. Therefore, he concluded that this was possibly the final test that he must endure to achieve God's blessing. Something would be done, such as the raising of Isaac from the dead, or maybe God would provide an alternate sacrifice upon his arrival at Moriah.

The next concern would be just how he could persuade Sarah to let him have Isaac for several days without upsetting her. Unavoidably, he must insist on taking Isaac with him to the sacrifice area. Nevertheless, for the peace and comfort of the residents in Hebron, Abraham knew he had to formulate a plan that wouldn't arouse any of her suspicions. Not an easy task, considering she was highly sensitive to all of his motives. He finally decided he would have an aide request Isaac's presence in Beersheba to tour his prospective inheritance. Because Isaac hadn't been to Beersheba for a while, the extent of his inheritance had changed, and he was becoming old enough to start thinking about the scope of his goods. Abraham was starting to age; therefore, the plausibility of his death couldn't be denied—this despite the fact that he felt better than he had for years before.

Abraham and Isaac spent a few days reviewing the herds and production facilities around Beersheba. Abraham used that time to decide who should accompany him to Moriah. He quickly eliminated Eliezer from consideration because of his perceptiveness. Finally, he concluded that it would be best to take only young men with him. Fear of harm from attackers could be ignored, because this trip was a directive from God. Also, the accompaniment of the young men would appear to be a learning assignment for the sacrifice at a new area, and the omission of taking a sacrificial lamb would seem natural, because Melchizedek sacrificed in the area. Presumably, there would be a supply of lambs available there.

Eliezer and Keturah were present to see them leave on the morning of their departure.

"Husband, are you sure you have enough protection for this trip?"

"My dear, the area is quite peaceful at this time. The last reports from all of our scouts found no large group of outlaws, and there are enough of us to discourage any small group from attacking. Also, we are obviously not decked out in expensive clothing or carrying the goods of wealthy merchants. Even a large band would probably consider us unworthy of robbery."

Abraham noticed that Eliezer seemed puzzled about just why this older man was leaving with a son he seldom played with and other youths he barely knew. "Eliezer, you seem quiet. It's rare for me to go anywhere without your raising some kind of protest about not being included in the traveling band."

"Sire, I am curious why Moriah was chosen as a place of sacrifice. It was my understanding that Bethel was the holiest place for us. I know that Moriah is a place that you have generally avoided. Then suddenly, you tell us that you have been instructed to sacrifice there. I assume that you are perplexed by this command also, or you would have told us more."

"Yes, my loyal and perceptive servant, I have been given yet another command to act in a way that I don't really understand. As before, I must, however, obey this request. Any efforts to ignore God's will have always brought grief to me, while obedience has always brought blessings. Continue to be my good and faithful servant while I am gone. We should return within about a week."

As Abraham had predicted, the ride to Moriah proved uneventful. As they neared the area, he found a secluded place behind an outcrop to leave the young men and animals out of sight of the sacrificial altar. He then proceeded to the sacrifice area only with Isaac and the pack animal carrying the wood for the altar fire. The young men seemed disappointed not to be able to see the sacrifice they had been anticipating for the whole trip. Abraham informed them that this sacrifice was being performed at a very holy site, and only he had permission to take his son Isaac with him to the altar. Also, he told them, they should stay at this designated meeting point; they were not to view the sacrifice.

Upon arrival at the altar site, Abraham paused to look around, hoping to see a lamb that God might substitute for Isaac. When he saw no animal activity at all, he asked Isaac to help him build the altar and put the wood upon it. All during the building of the altar and preparing it for sacrifice, Abraham kept expecting God to intervene in some way, but nothing disturbed the serenity of him and his son at their work until the altar was ready for sacrifice.

*   *   *   *   *

Those few people who later learned of the binding of Isaac and his placement on the altar asserted that Sarah never learned of the incident. Neither did Abraham nor Isaac ever mention what must have been boundless relief when God informed Abraham that a substitute lamb was caught in a nearby thicket—a thicket that had revealed no lamb just moments before.

When Isaac immediately thereafter decided to live with relatives and friends near the well that had been revealed to spare Hagar's and Ishmael's lives, many wondered what had happened on the trip. Stranger still was Sarah's ready acceptance of Isaac's move. Because the area around the well had become a prosperous area, the ostensible reason given by Isaac was that he needed a place to thrive on his own.

Shortly after settling into his new home, Isaac received word that his mother was seriously ill. He considered informing Abraham of her illness, but decided it was best not to. Should his father attend her bedside, his presence could upset her and prevent any possible recovery.

Her death occurred a few days later. Abraham was quickly informed of it and raced to Hebron for the burial. Discussion over her final resting place would have to wait while a temporary burial site was found. Mamre no longer lived in the area, but the other chiefs were still in awe of Abraham. They tried to provide him with a free burial site, but Abraham insisted on payment for the ground. In accordance with his request, the former owner, Ephron, cleared the burial site and marked the site for consecration.

*   *   *   *   *

Ephron was a Hittite who had moved with his family into Canaan several years ago and wasn't familiar with Abraham's reputation. Hence, he was puzzled when one of his older neighbors rebuked him for his comment about Abraham always being adamant against accepting gifts, except when seriously embarrassing a fellow peer.

The criticism instantly upset Ephron, who broke the tradition of avoiding the strong reprimand of an older person. His neighbor ignored Ephron's protest and stressed that Abraham had been forgiven by his overseer, Abimelech, making criticism by anyone else to bespeak of jealousy. The neighbor concluded with the admonition that the community should feel honored by Abraham's decision to bury his family in their land.

Ephron then assumed correctly that his former property would be the final burial site for Abraham's family.

*   *   *   *   *

When Isaac asked about when and how his mother's bones would be taken back to Ur, he was displeased with his father's reply.

"Isaac, this is the land God has chosen for our descendants. The sojourn of your fathers in Ur has no continuing significance for us. With the passage of the few years since we left Ur, our interests no longer coincide with that of my brothers and your cousins."

"Father, I have heard some remarks by my mother that a superior being contacted you and also asked you to do certain things. She told me few specifics, even mentioning some things with a tinge of bitterness."

"Yes, I have had rather frequent contact with God for many years. This God guided both my and your mother's life. Although he sorely tried our faith, your mother and I remained faithful to him. When God assured your mother that she would have a child, she overcame her doubts and fears of giving birth at an advanced age. Any bitterness toward God for waiting so long to bless her was never mentioned. I sense that many people in our communities held resentment toward her because of a disposition that could be upsetting at times. I can, however, truly say that she was a good and faithful wife. Her estrangement from me late in life may well be the worst tragedy I have experienced. I also sense that you think that she didn't love you. Please know that you are wrong. I feel full confidence in saying that she loved you far more than she ever expressed to you."

With tears in his eyes, Jacob replied, "Father, you have never shown me the close attention that you gave to my brother Ishmael ... or so my mother said. What I don't understand is, why are you promising most of your inheritance to me when you have other deserving sons also?"

Abraham explained that Isaac was the heir that God had chosen. Given that selection, no other consideration would be made regarding the inheritance that Abraham would bestow. Ishmael was prospering without help of an inheritance and was to be excluded from the inheritance anyway. God had promised that Ishmael would prosper through blessings from him. Any children that Abraham had by Keturah would be given generous gifts, but the major part of Abraham's final goods belonged to Isaac.

"Father, I am pleased that at long last, we have had a serious talk. I must be returning to Lahai-roi, but I promise to keep contact with you from time to time. Perhaps an occasional meeting can ease some of the sorrow I feel from losing my mother."

*   *   *   *   *

The marriage to Keturah had been a rewarding event in Abraham's life, but the death of Sarah brought back old and unpleasant memories. Both Keturah and Eliezer seemed to notice that some cheerfulness had gone from his demeanor and tried to engage him in activities to occupy his mind. Their appraisal of his mood was somewhat accurate, but they didn't realize that Abraham had other preoccupations besides Sarah's death. The long talk with Isaac had brought to mind just how the promise to his distant progeny was to be fulfilled. Isaac was still single—a status that had to be corrected if any descendants were to thrive in the future. Nevertheless, Abraham's ideas on how that progeny should be generated had failed in the past. Isaac's marriage must be a union blessed by God. There could be no failure this time in producing an heir for God.

While thinking on how Isaac should be married, Abraham recognized the need for a retreat to Bethel to commune with God. He needed solitude, not the commotion of the camp. He again took only some young men with him; he didn't want Eliezer along, finding jobs for him to do.

Abraham's initial impression at Bethel was that the site needed some repair, but the repairs would have to wait until he had finished his communication with God. After the evening sacrifice on the first day, he retired to his tent.

"My Lord God, you blessed me with an heir, Isaac, who needs to find a wife if he is to fulfill your promise. Isaac doesn't seem to have a clear idea of the great responsibility that he must accomplish. His interests all seem to run toward living a pleasant and unfettered life. I believe that marriage will have to be forced upon him; should he decide to marry on his own, he will likely choose a wife who will make a poor mother for his children. You know that my ideas on providing an heir have not always been favorable in your sight. I plead with you to help me find a wife for him—one that you would approve. He is also at a very vulnerable time in his life. The loss of his mother seems to be affecting him even more than it does me—to my shame, I must add. Isn't now the proper time to find a wife for him? A loving wife would be a great comfort in his grief. Please heed my plea and help me."

Abraham prayed well into the night until he fell asleep. He awoke the next morning quite stiff from sleeping in a kneeling position. The young men had arisen, fed the animals, and eaten breakfast by the time Abraham managed to stumble out of his tent. They looked up from the board game that they were playing, somewhat astonished at his effort to walk. They were relieved when he assured them his condition wasn't serious. He needed only a slow morning walk to correct his equilibrium.

Because he still had no satisfactory answer from God, Abraham decided to remain for several days of entreaty if necessary. And since they would be there for a while, why not put the young men to work cleaning up Bethel? To his mind, straightening up God's place superseded playing board games. He also suspected that gambling was occurring with the games. This was an activity that he couldn't allow to continue in this holy spot.

After he was out of earshot of his companions, Abraham resumed his pleading of the past night. After a long walk, he retraced his path to camp. Although he hadn't eaten any breakfast yet, he still wasn't hungry. Nevertheless, he didn't want the young men fearing that some tragedy had befallen him.

The trip back to camp caused his mind to drift to a state of reverie over the time of his first sighting of Bethel, and the tinge of wonderment he had felt about why God had chosen this place to designate as holy. To his mind, Shechem was far more impressive and mystic than this rather ordinary-looking area. Abraham knew that many of his contemporaries were somewhat jealous and maybe a little amazed that God had chosen him as his main representative on earth. What those people didn't realize was that the blessings and honors carried with them a burdensome responsibility—a responsibility that he hadn't always performed well, causing him to receive some sorrowful discomforts. This God who blessed him and whom he honored was a being that was hard to understand—a God who now seemed to be ignoring him in a time of great need for help.

Abraham waited nearly a week before issuing a request to return home. He spent several hours each day pleading with God without response. He had a sense that God wasn't currently dissatisfied with him and was listening to his pleading, but no explicit recommendations or instructions were given to him. As the young men became more and more restive over doing chores that had grown to seem useless or extreme, Abraham concluded it was definitely time to head back. He had honored God by sacrificing at his holy site. If God hadn't answered Abraham's desire for Isaac's marriage, maybe the time for the marriage wasn't now.

Upon his return to Beersheba, Abraham resolved to wait for a message from God by showing a close interest in his daily activities. Nevertheless, try as he might, his absentmindedness was still highly evident. Long years of close association must have helped Eliezer realize that Abraham was bothered by a serious problem—one more serious than anything that Eliezer could imagine.

"Lord Abraham," Eliezer began, addressing him more formally than normal, "I know something is bothering you. Would you like to talk about it?" Abraham stood silent for a while before he agreed to discuss his problem. They both resolved to finish their chores early, so they would have much of the evening and early night to talk.

Abraham started the discussion by formally describing the trip to Moriah. He was surprised, even startled, when Eliezer told him that a few people in camp already had heard about the intended sacrifice of Isaac. When Eliezer himself had first heard of it, he considered it to be a vicious rumor. He then persuaded those who asked him about the trip not to spread the rumor any further. He even tried discreetly to find out the source of the rumor but was unsuccessful. He was disappointed at his inability to discover the source, he told Abraham, but he believed that the stopping of the rumor was more important than finding out who started it. He had made everyone swear to convey his edict on suppression of the rumor back to the person from whom they heard it.

"It seems that one of the young men who accompanied me must have started it," Abraham ventured, "because I don't think anyone else could have seen the sacrifice. I am rather sure that Isaac didn't mention it, or I would have heard about it when I attended Sarah's burial."

"Sire, that's my guess, also, but I couldn't find out enough information to be sure. Nevertheless, because the outcome of a substitute sacrifice is good, shouldn't you reveal the full reason for the trip? If you don't, there's still a danger that a garbled account will be circulated around the camp. Despite your high status in the community, people are still inclined to believe the worst about even the most noble of us."

"For now, let's do nothing. If anyone new asks you about the incident, go ahead and reveal the full story to him. If it should become obvious that many in our communities know about the matter, we can have a meeting to tell everyone else then."

After summarizing his conversations with Isaac for Eliezer, Abraham finally addressed his concerns about his son still being single and just how he should proceed in finding him a wife, while doing so according to God's will. He particularly stressed how his pleas to God had gone without a direct answer.

Eliezer asked for a break to obtain some repast while he thought on this difficult request. After several sips of a ciderlike drink, he replied, "Sire, have you considered that God believes you are qualified to make your own decision? The very fact that you have approached this thing with grave concern means that you will consider who Isaac marries quite carefully. Over the years, I have seen you grow ever more considerate, even to a fault—a point that needs no elaboration."

"Eliezer, I am not so sure. I have only recently come to regard Isaac as I should. It took serious events, such as God's call for his sacrifice and Sarah's death, to realize fully that Isaac was God's choice. I have maintained a deep desire—one that I was essentially unaware of—for Ishmael. Although God didn't directly chastise me for doubting Sarah's and my ability to have Isaac, I have to admit I also had some doubt."

"Sire, I have an idea. We know that Isaac is your heir, as chosen by God. We also know that you have spent many hours pleading for God's guidance in selecting his wife. We also know Isaac is of marrying age. Finally, let's assume that you proceed with your plan to seek that wife, and as a consequence of that search, you do make a mistake and choose an unsuitable wife. I think we can be sure that God would intervene and tell you to avoid the marriage. It is totally unbelievable to me that God will let Isaac marry an unfit bride."

"Eliezer, you do make a convincing argument. Let me think on what we have discussed for a few days. I don't see any immediate need for me to act on this marriage, or I would have been given specific instructions by now."

"Sire, I agree. Why don't we attend some festivities tonight? Your mind has been focused on so many serious problems of late. A little relaxation of mind could help clear your senses for some difficult decisions ahead."

Abraham set no specific time for the resumption of the search for Isaac's wife. Within less than a moon, however, an unexpected visit from a friend of decades ago soon started the search in earnest.

As Abraham stood talking to a shepherd about how sheep should be gathered for shearing, some riders approached from the north. Accustomed to scouting troops riding into camp at almost any time, Abraham only briefly glanced at the riders, who rode close by and stopped to dismount. As the riders dismounted, he suddenly noticed something unusual about the group that his consciousness had not detected at first. The latent realization was that one of the riders was a person who hadn't been around the camp for many years.

Taking time to pause in the conversation to look directly at the riders revealed clearly, to his great pleasure, that one of the riders was Mamre. Showing speed that rivaled that of some young men, Abraham rushed to greet, embrace, and kiss his friend of so long ago.

"Chief Mamre, I thought I would never see you again. I have heard so little about you in recent years that I almost feared that you were dead. While I am happy almost beyond bearing to see you, I must ask what brings you here. I heard many years ago that you had settled back in your old estate for the rest of your life."

"My Lord Abraham, I was contacted by some of our people still at Hebron about the growing belligerence of Egypt. I wanted to come and see for myself just what the situation is here. We have the Assurites and their actions under constant surveillance. I felt that our warriors back home could spare me from my duties in observing them for a while. Hence, I headed here after I visited your relatives in Ur, who seem to have lost nearly all contact with you.

"I have some news about them that you will want to hear. I am sad to tell you that your brother Nahor is dead, but he left twelve children—eight by his wife Milcah. His son Bethuel was our host during the stay in Ur. Bethuel's daughter Rebekah was a particularly gracious hostess. She is so kind and beautiful that he is concerned over whom she should marry. I don't propose to be a matchmaker, but I believe that she is about Isaac's age. I doubt he could find a better wife than she would be. As for the rest of the community, many of whom were born after you left, they are doing well and prospering. I told them about your communities in Canaan, but none of them seemed inclined to leave the pleasant countryside of Ur."

"Chief, I am sad to hear about my brother's death but pleased that he has much progeny to succeed him. I am certain that your trip here is not by chance. I have only recently become concerned about my son Isaac's need to find a good wife. It's my belief and hope that I should seek out Rebekah to obtain her assent to marry him. I know coming to that conclusion so soon after hearing about her may sound rash, but it isn't."

Abraham proceeded to give a brief history of his life since the two men had last met. He explained the substitute sacrifice for Isaac in graphic detail. He was aware that Mamre still had contact with tribes that conducted child sacrifices. He stressed how this incident proved that God abhorred child sacrifices.

When Abraham finished telling about Sarah's death, Mamre said, "I am also sad to hear of her death. While we never did have a close relationship, she always treated me respectfully. I am a bit sorrowful that I always tried to avoid her as much as possible. Had I seemed friendlier, maybe she would have been more open with me."

"Chief, it was probably best that you acted as you did. Sarah likely didn't like you. I grew to know her likes and dislikes and tried to keep certain acquaintances away from her. In your case, our relationship was so close that you had to interact with her at times."

The talks with Mamre lasted for several days as aspects of bygone and recent history were discussed. The festivities around the camp presented such an added burden that most of the people were glad to see Mamre ride out of camp. Realizing that most of his people were tired from working and partying, Abraham wisely waited a few days to talk to Eliezer about the trip to Ur.

"Sire, are you sure you want us to journey to Ur? Are you sure that Rebekah will make a better wife than could be found in Haran, or even Hebron?"

"Yes. I am convinced that Mamre was led by God to bring me the news about the daughter of my nephew Bethuel. Even Mamre himself suggested that she would make a good wife for Isaac."

"Then it's to Ur we go! I accept your resolve that Rebekah is the one for your son to marry, but we do have at least one problem."

"What is that?"

"We have an excellent description of Rebekah and her quality as a prospective wife. Mamre's description was so good that I can picture how she looks in my mind. Assuming that Mamre is close in his description, she is almost as pretty as Sarah was. Nevertheless, how can we ensure that our request for her acceptance of marriage can be granted? Her family has never seen Isaac, nor are you that well-known in Ur anymore."

"Eliezer, I trust that God will cause her family to favor your request; I intend for you to lead the invitation party there. I also think we should ask for some sign from God before the proposal is made."

"Sire, are you aware that you might be tempting God by asking for a sign? I am not comfortable with that approach."

"Please don't be concerned. I have pleaded with God about this marriage, as you know. And how does he answer that plea? Not with a direct answer, but by sending an old friend who I had thought I would never see again with the news of the perfect wife—at least as nearly perfect as one is likely to find. I am certain that if she is the one for Isaac, God will perform some sign to prove it."

"Just what kind of sign should I look for?"

"I am not sure. Why don't you prepare for the trip? When everything is ready to go, we can discuss this one last time and make the decision about the sign then."

Eliezer promised to assemble the goods and animals that would be needed for the trip. Proceeding under the assumption of a successful outcome, he selected a small herd of camels to carry the gifts and to provide transportation for Rebekah and her attendants for the trip back to Beersheba. Having received tacit support for the use of any resource he desired, Eliezer assigned the three best warriors to the trip. One of the three resided in Hebron and would be picked up en route. Another one was on patrol, but his prowess was so important that the start of the trip could wait until he returned from patrol.

Eliezer's activities were readily noticed not only by his close community but also by the scouts of Abimelech. The news about this activity aroused Abimelech's curiosity to the level that he had to seek out what Eliezer was doing.

"Lord Abraham, my scouts tell me you are preparing for a trip of some kind."

"Chief, I am not going anywhere. Some of my servants are preparing for a long trip back to my homeland of Ur. The purpose of this trip is to get a granddaughter of my brother Nahor to accept marriage to my son Isaac. Because I anticipate a positive response to our request, my servants are taking extra camels to provide transportation for his future wife and her attendants."

"I was aware that you had a son of marriageable age. What I don't understand is: why you are traveling so far to find him a wife. I think there are several women around here who would make him a good wife. In fact, I believe that your wife Keturah has some lovely cousins who need a good husband."

"Chief Abimelech, please pardon my response, but I am convinced that my grandniece Rebekah is the wife that God has chosen for Isaac."

A rather heated exchange developed between the two men. Abraham hadn't seen Abimelech so angry since he had first met him and misled him into thinking that Sarah was just a sister and not also his wife. Abraham argued that he was not prejudiced against surrounding neighboring tribes. After all, he wasn't choosing a wife from his own communities in this land, either. This logic helped avoid having to bring up his disdain for a marriage between his immediate family and a pagan spouse.

Abraham left the conversation not only angry but also disturbed, although his consternation was somewhat greater than his anger. He saw Abimelech stop and carry on a conversation with Eliezer for a good part of a twelfth-day. Just what Abimelech would have to say to Eliezer—a man he rarely gave more than a quick greeting—perplexed Abraham. He decided not to interrupt but to find out the nature of the conversation before Eliezer departed.

Within about a week, Abraham received word that everything was ready for the trip. "Eliezer, there are two items of interest besides the details of the trip that I must ask you about. I want to know just what Abimelech talked to you about a few days ago. It must have been important, because I don't think that I've ever seen him talk that long to you before."

"Sire, he wanted to know why we were going so far to find Isaac a wife when he had eligible close relatives of marrying age close by. He wanted me to convince you that a marriage relationship between your son and a relative of his would strengthen the governing of the tribes in Canaan for many years, maybe ensuring that Egypt would never be a threat to the land."

"What did you reply?"

"I told him that my lord was convinced that Rebekah would be Isaac's proper wife. I also told him you were resolute in your assumption about whom Isaac should marry."

"Did that convince him that further pleading wouldn't work?"

"No. He kept on bringing up reason after reason—some of which were ridiculous. After I became nearly exhausted listening to his near rant, I told him that marriages for expansion of power didn't always work. Often the offspring is weak or decides to overthrow the power of their sires. Rebekah would bring no relatives with her who would start another line of authority in this land. It was my opinion that this arrangement of marriage should bode well for the rulership of both camps."

"From what I saw, I assume that didn't upset him very much, although I wonder why not."

"Surprisingly, he seemed pleased with that statement and soon left."

"Eliezer, once again you have been a peacemaker between us and our friends or enemies. There is no way that I can express the gratitude I have for your help. Before I mention the next item, however, I must get you to swear to me that you will *not* let any of the rulers along the route of your trip to change your mind about the selection of a bride for my son. Isaac must *not* marry any of these people. Although we are joined with them in protecting this land and in trading of goods freely, we mustn't allow them to bring paganism into our camp."

"Sire, I don't fully understand, but I will swear to that oath. Nevertheless, some of our people have been allowed to marry into our neighboring tribes."

"Eliezer, that's right, but you should consider that none of the families from those marriages are living in our camp. All have been told to live with our neighbors, even when the groom was one of us. I have tried to persuade my people to avoid marrying members of the surrounding pagan tribes, but I have occasionally been unsuccessful in my persuasion. I never forbade it absolutely. Only when it comes to my immediate family do I expressly forbid marriage with pagans … but pagans are not welcome to live within our own family community."

Eliezer promised by oath for a second time not to let Isaac marry a woman from a neighboring tribe. After a short pause, Abraham addressed the second item: he wanted to know if Eliezer had thought of the sign he would expect from God when he met his nephew's family.

"My Lord Abraham, I have thought on this subject every day since we first talked about it. I am disappointed to say that I am no surer of what to expect than I was that day. Please forgive me in this matter, for I fear I have failed you in this vital assignment. Nonetheless, I can't just give some suggestion that I feel wouldn't carry proper expectations from God."

"Please don't concern yourself with this matter now. I beg of you to have faith that the proper inspiration from God will come to you when you arrive in the land of our forefathers."

"My Lord Abraham, the burden you put upon me is great. What shall I do if I don't receive a proper sign from God or if Rebekah refuses marriage? Do I take your son back to some other place so that he may find another wife?"

"No. I am convinced that Rebekah is the one. If we fail—but my faith convinces me that we will not—do not remove Isaac from his home. I will think on no other outcome but our success in this endeavor; I cannot accept any other result. Be faithful to my request and toward our God, and we will succeed."

None had ever seen Abraham so fussy about the logistics of any planned trip, especially one arranged by the trusted Eliezer. His requests for additions and subtractions of goods and animals delayed the start by two days. Just as everyone's patience had about reached its limit, Abraham pronounced everything ready to go. Only the warrior returning from the scouting trip actually thanked him for the delay, which had given him extra rest.

THREE

RETURN TO UR

T HE CLOSE FRIENDS OF the members of the marriage party gathered to hear Abraham's blessing for a safe trip and return from Ur with Isaac's bride-to-be. After a brief stop in Hebron to pick up the last member of the party, they met an eastbound caravan.

To Eliezer's delight, he quickly discovered that the caravan leader was the son of Aramus whom he and Abraham knew well from the days of the community's move from Ur many years ago. Additionally, the travel schedule pleased him. They would have an extended stop in Damascus, his boyhood home. He would have a chance to visit some old acquaintances.

On the afternoon of the departure, Abraham had ordered another contingent be put together for a trip. The acting camp leader had complained that he couldn't afford to lose any more workers for the next several days. When told that this trip would be a short one to visit Abimelech and Isaac, he withdrew his complaint. They would be close by and could return quickly if anything untoward arose.

Not unexpectedly, their arrival at Isaac's home found him engaged in games of sport with other young men of his area. Isaac's immediate surroundings showed some signs of neglect, and the herds hadn't grown much from the number given in reports Abraham had received in the past year.

Isaac politely dismissed his friends and addressed his father. "I am happy to see you, but I hope that you aren't bringing me bad news."

The implication hurt Abraham a bit, because he quickly realized that Isaac had come to expect Abraham to contact him only when there was bad news to report. "No. Isaac, I have brought good news—actually, wonderful news. I have recently heard that you have a beautiful and gracious cousin back in the family's homeland of Ur. From her description, delivered to me by an

24

old friend whom I had never expected to see again, I believe she would be an ideal wife for you. To that end, I have sent a party to ask her to be brought here to Lahai-roi to be your wife. You know that it's time for you to marry, and I don't believe that you can find a better wife than Rebekah. That's her name."

"Father, I have mixed feelings about your request for my marriage. My first feeling is that I am not ready for marriage, and I also hate to lose the freedom of my youth. The time has come, however, for me to take on a family responsibility. As I can tell from your countenance, you don't like the condition of my home; I promise that I will be more careful now that I am to be married."

"Son, I am pleased that you have received this news so well. Although none would dare say they feared your refusal of Rebekah, I am sure some doubted. But I had confidence that she was the wife for you and that God would lead you to accept her."

Abraham continued on to agree that Isaac's environment showed the signs of indifference, if not neglect. He suggested they could help him straighten and clean up the area and make it more pleasing to Rebekah's sight. Isaac should realize that even a slightly slovenly place would shock her, Abraham explained, because she had grown up in a clean and prosperous community. Nevertheless, he didn't need to worry about impressing her with riches, for numerous gifts would be delivered to her and her father, Bethuel.

Abraham only stayed with Isaac for two days, because he had to get back to Beersheba to assemble goods and materials to provide additional shelter for Rebekah's attendants. The stopover at Abimelech's delivered the message that Isaac was to marry Rebekah. Despite the risk of angering Abimelech to an extent that would make him an enemy, Abraham felt that being secretive and silent about the matter to which the other man had been emotionally attached would anger him even more. To Abraham's delight, Abimelech accepted the invitation to Rebekah's wedding politely and even blessed the future marriage while admitting that Isaac couldn't be more fortunate in finding a bride. He humbly apologized for being so stern in his condemnation of Abraham for seeking Isaac's wife in a distant land.

*　　*　　*　　*　　*

Meanwhile, Eliezer's band had started its trip to Ur. Every member expressed their condolences when they found out that this trip was the first one for the caravan leader since the death of his father, Aramus. Nonetheless, Eliezer was quite pleased when he discovered Aramus had named his son after him.

"It's true; my father thought to honor Abraham by naming me after your master's chief aide—you. He died of some disease that the physicians couldn't understand. He was quarantined during his last days, and I didn't have a chance to be with him when he departed this life. I can hardly believe that a vigorous man as he would die this way. I had always pictured him as dying from a trampling by a camel, or such like. I could never see him as frail and weak, more like a skeleton than a finely muscled man."

Eliezer spoke familiarly to his namesake. "Son, I didn't know your father closely, but my master liked him immediately from the meetings they had. I am also most honored that he would choose to name you after me. I addressed you familiarly because I feel as if you are my son. I will try to keep in contact with you, if you don't mind."

"That would be nice, and if you would pardon my imposition, I would like to see Abraham sometime. That meeting will have to wait, however, because I plan to take this caravan all the way to East Khatti if the caravan owners will let me. This long trip back and forth over the entire trade route is in memory of my father."

"You most certainly are welcome in Beersheba when you return. We will keep posted on your return and will accompany you to Beersheba then if you wish."

"Sire, I don't equal the youthful strength of my father and will need a long rest upon my return. It could be many a moon before I can come to Beersheba."

"Rest you should have, but why not recuperate in our camp with some good fellowship?"

The stop at Chinnereth afforded an opportunity for one member of the party with artistic talent to sketch the lake area before nightfall. They arrived at the lake at the time of the new moon, precluding any moonlight scene for the drawing. Fortunately, the artist's photographic mind permitted him to sketch a sunrise scene at the midday rest stop. When asked why he was producing a picture of Chinnereth and not other sites on the route, the artist reminded his companions that Abraham loved the place and might not travel there again. These drawings would be the next best thing to a trip there.

Upon their arrival in Damascus, all continuing groups were informed of the gathering spot for resumption of the trip. They would have a three-day stay in this city, which had recovered well from past problems. No centers for distribution of goods to the poor could be seen. The prosperity of the city had also shut down charlatans posing as providers for the poor. Assistance to the poor was now a matter of individual action.

* * * * *

Eliezer awoke late the morning after their arrival, supplying his body with some much-needed rest. This son of Aramus, Eliezer's namesake, drove the caravan at a faster pace than Aramus would have. His father had had enough standing with the caravan owners to allow him to ignore their urging for a fast-paced trek. After a leisurely morning meal, Eliezer decided to attend the town-council meetings. He thought that at least two of his old acquaintances were still serving with the civil organization. When he walked into the observation area, one of them immediately noticed him, excused himself from the bench, and greeted Eliezer with thanks for the past management of the city by Abraham and his close aides while apologizing for the current lack of remembrance of him by the current residents.

"Joktan, my master is a man who doesn't like to rule by presence of being. His reticence in dealing directly with the people of your city didn't give him broad recognition by its inhabitants."

Because of a long absence of any contact with members of Abraham's community with Damascus, Joktan asked if Abraham had issued a decree to avoid the city.

Eliezer promptly explained that no orders existed for their people to shun Damascus. Irreconcilable differences in the conduct of worship services had caused their departure; they had just removed back to Canaan and had never had a reason to return here until now. He then went into some detail about the trip to Ur and its purpose.

Joktan chortled about Eliezer's role as a matchmaker but reckoned that his assignment did make sense.

"Indeed it does," Eliezer agreed. "Oh, before I leave here today, I would like to find the place of some addresses that I have. They are the residences of my father's descendants; however, I am not familiar with the names of the streets. They must be new additions since the days of my childhood."

He was told to go see the tax collector, who knew where everyone was. No place existed in the city whose location he didn't know. Joktan then motioned for the other acquaintance of Eliezer, who was now standing near the bench and eyeing them. Eliezer quickly went through the introductions and his statement of why he was in Damascus before excusing himself to seek out his relatives.

Eliezer first went to home of the nephew of his youngest sister, who lived closest to the council chambers. The nephew's name was Abram—none had occasion to change his name, as with his namesake.

The nephew was excited to see Eliezer, although he barely remembered him and promptly asked Eliezer for an extended stay.

"I am sorry that I have only two more days here before our caravan leaves for Nineveh. I am on a mission back to the original homeland of my master and your namesake." When his nephew proudly commented on being named after the great man Abram, Eliezer neglected to mention that, since the elder Abram had become Abraham, the younger man was no longer quite a namesake.

His nephew decided that a family reunion should be scheduled for his uncle on his last day in town. Nearly all of Eliezer's close relatives lived within a couple of twelfth-days' ride from his place. One elderly aunt lived only a few streets over but would not be able to attend the reunion because of ill health. After Eliezer settled into his quarters at his nephew's home, he walked over to see her.

"Eliezer, your father would be proud to see your prosperity," she told him. "I wish that he could have lived to see you again. Can we persuade you to retire from your service to Abram and return to the higher civilization of our fair city?"

"My dearest aunt, I cannot do that. I have a job serving who I believe to be the best man on earth and God's chief representative. As long as he wishes to employ me, I must serve him. Only his dismissal, or my death, would terminate that commitment." He came close to mentioning the infirmity of old age but realized that he shouldn't remind his aunt of infirmity. Before she could speak, he continued, "Incidentally, my master was renamed Abraham by his God. The renaming was done because he has been promised to be the progenitor of nations ... but don't mention the renaming to my nephew Abram."

"Very well. However, may I ask what brought you here?"

"I am starting a three-day stay today before resuming my mission to Ur of the Chaldees to bring back a young woman to be the wife of Abraham's son Isaac. This mission is possibly the most important one of my life. My master assures me that the young lady Rebekah is the wife that his son must have. When one considers the promise I just mentioned, one could assume I am on a mission for God also."

"You know that you were your father's favorite child. I believe he saw something special in you. I wish you would return to your family, but I see that you must do what you were destined to do. From what I have heard of your master, his religion must be superior to the ones observed around here. I wish I could join you, but you know that is impossible. I want to thank your God for allowing me to see you before I died."

Eliezer had added several gifts to the loads on their pack camels other than those to be given to Rebekah and her family. Hence, he was able to promise his aunt that he would bring her a fine robe on the day of the reunion.

Because of the need for constant surveillance of their goods and animals, Eliezer couldn't invite many of his companions to the reunion. Therefore, he chose to attend the reunion alone. His nephew Abram formally introduced every one of his relatives to him with a brief description of the life of each family. Certain comments told him that the scope of oppression from taxation and control of daily activities had broadened from the days of Abraham's rule in Damascus. When confronted by one cousin about Abraham's abandonment of rulership, Eliezer confidently asserted that it was necessary. He explained that the people had wanted the type of government that would lead to the plight of the city's citizens of today. This explanation naturally upset this cousin and others. Nevertheless, Eliezer felt no remorse, because he hoped the truth would still help to guide his relatives out of paganism. Sadly, none showed any interest in changing their way of worship as his elderly aunt had.

His nephew Abram prevailed upon the relatives to act civilly toward his uncle, who obviously had been blessed by God. Even though Eliezer was antagonistic to their gods, they shouldn't offend his God. He had a narrower view of the godhead than they did, and because they revered all gods, they couldn't discriminate as Eliezer did. The reunion ended with a sumptuous meal and pleasant farewells. Eliezer gave his host nephew a parting kiss and returned to the meeting area for the caravan.

The light of the flares illuminated Eliezer's troubled countenance as he greeted the night watchman with the daily password.

"Did you see some intruder as you entered the camp?" the watchman asked.

"No. I guess my countenance does seem troubled to you. I ran into a confrontation with my cousins at the reunion and haven't relaxed yet. If everything is all right, I must get some sleep before our departure in the morning."

The caravan leader started to put their group in the lead position of the caravan train. Eliezer suggested that they would do better at the center of the train, because some of their spirited young camels liked to follow their own trails unless they saw other camels head somewhere. While this statement was somewhat true, his real reason for taking a middle position in the train was to hide the load on his camels as much as possible. He did promise the caravan leader, however, that he would like to ride by his side for part of the trip.

After the train was under way and all of the animals were behaving by following those in front of them, Eliezer rode up beside his namesake and asked, "I suppose our next prolonged stop is in Nineveh?"

"Yes. It is really impossible to bypass that city even when it's congested— which is most of the time. Most caravans that try to avoid the city are caught and heavily fined. The escape rate is so low that I doubt any caravans would dare try to bypass it anymore."

This statement brought the conditions in Shinar back to Eliezer's mind. After some idle chatter about hating to pay fees and a lighthearted description of how he had gotten the Elamites to reduce their fees on a trip to Haran many years ago, the elder Eliezer asked a casual-sounding but probing question: "I suppose Nineveh is completely walled by now?"

"Yes. The city is actually a fortress. The wall and battlements take up space and force the travelers and citizens to compete for room to live and care for their flocks. This occurs despite the fact that the city is a mighty, sprawling city. The problem is that it's not growing as fast as needed to accommodate the people."

Still probing, Eliezer commented, "That doesn't sound good; we may decide to leave the caravan at Nineveh instead of a stop thereafter. I would also like to know if there are any new customs or standards of conduct that we should follow."

"I probably don't know all of the laws myself. I follow a code of treating everyone as I would want to be treated, and I carefully obey and politely address the officials—even the minor ones."

This free flow of information kept prompting questions in Eliezer's mind. "Who are the rulers of the city? My last information had it as a contested city when it came to government control."

"The Assurites have taken over the top leadership of the city, but you will see an assortment of tribes running the lower-level activities. Surprisingly, I have seen some Ethiopians running some of the livery and hostels. Oh, that reminds me: make sure that you drop all your prejudices toward other tribes. The Assurites don't countenance any insubordination against any of their people in authority, regardless of country of origin."

"Thanks for the reminder, but our people live with mixed tribes. Prejudice is not a part of our culture."

He felt a twinge of conscience from making that statement but immediately realized that it was accurate. True, he was on a mission for a bride living in a far land, but the discrimination expressed by his master, Abraham, involved avoiding improper personal conduct. No objections against Isaac's marrying his neighbors had been based on physical characteristics—at least as far as he knew. Nonetheless, many tribes of distinct physical characteristic were starting to avoid intermarriage with tribes of contrast to them. He couldn't help but wonder if Abraham may have started to discriminate in that way also, even though he had children by Hagar and Keturah.

One of Eliezer's companions, Yosef, spotted a bedouin group composed entirely of grown men when the caravan was still several days' journey from

Haran—a sure sign of renegades. A warning blast on a ram's horn brought Eliezer back to his section of the train. He complimented Yosef on his keen eyesight and told his men to prepare for an attack, even though it was unlikely. Assuming that Yosef had seen all of the renegades, they posed little threat to a caravan of this size. Caravans would often stop for days to pick up enough members to provide for a large contingent that renegade bands wouldn't dare attack. Eliezer exchanged places with Yosef by putting him at the head of the train. The renegades followed them throughout the day but kept away at a discreet distance. Many of the members of the caravan experienced a jittery night, which caused a sluggish preparation for the morning's start because of loss of sleep.

*   *   *   *   *

Yosef was assigned to the head of the train the next day. As soon as they were under way, he asked the caravan leader whether he should ride ahead to Haran for help. No government patrols had yet been seen and were assumed to be scarce or nonexistent.

The caravan leader must have tacitly agreed about the lack of governmental patrols, because he made no comment about it. "Yosef, I don't think that would do anything but deprive us of a defender in case of attack and put the messenger in greater danger of losing his life. A band of that size foolish enough to attack us during daylight would be a bunch of men gone berserk from drinking fermenting wine. I don't believe that these men are drunkards; they are too cautious in their tracking of us. It's my opinion that they will leave us today, trying to make us think that they have given up. They hope to lull us into believing that we are safe, so they can return to attack us tonight."

Yosef was silent for a long while before he offered a plan to rid the caravan of the renegades for good.

*   *   *   *   *

That night, a lone sentry was left to guard the main entry point to the caravan rest formation after everyone else appeared to have gone to bed. Stealthily, armed men were posted all around the perimeter of the formation. They hid themselves by crawling to their positions and lying flat on the ground. Shortly after the night meridian, the renegades appeared out of the night, headed directly toward two of the more lucrative units of the caravan. The archers waited until the intruders were upon them before they rose up and let fly their arrows.

None of the renegades had a chance to offer resistance. Within a few heartbeats, the skirmish was over. Some of the defenders weren't expert marksmen and missed a couple of the renegades who were able to escape into the night, undoubtedly determined not to engage this caravan again. Three of the attackers were treated for their wounds and transported as prisoners on a travois to Haran, but only one of them would survive the trip.

*   *   *   *   *

Eliezer concluded that he had obtained about all of the intelligence information that his namesake had to give, so he decided to let Yosef ride at the head of the train for the rest of the way to Haran, just in case more renegades appeared.

The closer he got to Haran, the edgier Yosef became. When the caravan leader asked him what was bothering him, he replied that the prospect of a one-day stay in Haran was causing him some consternation. He would like a longer stay to visit relatives that he hadn't seen in years, but he wasn't sure about suggesting that they lose time by waiting for another caravan, especially since he enjoyed the present caravan leader's company.

"Yosef, I had planned for only a one-day stop, but you have changed my mind. Those renegades have sapped all of us of our strength through lost sleep and anxiety. We need more time to recuperate. Would a three-day stop be enough?"

The announcement of the increased time in Haran upset Eliezer so much that one of his companions asked why he looked displeased. He just smiled while thinking, *His wonderment is valid. Suddenly, I can hardly wait to fulfill my assignment—an assignment I dreaded at first.*

The caravan accommodations were so spacious and pleasant that Eliezer recommended that they invite their Haran friends and relatives to their camp. In that manner, their friends could meet everyone. Otherwise, they would only be able to send one at a time to the city. Eliezer's family members in Damascus had been confrontational but basically friendly. Here in Haran, the old friends and family members were subdued but didn't show any real delight in seeing them. Yosef was given a particularly cool reception from a former childhood sweetheart. Even the news of Sarah's death didn't elicit much sympathy. This helped confirm a deep-seated feeling that Eliezer had held for many years: despite the great respect and deference Sarah had received from everyone but Hagar and Ishmael, most of her community didn't really like her. Over the three-day period, all of the friends and family that they could find in Haran were invited to the camping area.

When all of the visitors were gone on the last day in town, Yosef observed that the past three days had been pleasant but tiring, while expressing the hope that wouldn't encounter any more renegades for the rest of the trip, because he had to rest when not on duty.

Eliezer eased his mind with an assurance that the rest of the trip should be peaceful, at least to Nineveh. "As I have few close friends here, and I saw indifference from the start, I excused myself and went to the town council for consultation about the countryside conditions between here and Ur. Because of the concern over events to their east and south of east, the government has neglected guarding the caravan trails coming from the Great Sea route. Conversely, the route to Nineveh is carefully patrolled all the way to that city. Also, Nineveh and areas to its east constitute a giant sieve that winnows out all of the chaff, so to speak. The rulers don't allow anyone who even appears to be unlawfully inclined to enter or leave their city. Any undesirables are shipped to various places in Shinar."

After a member of the group reckoned that all renegades knew to stay out of Haran and places east, Eliezer replied, "Yes. The town council took our prisoner into custody, but they were rather surprised that a caravan as large as ours was attacked. They suggested that the restriction of the area of operation was causing some of the renegades to fail to find enough travelers to plunder. Hence, they may have become more emboldened. The council members suggested that we might want to hire some mercenaries for our return trip to Lahai-roi."

Yosef initially insisted that they were able to protect themselves but relented when convinced that the recent attack indicated the need for mercenaries. Nevertheless, he wondered aloud whether those mercenaries could be trusted not to turn on them in battle.

Eliezer answered thoughtfully, "Let's wait and gauge the capabilities of the return caravan. If that caravan is as good as the present one, we probably shouldn't risk hiring any mercenaries. Very few hired fighters have the desire to fight that their customers have, except for the more belligerent ones who are difficult to deal with." Eliezer yawned and suggested that they retire for the night, because everyone needed some rest before the trip resumed the next day.

The caravan had scarcely cleared Haran when they saw a contingent of soldiers patrolling the route ahead of them. When the contingent continued to keep a constant gap in front of them, Eliezer, who had resumed his position by the caravan leader, asked, "Are those soldiers escorting us?"

The younger Eliezer replied, "They probably are. I had an occasion to meet with several caravan guides during our stay in Haran. They told me there are so many soldiers between here and Nineveh that every caravan usually receives a military escort. Sometimes they will depart the route temporarily, but they usually return soon. Nobody seemed to know why they appear and disappear—possibly to eat or rest."

"I am happy that we will have an escort. My companion Yosef was upset by those renegades we just disposed of. I'm sure that his keen eyesight has seen the soldiers also. Maybe he will relax now."

Actually, the elder Eliezer wasn't as relieved as he had expressed, but somewhat annoyed. While he appreciated protection for safety's sake, he wanted to find out just who his benefactors were. With the mixing of people in this area, it was no longer possible to tell the tribe of the riders by silhouette. This was particularly true of soldiers who tended to be similarly armed and trained to use a standard riding profile. As he mulled over the situation, he said a silent prayer of thanks that God had led them to Canaan. What had appeared foolish upon their move from Haran to Canaan turned out to be a blessing. The sullenness of the people in Haran and the regimentation obvious from the numerous military units spoke loudly of an unpleasant living environment.

That night the tone of conversation was stilted rather than happy. Eliezer mused over and accepted a suggestion that the number of watches could be reduced because the numerous patrols greatly increased their safety.

*　　*　　*　　*　　*

A subdued, if not unhappy, mood persisted until one day they espied a large city in the distance. The outskirts consisted of low-profile buildings, but Yosef thought that he could see a tower in the distance far beyond the nearest buildings. As more and more members spotted the buildings, a murmur arose along the train of the caravan. The excitement in their voices far exceeded that of the sighting of anything else so far.

Eliezer, the caravan leader, soon halted the train and ordered it into rest stop formation. "It's late in the day, and I thought it wise to halt now and talk about Nineveh while the excitement exists. What you see nearest to you is actually not part of the main city. Once we reach this nearest cluster of buildings, we still will be almost a day's journey from the city gate and battlements. The entrance to the city isn't far from the distant tower that some of you can discern in the shimmering skyline. The tower was once a more imposing sight that would have stood out even in this haze. The city leaders have let their ziggurat lapse into disrepair."

A caravan member's question about being able to ascend the steps of the tower received an almost incredulous negative response before the caravan leader promptly resumed his conversation. "It now becomes most important that we keep close ranks from our entry into the outskirts of the city until we leave it. If any group starts to lag, you are apt to lose the rest of the caravan. I assure all that none would want to be stranded in this city. As a large group, we will be able to negotiate much cheaper prices for services than any individual or small group can. I have had my assistants surveying the train for the past three days. Some animals must be culled from the train and sold at an animal hospital located just before we enter the nearest outskirts. The group led by my namesake and our company has enough excess capacity left to handle the load of the weak animals."

This request caused a furor to arise in the camp that took nearly a twelfth-day to resolve before everyone could be persuaded to depart with some of their favorite animals. Those returning through Nineveh were soothed when they were told that they could board their animals until they returned if they wished.

Finally, the caravan leader was able to finish his instructions: "While this city may be the safest on earth, you still should guard your goods. The rulers haven't been able to deter some fools who are bound to engage in crime. There is always one or two around who believe that they can escape detection. My last instruction is this: don't be upset over our pace through the city. I plan to adjust our pace to arrive at the gate by mid-post meridian. The morning and late evening times are hectic, with some usually getting stranded at closing twilight, and I can assure you that the accommodations immediately outside the gate are not as pleasant and economical as those inside."

Even arrival well before twilight barely permitted the caravan to enter the city before closing time. Fortunately, this caravan had a favored status with the city fathers, giving them a rest area only a short distance from the gate.

Eliezer and Yosef had altered their appearances before joining the caravan near Beersheba by applying dark pigmentation. They knew that an encounter from a battlefield enemy of the past could bring retribution upon them. Shortly after reaching the rest stop, they headed for the side streets of the city. Confident in their disguise, they wanted to explore the support areas of the city rather than the business district on the main thoroughfare. Almost immediately they discovered storehouses constructed from mud brick, making them difficult to destroy with a rain of burning arrows.

Eliezer paused in his pace and remarked, "Everyone says that the battlements are formidable around the entire inner city. I think we have seen enough of the enclosed area to realize that this city could stand a long siege. The only possible vulnerability would be their water supply, but judging by the size of cistern at our rest stop, I am guessing that wouldn't be a problem, either."

After wending their way down many dark alleys, Yosef suggested that they return to the main street before they were caught and charged as thieves. Once again one of Yosef's many talents—sense of direction—proved valuable as he guided them through the darkest alleys to avoid scrutiny by the patrols. Eliezer couldn't help wondering how they arrived back at camp so quickly and directly. He was certain he would have gotten lost in this intricate city without using the lighted streets. Even the grid layout of the city wouldn't have helped him to find his way.

The next day's procession passed directly by the central ziggurat, constructed in bygone ages. It had definitely started to show decay; even the more recent additions were crumbling. Eliezer was riding with his group because only caravan employees were permitted to lead the train through Nineveh. Also, law required that all owners proceed through the city with their own goods. The government was prone to confiscating any goods questioned as inappropriate for commerce if those goods couldn't be immediately justified by their owner. An efficient city as this had no time to search for absent owners.

Eliezer eyed the ziggurat closely as they passed. His rhetorical comment drew nods: "It seems apparent that religion has a diminished status at this time. Everything impressive about this city has a military connection. From the battlements to the storehouses to the cisterns, everything is kept in good repair … except their former central place of worship."

As the caravan approached a government checkpoint, Yosef related a widespread saying that the ziggurat was destined to crumble and be covered over by sand, because the gods were mad at the original builders of the city and would eventually let it be completely destroyed.

When a city official suddenly appeared and motioned to the caravan leader to divert his train into an inspection area, Eliezer winced. The city generally liked for the traffic to flow freely, because the faster the traffic flow, the faster the collection of fees. This detour definitely boded some problem. Should he try to hide, or stay in front of his group? Given his ownership credentials, he had no option but to face the government officials. While all of these musings were passing through his mind, he turned his attention to seeing that his animals behaved.

A startled Eliezer turned to a deep-throated address: "Sire, may I see your list of goods and provisions?" His sudden outward reaction immediately turned to inner anxiety. The person addressing him was a somewhat aged version of a prominent prisoner he had met during the war to rescue his master's nephew Lot.

"Before I assess your inventory," the man said, "I must know if we have met before. You look like someone I should remember from a past encounter."

Eliezer was a bit relieved, because the man's countenance told him that the man didn't recognize him yet. Nonetheless, this fact posed a dilemma. He wanted to deflect the man's curiosity, but surely didn't want to lie, in case the man's memory became more lucid.

Eliezer, ever able to think his way out of almost any confrontation, replied, "It's possible we have met at some time. I have traveled extensively over these lands during my life." Immediately dropping his reply at that remark would enable him to justify any further response to the official.

The official continued to look at Eliezer for a disturbing length of time before he turned his eyes to the papyrus inventory sheet in his hands. Slowly a quizzical look grew on the official's face. Eliezer tried to contain his uneasiness until the official spoke. "This script is similar to that of the inhabitants of old Damascus, but you list your residence as Beersheba by the Great Sea. Where were you born, and is Beersheba your true residence now?"

This conversation wasn't going well. Eliezer made one of his fastest silent prayers to God before he replied. There was no way he could hide his origin—even his accent still belied the land of his birth. Nevertheless, it was important—maybe necessary—that he not reveal his birth in Damascus to any extent that would identify him as anyone other than a humble citizen.

"My Lord Townsman, I do indeed presently reside in Beersheba, but I was born in the servant district of Damascus. I was tutored from an early age by my dearest uncle." Serendipitously, his mother had been staying with a midwife in a poorer part of town at the time of his birth. His father had been out of town on an important governmental assignment as his mother's delivery drew near. As a precaution should the time of birth occur while he was gone, his mother had been sent to live with a midwife. Eliezer had also been taught by an uncle who was the headmaster of a prestigious school, not some half-illiterate uncle given the job of teaching his nephew because he was less deprived of knowledge than the other relatives.

"Hmm, I see you have much fine jewelry listed. Why isn't it listed in the merchandise section of your inventory?"

"Sire, none of this jewelry is scheduled for sale. I am taking it to some of our family living east of here. They have helped us in the past, and our family and community wishes to bestow some of the bounty we have gained in Canaan upon them."

Astonishingly, the official turned and paced rapidly back to the caravan leader and engaged in a short conversation. The exchange piqued Eliezer's curiosity, but the gesture of release delighted him so much that he let the thought pass from his mind.

The delay made it impossible to clear the city that day, which permitted an early stop for the night. Just as he had prudently timed the group's entrance into the city, the caravan leader didn't want to join the early morning crowd trying to leave the city. Traversing the remaining distance to the exit gate should take half of the next day's daylight hours.

*　　*　　*　　*　　*

That night Yosef, who had taken the opportunity to hide from the town officials, asked Eliezer whether the incident with the city official meant they should increase their disguises in some way without raising the suspicions of others in the caravan.

"No. I believe that we have taken proper precautions. I am convinced that God helped blind his eyes to my identity, although my change of complexion and aging should have thoroughly fooled him. I suspect that it was something in my voice or mannerisms that stirred his memory. Once we leave the caravan, I will try to change my voice and some mannerisms. Also, our return trip should not look so suspicious with an entourage of women accompanying us. You must admit that our group does stand out somewhat in this crowd. I am accompanied by some quite stalwart men, which reminds me that we need to keep diligent. I suspect that we will have an agent or two observing us for the rest of the trip."

Yosef nodded agreement but suggested that Eliezer post extra guards that night. They both agreed that they didn't like the way that the official had looked at their jewelry cache. A city as completely controlled as this one must have greedy officials who took advantage of travelers on occasions. Theft by the powerful would be easy to cover up in this place.

Yosef lay down on a spot near the jewelry that was hidden from view by anyone passing their formation. He pretended to be asleep, should any rearrangement of goods or animals by others reveal his resting spot. The night meridian came and went without a suspicious stirring in camp. The night waxed late, and the darkness before dawn had set in when Yosef's keen eyesight caught a glimpse of two stealthy silhouettes approaching his way. He immediately blew a blast on a ram's horn.

This action risked a possible adverse reaction that fortunately didn't occur. To his delight, most of the animals some distance from him only stirred a bit, but a couple of nearby horses tried to bolt, resulting in one of the would-be thieves receiving a kick that sent him stumbling and finally falling prostrate at Yosef's feet.

By that time, more people than animals were stirring. Eliezer, who had spent a sleepless night, was the first at Yosef's side. They both quickly tied the hands of the fallen thief. Yosef then abruptly sought out the other culprit, who seemed stunned by the blast from the horn. He had escaped any trampling by the animals, but had lost his orientation in the darkness amid the commotion. After stumbling around futilely, he fell to knees, cringing in fear and seemingly bawling like a scared child.

By the time the second in command arrived at the scene, the prisoners were bound and all the animals were back in their place. His first words were, "Who blew the ram's horn and why?"

Yosef spoke almost sheepishly. "I was the one who blew the horn. I suppose the most important part of your question is why, and I do have a good reason for what I did, as hard as it may be to explain. First, I blew the horn to create confusion to stop two thieves from stealing our goods. Even in the darkness, I could see that they were not part of the caravan, and their approach by stealth and cover of darkness proved their intent to steal, at least to any reasonable person."

The caravan leader's assistant wasn't pleased with the response. "As there were only two thieves, I believe a safer way to capture them should have been followed."

"Sire, I fully understand your point. I wasn't sure there were only two thieves, and even two men can be difficult to overcome in the dark, although I am strong. Also, from my shepherd days, I learned that certain tones on the ram's horn don't disturb animals very much. You may have noticed only the two horses near me reacted violently, and I am surprised the horn startled them so much."

The assistant started to calm down some, but he wasn't ready to concede the argument. "But you did awaken the whole camp, and you should know that the events of the last few days mean that everyone needs as much undisturbed rest as possible."

Yosef was starting to become riled himself. "I agree, but I believed it was more important to disturb my traveling companions than risk harm or theft happening to them."

While this statement was slightly devious—Yosef had been far more concerned about the loss of the jewels than the risk of harm—it seemed to satisfy the assistant enough that he stopped arguing. The latter concluded that no harm had occurred, and the capture of two thieves had spared the camp from loss. He ordered more sentries posted and suggested everyone else try to get some more rest, as short as it would be, because they had to leave as scheduled this morning.

Before departing later that morning, the second in command and Yosef waited for some officials to arrive and take control of the prisoners, one of whom was beginning to show a prominent bruise on his seating posterior. The chief official requested that Yosef be detained to be present at the thieves' arraignment. Eliezer promptly told him that they would withdraw their charge of thievery if they could be allowed to continue with the caravan.

Eliezer and Yosef breathed a sigh of relief as the caravan reached the pace that would finally get them out of this oppressive city. Yosef remarked to his companions—not particularly privately—that his presence at the arraignment was a ruse to free the two thieves, who must surely be government agents. His companions nodded in agreement. Eliezer added with a sigh of relief, "The most important issue is for us to get to Ur with our gifts and to avoid detainment along the way. Demanding justice in this city can be a vain prospect for some people, including us."

*   *   *   *   *

Shortly after they cleared the exit gate of Nineveh, Eliezer decided that it was time to see whether Yosef's action of the previous night had upset the caravan leader, who wasn't in camp but at a friend's residence nearby. The elder Eliezer started the conversation by expressing his delight at being past Nineveh. The other Eliezer, the caravan leader, smiled and asked him when they would be departing the caravan.

"I had planned to go to the second stop and travel the less-used route," the elder Eliezer replied, "but our encounter with the thieves last night has caused me to change my mind. We will be leaving at the next stop. The road north from there is guarded better than the other road. We have ample resources to sustain us. We shouldn't be bothered by the competition for roadside services."

The caravan leader continued the conversation with praise and thanks for his help and camaraderie on the trip. The lack of comment concerning Yosef eased his anxiety about what the leader might think. He didn't want the caravan company to ban them from caravan travel. The only concern that the leader had was whether there would be a need to acquire more animals to handle the offload of items that Eliezer was carrying for others.

Eliezer let the caravan depart before his group prepared to head toward Ur, so he could guard his goods more closely. A favorite ploy of certain travelers was to distract departing members with good-byes while an accomplice would commit a theft that hopefully wouldn't be discovered until much later—too late for retrieval. Accordingly, Eliezer posted all of his companions to guard their goods while he performed the customary good-byes. He especially scrutinized the off-loading of the goods that he was carrying for others.

Fortunately, they were traveling during the part of the year with the most commercial traffic and soon caught up with a group of businessmen headed for Ur and beyond. With the addition of these men, they constituted a small caravan.

The nearer they came to Ur, the more the countryside looked as it had in the past. The familiar surroundings gradually eased Eliezer's mind of his troubles with thieves—belligerent and stealthy. He turned his mind to asking God for a sign to prove that Rebekah was the proper wife for Isaac. While he could evaluate her qualities, he had been instructed to trust God for the answer. Abraham's certainty about her made this trip absolutely necessary, but God must select Rebekah as Isaac's bride. After mulling over several different scenarios in his mind, Eliezer realized that each one was fanciful or foolish. With his frustration growing, he finally decided to put it from his mind for at least a day. There was a nice rest area less than a day's journey from Ur where he could stay if he didn't comprehend the solution before their arrival at Ur.

That night Eliezer decided to retire early. The mental processes of the day had tired him more than the physical journey. The next morning, he could hardly remember lying down to sleep, but he had vivid recall of the most clearly defined dream of his life. The setting of the dream could be no other place on earth but Ur of the Chaldees. He even recognized a few of the older people in the background, but all of the people in the foreground near the well were young people, some of whom couldn't have been born yet when he had last been in Ur.

The strangest part of the dream had to be a group of men approaching the young people at the well. The size of the group and the men in it looked familiar, but his dream psyche couldn't discern who they were. At first he felt dread and fear at what the men might do to the young people, but he slowly came to realize that the men didn't appear to be threatening. They were tradesmen carrying many goods. After what seemed to be a twelfth-day, the leader of the group approached the well.

Just as the man sat down next to the well, presumably to wait his turn to draw water, the dream got even weirder. Out of nowhere, a beautiful and rather tall young woman approached. She was clad in a resplendent wedding dress with a tiara of diamonds in her hair, along with a jeweled necklace and golden arm bracelets. The old man and the young woman looked at each other for a long time before she asked the man if she could draw water for him, his companions, and their animals.

Then, before he could draw another breath, the dream was gone, and he was awake in the near-dawn darkness, which was starting to brighten. Although the others wouldn't arise for a while, he got up with a smile. He now knew who the young woman, the old man, and his companions were. He also knew what the sign from God would be.

Eliezer's only remaining question was whether to travel with these businessmen the rest of the way to Ur or pick up the pace on his own. He would keep the details of this dream private, because certain features of it were bizarre. He knew some of his companions would deprecate the dream's significance. He would only tell them that he had resolved how he would do his introduction to Rebekah's family and that he was ready to follow a faster pace if they thought it safe. All of his companions advised him to stay with the group, which would stop overnight at their destination. The safety of this action was more important than gaining an extra day at a faster pace. If an attack should occur, they could wind up losing goods while gaining no time.

Eliezer wanted to argue for the faster pace but realized that his reasons were foolish. Yes, he must control his elation over the blessing of having received an answer to his prayer for a sign from God. It was an enormous relief to know that he was assured of making the right decision now. When the journey seemed to be going even slower than in the past days, a nagging doubt entered his mind that Rebekah would not accept the marriage proposal, but he dismissed the idea immediately. He knew of his master's faith in this endeavor. Now, with all the details revealed, Eliezer's mission was bound to be successful.

FOUR

MEETING THE
FAMILY

O N THE MORNING OF entry into Ur, Eliezer told his fellows that he must ride ahead to contact a friend before bringing his camels into Ur. If his friend couldn't provide them sustenance, they would have to stay at a roadside hostel and livery. Eliezer's real intent was to be the first one at the well.

He stayed with the group until Ur came into distant view, and then he rode swiftly to town. Once he left the group, he mussed his hair and applied some dirt to his clothing. He wanted to present the image of a weary traveler. His apparent condition and age should prove his need to a compassionate person.

Upon arrival at the well, he decided he should stand instead of sit. He didn't want to present a picture of a traveler wearied beyond the point of good health. He stood aside for quite a while, because none of the people at the well looked as Rebekah had in his dream. As he became apprehensive, he repeated the prayer silently to God for Rebekah's presence. He hadn't completed describing the scene in the dream before a young lady exactly fulfilling his inner perception of Rebekah walked toward the well, appearing as if from nowhere. Unlike the woman in the dream, she wore a colorful peasant dress, which still signified that she was from a well-to-do family.

As she arrived, he almost stepped into her pathway. She paused momentarily and smiled at him. Her look was so compassionate that Eliezer wondered whether he had made himself to look too bedraggled. When she lowered the bucket to draw some water, he asked, "Would you be so kind as to give me a few sips of the water from your pitcher? I am waiting for my companions to arrive with our camels, but I just realized how thirsty I am. I would like a bit of water before they arrive."

"Yes, I will. Are those camels approaching us yours? If you like, I can draw water for them also." This rather improbable gesture of kindness happened just as it had been revealed in Eliezer's dream. His only remaining job would be to sell Isaac to her and her family.

When she finished drawing the water, he asked her whose daughter she was. "I am the daughter of Bethuel, whose mother was Milcah, the wife of Nahor. My grandfather was the brother of a famous man, Abram."

Eliezer presented a generous amount of jewelry to her in gratitude for her help and in exchange for her promise to provide them and their animals with lodging for the night. Her household servants would help with the securing of the animals, she told him. Her father and brother should be home by the time that they had tended their animals and had refreshed themselves.

"I guess we do need to make ourselves more presentable," Eliezer said to himself almost inaudibly.

*   *   *   *   *

Eliezer assembled his animals as each one finished drinking, and Rebekah ran home to tell her family about the stranger. She instructed the head servant to tell her father and brother about her encounter when they arrived home and about her helping the men with occupying the guest quarters.

Before all of the animals were ready to be led to their resting place for the night, Laban heard the news and hastened to the well, where he met Eliezer and his sister. He appeared to be in shock when he saw Rebekah bedecked in jeweled neckwear and golden bracelets. He had just opened his mouth to speak when Rebekah repeated the news he had heard from the head servant, but in more detail. Laban immediately agreed with Eliezer that this marriage must be ordained by God, but they must get her father's approval.

Eliezer wore his best robe to the lavish supper that still was being prepared when he arrived at Bethuel's courtyard. "My honorable host, I have a request of marriage of your daughter Rebekah to her cousin Isaac. He is the son of Abraham, your father's brother."

Bethuel cheerfully responded that he was honored to have his daughter considered worthy to be the wife of the son of the great nobleman Abraham. He also agreed with his son Laban that this marriage was ordained by God. Nevertheless, he insisted on knowing more about the life of his uncle Abraham since he left Ur. He worried about Rebekah's leaving, because he had heard disturbing things concerning the land of Canaan.

Noting the way the name of the land rolled off Bethuel's lips, Eliezer feared that he might have more of a problem selling Rebekah's new home than he would the marriage to Isaac. He resolved that the best way to ease Bethuel's mind about Canaan would be to review the accomplishments of Abraham there since leaving Haran. Rebekah's family needed to hear and fully understand the environment in which she would live. Therefore, he would recite a long narrative about the happenings in Canaan.

Eliezer saved the most interesting events for the times when Rebekah was eating with them at the table. On the second night, she asked, "I am overjoyed at the opportunity to marry Isaac, but why isn't he here with us? I desire very much to talk to him."

Eliezer couldn't determine if that comment had made Bethuel mad at Rebekah for her impertinence or at him for trying to betroth Isaac sight unseen. For one of the few times in his life, he stuttered as he searched his mind for the proper response. When he did compose himself, he reminded her of the customs of the land and how children were promised in marriage without the two knowing each other. Nonetheless, whatever the custom of marriage might be, he was willing to describe Isaac to her in detail. Also, he promised, when he finished describing their history in Canaan, he would explain in detail the scope and breadth of the inheritance that Abraham would bequest to Isaac.

The mention of the inheritance caused Bethuel's face to become more pleasant. Regardless of what he had been thinking before, the man's countenance changed to a smile, and he asked Eliezer to continue his narrative. Eliezer could surmise that Bethuel was taken with the prospects of the dowry that he was to receive. He made a mental note not to forget to close his speech with the amount of gifts to be presented to Bethuel and the inheritance that awaited Rebekah.

On the third night Eliezer concluded his narrative. "My honored host, I am done speaking of family and community. I hope that I have given you enough information for you to understand just what awaits Rebekah should she accept the marriage proposal. I have pictured Isaac fairly to her also; I have mentioned his faults, as I have his strengths. Unless there are more items of interest to you about us, I would like to know when we can have your answer."

Bethuel again voiced his opinion that this marriage was ordained by God, but he supposed that Rebekah should decide whether she should marry Isaac. Mysteriously, he almost whispered that it was difficult to tell when Rebekah would be ready to answer.

After the next day came and went without a response, Eliezer asked again for a response. Bethuel replied that they wanted to keep Rebekah for several more days before making a decision. Suppressing some anger, Eliezer replied, "Your hospitality to us has been beyond anything that we could have asked. I must, however, have an answer on this matter sooner. We have been on a long, weary, and even dangerous journey. If I don't make a timely return to my lord, Abraham, he will become apprehensive over what happened to us. His advancing age makes it necessary that he not be worried over our fate."

Eliezer had been diligent in describing Isaac and the area around Lahai-roi to the family, but his best dealing was happening now. He was sure that Bethuel had already accepted the idea of marriage, and this ploy had been made as a means to obtain a larger dowry from him. The next request from Bethuel would undoubtedly be for more goods; Eliezer was calling his bluff. When Bethuel agreed to leave the decision of marriage and departure time to Rebekah, Eliezer knew that he had won.

Her father directed a servant to call Rebekah into the room. Rebekah nervously looked back and forth at her father and Eliezer. As she stood waiting after her bow, her father finally asked her whether she had reached a decision on marriage to Isaac. He told her there should be no good reason to delay her answer and that the decision was hers to make. He implored her to answer according to her desires, for this was the most important decision in her life so far. He trusted that she had had enough time to decide yes or no.

Eliezer smiled. *Clever. Blame me for forcing a decision and try to hint at more time to plan your fleecing of me.*

She looked at Eliezer without addressing her father. "I do wish to marry Isaac. Your humble handmaiden could never have hoped to have been able to marry the son of such a noble person as Abram—I am sorry, I must get used to his new name, Abraham. May I ask when you wish this marriage to take place? I can have a train of servants ready soon if need be."

"My dear Rebekah, you may have noticed that we brought more camels than necessary for our small group. We have sufficient equipment and animals to transport you and your maidservants back to Lahai-roi whenever you are ready to go. Please take the necessary time to assemble your clothing and household goods; however, we hope that you can be ready quickly. We do need to get back to your future father-in-law before he despairs over our fate."

"If you can help my servant load your camels, we can be ready two days from tomorrow."

Eliezer clapped his hands in a staccato manner, which brought two of his companions into the room. "Please help Rebekah and her servants load the camels for departure within three days."

Eliezer spent the rest of the time before departure touring the city of Ur and some of the surrounding countryside to reminisce over his past and to have one last recollection of the old homeland of his master. He had his fellow artist draw pictures of Abraham's relatives with the landscape in the background. He also brought out more gifts for Rebekah's mother and father. He had held some back because he wasn't sure how strong Bethuel would be in holding onto his daughter or just what price in gold he would deem her worth.

On the morning of departure, Bethuel and Laban were happier than they had been anytime during Eliezer's stay. *I guess our dowry met the extent of her father's greed,* Eliezer mused. *I just hope we get away before he changes his mind about letting Rebekah go.* His concern proved unfounded as Bethuel only reminded the group that they had a consignment more precious than jewelry to protect—his daughter Rebekah and her servants.

Eliezer nodded as he replied, "Don't worry, we will protect them with our lives. With the addition of the two menservants, we should be a group that none would want to attack. We will keep a watch for potential trouble, and I probably have the best lookout in the world in Yosef traveling with us."

They rapidly overtook a small merchant band that had stopped overnight near Ur, but left earlier than the latter did. As they slowed their pace to fall in line, Rebekah commented almost breathlessly, "I am glad that we caught them when we did. My camel's pace was starting to tire me. I envisioned falling off and injuring myself before I had hardly begun my journey for marriage."

Eliezer smiled. "I was watching you and was about to slow our speed before our hosts spotted us and allowed us to catch up. I had met their leader the night before and told him to keep a watch for our approach from the rear. I had expected we would have some delay in getting away from your father this morning."

"Indeed, Father can be rather fussy and time-consuming in preparing for anything new. I expect I am marrying into a family that is more active than mine. My father's carefulness has helped him prosper, but it does lead to a somewhat dull life. I didn't mention it to my father, but Isaac had an advantage in asking someone to marry him who was eager to leave home. It is just doubly fortunate that he is the son of a great lord."

"Rebekah, I don't plan to talk about your new home anymore, unless you still have some questions. I felt our three-night discussion gave a concise but informative history of our experience since leaving Ur."

"Master Eliezer," she replied, despite his instructions to address him more familiarly, "I don't wish to know anything else until I see my husband, Isaac."

Eliezer nodded with a generous smile and rode away. He then sought out one of Rebekah's servants to find out what his men needed to do to make the trip as comfortable and entertaining as possible for them.

On the third night out, as everyone sat watching one of the maidservants perform a veiled dance, Eliezer noticed an amused look on Yosef's face. "I see that you are enjoying the dance."

Yosef smiled as he stated his amusement over the differences he saw in Rebekah from Isaac. She was more fun-loving and vivacious than Isaac, although Isaac did have fun in his own way. His fun, however, was derived from besting someone in a sporting or hunting endeavor—even though he wasn't overly proficient at either one.

"Don't laugh at this fact, because it could pose a problem in their marriage," Eliezer admonished. "Nonetheless, I don't believe that their difference will be any problem. I think Rebekah is so tolerant and generous that she can live with Isaac. Also, Isaac is so despondent over the loss of his mother that he will appreciate the love of another woman who is capable of even a greater love than his mother. I see great wisdom in Lord Abraham's assertion that Rebekah is *the* wife for Isaac."

* * * * *

Rebekah eventually noticed that Yosef was always busy with some activity during their traveling hours and didn't seem to relax much during rest periods. She finally expressed her curiosity. "Yosef, why are you always doing something? You seem to always be either working or on permanent guard duty."

Yosef responded that her perception could be wrong, because the return trip had been pleasant and he was far more relaxed than on their trip to her home. He added that they had had considerable trouble with bandits and thieves on the trip to Ur; hence he was still wary and intended to remain so until she was delivered to her new home.

One of the other warriors jokingly chided Rebekah about bothering Yosef. He had the best eyesight of any of them, and too much wine and revelry by him would put all of them in greater danger if his faculties were impaired.

* * * * *

After their smaller caravan had merged with a larger one en route to Nineveh, Eliezer called a meeting of his companions. "We must decide what protection we will need when we leave Nineveh. The caravan leader has received an update on the expected size of the caravan to Egypt from Haran. He expects that it will be at least as large as the one we took on the trip up."

When a number of comments seemed to disagree on hiring more

mercenaries, Yosef mentioned that a former girlfriend in Haran had told him of some young acquaintances who might be interested in accompanying them to Canaan and setting up a home there. They were a bit rowdy but would make good fighters if needed. She was also certain that the young men would be loyal in protecting them.

Eliezer thought for a while before replying. "You know that Abraham left many of our people in Haran because they were pagan. We can dispatch other mercenaries back to where they came from, but relatives will want to stay with us. I assume they are pagan, and an invitation to our current homeland would violate our master's desire to keep pagans outside our camps."

Yosef reckoned the men were vagabonds and unlikely to want to engage in the life of a shepherd. He would expect them to become mercenaries for someone else—probably Abimelech—immediately after they were released from their duties.

Eliezer asked for a moment to think, as he was being pressed for a decision. After several minutes of thought, he agreed to the hiring of the young men with the stipulation that they understood that they must reject paganism or find other residences than the communities in Hebron and Beersheba. Yosef said he doubted they would reject paganism, but he could set up an existence for them around Lahai-roi. The growing and prosperous area should provide them a good living even if that they didn't become mercenaries for Abimelech.

The trip through Nineveh drew hardly a glance from the milling crowds or petty officials. Once again the knowledge of the caravan leader expedited their entry and exit from the city. They stopped just beyond the far outskirts to allow for some members of the caravan to retrieve animals from the boarding livery, including a few that had been left by individuals who had accompanied them on the trip to Ur.

That night, before everyone had settled in for their evening meal, the caravan leader informed each group leader that more governmental patrols had been installed between Nineveh and Canaan. Also, negotiations had been going on with various tribes in Canaan to provide more protection for the trade routes. He hoped, even believed, that ample security would be available all the way to Egypt.

Given this information, Eliezer and his companions decided not to contact any acquaintances in Haran for escort duties. Nevertheless, on their first day in Haran, two of those acquaintances sought them out and insisted on accompanying them. They also insisted on hosting a banquet for Rebekah.

Rebekah returned from the banquet looking more tired than anytime so far. When asked what happened, she replied, "They treated me as if I were the queen of a great nation. Everybody wanted me to do something or to go here or there at all hours of the day and for much of the night. I must go to bed early tonight if I am to travel tomorrow."

Eliezer smiled. "Our former community reacts quite differently depending on whom they entertain. They still hold a grudge against their relatives in Canaan from events decades ago. But you haven't antagonized them in any way. Nonetheless, I suppose that you are glad to see the descendants of your forefathers' friends and relatives."

Eliezer persuaded the caravan leader to make stops at Chinnereth, Shechem, and Bethel, giving Rebekah and her attendants a brief history of each place's significance. Otherwise, Eliezer hadn't spoken much to them during the entire trip, but on the last stop before arrival at Beersheba, he called everyone together for a meeting.

Looking directly at Rebekah, he spoke. "Tomorrow we should arrive at your father-in-law's abode. We will spend as much time there as he and you wish for preparation for the trip to Lahai-roi. You also may wish to rest there awhile before completing the last leg of our long journey."

"I do wish to rest and wash away some of the dust from the trail before I see my husband. Your description of Isaac makes me believe I should present a good appearance. I want him to have a good first impression of me before his life changes through marriage."

Since shortly after their arrival in Canaan, the contingent had had daily contact with Abraham's or Abimelech's scouts. On the last morning, Eliezer dispatched a scout to tell Abraham of the approximate time of their arrival, so a host of greeters would be available at the caravan stop.

Eliezer momentarily couldn't believe his eyesight when he saw Abraham bow to Rebekah.

"My dearest lady and daughter, welcome to our fair land." While Abraham was a humble man, he could unashamedly promote his land, people, or himself when appropriate. He continued, "I hear that you have had a pleasant journey, although I must say that I was getting anxious by the time I first heard of your arrival in Canaan. I suspect that you and your servants will wish for time to rest and refresh yourselves before you meet my son. I have some servants ensuring that Isaac stays in Lahai-roi. You may take as long as you need to rest and prepare for meeting him. In the meantime, please ask my servants for anything you need."

"My Lord Abraham," said Rebekah, remembering to use his new name, "I have no ability to express my gratitude for your choosing me to be your daughter-in-law. Once we are settled in here, I will give my head servant a list of things that we need. Mostly, we planned well for this trip and are not in need of many goods."

Eliezer quickly instructed Abraham to keep all greetings brief, because he suspected that everyone in his band was weary and needed rest above all else. On the third day, Rebekah sent her closest personal maidservant to tell Eliezer that she was ready for the trip to Lahai-roi whenever Abraham wished.

Rebekah's quick readiness to travel surprised Eliezer. Abraham also showed promptness by announcing that they could leave to see Isaac on the next day. They would time their departure for arrival in Lahai-roi in the evening hours, because it was assumed that Isaac and his servants would be busy with preparations of their own during the day.

*   *   *   *   *

Isaac had quit working earlier than usual, almost from a premonition that this could be the day he would see his bride. He sat contemplating his immediate future as the streaming rays of the sun that had just set still generated rainbows in the eastern sky. He still had fleeting doubts about his residence. *Is it clean enough? Is everything in good repair? I still haven't repaired that breach in one of the lamb cotes.* He quickly reconciled each doubt with the knowledge that Rebekah would be tolerant. He could help reconcile any disappointment with the argument that he had already improved his place considerably since he learned that he was to be married.

As all of these thoughts flowed through his mind, he noticed some dark figures in the distance, which soon became recognizable as riders on camels. *Finally, the time has come for the next great step in my life.* He called to a nearby servant and ordered him to run to greet the riders while he walked slowly toward them.

As the servant neared Rebekah's mount, she directed the contingent's leader to allow her to dismount. She landed as Isaac's servant greeted her and had barely returned the greeting before asking, "Who is that man walking toward us?" The servant smiled and told her that the man was his master, Isaac. Following the custom of her people, she covered her face with a veil. She wouldn't reveal her full face until after the wedding ceremony, which occurred the next morning.

*   *   *   *   *

Abraham and all of the unneeded servants started their return to Beersheba the same day as the wedding. As they rode off, Abraham asked for a stop, so he could give a formal prayer of thanks to God. When the return trip resumed, his entire entourage was silent. He knew they were waiting for some comments from him. "My loyal servants, this is truly one of the great days of my life. A test of my faith in almost arriving at despairing over whether Isaac would ever marry properly has passed. Now everything is in the hands of God. I am confident that Isaac and Rebekah will fulfill the promise to procreate my descendants."

*   *   *   *   *

Meanwhile, Isaac's elation over the beauty and compassion revealed by Rebekah following the wedding was beyond anything he had ever experienced. Deep within his psyche, he realized he had not been a favorite child of either of his parents. His feeling of reduced worth had been further assaulted by some of his servants who occasionally brought up how Ishmael had mistreated him. At last, he had someone who loved him, although she had known him for less than a day.

Isaac had been rather quiet until his father's group disappeared, and then he spoke at length to his bride. "Rebekah, I hope I will prove to be a husband you can love. I could never hope for a better wife than I sense that you will be. I have lived a life without the love that you have. Although my mother never loved me deeply, she did see that my life was protected. I now have a comforter dearer than my mother."

LAST DEEDS

Isaac's wedding day was the beginning of another period of contentment in Abraham's life. Keturah's fruitfulness provided several children for his distraction and amusement in old age—at least for a long interlude.

As time passed, Keturah's children started to reach adulthood while Rebekah and Isaac remained childless. Keturah eventually began to wonder why Abraham kept his inheritance, which their children could use. One day she scolded Abraham for not using some of his abundant wealth to help their children. She knew he was generous with his wealth when helping other people. Because their children were ready to start their own families, she couldn't understand why Abraham hadn't given them some of his estate already.

Abraham gave her a noncommittal answer—something to the effect that he would consider her request. He immediately went to a place of meditation. He was bound by a request from God to hold most of his goods for Isaac's inheritance. Nevertheless, nearly everyone around him considered Rebekah to be barren. Already several of Abraham's closest servants had made discreet inquires into how he was to dispose of his holdings. He was definitely starting to age now, and all knew that his life was drawing to a close. Before ending his mediation, he resolved to provide some help to Keturah's children while reserving the major part for Isaac. Thankfully, the mediation gave him a renewed faith that Rebekah would yet bear children.

Abraham rarely traveled anymore, so he sent servants to call Isaac to his residence. "My son, I want to talk to you about the lack of a grandchild from you. Keturah is asking for the bequeathing of my goods to her children. As you know, I can't do that, because you have been promised by God to inherit what I own. Nonetheless, Rebekah's barrenness causes me to appear to be a miser, as I have no other heirs on whom to bestow my wealth."

"Father, we are aware of the condition—a condition that is making me despondent. I know not what to do!"

"My dear son, we—you, Rebekah, and I—need to plead to God to remove her barrenness. God has promised that you will be the one descendant of mine who will have my main inheritance and his main blessing. I didn't call you here to scold you or condemn you, but to encourage you to increase your supplication to God."

Not long after this meeting, Rebekah became pregnant with twins. When this joyous news reached Abraham, he organized a feast to give thanks to God. Abraham was so happy that he totally missed the scowls that passed across Keturah's face in the days and months that followed.

When Keturah heard of the successful birth of the twins, she decided it was time for more pleading. Hardly allowing Abraham to enjoy the announcement of the birth of Jacob and Esau, she accosted him about his continued lack of support for their children. Even though Isaac now had children, he surely wouldn't need all of what Abraham owned.

Abraham agreed that he could spare some of his goods and animals and promised a response the next day. Abraham's resolve the next morning was as firm as any resolve in his life, including regarding the rescue of Lot. He spoke to Keturah and her children with a stronger voice than he had had for many years. "I have directed my servants to set aside money, goods, and animals for each of you, my children. You are to arrange for transportation of your gifts and depart our community before the next new moon."

Each of his children stood with various degrees of incredulity showing on their faces. The passionate but usually cheerful Keturah became upset. Replying gruffly but outwardly politely, Keturah demanded that their children be given more than just gifts. She could understand giving Isaac a larger portion of the estate, but she couldn't understand why he deserved the majority of Abraham's holdings.

"Keturah, I am bound by God to dispose most of my goods upon Isaac. I have been generous in my giving to our children. I am sending them to lands to the east, because they should be able to lead a prosperous life there with what I have given them. I am also sending them away because I don't want any conflict between their children and Isaac's children. I allowed Ishmael to live with me after Isaac's birth. Having to send him and his mother away as I did—an action that could have cost them their lives without help from God—disturbed me greatly. I am avoiding repeating that action. They must depart, but they will have adequate goods and belongings to survive, even prosper."

Keturah and some of her children continued to complain and petition him for a larger share of his wealth, but Abraham made no additions to any of their gifts. As each child departed with his family and belongings over the succeeding days, Keturah stayed by her husband's side, despite once having threatened to leave with her children.

*   *   *   *   *

Meanwhile, the birth of the twins to Rebekah proved a major turning point in Isaac's life. Abraham—probably with good reason—hadn't bestowed much of his goods on Isaac, either. Isaac had reverted back to a languid lifestyle, but the birth of the twins prompted him into industrious action.

Rebekah was delighted by the change in her husband and the prospects of increased wealth; she was getting tired of waiting for Isaac's inheritance from Abraham. Nonetheless, her biggest concern wasn't financial. Almost from day one, the twins had showed different personalities. Esau, who had started to be born first, was grabbed by the heel in a seeming effort to pull him back into the birth canal and be replaced by Jacob, who, nevertheless, was born second. Jacob showed a subtle aggressiveness during play, while Esau displayed ambivalence toward most things, the exception being his strong reaction against Jacob.

After tolerating the twins' actions for a while, Rebekah told Isaac about them. Isaac smiled and wondered if she was just imagining the conflict between the twins; they were too young to be enemies already. When Rebekah insisted she wasn't imagining their behavior, Isaac suggested that they would grow out of it. Rebekah reluctantly accepted his speculation but resolved to watch the children carefully as they developed.

*   *   *   *   *

With several longtime worries off his shoulders, Abraham settled into an old-age mode. He never traveled out of his immediate camp area. Eliezer also became weary of managing his master's holdings and, with Abraham's approval, appointed a younger caretaker to work with Isaac in preserving his inheritance.

As Abraham's health continued to decline, Isaac visited his father more often. Nevertheless, one morning Abraham awoke with a resolve to visiting Isaac's home, although he had seen his son rather recently. A servant stood motionless at his command, telling him he shouldn't make such a long trip. His health wouldn't allow him to withstand the exertion.

"Don't consider me to be so helpless! I feel better than I have for a long time. I want to see Isaac's home one last time."

Several others tried to persuade him not to make the trip but to no avail. As Abraham was being helped to mount the gentlest camel in the herd, he started to twitch. Those twitches soon became strong spasms. He was gently placed on the ground and held from harming himself until his body relaxed.

By midday Abraham was conscious and resting on a comfortable bed. He couldn't sit up, however, without pillow support. Realizing he would never rise from this deathbed, attendants immediately sent messages to Isaac, Eliezer, and other friends. Because Abraham's physician didn't want him bothered by a lot of people walking through his tent, straws were drawn for the privilege of seeing him for the last time; otherwise only Isaac and Eliezer would be allowed to see him.

Upon awakening the next morning after a restful night, Abraham requested a talk with Eliezer. His physician started to deny the request but quickly agreed that there was no use trying to preserve his waning strength now. Eliezer, who had moved into a neighboring tent, asked for a scribe as he entered Abraham's tent.

As the physician escorted Eliezer to the bedside, he told Eliezer that this could be the last time he would see his master alive. Abraham was feeling better today, but this improvement could be his final rally before death.

Eliezer had just finished greetings when the scribe arrived. Abraham looked at the scribe and shook his head. "If you please, I don't wish for my final words to Eliezer to be recorded. I am now powerless to change the future, and I don't want my legacy influenced by anything that I might say on what could be my last day in this phase of my existence." Eliezer immediately motioned for the scribe to leave.

"What I am about to tell you is an unburdening of my spirit. I believe it's truthful to say that I have had a relationship with God like no other man before or after me. Yet those early promises from God have been largely deferred to a time long subsequent to my death. Because of my absolute faith in God, I can still rejoice in his blessings in my lifetime and those to come. Nevertheless, I can*not* but believe that if I had been fully subservient to his will, my son Isaac would be inheriting a world that would experience those blessings now, rather in a distant future. Additionally, I would be receiving my reward instead of spending a long sleep separated from my Benefactor.

"And speaking of Isaac, I have given my inheritance to him only because of God's command. The expulsion of Ishmael and the sending away of Keturah's children with gifts far less valuable than Isaac's inheritance ran counter to my natural inclination. Of all my children, I feel that Isaac has the least natural tendency to guide his offspring to preserve an inheritance, but I implicitly trust God that there's a good reason for Isaac to have my wealth."

When Abraham paused in reflection, Eliezer spoke. "Should you really believe that God's promises were meant for this age? Didn't you tell me some years ago that God was withholding fulfilling your blessing because the sins of the Amorites, your allies, weren't full?"

"That makes a good excuse, but I am sure that a way could have been worked out to fulfill those promises at this time. That is my belief despite of what I know of the mercy of God toward all, including the Amorites—a mercy that exceeds human comprehension, although such speculation is really little more than idle reasoning.

"As a final admission, I believe that my affair with Hagar sealed my fate. It's really strange that the children of the only woman who truly loved me, Keturah, were never involved in an extended controversy over inheritance. In retrospect, I must acknowledge that I let my lust get the best of me when I listened to Sarah's reasoning about engendering my heir through Hagar. I also accept your supposition that she was setting me up for failure, although I don't believe she understood her own motives at that instance. The consensus of some is that her entrapment, as they word it, was done to give her an excuse to justify our ultimate estrangement. I would cite that our continued state of conjugal living for several years thereafter proves otherwise. I think she made the suggestion without a lot of consideration and didn't realize she had ulterior motives."

When Abraham seemed almost to faint, Eliezer called for the bedside attendant, but Abraham asked for a moment's rest before continuing his talk.

"Despite my personal failures in interacting with my father, Lot, and Ishmael, I have had several fulfilling associations in my life. In some respects, I would say that my association with you was my greatest social experience other than my walk with God. Unbelievably, he never did directly rebuke me, unless you consider his demands for me to stop pleading and to do something that I didn't want to do to be a rebuke.

"My close walk with God hasn't been the only unusual facet of my life. Of my relatives who became offended, only Shem reconciled with me. I suppose he came to realize shortly before his death that his offense was mostly caused by his own jealousy over our success in Aram. Unfortunately, some of the greatest animosity toward Isaac is being expressed by the children of my nephew Lot and son Ishmael.

"The only associate of stature outside of my immediate community to remain faithful throughout my life was Mamre. Even my choosing of a wife for Isaac from my distant homeland instead of from among his nearby relatives didn't offend him—at least not visibly.

"I am starting to tire and must sleep soon, but before my last comment: would you convey my regards to Eber? I suppose I should include him as a constant faithful associate, although I had limited interaction with him. Do you remember the time he snuck into our camp disguised as bedraggled bedouin?"

After Eliezer nodded to both questions, Abraham closed with several reminiscent stories about the lives of his father, Terah; first wife, Sarah; and the noble Shem.

The message received by Isaac had only indicated that his father was sick; therefore, his lack of haste brought him to his father's bedside late in the evening of the same day. Abraham awoke from a sleep only able to speak a few words of greeting and to squeeze Isaac's hand weakly. When he was told that Rebekah had not been able to make the trip to see him, he managed to request that Isaac convey his final blessing to her.

Isaac motioned for Abraham to be silent. "Father, please don't speak further. I have much to say to you before you go to your reward. I know that you are interested in Rebekah. I will indeed give her your final good-bye." Isaac proceeded to highlight their recent life and how the twins were prospering. He specifically stressed how Abraham's heritage was assured through his two grandchildren, Esau and Jacob.

Abraham stayed alert for about a twelfth-day, listening to Isaac reassure him of the generations to come and his good deeds of the past. Then he slowly began to drift in and out of consciousness. After about another twelfth-day, he lost consciousness for the last time. Isaac and his physician sat by his side until the dawning of the next day, when Abraham's last breath seemed to coincide with the first peek of the sun's disk above the horizon.

*　　*　　*　　*　　*

Eliezer and the scribe had remained in a nearby tent overnight. The next morning, as they were preparing to leave, a rider approached with the sad news of the death of the imperfect but great man of faith, Abraham. Eliezer rent his tunic and requested a tent in which he could spend some days of mourning in sackcloth and ashes. Before the servant left, he inquired as to how he should conduct the burial of Abraham. Eliezer promised that he would arrive at the deathbed within a twelfth-day.

When he did, he greeted all attending the body. "May I express my deepest sympathy to everyone. My own sorrow is so great that I wish that I could have died in his place. While I have yet to express my mourning, I wish to be involved with the proper respect in burial."

A distraught Isaac immediately gained his composure. "Eliezer, as my father's lifetime advisor, you should direct all preparations for his burial, assuming that you're able."

Eliezer suggested that the burial preparers, who had been summoned the day before, be allowed to start their work. Although a memorial service was necessary, it would have to be after Abraham's burial. Many people must be invited to attend, and there was no hope of contacting all of them before the allotted time for burial. He further stated that Ishmael had been sought from the time of Abraham's first attack of weakness. Hopefully, he would be found in time to attend the burial.

Isaac seemed shaken at the mention of Ishmael's name. "I understand that he is my brother, but of course I don't remember him. Our paths have crossed a couple of times, but I never did get to see him, except at a distance. I also understand that he departed our camp when I was a baby, but neither my mother nor father would discuss the reason why he left our camp. I surmised that the occasion of his departure may have been under conflict. I wonder how he will treat me, and how I should act toward him."

"Isaac, I would like to talk about the circumstances of Ishmael's departure after my mourning days are over. I have much to tell you about him. I would suggest that you have your servants handle all of the billeting chores necessary for his comfort during his stay. You should allow for an audience with him of short duration. If he has any questions about your father's estate, you must tell him to talk to me or the estate's chief scribe."

"Thank you for that advice. I was concerned that he may yet want part of our father's inheritance."

"Should he or any of Keturah's children who might attend broach the subject of inheritance, refer them to the scribe, who has sworn documents consigning Abraham's estate to you. Although I won't advise you as to any gifts you might wish to bestow upon your brothers, please don't in any way indicate that they should have a share of his estate."

"And why should I be so hoarding with our father's wealth?"

"Because once you concede that they should inherit with you, their demands are likely to be boundless until they have demanded most of the estate, probably not even leaving you an equitable share. Remember, your father gave his wealth to you to manage. It is your responsibility to be a good steward of his largesse."

When Isaac probed for further advice, Eliezer told him that they must attend to the burial plans now and again reminded Isaac to see him after the mourning days were completed.

Before the burial cortege had reached the burial site of Machpelah, it was overtaken by a small host accompanying Ishmael, who immediately asked where Abraham was being buried and why that location had been chosen.

At Eliezer's nodding, the chief scribe informed Ishmael that his father, Abraham, had purchased a family burial plot at the time of Sarah's death. It had been consecrated for use by all his immediate descendants.

"Does that mean that I can be buried there, or was my expulsion of so long ago also an expulsion from the family?"

After noticing Eliezer shaking his head, the scribe assured Ishmael that no edict existed to prevent his burial next to his father.

"Don't worry, my people wouldn't dare bury my body anywhere near that of the witch who expelled my mother and me from the camp. Although we nearly died from her action, God blessed me and my mother. He turned our disgrace into good for us. We soon prospered many times over what we would have gained from staying in a place where we were not liked and had to fight for most of what we did receive."

After a long pause, Eliezer spoke. "Ishmael, I am sorry that you still carry a grudge against Sarah beyond her grave, but I am pleased that you have done well."

The caretaker appointed by Ephron always kept a burial niche available for reception of a body. Because no designated priest was available, the ceremony consisted of a silent prayer by those individuals accompanying the body. The burial preparers then placed Abraham in his resting place and closed the crypt.

*   *   *   *   *

Isaac started to leave before Ishmael could speak to him, but decided he was morally bound to speak to him and that now was the proper time to do so. "I am Isaac, your younger brother. I am sorry we have never met formally since my babyhood. I have often wondered what my brother was like, but my father always intimated that I shouldn't contact you. Because of his death, I see no reason to continue to shun your presence."

"I am not surprised. Nevertheless, my mother always scolded me when I spoke ill of our father. She honored him to the end of her life, which ended a few moons ago. Conversely, she instilled me with a hatred of your mother. Out of deference to you, I won't speak of your mother again, but I will pay my final respects to our father and be on my way. Also, don't be concerned with any request concerning our father's estate. Other than her final good-bye, my mother's last action on her deathbed was to make me promise to honor Lord Abraham, as she addressed him, and not to contest the bequeathing of his estate to you."

Isaac thanked Ishmael for his civility. He started to utter an invitation for a lengthy stay so that they could become acquainted but decided not to. A quick departure would prevent Ishmael's suppressed anger from bursting forth into embarrassing or dangerous arguments.

Ishmael declined to attend the memorial for Abraham. "No. I have given my respects to my father, Lord Abraham. I don't need to associate with his peers and friends, some of whom never showed me any respect. The burial site reminds me of my great father; the memorial would remind me of a part of my life that I should abhor." Eliezer nodded and waved a silent farewell as Ishmael's band rode away.

Several days later, commotion arose around the tent where Eliezer had spent his period of mourning. He had arisen from his previous night's sleep and had been preparing to meet Isaac, who had returned from Lahai-roi, later in the day.

"What happened?" Isaac inquired as he arrived at Eliezer's tent.

A physician looked up from Eliezer's prone body while explaining that Eliezer had fallen as he left his tent to come to see Isaac. Except for some abrasions and a possible fracture of an arm, the physician said, he was probably all right.

The physician signaled for some attendants to bring a carrying litter for transporting him to a convalescent tent to have his wounds dressed and his arm set. He was given a generous serving of strong drink to sip while his wounds were being attended to. When Eliezer had clearly entered a state of low-level euphoria, the physician skillfully stretched and contracted the arm while eliciting only a slight moan from the patient.

The next morning, Isaac came to see Eliezer. "I guess we need to postpone the memorial until you heal."

"Isaac, I think you should proceed with the memorial as soon as possible. Abraham had many friends who didn't get to attend his burial, and they are anxious to show their respects. Memorials to lesser individuals can wait, but not for a man of Abraham's stature. Also, by the time all of the invitations have gone out and the guests have arrived, I should have healed enough to attend. If not, I was at his burial ceremony; that would be enough."

Both agreed to summon a scribe to draft the invitations and memorial speech for the ceremony. When Isaac began to name the people who would receive invitations, he was stopped from talking. Eliezer reminded him that several of his relatives, including all of the children of Ishmael and Lot, must be excluded. He recounted the belligerence of Ishmael at the burial ceremony and informed Isaac that recent intelligence reports indicated that Lot's descendants could be planning a raid on his home. He also advised him that some of Keturah's children dwelled in an area unsafe for casual travel. Nearly all of the people who made the invitation list were friends or associates, not close relatives.

*　*　*　*　*

As Eliezer carefully walked to the memorial site, he noticed that Isaac had a look of despondency not usually characterized by grief. "Isaac, is something bothering you?"

"Yes, I guess so. Ever since we started drafting the invitation list and excluding those who shouldn't attend, I have been concerned that my father had a lot of antagonistic relatives and almost no friendly relatives. I then began to wonder if I were the cause of all this. I, a major miracle of birth, wind up causing all of my brothers to hate me."

Eliezer thought for a moment before answering. "First, you are *not* to blame for this hatred. Except for the perceived hidden jealousy and resentment by your uncle Nahor in Ur, your father brought most of his family problems upon himself. His inability to keep from making mistakes with family matters was a problem I was never good at stopping. I noticed a growing interaction with Hagar that I told myself was just normal for job assignments. Nonetheless, I was not very surprised when her pregnancy became obvious. I was also too eager to get rid of Lot when Abraham told him he should leave for the Vale of Siddim."

"Do you think my father would have acted any differently toward his family had you advised him against those actions?"

"In fact, I did advise him to wait for God's answer when he received a message from God that told him he would engender his own heir. I did warn him, but it's strange that only now am I wondering if I could have done more. I guess a certain amount of hero worship caused me not see some of his faults."

"Eliezer, don't you think a man as close to God as my father should have been able to handle family matters better?"

"We can discuss this further after the service, which is about to begin, if you wish. I believe that you are asking a question I can't answer. Had I been that capable, I would have helped him solve some of his life-long problems with your mother, Sarah."

During the closing hours of Abraham's death, no thought had been given to the place for his memorial; he had only mentioned that his burial should be at the family plot at Machpelah. After his burial, several places had been discussed before an expanse of ground on the shore of Lake Chinnereth was chosen. Nevertheless, when the time had come to finish the invitations, an orator scribe had proposed that Shechem would be a better place for projecting any speaker's voice. Hence, Eliezer was now seated on a small rise between the mountains in the valley of Shechem and near the speaking platform.

To avoid hurting any feelings, only Isaac, Rebekah, Esau, and Jacob were scheduled to be seated on the platform, but suddenly Eliezer noticed that five people had taken seats there. A second look revealed an elderly man who looked familiar but remained unidentifiable to Eliezer. He had seen Isaac's family mount the steps to the platform but hadn't noticed how the elderly man got onto the platform. He inquired of others around him, but none could discern who he was, either. *I guess they will tell us who he is soon, because the first speaker is prepared to start*, Eliezer resolved.

"Friends and family of Abraham, at last we have gathered for the last formal honoring of the great man. I will give a brief history of his long life, which will be followed by tributes from the people seated behind me. They are his son Jacob's family and the aged gentleman who really needs no introduction: Eber."

The announcement of Eber's name caused a gasp from Eliezer and a feeling of chagrin. *How could I have not recognized him? Who else so aged would be here in a place of honor? But it has been a long time since I have seen him, and his visage has changed considerably since then.*

The speaker, who was the chief scribe for Abraham's estate, started the history by describing the world into which Abraham was born. The death of Abraham's forefather Peleg in battle about four years before his birth was generally considered to have marked the beginning of a great conflict in the world. The death of Noah about two years later seemed to cast a pall over all of the earth. The death of that man who had saved mankind's very existence through his favor with God distanced all of them even further from God.

As the history continued, Eliezer marveled at how many influential people had intersected Abraham's life without his gaining a close relationship with the world in general. His reputation was far more widespread than was the knowledge of his person. The recounting of his actions with Mamre and Isak, now both deceased, were particularly poignant. The mention of their names caused Eliezer to cry for the first time since Abraham's death.

Even though he wasn't family, Eber was given the honor of being the last speaker. The scribe and the members of Abraham's family had barely mentioned Eliezer's name. He had not, however, been able to tell Eber not to. Eber, a man whom Eliezer had worked with many times, made Eliezer the highlight of Abraham's associations. Nevertheless, Eliezer was happy to hear Eber invite him for an audience when the memorial was over.

"General, I would never have believed that you would have tried to attend this memorial. Really, I was so disbelieving that I wondered who you were until your name was announced."

"Master Eliezer, this is my first effort at travel in over a decade, and I am rather sure that it will be my last, assuming that I make it home again. Nevertheless, I just had to risk my health, and even my life, to attend this memorial."

"Oh, I am sure you will make it home; you look well despite your decline since I saw you last, long ago."

"Decline it is! I haven't been involved in military matters for at least twenty years. It may surprise you, but I am jealous of you. You were involved with Abraham in the most significant military success of my lifetime. Even the slaying of Nimrod has to take second place to your victory over the four kings."

"I know whatever jealousy you held against Abraham was none or never expressed. However, such was not the same with Shem. Abraham mentioned how the jealousy of Shem was nearly carried to his grave. Nonetheless, it is truly tragic that all of the noted warriors of the past are now gone or passed into dotage. But a further and greater tragedy is that all of our efforts seem to have had no lasting value."

Eber graciously refused an invitation to stay, stating that his assisting travelers were leaving immediately, and he must accompany them. Eliezer scarcely had finished a tearful good-bye when he saw Rebekah's father and brother.

Bethuel was the first to greet the weeping Eliezer, supposing aloud that Eliezer's release from grief had finally come.

A number of thoughts quickly crossed Eliezer's mind. It was all he could do not to ask Bethuel if he were there to solicit some of the bounty that Isaac had just inherited. *If there's wealth to be had, Bethuel will soon be there,* he silently chortled but calmly replied to Bethuel's greeting. "I guess I have been crying, but great as my grief is for the loss of Abraham, my tears are for the failure of our hopes in this time. The meeting with Eber brought back memories that can only be described as sorrowful."

Bethuel displayed an uncharacteristic compassionate look as he wistfully expressed sympathy for the trials that had afflicted other members of his family. His grandfather's assignment of his family to Ur had given him a life of prosperity and peace. Of course, his life had been quite ordinary, without the interesting upheavals that Abraham and Eliezer had experienced.

When Isaac approached him with a request for travel preparation back to home, Eliezer asked Isaac to see if the maintenance crews could provide Eliezer a way home. The affirmative response allowed him to stay behind for final private tribute. He gingerly walked to a spot away from the cleanup activities to give his final oral dialogue to God.

"My God and Comforter, I want to thank you for a long life in service to the greatest man on the earth in my time. Although you didn't see fit to extend your fullest blessings during his lifetime, he was most appreciative to be the progenitor of your people. If there's anything I may yet do to further your plans through Isaac, please guide me to their fulfillment. Though my body is frail, my spirit is yet strong for you."

SIX

TEENAGE PROBLEMS

ELIEZER HAD SCARCELY ARRIVED home before he became quite ill. *My God, have I only lived to pay my last respects to my earthly master? If so, I thank you for sparing my life until now.*

The physician who had attended Abraham's final illness was soon by his bedside. After careful examination, he exclaimed, "I believe that you can live many more days if you follow my advice. Your bodily constitution can no longer stand long trips. Another trip like the one you have just taken could kill you."

"Sire, I felt well all during the trip to and from Shechem. Are you sure there isn't some other problem with my health?"

"When people are faced with tasks they must accomplish, they often perform well beyond their abilities. I am not surprised that you held up well during the trip, especially the trip up. My guess is that your mind considered your return trip important also. Then, once you were home, the mind relaxed to its normal state, which permitted your overused body to assert its weakness. I am prescribing several days' rest and some special herbs to use for tea. I am also assigning an attendant who will tend to your every need until you are well again."

To his physician's surprise, Eliezer was feeling well by the third day.

*   *   *   *   *

Unbeknownst to Eliezer, a servant of Isaac had been watching Eliezer's tent nearly constantly since the moment of his return. When the servant saw

Eliezer leave his tent, he approached Eliezer with an urgent request from Isaac for an audience with him.

Eliezer seemed to suppress a negative response before replying, "I understand. I had planned to go to Lahai-roi to see him after a short rest upon my return from the memorial. Now my illness has left me too weak to depart our camp for a moon or more. I can, however, talk to him if he could come to see me."

The servant thanked him and left to send a message to Isaac.

*   *   *   *   *

Upon arrival, Isaac asked one question after another until Eliezer politely asked him to stop. Eliezer then told him the full story behind Ishmael's expulsion from camp and also about Lot's departure.

Then he answered Isaac's other questions. "You asked me about the level of protection you will need. As inheritor of your father's estate, you have control not only of his wealth, but also the consignment of his forces. Assuming you still wish to live at Lahai-roi, you could transfer some of your warriors there. None of the tribes in the area would allow a large army to approach to attack anyone. Therefore, your only danger from Lot's forces, if his blustering is anything more than an idle threat, would be a small group disguised as desert raiders. Hence, I would suggest moving a few more soldiers from Beersheba to serve as watchmen in your area."

"What about Ishmael? He wasn't exactly civil at our father's burial. Also, his denial of any interest in my father's estate didn't seem to exclude anything he could take by force."

"Isaac, your home is relatively secure for now, but you must talk with your advisers about protection in the future. Your nearest enemies are the children of your cousin Lot and of your brother Ishmael. They aren't strong enough now to pose a significant threat, but they are likely to strengthen. Their progeny are multiplying rapidly, and they are likely to grow much more numerous than your family. This is not meant cruelly, but the wives of your cousin and brother are fertile. Therefore, it behooves you to form an alliance with your neighbors for protection. I can no longer advise you in these matters because of my failing health. My physician has promised me many more days, but I believe he is too optimistic. Of course, as long as I have any degree of health and sound mind, I will be available for consultation. I just can't handle any constant daily chores."

Isaac continued to ask questions about different aspects of the estate, but Eliezer referred all matters to his advisors. Just before departing, Isaac posed one final question: "As my father was slipping into his final unconsciousness before death, he mentioned something about 'paying Eliezer his wages.' Do I still owe you more wages?"

"No. I think what occurred was a remembrance of long ago, before you were born. He had just received a message from God that his ultimate blessing to you and your descendants would be withheld for many years into the future. This news caused him to decide that his current heritage didn't need to be so large, given the far future fulfillment. He then bestowed a tenth of his goods upon me for what he called unpaid back wages, although I tried to persuade him to give me only half of that amount. Since then I have been well compensated, so there is nothing owing to me."

"I wish to thank you for what you did for my father one more time. I will keep in contact with you, because I am sure I will need your wisdom. May God grant you many days! I know there may be some selfishness in that blessing, but your death will be another great loss to our communities."

Isaac approached Yosef to request a transfer of troops to Lahai-roi. "Yosef, I have been told I should ask you about assigning troops as lookouts around my home. I understand there have been threats of attacks against me. I was hoping to take some soldiers home with me."

When Yosef told him that all of the warriors were away on assignment, with the first contingent not due back until the day after the next, Isaac replied after some thoughtful consideration, "I must get back home, given the possible threat of attack. Just send them as soon as you can."

When Isaac had turned his mount to depart, Yosef called to him to wait. He told Isaac that he could be spared for a few days. He would also leave word for certain warriors to change their billeting to Lahai-roi after a short rest upon their return. If Isaac would give him another twelfth-day, he could ride home with him. That way Isaac would have one more protector the moment he arrived home.

As Isaac and Yosef rode into the former's homestead, Isaac noticed that Rebekah was having trouble corralling some contrary goats. He motioned to Yosef for help with the wayward goats. When the goats were confined, Isaac addressed Rebekah concerning where all her help had gone.

"Esau has all of the servants not handling household duties with him on a hunting trip, and who knows where Jacob is. The boy seems to wander off all of the time, with only a waving of the hand to show that he is leaving."

"Why did you allow Esau to take all of the servants hunting, or why didn't you call some of the household servants?"

"I didn't call any of the household servants because I thought I could handle the goats myself. They usually are easily herded. I suppose they noticed I was alone and thought they could get by with something. Also, Esau has spoiled most of our outside servants; they are too eager to accommodate him on his hunting trips. In addition, you are no help. I believe your declaration of liking venison over domestic meats gives Esau an excuse to spend nearly all of his time hunting. He claims that his efforts at hunting provides food for the family and pleases you."

"Rebekah, I like what I like. Have I ever told Esau he should spend all his time looking for deer to kill? Also, why isn't Jacob here? It seems to me that he is away much of the time also, and I am sure I haven't encouraged him in whatever pursuits he is following."

"No, but you haven't given Esau the proper direction in being a herdsman, not to mention your failure to reprimand his neglect of learning to read and write. Concerning Jacob, he spends a proper amount of time with his chores, although his wanderings are a mystery. For instance, he asked me if I needed anything done before he left. I told him no, because I wasn't aware of the problem with the goats when he left. Also, Jacob is progressing well with reading, writing, and counting. His tutors have someone to teach, unlike the tutors for your eldest son, who are probably skillful huntsmen by now."

"I see. Esau is my son! I guess I am unaware of who his mother is, because you are not claiming him!"

*   *   *   *   *

Rebekah scowled and walked away to finish securing the holding pen for the goats. *The women in Abraham's immediate family are certainly strong-willed,* Yosef thought while barely suppressing a smile

Isaac appeared both angry and perplexed, but he remained silent for an awkwardly long time. Just as Yosef was about to speak, he said, "I didn't intend to involve you in any of my family squabbles. You may think that Rebekah is like her aunt Sarah, and she is somewhat, but she is much more loving. This problem with Esau has been building for many, many moons, even years. Everyone has a breaking point, and I suppose that a whole set of circumstance happened to cause her to reach hers. After spending many decades of my life without any close love, her few tantrums are less annoying than a bite from a stinging fly."

From the mention of Esau's name, Yosef felt he might be able to help with this situation and asked Isaac whether he could make a suggestion.

"What is it? I am ready to accept almost any advice."

Yosef started by explaining that he would be able to devote himself to helping with Esau once the new warriors arrived—that is, if Isaac could get the estate manager's approval for him to stay at Lahai-roi for a while.

When Isaac assured the approval, Yosef recounted his days as an overseer of Ishmael and how he had tempered him toward civility. He admitted that some might consider him to have been a failure because of the final incident that had caused Sarah to expel Ishmael from camp, but his successes with other children proved his abilities; not every child could be tutored. It was true that he wasn't very good with babies, as his wife frequently told him. Nevertheless, when a child grew old enough to start believing himself capable of adult actions, Yosef was good at modifying bad behavior.

"But Esau has long since expressed his assumed maturity. He is bigger, stronger, and more capable in many things than I am. I know he is still a few years shy of adulthood, and I hate to think of what he might become, considering that he still has growing to do. Assuming I accept that you can change people's behavior, how do you propose to handle Esau?"

Yosef agreed that beginning to tutor Esau at this age posed a major problem, but regardless of a person's age, everyone had some vulnerable areas where the right influence could usually change them—not always, but often.

The first thing that Yosef would do, he explained, was find an area of Esau's life that he didn't want anyone restricting. Based on what Rebekah said, it would seem that Esau enjoyed hunting almost above everything else. He also seemed to want hunting companions. Given the increased need for protection here, it was feasible to require all servants to desist from hunting, except for occasional trips to provide a taste of venison. This plan would cause Esau to stay home more.

"Yosef, I am not sure that he won't find some hunting companions from among the tribes around here. He has already invited some of them on hunting trips with him. He is also so precocious that he is starting to notice the daughters of those tribes, especially the Hethites. I am afraid he has too many associations to restrict his activities effectively."

Yosef suggested that they might have to get creative if Esau tried to thwart his plan. He could be assigned secondary guard duty, which would not require constant lookout. One stipulation connected with that duty would be to avoid idleness when not called upon to turn away some enemy. Sessions with a tutor could then be assigned.

"What you are suggesting sounds good, but if I know Esau, he will thwart us in some way."

Yosef and Jacob agreed that they would wait to try their plan until after the transferred warriors arrived. Despite the turmoil of the day, the evening meal passed pleasantly, without any argument of any kind. Rebekah was as pleasant as Yosef had seen her on the trip from her homeland. *Although strong-willed, I suspect that Rebekah gives Isaac little to be upset about, and I still suspect that Isaac is finding it hard to act as head of a family,* Yosef mused before being interrupted by Esau, who asked him if he had time to hunt for venison.

Yosef mumbled several words before he was able to speak plainly. He told Esau that he seldom hunted, because he had spent his life as a warrior or tutor. His hunting endeavors had been few and short, because his troops had seldom run low on supplies. A good warrior always tried to ensure that he and his fellows had adequate food on hand and nothing more, because his goal was to fight the enemy, not hunt food to survive.

Isaac smiled and remarked almost rhetorically that most people didn't have time to pursue hunting as a daily job.

Yosef's mild regard for hunting didn't appear to faze Esau even slightly. He promptly interrupted, "I believe it is now possible for someone to live his life as a hunter. The growing prosperity around here has several families living a life of idleness, but they still have a taste for wild venison. Some of my friends say they can sell all of the venison that they can cure."

Rebekah had been suppressing a growing look of contempt for the direction that the talk around the evening meal was taking. "My son, how can you talk of a lifetime of hunting when our flocks are so large that we need your help? Also, the life of a hunter is dangerous and taxing on his health; not surprisingly, many hunters never reach old age. For all of the thrill of the hunt, the heat, the cold, and the wet make for a miserable life most of the time. I must insist that you start spending more time at home, or maybe we should assign you to a herdsman in Beersheba. I am not asking you to stop hunting completely—just don't make it your only job."

Amid the chores of touring the expanse of the area around Isaac's home for vulnerability from attack, Yosef talked to both Esau and Jacob. Discreetly, he inquired into Jacob's activities—Esau's had already been thoroughly discussed. He found that Jacob was an avid observer of nature. He could recite descriptions of the habits of many animals and distinguish differences in some plants that others would consider to be the same variety.

When told that his mother didn't understand where he went on his excursions from home, Jacob reacted with obvious amazement. "I talk to my mother about all of the things that I see on my trips. I guess that she's too busy to comprehend the amount of time and effort that it has taken to gain my knowledge. I'll tell her at once about my observations of nature."

*   *   *   *   *

Within a few days, the full assignment of warriors had arrived at Lahai-roi.

The day after the last arrival, Yosef gave all of the warriors a final tour of the area, pointing out potential attack routes as they rode.

With his military duties finished, Yosef chose a midmorning break to recite his plan for Esau to Isaac. It basically consisted of transferring Esau to a herdsman's apprenticeship at Beersheba. He stated that he had changed his mind and thought Rebekah's suggestion was better than his original idea; he explained how this move would accomplish several goals. It would remove Esau from his familiar hunting grounds, separate him from those who would placate his every whim, and teach him some skills he needed to learn.

Isaac looked pleased, and then perplexed, and then skeptical before replying, "I agree with you and Rebekah, but I am doubtful we can get him to do what you are suggesting. You can probably get him to Beersheba without a great deal of effort. But once there, he is almost certain to run away. He is so competent at blending into the wilderness that his pursuers aren't likely to find him."

Yosef suggested that they coerce Esau into acceptance by threatening to deny him an inheritance—to which Isaac uttered a sardonic reply that Esau really didn't care about his inheritance, especially if it denied him any hunting privileges.

Yosef promptly disagreed by citing that Esau had talked to him about his life in general. The words had come out of his mouth did indeed deprecate his inheritance, but also occasionally revealed resentment over sharing things with Jacob.

Isaac wondered whether Yosef was suggesting that Esau be watched as a virtual prisoner until his selfish nature appreciated what he had to inherit.

Yosef startled Isaac by proposing that Esau be given freedom of movement, even though this action would probably result in his fleeing Beersheba. Nonetheless, whether he decided to hide out in the wilderness or head straight back to Beersheba didn't matter. He was quite able to care for himself either way. Yosef guessed that Esau would return to Beersheba within less than three moons. He wouldn't find any companionship in the wilderness—even the animals there didn't like him.

When Isaac loudly proclaimed that he couldn't accept the possibility of his son getting killed or captured as a slave of some bedouin tribe, Yosef assured him that Esau was too clever to be caught by any bedouin. Alone, he was slippery as a desert fox—and as invisible as one. Next to a shepherd's life, the life of a bedouin was repulsive to Esau. He liked to roam and hunt, but he also liked to return to the comfort of a nice home after a few days. That was another reason why he would likely only stay away from Beersheba for a relatively short time. Yosef begged Isaac to trust him on this matter. Although he couldn't be absolutely certain that Esau wouldn't die in the wilderness, Esau had great survival skills and an aversion to danger.

*   *   *   *   *

Around the evening meal, Isaac asked Esau to accompany him on a trip to Beersheba. He had to see the lead scribe for Abraham's estate, and that scribe also wanted to get his signature on some documents. Yosef would also accompany them to check on his duties there. To every adult's amazement, Esau readily agreed to the trip without a word of dissent.

After several exchanges of conservation, Esau revealed why that he had accepted the trip: "I have been wondering about the hunting opportunities around Beersheba. I wouldn't mind staying there for a while to take a couple of hunting trips."

Yosef saw a look on Isaac's face indicating that he was on the verge of making a scolding statement. Yosef quickly signaled for him to stay silent. Then Yosef told Esau he would be happy to accompany him on a couple of hunting trips if his parents didn't object. Yosef also took the opportunity to hint that Esau was old enough to be assigned a guardian at Beersheba for an extended stay. A knowing wink at Rebekah eased her concerns.

Isaac and Rebekah then calmly discussed with Esau how an assignment in Beersheba would be good for him. They also suggested that Esau should be given a thorough tour of the area around Bethel, at which point Yosef agreed with all of their stipulations.

To discuss the situation alone with Yosef, Isaac used the excuse that he was needed to accompany Yosef for an inspection of the camels to be used on their trip to Beersheba. "I nearly spoiled your plan by denying Esau this stay in Beersheba. Nonetheless, I don't fully understand what your plan is. This action of taking him on hunting trips seems to thwart what we agreed upon."

Yosef respectfully countered that the plan was thoroughly consistent with what they planned. They needed him to like the area before they sprung the herdsman job upon him. Yosef knew some good hunters back home who could help out with the plan. He felt that Esau would fall in love with the area by the end of the second hunt. There was one thing, however, about Esau's acceptance that he wondered about: why would Esau want an inexperienced person as Yosef to accompany him on a hunt?

"I know my son. I think that he wants to impress you with his hunting skills while embarrassing you for your lack of hunting skills."

Yosef smiled and reckoned he would have to swallow some pride. He then asked Isaac whether he had determined the right time to broach the subject of a herdsman's job to Esau. He was sure there would never be a good time to tell him, but an immediate confrontation about the job would likely upset Esau even more. There was no urgent need to remove all hunting activities from his life at his age—or maybe ever. A division of his time between herding and hunting should be acceptable.

"Yosef, you were known as a man of wisdom and talents from an early age. To some people, you were more popular than my father; therefore I trust you. I suppose that I should tell Rebekah of your new plans."

Yosef shook his head and asked Isaac to delay telling her until they were ready to leave and he was are sure that Isaac wouldn't be overheard. Rebekah probably already suspected what they had planned for Esau. Yosef had seen no signs of doubt on her face as they left the evening meals.

The preparation for the trip to Beersheba occurred with only one minor incident. Just before they were to start the trip, Esau and Jacob got into a wrestling and kicking brawl. Esau had made fun of Jacob for being a sissy for staying behind in his mother's care.

Yosef, though beginning to age, was able to grab both boys by the collars of their tunics and present them to Isaac while asking them to explain this "serious" dispute to their father.

Both boys stood pouting during the long pause before Isaac spoke. "Your silence indicates that you are acting as pampered children desiring the same plaything," he finally said. "If I am wrong, I am still waiting for a good excuse for this fight."

Esau looked down at the ground, but Jacob's eyes suddenly sparkled as he spoke. "Esau called me a sissy for staying behind with my mother. I told him to prove that I was a sissy. That's when he kicked at me before I grabbed him and wrestled him to the ground for my protection."

Isaac looked at Yosef as if to ask him to lecture the two boys on what they had done wrong. Yosef almost started to scold them but said nothing. This was a good time for Isaac to accept the responsibility of fatherhood.

Yosef decided to force Isaac into that responsibility by asking, "Do you have any words that you wish to say to your sons before I release them?"

Astonishingly, Isaac gave both boys a convincing reprimand. He told Esau that everyone in the community had a job to do. There were important chores to perform here, and Jacob's remaining at home in no way made him a sissy. Rather, if Esau didn't apologize, Isaac wouldn't take him on the trip and make him do household chores instead. The lead scribe could come by within the next moon to get his signature; there was no absolute need for Esau to accompany them on the trip. Isaac then told Jacob that he should be more tolerant of the insults of his brother. If a polite request for retraction wasn't complied with immediately, he should walk away and consult an adult about what he should do.

"But Father, Esau attacked me before I could have asked any adult."

"Jacob, that's true, but he might not have been so belligerent toward you if you hadn't provoked him. Remember, I said that you should have asked politely for a retraction."

*   *   *   *   *

After looking over Beersheba with the estate manager for two days, Esau became restive and demanded a hunting trip. Esau insisted on taking camels only; they made better supply carriers. He always hunted on foot and never from horseback. Hence, horses were unnecessary.

Yosef was surprised when Esau requested that Yosef lead the hunting formation. When an antelope bolted well before anyone could get in bow range, Yosef noticed a scowl on Esau's face, but thought it signified nothing more than a mild disappointment.

When midday arrived without any kills, Esau lost his temper. "I have never experienced such futile attempts at acquiring game. I thought you were experienced hunters. The only time I had a chance to bring down a deer was spoiled by someone being in my line of sight to the deer."

This indirect type of oral assault was something Yosef had rarely experienced at any time in his life. This attempt at humiliating him immediately brought Isaac's warning to mind. Obviously, Yosef had to admit that his clumsy attempts at stalking game were the main cause for their lack of quarry, but he also must not let Esau usurp his authority. He had to teach the child a proper respect for others who might lack some of the abilities that the child possessed. Esau's superior skills at hunting didn't make him a superior person overall.

Yosef began with a hidden reprimand for Esau. He wondered aloud why Esau wanted him near the lead of the formation. His warrior skills at stealth weren't appropriate for hunting animals, as most of his companions must have noticed. Keeping out of the line of sight of an enemy didn't seem to work the same for hunting animals. Therefore, Yosef decided to place himself at the rear of the formation or remain at the campsite while the rest of them hunted. His vigor of youth had started to wane; a full day of hunting was more than he could easily endure.

Yosef wasn't as exhausted as he had just indicated, but he hadn't lied, either. He felt that a rest until evening was better than continuing with an exercise that had become boring. He hadn't confronted Esau's arrogance directly and wouldn't unless Esau continued to display contempt.

The post meridian hunting results were quite successful, with an antelope and two deer kills. Yosef's closest friend signaled to him upon return from the day's hunt that Esau had acted civilly. *Good. I'll wait for a more appropriate time to correct his arrogance. I should never have invited myself on this trip anyway,* Yosef silently and remorsefully concluded. The ride home that evening concerned mostly what kind of feast they should have to enjoy their kills.

After a week of giving Esau his choice of daily activities, Isaac told his eldest son that he was scheduled to report to the lead shepherd the next day for work duty.

"Why should I have to work with a bunch of goats?" Esau protested. "Haven't I provided ample food to the community by hunting? Father, I know you enjoy the meat from deer, wild sheep, and antelopes more than the insipid taste of kine. I must get back to the hunt; last night's meal was quite distasteful."

Strangely, the adamant insistence by Isaac and Yosef eventually changed Esau's belligerent attitude to one of ready acceptance.

As Esau meekly walked away, Yosef sardonically observed that in no way had Esau accepted the assignment without a long argument. He would be very surprised, he told Isaac, if Esau reported to work the next day.

Isaac pleaded, "Do we have to allow him freedom of movement? After all, he is still child, not yet an adult. Should anything happen to him, I would feel liable and appear so in the eyes of my friends."

Yosef eased Isaac's mind when he told him that some descendants of his father's friend Mamre had been contracted to watch and to follow Esau's every move. They were skilled stalkers and would keep in communication with roving warriors. Esau shouldn't even realize that he was being followed.

As predicted, Esau sneaked out of camp at the start of the darkness before dawn. Esau had managed to acquire a confederate who had tethered a camel loaded with supplies on the outskirts of camp. He quickly led his transportation out of hearing range before mounting and riding rapidly into the waning night.

*　　*　　*　　*　　*

Esau defied Yosef's prediction on how long he would stay in the wilderness for at most two moons. The report from his stalkers, who actually lost sight of him on a couple of occasions, told how his enthusiasm for the hunt waned after the third moon. He began to hunt less and less and soon appeared to be living mostly on vegetation. Gradually the robust young man turned into a somewhat gaunt person who appeared much older than his teen years. Just when the stalkers were about to contact him and offer him some meat, he headed straight back to camp. Esau did kill a small deer before returning to camp, feasting on it to restore some vitality to his visage.

When Isaac received word that Esau had returned to Beersheba in generally good health, he immediately left to see him. He sent a servant ahead to contact a camp leader, so he could get a complete account of Esau's health before meeting him.

The camp leader tried to calm Isaac's anxiety by explaining that his son had returned to camp in a thin but otherwise healthy condition. The physician had commanded him to rest for a week before engaging in any camp activities. He had also put him on a diet designed to give him maximum strength for the amount of food eaten. This diet was important, because Esau needed to build strength without overindulging in a large amount of food. He had probably been subsisting on an insufficient diet for over a moon. The volume of food intake needed to be gradually increased; he would get sick if he were to eat too heartily.

"I am happy that he survived without serious injury or sickness," Isaac said. "Could I see him?"

The camp leader consented but advised him not to mention anything about future duties or criticize him for what he had done. There would be time for reprimand later if needed. The physician believed that Esau had suffered enough to have learned a needed lesson in life; further criticism might depress him to the point of despair.

Isaac found Esau sitting under the shade of his tent, enjoying a drink of sweet tea. "My son, I am overjoyed to see you. Your mother and I have been worried—it seems forever."

"I assume that my mother didn't come with you?"

"No, please. Your mother was as concerned as I, but the message said that you were well. There was no reason that both of us had to come to see you. Nevertheless, I left an important job to see you. You must understand that we love you and want you to succeed in life."

Esau just scowled. "Succeed ... but I suppose that I must undergo some endless scolding before that."

"Son, I believe that you have suffered enough. If you haven't learned that running away from your family produces bad things in your life, there's probably nothing I could say to convince you otherwise. I want you to relax and regain your strength."

"May I come home when I feel better?"

"If that's what you really want, but you have yet to complete your assigned stay in Beersheba."

Isaac stayed in Beersheba until Esau had recovered in strength and attitude. After a week, he decided to talk to Eliezer, whom he hadn't met since arriving in camp. When he finished explaining Yosef's plan to Eliezer, Isaac asked for his opinion.

"I am reluctant to get involved in this matter. I feel that I failed your father when it came to advising about family matters. All I will say is that Yosef usually has good wisdom when it comes to working with people."

When Yosef returned from a trip to Bethel, Isaac requested that Yosef ask Esau about taking the apprentice job that had been spurned previously. Yosef declined to make the request, because Esau could still hold some resentment toward him—he hadn't fallen for Esau's trap during the hunting trip by justifying his lack of hunting skills. This request was Isaac's to make or not.

*   *   *   *   *

Isaac stopped by the recuperation tent before the morning meal. "Son, I guess you get to move in with me today." Esau managed only a nod and a couple of one-syllable assents. The meal passed with little conversation. Isaac didn't want to broach the subject of the apprentice job over the meal, assuming that it might upset Esau again.

Esau later accepted his apprenticeship without dispute and within a week thereafter, Isaac departed for home. Esau's only slightly veiled hostility toward his mother prompted Isaac to observe how she treated Jacob. Within less than a moon, he noticed how Rebekah favored Jacob, treating him almost as a toddler. He tried to convince himself that she wasn't playing favorites with her children, but he couldn't avoid accusing her.

"Husband, I don't favor Jacob over Esau. It's true that I scold them differently, but that's because they are two very different individuals in their deeds and actions. Some offenses merit sterner punishment than others."

"My dear, what you say is hard to deny, but I believe that Esau has noticed favoritism by you toward his brother. When he returns, you should be especially kind to him."

"There's a problem with that suggestion. I have tried since he was a toddler to show him love, but he rejects it almost all of the time. He is self-willed and rude. Do you remember how I saw a different nature in the two boys almost from the day that they were born?"

"Rebekah, are you sure that you aren't listening to the midwife who tried to warn of dire consequences from Jacob's grabbing Esau by the heel during the birth process? Has that prediction of conflict between the two influenced your thinking? Their conflict must be nothing more than what you would normally see between two children of similar ages—even exact ages, as with these two. Please try to treat Esau well when he returns. Also, if you would treat Jacob more like an older child and then Esau likewise, maybe Esau wouldn't reject your attention. I believe that he is more resentful of coddling than Jacob."

Rebekah replied with a sulking expression, "I will try to do as you say, but you will see that there's more to Esau's rebellion than the way I treat Jacob or him."

Esau served as a herdsman's apprentice for a year—a year of frustration to his overseers. Esau was good at spotting wild animals that threatened the flock, but he would often pursue one predator too far at the expense of leaving the flock unprotected. His herding management allowed several animals to suffer injury through Esau's failure to keep fighting animals separated from the weaker ones.

Isaac was upset over the report given to him by the head shepherd when he arrived to take Esau home. "Are you sure you have properly evaluated my son? Our flocks are so large that some losses are bound to occur."

The head shepherd politely insisted that he was accurate in his evaluation. He cited the fact that he had tended flocks for many years and knew how apprentices were supposed to progress with the care of flocks. His son was capable but hadn't developed a love for the animals in his care. Therefore, he had become careless. Until Isaac's son changed his attitude toward caring for animals, he would never succeed as a shepherd.

"He is such a strong boy, a good bowman, and a strong runner—all qualities useful for a shepherd," Isaac mused, perplexed.

The lead shepherd firmly replied that all of those fine qualities couldn't compensate for an uncaring attitude. He repeated again that until Esau changed his attitude, he couldn't succeed as a shepherd. He suggested that Isaac find other duties for his son.

When almost daily disputes broke out between Esau and Jacob upon the former's return, Isaac suggested that Jacob needed to spend an apprenticeship at Beersheba.

Rebekah replied with mild disdain, "Jacob works well with animals. I see no need for him to perform the duties of shepherd away from home. He has many of the qualities of his grandfather Abraham. I see higher duties for him than being a shepherd. Are you sure that your only reason for sending Jacob away isn't just to separate the two boys? You need to assert your duties as a father and put a stop to their quarreling. Incidentally, you should notice that I am treating both boys the same, and that equal treatment hasn't changed Esau's attitude."

Rebekah's expression then changed. She belatedly answered as if deep in thought, "You may have a good idea about separating them. Assuming the lead shepherd and you are correct, the talents of the two boys are quite different. There's no reason they shouldn't be pursuing different jobs at different locations. We both know that Esau can take care of himself—and Jacob can, too, with proper guidance. Also, a few moons of shepherd duty would provide Jacob with some needed experience. And speaking of your father Abraham, he wasn't above performing shepherd duties whenever needed."

Isaac smiled in agreement, and within a week, Jacob traveled to Beersheba to start his apprenticeship. Whereas Esau served for a year and learned little, by the end of the first moon, Jacob had progressed well in learning shepherd duties. His knowledge of how to keep animals that would fight segregated from each other matched that of an experienced shepherd.

The attitude of the lead shepherd was far different when Isaac arrived to pick up Jacob. He declared Jacob to be a born shepherd. He had never seen a young man learn to shepherd animals as rapidly as Jacob had. It was almost as if he knew every member of the flock and its needs and wants. He was also excellent at spotting domineering animals and turning them into docile creatures. The lead shepherd jokingly encouraged Isaac to take him home, because if he stayed there, he would soon have the lead shepherd job.

"I am glad he worked out well for you. After having to put up with Esau, you needed a good worker. I do think that he was well prepared for this job before he started. My wife tells me he handles our own flocks well. I suppose that I should promote him to a higher position over my herd at home."

The day after Jacob arrived at home, Isaac called for a family meeting. He started off by saying that the two boys had to stop their quarreling. He then proposed that the two work at different jobs. A logical assignment for Jacob was to be an assistant to the overseer of the flocks. This job would require more time with the animals and less time roaming the countryside. Because Esau didn't like to shepherd animals and liked to hunt, his logical assignment would be with the sentries as a roving scout. That way, his job and hunting skills could be performed at the same time. While this arrangement would keep the two apart much of the time, they were to learn civility toward each other for those occasions when they were both home at the same time.

Isaac noticed that Rebekah, Esau, and Jacob all left the meeting with a smile on their faces. He couldn't recall when he had last seen all three smile at the same time.

SEVEN

A DARK INTERLUDE

OVER THE SUCCEEDING DAYS, weeks, and moons, Rebekah's frustrated countenance changed to a radiant pleasantness. The lack of frequent, seemingly constant, quarreling by her sons was the obvious reason. The increased peace, however, didn't solve all of the family problems.

Jacob wound up bearing most of the duties of maintaining the flocks. His overseer had obtained his job largely because he had been one of Isaac's hunting friends; the sickness and deaths among the flock would have caused anyone else to have lost his job. Jacob was soon able to improve the general health of the animals, but he realized that the management techniques he was forced to use wouldn't allow for an efficient increase of the flock. A man who wouldn't despair over the loss of prized kine wouldn't allow for Jacob to cull weak animals from the breeding stock. He also forced Jacob to allow animals of disparate traits to breed.

When Jacob complained to his father, he received a dismissal of his ideas. Finally, he tried to enlist his mother's help. "Mother, I am in distress over my job."

Rebekah responded, "Why, son? I hear you are doing quite well."

"Oh, I have improved the state of our herds, but it has been an effort, because the lead shepherd has done little but spend his time talking and drinking with his idle friends. These friends consist mostly of those unable to work—from whom, he says, he gets good ideas about shepherding. It is strange that I don't see any ideas put into use. His idleness, however, is not my main concern. I am capable of handling the control of the flocks and herds. What I perceive to be the problem is that he will not allow me to cull weak animals from the breeding stock. We still have inferior and weak young animals being born. I have petitioned my father to allow me to correct this, but he just tells me that my overseer has more experience than I do and to follow his instructions."

"Jacob, I am afraid I can't help you. I tended flocks as a young girl, but my father and brother did all of the managing of them. I doubt I would be a good advocate, because I lack knowledge you seem to possess. I am sure your father would just assume my argument was nothing more than my favoritism toward you."

"But Mother, I know what I am talking about. I have been criticized for the time I have spent in the wilderness. My days spent there weren't wasted. I noticed how the strong animals almost always mated, and the weaker animals were seldom with young."

"Can't you still segregate the weaker ones in our flocks and prevent them from breeding?"

"No, not easily. During breeding season, it is hard to keep specific animals from one another."

When Rebekah shrugged, showing that she wished not to discuss the matter further, Jacob left perplexed and despondent. He would have to work with what he had. For the next few days, he would mull over his mother's suggestion about ways to segregate the weaker animals from the breeding stock. It wouldn't be easy, but even partial success with the separation could help the quality of the flock some.

* * * * *

While Jacob was having problems with his overseer's incompetence, Esau's life wasn't unfolding as well as he had expected. First, the roving assignments always had him riding with warriors who regarded hunting as strictly a pursuit that one undertook to keep from starving. They took enough supplies to complete each mission without the need to search for food, although any careless deer usually became meat for the next evening meal. But because few careless deer crossed their path, not much hunting happened on any of his excursions.

Esau was awakened from a short sleep early one morning while trying to recuperate from a lengthy hunting trip that had been allowed to him because of his complaining about being overworked. He gruffly told the servant shaking him from his sleep to leave him alone, because he still had some idle time remaining before any assigned sentry duties. The servant continued to arouse him while telling him that their community was about to be attacked by some thieving bedouin, and the sentries on duty needed his help.

Suddenly Esau was wide awake. His fatigue from the hunt was replaced by a surge of energy as he bolted from his room while still putting on his garments. He immediately spotted a vantage point that gave him clear shots at the attackers. His volley of arrows quickly wounded two of the leaders of the thieving band. The whole band fled when they realized they couldn't gain an advantage without the danger of some of them losing their lives.

The lead sentry commanded everyone to hold their positions until the full light of dawn. The scurrying sounds of retreat indicated that all had departed, but raiding groups of late had been using partial retreats to lull their victims into dropping their defenses and suffering a renewed attack, often with disastrous outcomes.

* * * * *

Even Rebekah looked pleased at the morning briefing concerning the attack when the lead sentry commended Esau's heroics. Isaac wanted him brought forward for a special recognition, but agreed to do it later when told that Esau was still resting after an exhausting hunting trip.

Isaac turned his attention to the attack and its implications for his family and community. "Were you able to determine who these raiders were? And are we in danger from a growing force? Eliezer told me not long ago that attacks might happen. I was starting to think he might have been sounding an unnecessary warning. It seems that he wasn't wrong."

The lead sentry shook his head and told them he wasn't sure, but from the size of the group, he believed them to be some of the descendants of Lot. His intelligence reports told him that Lot had instilled hatred for Isaac in all of his succeeding generations. They had spotted Lot's people roving the area over the past few days. Based on the dark forms of the assailants and the debris left behind, the raiders were likely they.

Isaac spoke promptly. "What should we do? It's my understanding that my grandfather Abraham never wanted us to contact them in any way. I wonder, however, whether his warning is still valid. I suspect that Lot has little influence over them anymore, and we could be dealing with a very different sort of people than in past decades."

The lead sentry thought Isaac could be accurate in his assessment, but he also opined that talking with them wouldn't do much good. If intelligence reports were true, Lot had become quite senile and didn't even know who or where he was sometimes. It is believed that a grandson was running the tribe now. The reports also said that the grandson was headstrong and uncontrollable, even by his own people.

When Isaac expressed his fear that they were going to be in constant danger from the tribe, the lead sentry tried to console him. He was rather confident that they were just bullies. Now that they had been overwhelmed by some opposition, he said, they should retreat for quite a while. The retreat didn't ensure that they wouldn't pester Isaac occasionally, but their attacks shouldn't be persistent. The sentry proposed that increased caution, including Esau suspending his hunting for the next few weeks, should ensure the safety of Isaac's family.

Around half past post meridian of the day of attack, a wounded man came staggering into camp. He identified himself as one of the morning attackers and begged for treatment of his wounds and sparing of his life for his transgression. He asserted that he deserved such mercy because none had been killed and because he had received punishment through being wounded.

The lead sentry told him that the sparing of his life depended upon what the master of the household said. Assuming that Isaac spared his life, the physician would be called. Also, any consideration for leniency would require that he answer any questions that Isaac might have about his comrades.

Through pain the wounded man agreed to the sentry's request. The wounded man began his questioning with a discourse about why he wasn't honoring the code of his people never to reveal anything about them to their adversaries. Their leaving him when he started to faint had removed any obligation that he had to them. He begged for assistance, to be tied to his camel, but they refused. He could hardly believe that they would leave a valuable warrior behind. He didn't get along with the leader of his clan. Obviously, the leader saw a good excuse to get rid of him without having to kill him.

The physician treated the willing captive with a sedative herb before removal of the arrow from his shoulder.

The induced sleep had the captive feeling so well by the next morning that even the physician agreed that he was able to answer questions. He confirmed all suspicions that the group of marauders was mostly the descendants of Lot, but they also had had a few Ishmaelites join them recently. The Ishmaelites were often more trouble than help; a coordinated effort was almost impossible to achieve with them. Yesterday's raid had been ruined by one of them breaking cover too soon. He felt that his clan would expel the Ishmaelites soon and follow peaceful pursuits for a while. His immediate clan was too small to attack large herd owners without help from the Ishmaelites, and the small herders were also banding together to form too much resistance.

Isaac continued the questioning. "I have been told that your clan is motivated more from hatred toward me than from a quest for booty."

After an affirmative nod, the captive revealed that his forefather Lot had developed a growing hatred for Isaac over his lifetime. When he was very young, Lot had spoken well of his father and his uncle Abraham but eventually started to condemn him. He gradually had become more hateful toward Isaac as the years passed.

Isaac again inquired, "I would like to know why, because I have had no dealing with him. I suppose he could be mad at my father for sending him to a land that eventually was destroyed, although it was very prosperous for several years after he arrived there. I can only imagine he somehow reasons that part of my inheritance is due him. He could conclude that my father owed him for his losses in the Vale of Siddim."

The wounded man concluded by telling Isaac that he seemed to be a pleasant man. He was glad that he hadn't met and recognized Isaac when he had entered their camp; he might have futilely tried to kill him. His forefather had instilled a hatred of Isaac in his people.

*   *   *   *   *

An uneasy peace settled over Isaac's household as all marauding bands were spotted and told to leave before they had any chance to attack. The effort to keep them at bay, however, became more and more difficult, because the area started suffering from increasing dryness. This condition necessitated an increased effort by some people to find sustenance for their animals and themselves. Jacob succeeded in keeping flocks healthy, but the reduced forage supported flocks that were leaner than normal. The drought was countering his effort to prove his herd-management methods.

One day as Isaac discussed new grazing arrangements with Jacob, a messenger interrupted their conversation by handing Isaac a papyrus message. Its contents had to be important, because it was enclosed in a bitumen-cured bag of expensive lambskin and sealed with a costly grade of wax. Its origin seemed to be from the Isles of Elishah in the Western Sea.

Isaac immediately ended the conversation by telling Jacob to inform the lead shepherd that he agreed with the new grazing changes. He then rushed home to read the message. He was rather sure of the contents of the message. On his last trip to Beersheba, he had overheard Eliezer talking to an elderly community leader who was saying that Eber had moved to his former home of Sicyon and was in failing health.

The lead sentence stated that Eber was indeed dead. It went on to describe his last days and list several major accomplishments in his life and, finally, give an invitation to a memorial to be held in Haran within the year. *I guess this is one memorial I won't be able to attend. Maybe Eliezer will get to attend. I heard that he has returned to his boyhood home in Damascus. Eber was our last contact with the ancient world—a world of turmoil like ours.* When Isaac revealed the contents of the message pouch to the members of his community, few knew who he was talking about.

*　　*　　*　　*　　*

As the drought caused further difficulties in keeping animals alive, Isaac's wealth declined through forced reductions and losses from sickness in his flocks brought on by reduced nutrition. Meanwhile, Esau found wild game to be elusive. Although flock reductions provided adequate meat for the table, he still spurned the taste of domesticated sheep and kine, causing the determined and headstrong hunter to take increasingly dangerous chances with his hunting range. He had always taken minimal supplies with him because he wanted to move swiftly when tracking or chasing game. Esau kept ignoring his father's warnings about futile attempts to find game anywhere near their home.

He had just resolved that his latest hunting effort was useless and headed home with the resolve to persuade his father to let him move to the outskirts of Gerar, where hunting should be successful.

His water and food were low, but he could make it home by traveling in the late evening and night, when less water would be required for drinking. Just before stopping at a resting place from the heat on the next-to-last day from home, Esau serendipitously espied a wayward deer. He stealthily crept within bowshot and carefully inched forward toward a level, secluded spot from which to take the shot. He had started to raise his bow when he fell through a cleverly concealed animal pit.

Athletic abilities developed from numerous days of hunting enabled him to grasp one of the poles and turn it so that its end stuck into the bottom of the pit. This action helped not only to break his fall but provide a means of ascent out of the pit. Resisting the urge to faint, he climbed the pole and collapsed prostrate on the ground as he finished scaling the walls of the pit. His last effort did result in fainting, which exposed him to the sun long enough to cause a strong thirst when he regained consciousness. To his dismay, he discovered that his water bag had partially opened, spilling most of his remaining water. He immediately decided to get out of the sun, drink most of the small amount of water left, and rest until evening. There was no need to panic, because a well awaited nearby at which he could refill his water bag.

Esau awoke startled from a fevered nap. The ambient light of day hinted that he had overslept until he realized that the sun was obscured by clouds that had arisen while he slept. The hint of rain shafts overhead disappointed him, as only an occasional drop hit his brow. Elated at the chance for an early start, he began to race toward the well before slowing his pace abruptly. His strength was low and must be expended carefully if he were to make it home.

Upon reaching the well, Esau was stricken with the first real fear of his life. The well had been filled with sand and contained not one drop of water. What was he to do? He was already thirsty and had no more than two sips of water left in his container. He had tested some salt bushes the previous day; they were all dormant. What little water any of the plants possessed was retracted to the roots, which required an effort to extract—an effort that he couldn't afford to exert.

Gradually his terror turned to determination. He would fight to stay awake and resist falling asleep during rest periods from walking. If he made good progress during this night's journey, he would be close to home and possibly even find some sustenance from some nomads roaming the area around his home. Also, he would try not to urinate during the day. His body waste could slack his thirst for a short time.

Unfortunately, Esau met no people on his trip until he reached home, where he collapsed at his brother's feet. A startled Jacob looked aghast at his faint brother. Being unable to determine what was wrong with him, he finally exclaimed, "Esau, are you sick?"

"No. I'm starving!"

"Then why don't you avail yourself of the porridge I am cooking? I am preparing our evening meal. Our parents should be returning shortly after disposing of most of our animals. This may be the last meat we have for a while, unless we have to kill the rest of our flock."

"Jacob, would you be so kind as to prepare a bowl for me? I am too weak to reach the pot. I spent the last of my strength in reaching home."

Jacob speared a small morsel and gave it to him. He proceeded to fill a small bowl and began the motion to hand the bowl to Esau when he suddenly withdrew it.

"Brother, do not tease me! I am about to perish in the presence of your food. The morsel I have just tasted is more delicious than anything that I have ever eaten—including venison."

"I have just decided that I should be compensated for saving your life. Exchange metals or animals are not my desire. Your life, however, should be worth your birthright. I have even heard our parents talking about a midwife's prediction that I would somehow acquire it from you. I had looked upon the predictions as those of a senile old woman until just now." Jacob turned and ran to obtain the papers describing his inheritance. Rushing back, he commanded Esau, "Here, sign this paper signifying the sale of your birthright."

"Would you deny sustenance to a dying brother unless he gave up his birthright? Isn't our friendship itself, not to say decent human kindness, enough to prompt you to give me a life-saving bowl of food?"

"What friendship? You have striven to make my life miserable almost daily. I am doing this not for myself, but for the good of the family. Your actions toward our mother and your catering to our father's weaknesses demonstrate that you don't deserve the birthright. Therefore, I am doing what needs to be done, because I know my father won't do it."

"Okay! I will sign. What good is my birthright anyway? Our father has been so neglectful of the inheritance from our grandfather that before the drought is over, there may not be enough left to inherit. He will probably die a pauper."

Jacob gave him the bowl of porridge, which he started to eat voraciously until Jacob forced him to slow his eating process. Esau had recovered enough strength to sit up by the time Isaac and Rebekah returned. The look on the faces of their parents caused both of the boys such concern that they asked their parents what was wrong.

The pleasant smell of the porridge seemed to lighten the mood of their parents, who began a discussion about what the family was to do. Many of their servants had been released with a supply of animals and goods to search out a place for survival. Time was past due when the family itself had to decide what to do if they were to remain prosperous—though at a greatly reduced level compared to what they had had at Abraham's death.

Isaac finally ended the discussion with a plan. "Rebekah and I will prepare to go to Egypt, taking only a few sheep and goats with us. We will give them extra provender for the next week, which should give them enough strength to reach Egypt even with the meager grazing between here and there. Jacob, you may stay here with the one servant family we still have. I know you are adept at finding forage for the animals under your care. Try to save as many as possible, but it's more important to have a few healthy members than a larger flock that are all sickly. Esau, you may go work for Mamre's descendants. I know your mother doesn't like this assignment, but the terrible times dictate it. That job is the best one for you that I can see. Please remember the ideals that you have been taught, and don't partake of those ways that you should know to be evil."

Isaac concluded the evening meal with an apology for the suffering caused by the loss of wealth. When Jacob saw that the consolation Isaac received from Rebekah did nothing to lift his spirits, he interrupted. "Father, I believe that some good has come from this drought already. I have had time to talk with some observers of weather with knowledge of the drought that struck at the time of grandfather's entry into this land. They tell me that the worst is over, but not to expect any quick improvement. If this is true, the drought has caused your incompetent friend to move on. I should be able to maintain a small, strong flock with which we can recover within a few years."

*   *   *   *   *

Isaac and Rebekah busied themselves with preparing the flock for travel and straightening the household for occupancy by the last family in their employ at Lahai-roi. Jacob would also occupy a room in the house.

"Jacob, you take care to keep your room clean. The servants will have enough to do without taking care of you."

"Mother, you are treating me as a child once more. I plan to spend most of my time—day and night—with the flocks. I will probably seldom be home, except briefly to see that things are all right with the family and to let them know that I am doing well."

Whether from elation over the prospect of new hunting grounds or a true lack of regard for his birthright, Esau mentioned nothing about his deal with Jacob. Esau had even managed to hide his nearly fatal hunting experience from his parents. He managed to procure a few extra things to eat between meals without Rebekah's knowledge and was quite well by the time of his parents' departure.

Isaac didn't notice Esau's listlessness because of his concern about the strange dreams that he had started having on the very night of the family assignments. His first dream involved a scene of roving bands of soldiers attacking villages that seemed to be located in the land of Goshen in Egypt, of which he had heard about from his father Abraham. His next dream pictured a nomad family entering Egypt. While the man and woman looked like him and his wife, they had several children, including a baby. The family had scarcely crossed the border when soldiers grabbed the children and rode off with them. The parents were so constrained that they did nothing but stand and watch the kidnapping.

Isaac spent a portion of the next day in prayer to God. He couldn't let a couple of weird dreams dictate his life, but he also couldn't reconcile the scene of the kidnapping of the children in his mind. Maybe it was just a remembrance from what Eliezer had told about his father's deathbed remark of his descendants living in Egypt, and maybe it was some other omen. When he completed his prayer, he resolved in his mind that he had done all that he could about the plan to flee to Egypt. If God didn't want him to go there, he would surely give Isaac the answer soon. Departure was just a few days away, and Isaac and Rebekah couldn't afford to delay their leaving because of the need to get their accompanying animals to greener pastures.

On the third night, the answer to his prayers came. God appeared to him in another dream, ordering him not to enter Egypt but to stop in the land of Gerar, which was still ruled by the aging patriarch Abimelech. Like his father, Abraham, Isaac readily accepted the dream, although his heart had been set on residence in Egypt. Also like his father, he asked why, but to no avail; the dream was over.

The next morning, Isaac excitedly addressed Rebekah. "We will not have to travel so far. We will ask the Philistines for residence in Gerar." He had concentrated on the change so deeply that he had forgotten to mention the reason for the change.

"Husband, may I ask why Gerar and not Egypt? You had seemed so set on that mysterious land that I can only wonder if the recent worries have you delusional."

"Rebekah, I spent much of yesterday in prayer to God concerning some disturbing dreams that I thought involved our entry into Egypt. Then, last night, God appeared to me in a dream telling me to sojourn in Gerar instead."

"Did he say why we aren't going to Egypt?"

"My dream ended just as I asked that question. You do need to remember that my father was expelled from Egypt. Maybe the land wouldn't be accepting of us if they found out I am his son."

A few days later, Rebekah, Isaac, and Esau left, but the latter couldn't hide his disappointment that his parents would be living close to him. The displeasure expressed by his son, however, didn't affect Isaac's mood even slightly. God had once again repeated the same promise to Isaac that he had to his father. God had renewed the promise that his descendants would inherit the lands of his father's travels and would multiply like the stars of heaven.

*   *   *   *   *

Jacob was at home to see his parents and brother leave, but he promptly returned to his flock the moment they left. *Now is the time for me to prove my value as a shepherd. My father doubts my abilities, and my mother believes that I am still a child*, he thought while sighing. During the past week, he had realized that the flock still contained some weak members that would only use up precious grazing without improving it. They were likely to cause the loss of nearly all his animals. He immediately had the servant family contact needy nomads for the disposal of these animals.

*   *   *   *   *

Upon entering Gerar, Isaac was directed to the elderly ruler, Abimelech. "I have been told that you are from Lahai-roi," Abimelech said. "I know the drought is severe in your land, but I wonder why you are choosing our country. Most of the refugees have bypassed us for Egypt."

Isaac had never been placed in a situation where his answer must be carefully worded. He certainly didn't want to lie, but the complete truth wouldn't do, either. If he were to say that God had directed him to stop in Gerar, there was no way of predicting how this pagan ruler would act. Such a revelation might also reveal Isaac, whom Abimelech had never seen at close distance, to be Abraham's son. Not knowing how the hatred of a son of Abraham by Sarah might have spread by the descendants of Lot and Ishmael, he decided he must keep his command by God and his identity secret.

The reply from Isaac specified that he had heard many good things about the land, and it was close to his homeland, where he still had some family. He also felt that Egypt might impose severe restrictions on future refugees entering their country. He had heard that it was often on the brink of internal turmoil, which he had no desire to witness, should unrest erupt there.

Isaac's answer seemed to please Abimelech, who assigned the trio to help with his court. The assigned workload allowed for considerable free time in the early post meridian, which puzzled Rebekah. Why had they, she wondered aloud, as strangers, been given such easy but important jobs? Her curiosity affected Isaac hardly at all. He spent most of his spare time during the first moon after moving taking a nap during this free time. Soon thereafter, he had recovered from the stress of his immediate past and became bored.

The only really unpleasant aspect of their life in Gerar was the lack of privacy. They shared a servant house with another family whose rooms had open access. Given the recovery from stress and lack of privacy in the living quarters, Isaac's post meridian desire turned from a nap to intimacy with his wife.

Isaac had already noticed a small, reed-filled glen offering privacy from the daily traffic on the grounds. The glen also contained a small, grassy area where animal skins could be spread for intimate pursuits, but Isaac had failed to notice that the seclusion in the glen didn't block every line of sight. A tower room in the main palace offered a partial view of the spot where Isaac and Rebekah lay.

The aging ruler seldom ascended the steps to that room because of his age and health, but the beauty of the day not only inspired Isaac to new pursuits but also inspired Abimelech to climb the steps for a bird's-eye view of his grounds from the tower once again. As his gaze scanned the grounds far and near, he espied movement in the area of the glen. Because his view was partially obscured by the reeds, he concentrated his eyes upon the movement. He wasn't sure what he was watching and decided to send a sentry to inspect the area when he completed his viewing. Whoever the people were, they didn't appear to be threatening. He suspected that one of his soldiers was enjoying some needed therapy. He would have the inspecting sentry be discreet in his surveillance.

When Abimelech had decided to return to his court, he took one last look at the glen. Just as he started to look away and descend the steps, a gust of wind flattened the reeds to reveal a full view of the grassy area in the glen. There was no doubt who the people in glen were and what rituals they were performing.

Abimelech's shock came from the sight of Isaac and Rebekah and not from their actions. Suddenly, a vivid image of another man and woman found pursuing the same act came to mind. *I thought Isaac looked familiar. I guess my mind is getting so weak from age that I don't see things as I should.*

He hurried down the steps from the tower, becoming more out of breath from the descent than from the previous ascent. He espied his chief aide in the courtyard and called to him.

"We have a serious situation that must be corrected. I have just seen Isaac and Rebekah acting as husband and wife and not brother and sister, as I was told by Isaac at our first meeting. They are lying in the secluded glen. Please dispatch someone to bring them to me in my private quarters. Inform the messenger that he is to approach the secluded area slowly and make a lot of noise as he approaches."

*   *   *   *   *

The messenger found Isaac and Rebekah standing as he met them. Wanting to let Abimelech be the person to inform them that their supposedly private act had been seen, he simply told them that Lord Abimelech wanted to see them.

Rebekah whispered her relief that the sentry had been so clumsy that they had time to conceal their activities. Isaac, however, had noticed a suppressed smirk on the messenger's face and realized that something wasn't as it seemed. As they were walking toward Abimelech's chambers—a most unusual invite—he happened to look at the tower.

When he paused in his pace, Rebekah exclaimed, "Isaac, what are you doing? We mustn't keep our benefactor waiting."

Isaac remained standing and then motioned for Rebekah to come closer. He whispered so softly that Rebekah asked him to repeat what he had just said. "Rebekah, I think that I know why we have been summoned to the ruler's private residence. We may be in trouble."

Rebekah's face turned almost ashen as she replied, "I did wonder why he wanted us in his private living area and not the court. I thought it might be some award or advancement that he wanted to give us."

Isaac couldn't suppress a worried smile at the naïveté of his wife. "I very much doubt that he wants to bestow any honor upon us. He would almost certainly do those actions at court. Please don't be shocked, but I believe he saw us in the glen. I just noticed that the view from the tower would reveal the glen, especially on a breezy day like this one."

Rebekah's expression turned incredulous of Isaac's comment. "I thought he wasn't well enough to climb the steps to the tower. You are just letting your imagination run wild."

"Rebekah, I don't think so. I overheard him say to an aide the other day that he longed for another view from the tower. It's possible that they helped him up there for the fantastic view that today would afford him."

"Isaac, you must be wrong! How can I stand the embarrassment?"

"My dear wife, if I am right, your embarrassment might not be our biggest problem. Remember, we told him we were brother and sister. If he saw us, he knows that we aren't. Our identity has been at least partially revealed. We have nothing to do but attend his audience and ask for forgiveness."

When they entered the courtyard, the messenger who had noisily approached them in the glen directed them to a sumptuously appointed room. As Isaac's eyes adjusted to the faint light in the room, he first felt awe at the finery of the surroundings and then fear at the first sight of Abimelech, who sat on a raised platform immediately opposite the entry. Finally, Isaac felt confusion as he discerned a smile on the ruler's face. Isaac looked at Rebekah but couldn't determine anything about her thoughts other than apprehension. The whole scenario unnerved him, but he suppressed an urge to speak and waited until Abimelech addressed him.

"You may have wondered why I gave you easy jobs at our first meeting. I thought you looked familiar. You didn't look like an ordinary shepherd; there was a regal mannerism in your bearing. I choose not to embarrass you with any details, but I know that you are husband and wife. Almost immediately after realizing that, I guessed who you are. I have heard of an Isaac who was the son of my friend Abraham. I have met his other children, but not you. Am I correct in my identification?"

"Yes, Lord Abimelech. I am Isaac, and this is my wife, Rebekah. She isn't my sister but a cousin. I am sorry I misled you, but we thought it best for us to conceal our identity."

"You have made me relive a similar incident with your father. Your ruse was totally foolish. While your wife had no fear of any advance from me, as your mother did, several lusty young men roam the ground. I must see you on the first day of next week. I need to talk to my advisers about your role in our country. I do assume that you still wish refuge from the drought here."

"Yes, Lord, please forgive us. And may I once again offer our appreciation for your kindness?"

Rebekah left the meeting smiling until she realized once again that their intimacy had been seen by another person. Isaac consoled her, "Only the ruler saw us, and I doubt anything we did shocked him. Hopefully, one good thing comes from this. I believe that he will give us private quarters next week. Just suppress your embarrassment, and our chances for future intimacy should soon increase."

As they approached the courtyard on the first day of the week, Isaac noticed a rare nervousness in Rebekah when Abimelech addressed a bowed Rebekah and genuflected Isaac, "Please rise. I postponed this meeting until I consulted the managers of our lands. Your father and father-in-law became a dear friend, although he doubted my civility, as you did. I was surprised that you would doubt me after what I did for your father, but I suppose he didn't tell you about me, or you thought our country had become more belligerent toward strangers. What I am doing today should resolve any doubts by you and your wife. I am giving you some choice land and an assignment of animals. You will no longer have to attend court, because your full time will be needed to tend your flocks."

RECOVERY

A S PART OF THE deal for Abimelech's gifts, Isaac agreed to live in Gerar. After becoming familiar with his home and animals, Isaac asked Rebekah about having Jacob to bring the flock he was tending to join them, so the family could maintain all their flocks in one place.

"Husband, I am curious why you want Jacob to tend our flocks, although I think he would be the best choice. He did an excellent job in keeping as many animals alive as he did during the drought. Also, is there enough grazing area for the increased herd?"

"I have changed my mind on his abilities, or I wouldn't have left him in charge of our remaining flock. Abimelech has been very generous in allotting us land. We should have enough grazing area when we eliminate all of the weaker members. I now realize Jacob is knowledgeable in judging the quality of an animal, and he is efficient in the proper use of grazing areas. Those two qualities should mean we will have an excellent flock of animals from now on. With his help, we should regain much of our wealth rapidly. I even hope we will have extra land on which we can grow plants for food to support a varied diet for us and others."

Isaac dispatched a message by confidential pouch intended for the servant family or Jacob; however, the messenger understood that the message was for Jacob only. He also misunderstood the directions on how to find Jacob, which were given to him by the servant master.

*   *   *   *   *

Late in the next day, as Jacob was moving his flock, he noticed some of the lead members acting skittishly. He had scanned the area just previously and was certain it harbored no dangerous predators. While cautiously scanning in all directions again, he spotted what was upsetting the lead sheep. A nearly prone man lay in their path, seemingly in distress. Jacob rapidly assembled his flock again to ensure that they were safe before running to the man's side.

"Sire, are you in trouble?"

"Yes, I am. I am very thirsty and hungry. I left the house of a man called Jacob yesterday after receiving directions where I could find him. Obviously, I failed to heed the specific instructions of his servant and became lost. I had expected to find him soon and return later in the day for some water to get me back to my home. Could you spare some water and a morsel of food? Also, would you happen to know where I can find Jacob?"

"Here's some water and dried meat and a cake of fruit. As to Jacob, I am he."

"Praise be to the gods, I am spared. Here is the message pouch that I am to deliver to you."

Jacob was overjoyed at the invitation to join his father. After reading the message and shouting so loudly that he scared the flock, he calmed them and invited the messenger to accompany him for the short distance home. The messenger had been walking in tighter and tighter circles until he was almost too tired to traverse the short distance to Jacob's home, where he rested for a day before leaving on his return journey.

The servant family and Jacob did a much better job of following directions to Isaac's home in Gerar. They were soon approaching their destination.

*   *   *   *   *

Isaac was preparing to leave to relieve the attending shepherd when he saw a moving flock he thought was the one he had been given by Abimelech. After a momentary fear that something dramatic, like a major raid, had reduced his flock, he slowly came to realize that the emerging animals were the ones he had left with Jacob.

He called to Rebekah, "My dear, Jacob has arrived. I see our old flock approaching from the north."

Rebekah, who had been preparing flour for use in pies for the evening meal, ran out with her hands covered with flour. "Oh! I believe I see our servants, but where is Jacob?"

Isaac replied with jocularity, "If I know him, he's already around here somewhere, looking for a place to billet his flock. The servants don't seem upset, so he must be close by."

While Jacob worked at merging the herds and flocks, Isaac busied himself with preparing to plant emmer, mandrakes, leeks, and other grains and vegetables. He had also used some of the proceeds from the sale of the weaker animals to buy quality fruit trees. At the end of the first year in Gerar, the family's fortune was blossoming.

On the day after Jacobs's arrival, they received the most soaking rain that the area had experienced in years. The fields produced so abundantly that Isaac was forced to sell some of his harvest at cheap prices, because he had no place to store the yield. Fortunately, his grain harvest was greater than he could have hoped for, because his flock also multiplied dramatically, with many sets of twins being born to the breeding stock.

Isaac had been so appreciative of having ample food that the desire for venison had been forgotten until he saw his great fortune with his first harvest. Within a week of finishing the harvest, his old longing for the taste of venison returned. At the next evening meal, he asked without introduction, "Why don't we find Esau and beg him to return here? I suddenly have a desire for venison. I don't know whether it is the relief from harvest duties or my noticing of some wild deer in recent weeks that has caused this desire for wild meat again."

Rebekah looked puzzled, hardly knowing what to say. Jacob knew that his mother appreciated the family peace without Esau, but also had a desire to see her son, even though he had given her much grief in rearing him. She gave a noncommittal reply: "If you send a messenger for him, I expect the messenger would have more trouble finding him than the one you sent to find Jacob."

"My dear, I have kept informed of his employers—he changes them rather often. All we should have to do is contact the last employer, who could give us directions to Esau's whereabouts. I propose to make the trip myself. Now that the harvest is over, you and your servants can spare me enough time to find him and bring him home."

Jacob listened intently to the conversation and decided that he didn't want to deal with Esau. "Finding him shouldn't be a problem. But when you do find him, can you persuade him to return? There's not much work here that doesn't include attending animals or crops. Neither of these two jobs are anything that my brother would want to do."

"Jacob, that's true. I don't believe, however, that he would have to do either of those two jobs. The growing prosperity of this land should allow for a profitable career as a hunter. His skills should help him to support himself from selling most of his kill. Really, he probably could get a job as a hunter for our landlord."

When Rebekah countered with her old argument about the dangers of hunting, Jacob almost blurted out the story of the incident that had caused

Esau to sell his birthright to him. The thought took him to the realization that Esau might become extremely angry were he to see his father's growing wealth. A series of thoughts followed from wondering why Isaac hadn't seen the sale signature on his inheritance deed to what would happen when Esau found out about his father's wealth. The discovery would surely happen someday, even if he could keep his father from seeking Esau now.

Jacob was so deep in reverie that Isaac had to raise his voice to get his attention. "Jacob! Are you asleep?"

"No. I was just thinking about Esau's return."

Although Jacob gave no details about his thoughts, Isaac assumed his consent. "Then you want to see him also?"

Jacob had to agree that it would be good to see Esau again; he dared not tell his father otherwise. Although all three left the evening meal smiling, only Isaac's smile was caused by genuine joy.

Rebekah used the excuse of needing Jacob's help with an outside chore to get him away from Isaac's hearing. "Why did you agree to Esau's return? Hasn't he troubled you enough during your life? I couldn't disagree, because I am his mother, and your father still believes that I favor you too much."

"Mother, I haven't told anyone this, although I wonder why Father hasn't discovered it. On the day you decided to leave for Egypt, which was changed to Gerar, Esau sold me his birthright. I was cooking our evening meal when he returned from his hunt nearly dead from starvation, or so he thought. I could see that he was just famished, and I withheld food from him until he sold me his birthright. I don't want him to return and see what he has given up. Nevertheless, I can't imagine his not finding out about our good fortune here in Gerar. I doubt anyone has had a harvest and birth of animals ever in this land like we had this year. Assuming our continued prosperity, it surely won't be long until he finds out about our success anyway. I thought I should face his wrath, which is almost certain to occur, now rather than later."

Rebekah's tone became even more upset when she heard this news. "Jacob, what have you done? When your father finds out about this, he is going to be angry—not only at what you have done, but also at your silence in keeping this thing from his attention."

"But Mother, Esau didn't tell him about it, either. It seems that he didn't care for the birthright. He surely knew he could last until your return that day. I believe he was more ashamed of the prospect of his parents seeing his plight of near starvation from the foolish pursuit of game than he was over losing his birthright. I felt at the time that I was more deserving of it than he was. Just a few moments of birth order shouldn't override the inheritance's receipt by someone who appreciates what his grandfather and father have to bestow. That appreciation doesn't involve wealth only, but also the promises given by God. The birthright carries an obligation to future generations that I believe Esau doesn't see. Can't you see his disregard by the company he associates with?"

Rebekah and Jacob stood in silence until she motioned for them to return to the house. "When I married your father, I was overjoyed at the prospect of being a mother in the lineage of Abraham. Although I have never regretted my decision to marry your father, my life has been filled with more hardship than I could have imagined as a bride. It seems that some of the greatest strife may be ahead of me—and you—yet. Nonetheless, I agree that the birthright should be yours by merit. Your breaking of tradition, however, may bring you some grief. I do hope and believe what you did is worth any trouble that we must endure."

Just before entering the house, Jacob whispered, "Don't worry, Mother. I won't give it up. This is one thing that I am prepared to cling to until death."

*   *   *   *   *

Isaac arose early the next morning and busily prepared to ride to Esau's last known location. As the servant commanded the camel to kneel, Isaac stopped short of mounting. The startled servant asked almost in fear whether he had secured the riding seat properly.

"No. Everything is tied as it should be, but I have changed my mind. I plan to contact Abimelech and some others around here about a job offer for Esau when I bring him home. I need to see them first. Will you change the provisions for a much shorter trip?"

To Isaac's anticipation and delight, he received at least three firm offers for a hunting job for Esau. Abimelech even made his job offer subject to rejection, so that Esau would fear no recrimination if he chose to reject the job offer.

After a day of rest, Isaac once again assembled some servants to help him resume the search for his oldest son.

Just as Isaac was about to call for encampment in the late post meridian of the second day out, his lead guide spotted a small party that he first identified as nomads until he saw there were no women accompanying them. The guide studied the "nomads" for a while before warning his companions to be wary of the party.

Isaac's eyesight wasn't as sharp as it had been in his youth, but he thought he recognized the silhouette of Esau as one of the riders. He asked the guide to draw closer to them.

His guide objected to the idea by suggesting that such action was perilous.

He cited that the group was carrying weapons that could be used against Isaac's party. Instead, he suggested that they ride away from the mysterious group.

"Wait! Let me give you a description of Esau. My eyesight is not really good, but I think we are close enough for you to see the features I will describe for you."

The guide scanned the party several times before agreeing that the nearest rider looked exactly as Isaac had described him. He was confident that the rider was Esau. The guide also observed that they had no precious possessions to tempt thieving bedouin in case Isaac was wrong about the party's identity.

Before they had covered half of the distance while carrying their peace flag, Isaac could discern that the nearest rider was indeed Esau, to whom he shouted. By this time, Esau's group had taken defensive positions, not trusting the peace flag. Esau soon motioned for his companions to take their ease.

"Father, is there something wrong?"

"No, son. We have had a bountiful harvest. I now have the ability to support all of the family and several servants. You won't have to work as a shepherd or crop grower, because I have contracted several landholders around Gerar who will give you a job that will allow you to hunt extensively. Lord Abimelech has offered you a job investigating for the best hunting grounds. Other jobs are sentry jobs for landholders who also like to hunt. You would probably spend much of your time hunting if you chose to pursue one of those jobs."

Esau asked several questions but when assured once again that he wouldn't have to help shepherd animals or harvest foodstuffs, he returned with Isaac. Esau accepted the job whose landholder was most distant from his father. He still seemed to deprecate the birthright he had sold. He made no mention of the sale, nor did he show his usual belligerence toward Jacob. He did promise to provide his father with periodic supplies of venison and left for his employer within less than a week.

The excellent first harvest was exceeded by the second harvest, which in turn was exceeded by the third harvest. Before the end of the third harvest, a high official in Abimelech's court showed up at the reaping field with greetings from Abimelech. A request for an audience with Isaac immediately followed the brief greeting.

Isaac didn't want to take time from the harvest to talk to a government official. There was still much grain to stack, and the sky wasn't looking promising for continued harvest work. He consoled himself that any loss of grain that might result from his talking with the official would be quite small compared to the harvest so far. He motioned for the official to accompany him to a nearby rest area.

"How may I help you?"

The official started his discourse by relating how Lord Abimelech had assigned these lands to Isaac because they had been nonproductive in the past. For that reason, his landlord had given him a generous allotment of ground, because much land would be needed for Isaac to survive well. Isaac's status as a son of a dear friend had prompted Abimelech's desire that Isaac live well. To Abimelech's surprise, and surely Isaac's, this land had produced far more abundantly than anyone could have hoped. His Lord believed that the lease fee of only one portion of harvest in ten was too liberal for the current production from the land. He wanted to establish a fee basis that would increase as the yearly harvest and flock growth increased. At current yields, or higher, the fee would never exceed three in ten.

Isaac's first impulse to bargain for lower fees, if not the current flat rate of one in ten, was quickly replaced by tacit consent. His harvest levels for the past three years had forced him to sell much of his produce at cheap prices that did little to increase his wealth significantly. He asked for each specific level of fees to be stated. A rough mental calculation revealed a still-prosperous return for him.

While he doubted that his yield would continue to increase, Isaac feared that Abimelech's greed would grow even for yields like that of the current year. "You may tell our Lord that the new fees will allow me to continue to live in your land and not be forced to move. They seem high, but the bountiful harvest should permit me to repay my benefactor for all that he has done for me."

*　　*　　*　　*　　*

Rebekah and Jacob were upset over Isaac's agreement. They reasoned that landholders typically required only one in ten rates for their excess land. Their good fortune shouldn't be discriminated against. Even with the rate of one in ten, they were profiting their landlord much more than his other tenants. Isaac should have argued that they provided more goods to him than any of those other tenants, they said. They also warned him that continued abundant harvests would only increase the greed of Abimelech. Isaac countered with the statement that he had told the official that the new rates were high and hinted that his family might have to move if they increased any more. When he repeated his calculation of return from future harvests as this one, they agreed that the family would still prosper.

The fears of increased fees were not realized. The moving hint seemed to work. Nonetheless, the growing prosperity, even with the higher rental fees, soon posed a problem. Isaac's wealth increased until he surpassed even his landlord in wealth.

Years later, during harvest, another official entourage approached Isaac. The setting was different this time, however. Isaac no longer performed many harvesting chores. His eyesight made it impossible for him to work alongside other workers. Also, the official entourage was led by the aged ruler Abimelech.

"Master Isaac, I have been lenient and generous to you during your stay in our land. Nonetheless, the time has come for me to reclaim the land on which you reside and give it to my people. You will be given time to complete your harvest. We have also arranged for a place for you to move some distance north of here. I hate to require this of you, but I must."

Isaac readily accepted the eviction without protest. For several moons, considerable strife had existed between Isaac's shepherds and the Philistines who filled several wells. Whenever a well was dug and became functional, Abimelech's subjects soon filled it with dirt. It seemed that at least one shepherd left every duty period covered in mud from cleaning out a well. The wells they could protect from the Philistines didn't provide enough water for the flocks. Only providential rainfall on several occasions had spared the animals from suffering.

Isaac bowed before Abimelech. "It's time that we should leave. Our strife with the shepherds of your land has been difficult and has put our flocks in danger of dying on several occasions. I had resolved to see and tell you within this week that we had to find pasturage elsewhere. Despite our current distress, our stay in your country has been mostly pleasant, and all of us wish to thank you for the hospitality we have received. I have prospered in your land like at no other time in my life."

"I am sorry for your troubles," Abimelech said. "You are a greater man than any of us. It is your good fortune that enrages my people when they don't reap a harvest like yours, despite their every effort. The only solution is for you to depart. I am sorry that I have to evict a good and cooperative tenant. I had hoped to spend my last days without conflict, but that's not possible."

Abimelech gave Isaac a parting kiss just prior to heading back to his palace.

*   *   *   *   *

Some of Isaac's shepherds began their trip to the new home that very day, and everything and everyone were resettled by the following week. Jacob had advised his father not to stop at the assigned place, which was still a valley within Gerar. He asserted that the Philistines wouldn't let them alone until they were completely out of their land. Within a few moons, he was complaining to his father, "I told you that the peace wouldn't last. The Philistines are once again fighting over our new wells."

"Are you sure our shepherds haven't been intruding upon some of the land forbidden to us, causing them to retaliate? I trust Abimelech when he gives me a promise. True, he did change our fees for use of his land, but not before requesting an adjustment. Unless I hear from him, I am reluctant to believe these incidents aren't our fault this time."

"Father, please trust me. These struggles are *not* our fault. I am sure Abimelech means to treat you well because you are Abraham's son. He is, however, an old man who can no longer control his young men. The Philistines admire vigor and strength—something their ruler no longer has."

Isaac didn't give an oral assent to Jacob's contention, but Jacob knew that his father realized he was right. "I suppose Beersheba would be a better place for us. If we moved there, we would be removed far enough to prevent any intrusion by them. That arrangement should solve any problem, regardless of who is at fault."

Jacob walked away thinking, *I guess getting my father to admit that he is wrong will never happen. Well, I will settle for a proper action from him.*

*   *   *   *   *

The Beersheba move did stop the quarreling; lack of personal communication equaled lack of contention. The homeland of Abraham started Isaac's reminiscence about his father and the promises that God had made to him.

These thoughts were soon reaffirmed by God. A few nights after arrival in Beersheba, God appeared to him in a dream, not only with a renewed promise of blessing upon his descendants but also a command to build an altar. Isaac no longer knew anyone who performed this work. Nevertheless, he still had vivid memories of the altar at Moriah upon which his father had placed him so many years ago. Isaac readily concluded that he had received no specific building instructions because the details of that altar were still clearly visible in his mind. While he didn't trust his eyesight for fitting the stones together, he still knew some masons who could follow his directions. Then he could use his touch to inspect the altar as it progressed and after they had finished building it.

*   *   *   *   *

When Rebekah heard about the dream, she became upset. From what she had heard, no identification had been offered in the dream of which son should receive Isaac's blessing. She loved both of her sons, but she also knew that Esau had spurned his birthright—a fact that she suspected Isaac still didn't know. The mere thought of Esau's receiving his father's blessing without the birthright promise made her cringe. She didn't want to imagine what might happen if that occurred. She even became momentarily upset at God for not telling her husband who should receive the blessing.

By the next day, she had reconciled her thoughts. Surely God knew what he was doing. Also, Isaac had given no indication that he was ready to confer his blessing upon either one of his sons. She would just have to wait and see. Hopefully, she would be able to act on Jacob's behalf when the time came. Whatever happened, Esau must *not* receive his father's blessing.

*   *   *   *   *

If Isaac thought he had seen the last of Abimelech as his time passed in Beersheba, he was wrong. Before the end of Isaac's first year there, one day in the late post meridian, a Philistine band approached his tent. Isaac always stayed in the presence of a young man with good eyesight whenever he was outside from his tent. His eyesight was no longer good enough to warn him of the presence of danger from animals (even domestic ones), certain obstacles, or partially secluded steep terrain.

His young companion informed him of the approach and the possible identity of the riders. Isaac stood wondering what their business could be and started to get angry from the anticipation of more complaints from them. He could never have imagined that Abimelech would be with them and was startled to hear the voice of the Philistine ruler address him as they neared. Isaac couldn't discern his face well enough to identify him, but the voice was unmistakable.

"My lord, what brings you to Beersheba? I am glad that you are still strong enough to make the trip."

"Master Isaac, our recent problems that caused your departure from our land left some things undone. I have come to ask for a covenant between your people and mine."

"Pardon my disbelief, but you chased us from you, and some of your people treated us roughly and put our animals in danger of dying from thirst. I can't understand why you would want to make a covenant with us."

"I accept your reluctance to accommodate us. Nonetheless, I beg of you to remember the kindness that existed between your father, Abraham, and me. Also, when you entered our land, your possessions were quite small compared to what they became during your sojourn with us. It was most unfortunate that your prosperity caused the envy of my people. I have grown old and often unable to control the waywardness of some members of my community. You should remember that I countenanced slights of my civility by both you and your father. I was also generous in my gifts to your father as I was to you. Can all of the good that has existed between your family and me be considered of less worth than some recent harassment that I was unable to quell?"

Isaac stood crestfallen as his shame grew with every word from Abimelech's lips. "Lord Abimelech, a thousand pardons from me, please. I must admit my greed in staying longer in your land than I should have. My family's prosperity was growing so fast that I foolishly put much of that prosperity in danger rather than move to another place when the renegades among your people filled our wells with dirt. I also should have known that you didn't personally approve of their actions."

Abimelech accepted Isaac's apology with a hearty hug and a kiss. Both men agreed that Isaac's grazing requirements had been starting to strain the capability of the land to support everyone's flocks. Isaac also admitted that he had been encroaching upon the resources of the people who destroyed his wells. Conveniently, his move to Beersheba had extended the borders and territory of control for the proposed confederation.

The covenant that was witnessed by officials of both men called for mutual help from either one in case of attack against the other party. In addition, Isaac's forces needed to be strengthened and trained, because his command consisted mostly of shepherds and tradesmen. Isaac agreed to seek military personnel from Aram—specifically from areas around Haran and Damascus. He still knew of relatives in both places. A meeting that had started out with rather strong words of confrontation ended with nights of feasting and camaraderie.

NINE

ALONE AGAIN

IN THE DAYS FOLLOWING the feasting, Rebekah seemed more subdued than normal. Isaac appreciated the kindness and unconditional love displayed by his wife, but her rather infrequent moody spells always disturbed him. These spells usually meant that he had done or not done something he should or shouldn't have.

"Rebekah, has the gaiety of the past days caused our present state of existence to bore you?" He hoped this somewhat facetious remark would elicit some response from her without further depressing her.

"No, husband. I am just concerned about Esau. He seldom has any contact with us. It seems almost from childhood, he showed a fascination for the tribes around us and disdain for his family. It pains me that he would take a wife from the sons of Heth or the Philistines."

Isaac once again thought his wife was displaying a less-than-proper trust in a son by his mother, but he tried to reassure her without scolding her. He further tried to soothe her concerns by stating that he would try to find Esau and talk to him about whom he should marry.

"My dear Isaac, pardon me, but he is so headstrong that I doubt he will listen to anything you say. To justify my concern, one of my servants told me that she overheard some gossip among the shepherds that he may already be married."

Isaac shrugged and smiled at his wife giving credibility to gossip. Within a few days, however, Rebekah's suspicions were confirmed. Esau showed up for a rare visit with two wives of the daughters of Heth, not one. Upon introduction, Rebekah almost fainted and barely controlled her tongue from a vicious scolding as she recovered from the shock of the news. Esau ignored or failed to notice the look on his mother's face; when he turned to look at his father, however, he stopped his train of introduction and exclaimed, "Father, are you ill?"

Isaac stuttered a negative reply and told him to continue with the introduction after a brief update on happenings in his life since his last visit. Isaac suggested that Rebekah show the two women around the camp while he showed Esau his new storage shed for the venison that Esau provided him.

*　*　*　*　*

They were scarcely out the hearing of the wives before Isaac scolded in unprecedented anger, "Why have you defied the wishes of me and your mother by marrying outside of our family? If you have done this to spite your mother, you have succeeded in offending your father, also. You surely must have known that I disapprove of these marriages as much as your mother does."

Esau appeared undeterred by his father's reprimand. "I felt that the daughters of Heth would be more loving to me than any of our community. Not only does my mother slight me, but so have Yosef and the other members of our community, including all of the eligible women. You may wonder why I don't visit more often, even to the point of sending supplies of venison to you with a friend. I stay away from here because I don't feel wanted. I have friends among the children of Heth, but not here."

Isaac shook his head and motioned for Esau to be still until he could think of a reply. He then told Esau that most of the dislike by his brethren had been caused by Esau's own belligerence. Had he shown even some civility toward the members of his community, they would have accepted him. As it was, nearly everyone—including his brother, Jacob—was afraid of him. Jacob still carried some scars from the beatings that he had received from him.

Esau had remained calm during the discussion up to the mention of the name of Jacob. "Jacob! Why should I show kindness toward Jacob? He made me sell my birthright for a bowl of porridge. He would have allowed me to die unless I gave up my inheritance. I can only assume you approved of his action, because I have never heard of even an apology from you."

"Sold your birthright! I can't believe it. I have said nothing about it because I couldn't imagine your doing a thing like that. You were tricked into this sale. I know Jacob, and I am sure he would have given you food and water, were he sure that you were near death. He took advantage of you during a dire circumstance in our lives. He assumed that you were so hungry that a bowl of porridge would seem worth more than an inheritance that appeared to have become worthless. Jacob had the faith and foresight to value what you didn't."

Esau answered scornfully, "I don't care about what I did then. I am interested in what you are going to do about it now. The birthright should be mine. He may have known that I wasn't near death, but I didn't. A bowl of porridge for life loomed more important than any inheritance I would never see."

Isaac signaled Esau to be quiet. "Did you sign your sale on Jacob's inheritance papyrus?"

"I did, but as I said, he forced me to sign it. I am sure the signature isn't valid."

"That may not be true. You can't prove he forced you to sign the document. Also, at the time of the sale, the inheritance could be considered to be so worthless that a bowl of porridge in the time of drought was just compensation. Additionally, your silence until now indicates that you didn't value your birthright."

Isaac asked Esau not to confront Rebekah and Jacob with his plea. He would find out exactly what happened and have the sale reversed if he could.

*   *   *   *   *

Jacob told Isaac why he had demanded the birthright and that Esau had not been near death, as he claimed. Isaac tried to reason that Jacob acted cruelly, and therefore he should remit the birthright. Jacob, however, held firm—more resolute than Isaac had ever seen him. After a long discussion that covered parts of several days, Isaac relented and resolved that there was no way to restore the birthright to Esau.

When Esau made a return visit about a moon later, he left despondent at the news that the sale was final and that Jacob was the first heir.

*   *   *   *   *

As the years passed and Jacob found no wife, another growing crisis involving the need for marriage arose—only this time, it involved Isaac's son Jacob and not Isaac himself. Rebekah became almost hysterical in her insistence that Jacob would not choose a wife from the daughters of the surrounding tribes. So many of their relatives had been dispersed by the drought of prior years that no compatible mates could be found close to home.

One morning, while Jacob was in the field, Rebekah decided to take him some buttermilk from a just-completed churning. The day was rather cool, but she still became tired before she reached the grazing grounds.

"Mother, you didn't have to bring this delicious buttermilk to me on such a chilly day."

"Son, I needed to talk to you about a problem for which we need to be alone for quite a while, and I understand that you are going to be farther from here tomorrow. Therefore, today seemed to be the best time to come to see you, and I have clothed myself for warmth." Jacob took the buttermilk and started to drink heartily as she continued, "You are past the age when you should be married, but I am glad that you haven't taken wives from the tribes around here. I have discussed with your father the idea of your going back to the land of my brother Laban to find a wife among your cousins. I understand that my family and your father's also are thriving back in Haran."

"Who will help my father? Even he now depends on me to run his endeavors. You know his eyesight is so bad that it isn't safe for him to leave his tent without a guide. He can't possibly manage his affairs without an assistant who knows how to run things."

Rebekah smiled and shook her head. "I believe that the lead shepherd, his other assistants, and I can manage his affairs. I have taken a close interest in family affairs for the last few years and know who the capable and honest members are. It's time for you to leave home and start your own family. I am certain that my or your father's family will provide you with that start."

After Rebekah deflected a few more arguments from him about why he couldn't leave home, Jacob agreed to seek a wife in Haran. With that problem settled, Rebekah next mentioned one that almost shocked Jacob—they must fool Isaac into bestowing his blessing upon Jacob.

"Mother, even if we could accomplish such a thing, is it right?"

"Jacob, Jacob! You thought it right to deprive Esau of the birthright, which I also condoned. You have seen Esau's disdain for his family and even for its possessions. He deserves neither the birthright nor the blessing."

"I still think it fair that my brother keeps some part of our family inheritance."

"Jacob, listen to me carefully. The birthright gives you the means to pass on the livelihood for your children-to-be. Those children will be responsible for continuing the lineage of Abraham—a part of the many nations I heard was promised to him. If you don't have the blessing, adversities could overtake you or them and endanger that promise that God made to your grandfather."

From that day, Rebekah thought about how to fool Isaac into giving the blessing to Jacob. She dared not mention or encourage him to bestow it while

Esau was around, because her husband could act immediately. She had to find some way to substitute Jacob when he thought that Esau was present.

Esau had recently moved closer to them, but he still visited infrequently. When he did visit, he seldom brought venison. Isaac began to complain about being without wild meat most of the time. Esau excused his lack of provision by stating that there was seldom any venison left over, because he had to supply so many other people.

After several moons of Isaac's complaints about Esau's failure to supply venison, Rebekah suddenly thought of a way to trick Isaac into giving the blessing to Jacob. The next time that Esau visited without any meat, she would suggest to Isaac that he bestow his blessing … but a requirement for that bestowal would be for Esau go kill a deer or antelope and bring him some spicy meat prepared from the kill.

While Esau was away, Rebekah would have Jacob fetch a couple of small goats that she would cook in savory spices. She had noticed lately that Isaac's sense of taste wasn't sharply discriminating. Because he liked spicy food, she regularly cooked all of his meat with heavy spices. He would occasionally wonder if Esau had sent venison or antelope. She also noticed that the flesh of a new breed of goat developed by Jacob almost always tasted like wild meat to him.

She must implement this plan soon, she knew, because Jacob needed to be on his way to seek a wife. *Everything should be ready.* She had fashioned goatskin coverings for Jacob's hands and neck shortly after talking to Jacob on that chilly day moons ago about his need to leave to start his own family.

Within less than a week after Rebekah had decided on the scheme, Esau visited them. He often used their home as a resting place during or after a successful hunt. As usual upon arrival this day, he ate a small meal and went to bed for a long sleep. This sleep period gave Rebekah enough time to begin her plan.

She suggested to Isaac that he bestow his blessing, but this time cleverly avoided mentioning Esau as the one who should receive it. Isaac argued at first that now wasn't the time for the blessing. Rebekah countered with the fact that their sons were grown. Esau was married, and Jacob was leaving to seek his wife after he had relinquished the rest of his duties to the lead shepherd and lead scribe. Therefore, Isaac's family was grown, and he would soon have descendants that needed his blessing. While Isaac was in good health, except for eyesight, it still wasn't good to tempt God in giving him more time to bestow his blessing. To her delight, Isaac soon relented and agreed to call Esau to him after he had finished his sleep.

In reality, Jacob had failed to relinquish some of his duties solely because he wanted to be around to steal the blessing from his brother. The lead scribe had even begun to seem confused about why he hadn't been informed of some items, because he expected Jacob to leave immediately.

Rebekah kept a close watch on the activities of her husband once she had his agreement on bestowing the blessing. She also told Jacob to stand by and be ready to act quickly when Esau left for the hunt.

When Esau awoke, Isaac asked to talk to him and made the request for the spicy meat in return for bestowing his blessing upon him. An elated Esau left prepared for the hunt. "Father, I will leave immediately to procure the venison. I don't have my companions with me. It may be a while before I can make the kill by myself. I am sorry that I once again had no meat to spare from the hunt that I just finished."

Isaac gave him a parting comment. "I'm sorry that I wasn't able to overturn your sale of the birthright to your brother. I can, however, provide you with some solace through my blessing. Take care and use as much time as you need to find the game. I will await your return with the spicy meat."

*   *   *   *   *

Before Esau was out of sight, Rebekah ran to Jacob. "Please fetch me a couple of kids from the new breed you have developed. I will cook some spicy meat from their flesh."

"Mother, do you believe that Father will be fooled just by the spicy taste? He will know that what you have cooked isn't venison."

"Yes, I can prepare the flesh of the kids in a way that will fool his taste, which seems to have become dull with age."

Jacob still wasn't convinced that other aspects of the plan would work. "Father may not be able to discern my face if I avoid putting it directly in front of him. He will, however, be able to touch me and realize I am not hairy like Esau. Also, Esau often smells like a deer or antelope. He should have that smell after he returns from this hunt."

"Thanks for reminding me about the smell of the hunt. I hadn't thought of that. There are some deerskins in the venison shed, now empty most of the time. Go and rub your skin with them. That should give you the smell of the hunt. As to his realizing that you aren't Esau through touch, I have fashioned some coverings of goatskin for your hands and neck. The fine hair of those skins should fool him. Please put these coverings and Esau's best tunic on before approaching him."

Jacob started to make further comments, but Rebekah insisted that he go slaughter the young goats. They must hasten, she explained, because Esau was a skilled hunter who might return sooner than expected.

Once the meat had been delivered to Rebekah, Jacob walked to a secluded spot where he practiced imitating Esau's voice.

When Rebekah had finished cooking, she called to Jacob, "It's time for you to steal the blessing from your brother. The lookout I dispatched earlier indicates that Esau is nowhere in sight, but he still could return soon. Actually, there is a distant campfire going that could be his cooking of his kill. If your father wonders how you found game so soon, tell him that God blessed you with a kill close to home."

Jacob knew that Isaac's eyesight seemed to improve from time to time, and that there was no way of telling when the improvement would happen. Hence, he decided to approach his father from the side and stay away as far as possible. Jacob had acquired the ability to imitate Esau's voice through his short practice period, but the required modification to his throat muscles didn't allow for a lot of volume.

*   *   *   *   *

When Jacob spoke, Isaac moved his head back and forth, as if he didn't know where the sound was coming from. "Who is it?"

"I'm Esau, and I have brought you the spicy meat that you requested."

"You have returned from the hunt quite soon. How were you able to find game so quickly? I have noticed that game has been scarce around here of late."

Jacob told him that God had blessed him by causing a lost deer to wander close to home.

Isaac still sensed that something might be amiss. To avoid giving his blessing to the wrong person—he didn't trust some of his servants not to try to steal the blessing—he called for Jacob to come closer. When he felt Jacob's hands and neck, they had the feel of Esau. Also, the tunic Jacob wore felt and had the smell of one of Esau's favorites. *He dressed in his best tunic for this occasion. Rebekah is wrong; Esau does appreciate the family.* As a final test, he asked for Jacob to kiss him. He had hoped to be able to discern the face enough to verify that it was Esau. Jacob, however, carefully approached from the side.

To Isaac's dismay, his eyesight on this day was worse than ever before. What he could discern revealed the face to be Esau's. *The beard is the same,* he concluded as he extended his hands for the ritual of the blessing.

"Your voice sounds higher than Esau's, like that of Jacob."

"Father, I have returned swiftly from the hunt to accommodate you. Perhaps I'm a bit breathless from hurrying."

*   *   *   *   *

Rebekah had judged correctly that she and Jacob had needed to hurry with the meat preparation. Jacob had just emerged from the tent after the blessing when Esau raced into camp with a container of spicy meat he had prepared at the kill site. "Father, this is Esau. I have returned with the spicy meat, as you requested."

At first Esau jumped back and then forward, as if to catch his father, who had started to tremble. Not sure of the cause of his father's malady, Esau waited to see if Isaac could speak.

Isaac slowly stopped shaking and exclaimed in a voice laden with anger, "Someone has just entered my tent and disguised himself as you. He has fooled me into giving your blessing to him. I had some doubt about who he was, but his hands and neck felt like yours, and he wore your tunic. He also provided me with some spicy meat, which tasted like venison. Strangely, all of my servants were away, with my closest aide being dispatched on some *important* errand. Therefore, I had none to verify that it was you. I either had to trust my senses or wait for a servant who might lie anyway. I chose to trust my senses, to my shame."

"Father, I think I can tell you who received your blessing. I caught a glimpse of someone with Jacob's profile leaving your tent just before I arrived. He seemed to be wearing some covering on his hands and wearing my tunic. I thought little of the spectacle, because the glimpse was brief, and I was in a hurry to bring the warm meat to you."

"Your brother has received my blessing in your stead. It saddens me that I have been so gullible."

"Father, can't you withdraw the blessing that Jacob has obtained under false pretenses?"

"I am sorry, my son, but I cannot do that. The act of bestowing the blessing is a sacred pledge. I am responsible for knowing and evaluating the person eligible for receiving it. It was my negligence in determining who I placed my hands upon. To my shame, I cannot withdraw the blessing from Jacob."

"My brother is correctly named. He has now acted these two times according to the meaning of his name as a supplanter. Father, do you yet have a blessing for me?"

"Not only is your brother properly named, but so am I. Isaac means mocking, and I have been cruelly mocked by my second son. I do, however, have a blessing for you, my first son, but it is a lesser one than what I have just bestowed. I can bless none as I have blessed Jacob. Please come closer, so I can place my hands upon you for the blessing."

Esau left the presence of his father after he decided that the shaking had been caused by rage and not some serious malady. Jacob also had departed for a stay with the flocks, giving the excuse that he needed to survey the grazing area for some reported predators. This was a convenient excuse that would allow him to stay away until Esau decided to leave. To that end, he left instructions with a servant to bring word of his brother's departure.

The toll of the second hunt immediately following an earlier very tiring hunt and the trauma of having Jacob steal his blessing sapped Esau of his strength. He stayed for a week, although he knew his employers would be angry at his prolonged absence. Nevertheless, he would be of no use to them until he regained his strength.

Esau's companions knew that he sometimes stayed with his parents after a hunt and, suspecting possible illness, decided to check on him when his absence reached a week's length. Esau greeted them cordially and told them he was ready for the next hunt. He had been sick but had recovered. When they kept asking about his illness, he told them the full story about what had happened to him.

His closest understudy expressed his violent feelings by scorning Esau for letting his brother rob him of what was his. He belittled Esau further by moving his hands in a circular gesture to demonstrate the wealth that Jacob had taken from him.

"I honor my father, and his last words as I departed from receiving a lesser blessing were not to harm Jacob. He emphasized that Jacob was destined by God to be blessed and any action by me to harm him would bring the wrath of God upon me."

Another one of Esau's companions sneered at his stupidity by asserting that no god would protect a thief like his brother. Esau's father was just trying to protect Jacob, although he deserved to die for his wrong toward Esau.

Esau smiled and then scowled. "I must honor my father while he is still alive. Upon his death, however, I plan to kill Jacob. That may be very soon, because my father has been quite ill ever since I confronted him with what Jacob had done to me."

*　*　*　*　*

Unbeknownst to Esau and his companions, a servant had just finished procuring some milk from a nanny goat to use for breakfast preparation. She had started back with the milk when she heard the threatening conversations.

She remained hidden behind a stack of grain until Esau and his companions rode off for the next hunt. She then raced to tell Rebekah what she had just heard.

*   *   *   *   *

Later the next day, a messenger approached Jacob with a request from his mother to return at once. Upon his arrival, Rebekah instructed him to prepare to leave before Esau got back from his current hunting activities. She had already convinced Isaac that Jacob should find a wife back in her brother's homeland; her expressed disdain over the prospect of his taking a wife from the daughters of Heth had finally convinced Isaac to agree to his leaving. She then told Jacob of Esau's threat and explained that she wanted to be sure that Jacob left while his father was still alive. Jacob suggested that he shouldn't leave while his father was so ill. Rebekah assured him that Isaac's despondency over being fooled into bestowing the blessing on the wrong child, as he saw it, was causing his illness and that he would improve with the passage of days to come.

Rebekah had correctly assessed her husband's illness. Isaac's first unstated impulse over hearing of Jacob's leaving now was to agree. He wanted to get rid of his son who had brought him much grief through self-righteous arrogance and willingness to commit wrongs under the supposition that the shameful acts were God's will. Nonetheless, he initially objected to Jacob's leaving, citing the need for his services, until Rebekah's assurance that they could get by without him soon convinced a mind anxious to get rid of an annoyance that was making him sick. Thankfully, Jacob had at least one good trait in that he had passed on his knowledge of animal and crop management to the rest of his workers.

Isaac agreed with the soothing feeling that he was doing the right thing. The competent stewards that Jacob was leaving behind should handle his wealth well, and Jacob's important job now was to find a wife to help provide grandchildren, because the one with the blessing must have descendants.

*   *   *   *   *

Jacob rapidly prepared to leave because of the obvious improvement in his father's health—a result that his mother had just predicted. The amount of relief and exhilaration felt by Jacob and his mother contrasted in direct proportion to the despair of his brother, Esau, and father, Isaac. Nevertheless, he had accomplished everything he could here; his destiny for at least the next few years lay in the land of his grandfather Abraham's first home upon leaving Ur.

With any immediate threat from Esau unlikely even if he returned from the hunt, Jacob's rush to depart was driven more by the feeling of regret that was quickly sapping his happiness. A change of scenery should help him regain the resolve that the end result of his actions justified his chicanery.

Rebekah noticed the elation expressed by Jacob wane almost by the twelfth-day. "My son, you appear to be downcast after looking so pleasant yesterday. Don't feel sorry for leaving us. You have been a son who has given me much joy. There comes a time in many children's lives when they must leave home, maybe never to see their parents again."

"Mother, it's true that there is certain sadness in leaving, but suddenly I am mostly suffering remorse from what I did to my brother. I know I did what should have been done, but I still have a hard time shaking the feeling of wrongdoing by me."

"Jacob! That's absurd. You need to get rid of those bad thoughts at once. The great heritage promised to your grandfather couldn't be allowed to fall to the lot of Esau. You have the traditional love for shepherding animals, a requisite for providing a heritage to descendants. Just look at the way he squanders his limited resources on rowdy companions. I despair that he will lose even the reduced blessing he did receive."

Jacob thanked his mother for the advice and held her close to him for a long time. The next morning, he held a meeting with all of the community leaders answering any final questions that they might have. He then gave his mother a final kiss with the promise that he would strive to gain a wife and property in Haran soon enough to retrace his grandfather's journey to this land before she died.

As Jacob turned to go, Rebekah called to him, "Jacob, you should give your father a parting greeting. I'm not sure he will appreciate your regards, but it's your duty as a son to extend them to him."

Jacob nodded and halted his small train of attendants by his father's tent. He dismounted and asked Isaac's personal aide if he could have a final audience with his father.

When the aide returned and nodded for him to enter, he walked to customary speaking distance before greeting his father. "Father, I am departing for Haran. I hope to return someday to see you again. Just in case we never meet again, I want to thank you for giving me the opportunity to manage your affairs since your sojourn in Gerar, and for all of the prosperity that I have received from being your son. I won't apologize for the fraud committed in stealing Esau's blessing, because I still believe that it was the right thing to do. I am truly sorry, however, that the incident brought you grief. For the other discomforts I have caused, I am also sorry. I don't think that either of us wants a long speech before departure. So, may God be with you!"

Isaac raised his hand in blessing. "You must go to your grandfather's relatives to find a wife. That is a command that has the full blessing of your mother and me, as you know. Rebekah may not have specified just who you should marry, but I know that she would be disappointed if you didn't select from the daughters of her brother Laban. Because you love your mother so dearly, I know that knowledge is enough guidance for you to select a mate. You will return to Canaan after you have prospered in our home of sojourn. I will get to kiss you again before I die—of that I am sure. Go now, and prosper."

Jacob kissed his father and turned to walk toward his mount with a renewed spring in his step. He was departing with the full blessing of his father. The rancor of the past few days had been lifted from him as a great burden off his shoulders.

The recent growth in population in Canaan provided the people with enough guards along the caravan routes to eliminate banditry. The frequent security patrols ensured that Jacob and his companions could travel apart from a caravan. Nevertheless, Jacob had contracted a retired caravan leader to lead their group. The leader's knowledge of the countryside would prevent their starting down any wrong trails. Most of his companions could get lost before they left Canaan.

The former caravan leader cited that his long years of experience in adjusting the pace of caravans might not apply here. Because none had specified to him the length time allotted for the trip, he didn't know the pace at which they should travel. He did, however, sense that they might be traveling too fast for the good of the animals.

"Sire, we do need to slow down," Jacob agreed. "You are right; our animals can't keep this pace. Sorry, I was so elated over the blessing of my family for this trip that my energy became unusually high. I didn't realize how fast we were riding. Let's rest for a while, and then I will resume the pace we should use before I relinquish the lead to you."

Jacob set a slow pace. They had plentiful supplies and exchange metals, obviating the need to hurry.

The prospect of a married life gave Jacob mixed feelings. His management of flocks took most of his waking life. He had also become apprehensive about how he would do as a husband. That concern had started from the day his mother had mentioned the need for nearly immediate marriage.

Not knowing how the rest of his life would unfold, he decided that this trip, at least, would be enjoyable and relaxing. Part of that enjoyment could be found in assessing the countryside he traversed. He drank in the scenery, noticing the nuances of the landscape even when passing terrain that others might consider bland and monotonous. Constructively, whatever he could learn about the lands now would be useful for the return trip that he must make someday. Starting with the first night, Jacob dictated important observations from that day to a scribe. He insisted that this recording of the trip be performed before any festivities began.

One day, in the early post meridian, Jacob told the leader to halt. The leader looked puzzled and gestured as if he didn't understand the reason for the command; his perplexity stemmed from the fact that the scouts hadn't indicated the presence of danger ahead.

"Sire, I want to stop here, possibly for more than a day. I sense that this place is mystical. We have adequate resources for well beyond the time when we should reach our destination; there's no need to hurry." Jacob added jokingly that his freedom was doomed soon enough, because marriage awaited him at the end of his journey.

*   *   *   *   *

That night, at the evening festivities, one of the servants approached the group leader, wondering what was wrong with Jacob. First, he had ordered them to stop with much daylight remaining, and now he didn't participate in any of the fun games. The past two nights, he had been the last one to rest for the next day. The leader just shrugged and continued to enjoy his goblet of wine.

*   *   *   *   *

Meanwhile, Jacob found a nearby hillock from which to look over the fascinating landscape. *What is it with this land?* He felt that he knew this place for some reason, but couldn't remember from where, when, or how.

Jacob felt strangely fatigued and decided to retire early. Whether from the noise of the reveling of his companions or the unsettled state of his mind, he slept fitfully, if at all, until after the nighttime meridian, when he fell into a deep sleep.

During this sleep, Jacob experienced the weirdest dream of his life. The first element of the dream revealed what seemed to be a nearby level area at the top of the hillock on which he had sat viewing the terrain. Slowly a ladder materialized and began to expand upward and upward. It grew past the scattered clouds and past the stars—strangely never diminishing in size with distance—until it reached a large throne barely distinguishable within the ambient blinding light engulfing it. Suddenly, a man appeared below the top rung and began to descend. He was immediately followed by another man, and then another and another. Jacob soon tired from counting the people descending the ladder. When the first man reached earth, he turned and starting climbing back up the ladder, to be followed by each person who set foot on Earth.

Amid all of the activity, one being remained in place at the top of the ladder. Jacob recognized the being as Melchizedek, of whom he had barely heard. Mysteriously, Jacob knew this member of the godhead so confidently that he didn't even question how he had obtained the knowledge of his identity. Strong emotions raced through his dreaming mind as Melchizedek repeated promises that had been given to his grandfather and father.

Jacob awoke the next morning with the certainty that his dream had been a message from God and that the ladder climbers had been angels. All of the mystical appeal he had felt yesterday made perfect sense now: this place was a gate to heaven. He informed the leader that they had to stay for at least one more day while he set up a monument to God.

As his companions pursued a day of hunting game, Jacob busied himself with stacking the stones for a pillar. He topped it off with the stone upon which he had rested his head the night before. After some retries at fitting the final stones, Jacob proved the pillar to be stable. His last act before joining the others in camp was to anoint the pillar with olive oil and say a prayer of dedication. In this prayer, he promised that if God protected him wherever he went, he would return again to this land and offer a tithe of his wealth.

*   *   *   *   *

Before departing the next morning, Jacob gathered everyone for a dedication ceremony, naming the spot Bethel—House of God—for, as he said, God was there. When the group started to leave the dedication spot, the guide thought he saw the corner foundation of an old building site through some vegetation. He hastened to push the overgrowth aside, revealing a well-preserved altar that showed signs of sacrificial offerings.

The eldest member of the group sensed the curiosity of some of his companions. He related the history of the altar. It had been built by Jacob's grandfather Abraham. He had heard tales from the past about this place being the original home of their people when they first came into Canaan. The description from those stories fit this place precisely. The place had been called Bethel then also; Jacob had just renamed it for what it was. This place could have no other name.

*   *   *   *   *

Jacob reverted to a festive attitude in the following days, although his jocularity diminished as they neared Haran. Upon entering Haran, Jacob's smiling face changed to a worried scowl. He had heard of the prosperity of the city from his mother, but her description of wealth didn't match the modest surroundings he saw. The city certainly had once been more prosperous, as evidenced by the decay. *Maybe I need to change my expectations. After all, my father makes the holdings of some of his neighbors look no better than this city*, he reasoned in rebuttal to his disappointment.

On the morning of the second day in Haran, the guide took Jacob and a servant to the section of town where he believed that Laban dwelled. After receiving a couple of negative replies to the location of Laban's property, Jacob asked, "Are you sure that you know where he lives? Maybe we should talk to the town assessor?"

The guide pleaded for another twelfth-day of searching before they asked for help. He was sure that Laban lived close by.

Within a short time, they reached a well that seemed to correspond to a description given by Rebekah about her brother's home. The people at the well identified themselves as Jacob's relatives and pointed to the younger of Laban's daughters, Rachel, who was approaching the well with her flock.

T E N

JACOB AS A SERVANT

I N THE DAYS THAT followed Jacob's meeting his cousin Rachel, his uncle
Laban, and other relatives, Jacob's companions caught a caravan back
home, except his nearest servant. The servant objected to leaving Jacob
alone. He wasn't sure that Jacob would be able to find work there. His uncle
didn't seem as prosperous as his mother had thought. Could Laban afford to
feed him, not to say provide a profitable job?

"You must return to my mother with the news that I have found her
brother and that I am all right. You don't have to lie about my finding a
job. Just tell her that I have begun my new life, and that I will be asking her
brother for marriage to his younger daughter within a few days."

The servant continued to express his concern about Jacob's decision to
stay with Laban. He felt that Jacob was destined to get himself into a dire
condition that could lead to servitude far worse than any his servants ever
experienced. His last plea was to stay until they saw how things worked out
with his uncle.

"My dear loyal servant, you must leave me, or you will be thwarting
God's will. On the night of my dream, he promised that he would provide for
and prosper me. All that I had to do was to trust him. You should be able to
remember that I took circumstances years ago no better than these and made
my father wealthy. I can and will do so with my uncle Laban. Go!"

*   *   *   *   *

Like his father, Isaac, Jacob usually had little insight into unstated human
motives. During the early days of Jacob's stay, Laban asked question after

question about how and what Rebekah and Isaac had done and were doing. He appeared to be more interested in them than Jacob. Jacob interpreted Laban's inquires as those of someone trying to become familiar again with his long-lost sister.

All of this rhetoric, however, was an expressed front that Laban would maintain throughout his long relationship with Jacob—a front that Jacob never did fully understand or seemingly believe existed. His trust in this instance prevented a preemptive defense that would have saved Jacob years of abuse.

Laban had regular contact with persons intimately acquainted with Jacob's role in producing Isaac's wealth. Laban had essentially been driven out of Ur by his father Bethuel, who had finally reached a conclusion after many years that he was a poor manager. When reduced almost to servant status, Laban couldn't abide staying around Ur, where Bethuel, if not others, would remind him of his failure. He negotiated a favorable settlement of wages with his father and headed west to Haran—a land that he, like his sister Rebekah, had thought to be more prosperous than it was.

In fact, this settlement had cost Bethuel so much that he had soon concluded that he needed to relocate to Haran also. Perhaps he could convince his son to give back some of the animals or at least help him make a living.

From the first day, Laban began to scheme in his mind how he could retain Jacob to work for him for very little wages and keep him for a long time. He didn't expect Jacob to duplicate his feat in Gerar; therefore, it would probably take several years to become truly wealthy. He could sense the instantaneous love that Jacob had for Rachel and her suppressed but obvious fondness for Jacob also. She would be a prize that Jacob would toil long moons—yes, years—to acquire. He had some pangs of conscience about essentially selling his child, but then men of greed like Laban had easy ways to assuage their conscience. By the end of the third day, Laban knew that his fortunes were soon to improve. He had the perfect commodity by which to extort onerous service from Jacob.

With rather uncharacteristic patience, Laban let day after day pass without the hint of requiring servitude by Jacob. Whenever Jacob would start to mention his reason for contacting Laban, his uncle would deflect the conversation to some casual subject. This routine went on for weeks until Jacob became so restive that he finally acquired enough nerve to ask Laban for his daughter Rachel in marriage.

*   *   *   *   *

Jacob was shocked when Laban refused a dowry for his daughter and demanded seven years of servitude. Jacob began to protest this effrontery that he felt toward himself and Rachel both. Nevertheless, before Jacob could utter a word, he concluded that this would be a good opportunity to prove himself and help his uncle to prosper. In a way, it didn't seem fair for him to take a fabulous prize as Rachel from her father without generously rewarding him for her. He had reached a conclusion that wealth and Laban were two items that had a difficult time staying together. A dowry would likely be soon squandered through poor financial deals. After making a minor complaint about being required to give up a part of his life, he agreed to the deal.

Jacob had no trouble taking control as the manager of Laban's flocks and herds. Laban never doubted Jacob's abilities as his father, Isaac, had. Also, the current herd managers for Laban had no deep care for the animals. When Laban gave the lead shepherd an easier job at the same wage, he immediately agreed to help, even welcome, Jacob as the flock manager.

Within a few moons, the flocks grew noticeably. From the first day, Jacob instituted an improved predator lookout system. This action alone increased the flock numbers considerably by the end of the first year. The spotting and quarantining of sick animals, the separation of violent animals, and other techniques made the first anniversary of Jacob's management a delight to Laban, who, on the morning of that anniversary promptly complimented Jacob on his success.

"Yes, Uncle Laban, I have toiled industriously to improve the conditions among and surrounding your flocks. I was appalled at the careless handling of the animals when I started. You may have noticed that I haven't been around the house very much. It has taken many days and many nights in the field to care for and condition the animals. I hope to have more free time from now on. Most of the shepherds have become caring and more capable at tending the flocks."

Laban responded by telling him how most of the other shepherds had expressed satisfaction in learning from Jacob. As a reward for Jacob's service for the past year, Laban had scheduled a three-day banquet which he and all of the shepherds could attend sometime during the festivities.

Jacob accepted the invitation with such excitement that Laban paused and looked back at him when departing. The festival had scarcely started before Laban realized what Jacob was excited about. Jacob had taken leave of his duties the day prior so that he could thoroughly cleanse himself of the smell and grime of the field. He took two long baths that day and another one before dressing for the banquet. Upon arriving at the feast, he immediately sought out Rachel.

Rachel almost shouted when she saw Jacob approaching. "Jacob, I have longed to see you! As my presumed betrothed, you are away far more than I would like."

After kissing her extended hand, Jacob replied, "It disturbs me to be absent from you also, but my job requires it, or it has in the past. I have trained the other shepherds to handle more of my duties. They should be able to make it possible for me to have more free time in the future."

*   *   *   *   *

While others started to feast, Jacob and Rachel were more interested in taking a long walk before eating. This action startled Laban, who thought that Rachel should have no close contact with Jacob until their wedding. Laban was torn between preventing contact now and waiting until after the feast. He could feign some problem with the flocks that would send Jacob back into the fields, but he decided against that action, because Jacob was due some relaxation. Instead, he had a servant watch everything that Rachel did. If Rachel were to stray too far from the crowd at the banquet, the servant was to call and tell her that her father needed to see her.

*   *   *   *   *

When both Rachel and Jacob realized that their every move was being watched, they decided to avoid any close contact for the rest of the festival. As they turned to walk back to the banquet, Rachel angrily told Jacob that she would soon talk to her father about his meddling in their lives.

*   *   *   *   *

By the meridian of the second feasting day, Jacob seemed to have had enough revelry—that is, revelry without Rachel, Laban guessed. He made an excuse that it was time for him to get back to the flocks. As he departed, Laban asked him why he wasn't staying for all three days—a deserved respite for him.

"Uncle, I have enjoyed my time off, and I am well rested. Really, the animals have been so cooperative of late that they don't tire me as much as they did a year ago. Besides, I don't feel that I should be away from them for three straight nights. There are still a few mean males in the flock that I am afraid will become belligerent again if they start to think their master has gone."

Laban smiled in agreement while suspecting that Jacob was upset over the chaperoning. He also saw an unpleasant expression on Rachel's face. He concluded that her countenance belied a suppressed anger toward him. He expected a confrontation soon after the banquet was over. He smiled at the chance to convince her that she needed to be discreet. His daughter must not act as one of the harlots whose trade was prospering in Haran—probably the most prosperous profession in the city.

At midmorning of the day after the banquet, Rachel asked for an audience with her father. She approached him with a quick bow and impolitely started speaking before being addressed. "Father, I am upset. I hadn't seen Jacob for almost three moons. Why did you have a servant observe our every move? He is just a good friend—a friend to whom I may one day be espoused. Because I am not yet betrothed, there is no reason why I shouldn't be able to see him. Are you going to insist that I have no contact with him?"

Laban told that her that she understood his opinion precisely, and because of the future betrothal, she should refrain from familiarity with Jacob. He had instructed the servants to inform him of any presence of Jacob, so he could ensure that she covered her face in his presence. Of course, she wasn't to talk to him unless necessary and in the presence of others. To do otherwise would be to act as a harlot.

"Father, I accept my fate in this matter, although I believe it to be cruel. There is much that I could learn from Jacob, and there is no good reason that I shouldn't see him."

Laban gave her a warning that she would be disowned if she disobeyed. His instructions were final.

Rachel bowed a deep bow and asked permission to be leave. Rachel walked away and became quite ill—so ill that she required close personal attention in her quarters for a week.

*   *   *   *   *

Meanwhile, Jacob took the separation from Rachel as just another disappointment in life and busied himself with work. Three days after Jacob's return to work, a trio of riders approached the glen where he was driving some strays back to the main herd. Jacob identified them before they reached greeting distance. The rider in the center was the dear servant he had sent home a year ago. Jacob started to run toward them, although he feared that he didn't want to hear the news the servant was bringing.

Before he dismounted, the servant told Jacob not to be alarmed. His parents and brother were doing well. He had just been sent to find out how

Jacob was doing and hoped to be able to stay with Jacob for a few days to gather news about him to take back to them. He assumed that there was much to tell about the past year.

"Nahum, you may stay with me, but you will have to spend most of your time in the field if you want to talk to me. Also, before I forget to ask, I am curious how my mother took the news of my surroundings last year. I know that I requested for you not to mention them to her, but I am sure that she demanded a complete description of everything. I also know that you rarely lie, so I assume you told her much more than I would have hoped for you to reveal."

His servant agreed that his initial report had not satisfied Rebekah. He had been met with constant questioning and the accusation that he wasn't telling her all that he saw and knew. She specifically wanted to know how her brother Laban was prospering and wanted to know it in detail. Reluctantly, he was forced to confess his concern for Jacob's quality of life. Surprisingly, she agreed with her son's optimism about his ability to increase Laban's wealth. She cited what had happened in Gerar after the drought as proof. Later he was informed that he would be assigned to make a yearly trip to see her brother and son while expressing regret that she or Isaac weren't able to make the trip to Haran.

"I am glad that you talked to Mother first. She has always supported me throughout my life. If not for her, my past life would have been miserable, and my future would probably be bleak. As you can see, I have been faithful to my word. I have given my uncle a goodly increase in holdings. He isn't wealthy yet, but I have made a good start in just one year."

When Nahum observed that Laban's increase wasn't as good as the one his mother described for Gerar, Jacob admitted, "That's true, but God doesn't always bless in the same measure every time. You should also consider that no specific blessing has been given to Laban. I presume any special blessing to accrue would come through me. Call it a lack of faith, if you will, but I don't need to acquire the same level of wealth for him as I did for my father—at least, not as rapidly."

Nonetheless, the servant departed after ten days with an upbeat report for Rebekah and Isaac. Jacob spent the next few moons immersed in his work while trying to fight despondency over not being able to see Rachel. Within weeks after the incident at the banquet, Rachel's sister, Leah, also dressed in a veil when in his presence. Jacob wondered why, because she wasn't to be his wife, but he let the puzzlement quickly slip from his mind, deeming her actions a result of Laban's prudery.

With his duties becoming less taxing almost daily and his camaraderie with Laban's jealous workers amounting to a nearly constant insult, Jacob became a bored and lonely recluse. He finally decided to frequent the roadside hostels for contact with business travelers. Not only would he get to know what was going on in the world, but also he would become known in business circles. The main thing he hoped to accomplish would be to teach himself business matters for the responsibilities arising when he married Rachel.

Another reason for acquiring this knowledge was to determine if Laban's business managers were doing a good job. Jacob expected they were handling the marketing of the wool and animal products poorly. The needs of the flocks had taken all of his waking hours during the first year, not giving him time to observe the actions of the business managers to any extent. He had noticed after the first shearing that the sheep came back with uneven stubble. The scraggly look of the animals insulted his sensibilities. This caused him to think that sloppiness in one aspect of business might indicate the same thing in other areas also. His supposition was reinforced a few days later when he overheard Laban remark about the wool production being less than he expected from the thick coats of the sheep before shearing.

When the servant Nahum arrived the next year, Jacob had a plan ready. His observations and overheard comments from workers and businessmen who knew Laban convinced him that there was more work to do than just caring for animals if he were to help Laban to become wealthy.

"My dear servant, I am happy to see you, more than ever before." Nahum's curiosity immediately showed on his face. "I see you are wondering why. My reason involves having you assigned to me as a personal assistant—just as you wanted to do from the start."

Nahum was delighted with the news, but he wondered what had happened to cause Jacob to need an assistant. The servant immediately expressed his concern that Jacob was overworked—or, worse yet, ill. He couldn't understand the request, because everything seemed to be going well without a servant.

Jacob told Nahum that he needed another person to investigate the workers handling Laban's business deals. From information he had pieced together, he was sure that wool and maybe animals were being stolen from the sale areas and sold separately by probably more than one worker. He was especially suspicious of Laban's closest administrator. He thought that Laban was suspicious also, but was either too careless to follow up or unable to set up a condition to catch the thieves.

Nahum readily accepted that Jacob's instincts about the matter could be trusted, but he was worried about putting both of their lives in danger by informing on the culprits. If Laban were reluctant to act on his own, he might even turn on him for condemning one of his pampered followers.

Jacob immediately dismissed the notion of any worker coddling by Laban. Laban was, as Jacob had just said, either too incompetent to catch the stealing or too lazy to put forth an effort. Even with the stolen goods, he was earning more than in the past. Perhaps he was willing to let the thefts persist if he received a certain amount of increase. Nevertheless, another person had an interest in stopping these thefts. That person was none other than Jacob himself. Ever since starting to work for Laban, he had been negotiating the wages owed to him at the end of his seven-year indenture. Although there was no guarantee that Laban would honor his pledge in full, the wealthier he was at the end of those seven years, the more likely he would be to pay Jacob in full. Therefore, Jacob had an interest in preserving Laban's wealth.

When Nahum still expressed doubt about their success in trapping the thieves without putting their own lives in danger, Jacob asserted that he need not fear. "Nahum, I think I have a scheme figured out that will have others do the incriminating for us. This plan will require some exchange metals—more than the meager amount I can ever acquire now. You will need to convince my father and mother to advance you the necessary amount when you return home. Your biggest job, however, may be convincing my father to let you return on permanent assignment."

* * * * *

To Nahum's delight, Isaac readily accepted his working for Jacob for most of the year. According to Isaac, Nahum only needed to return once a year to update them on what was happening with their son.

But Nahum got a mild shock when Rebekah objected to his leaving.

Nahum boldly countered her objections. He and Jacob had been good friends for years, and she had enough young men and women among her servants to handle any slack caused by his departure. He saw no reason for denying their fellowship. Jacob had no close friends at her brother's place, because he was denied any contact with Rachel or even Leah. The rest of Laban's people were boorish or jealous.

"I am denying your return because I am afraid that Jacob's scheme will fail," Rebekah explained, "and one or both of you will be injured or killed."

Nahum became both frustrated and emboldened as his persuasion continued to fail to convince Rebekah. He finally blurted out almost in anger that she hadn't been afraid to help Jacob usurp the blessing from Esau—and that action had probably been more dangerous than what they were planning. Actually, Jacob's role in their plan was quite innocent. He didn't think that any of the thieves working for her brother had enough sense to realize that Jacob was the person behind the scheme to reveal who was doing the stealing. Also, he would be gone from the area before the culprits were caught. The only sad thing about the plan was that its successful completion would mean that Nahum could never see Jacob again if Laban didn't send the culprits away. He would wear a disguise during the rest of his time with Jacob, but the thieves could still recognize him if he continued to stay around after he and Jacob had exposed their stealing.

Rebekah looked ashamed as she replied, "I suppose I am trying to protect him as I would a baby. My son is grown and must make his own decisions. Also, it's not right that my brother should continue to be the victim of theft. How much do you need?"

Nahum returned disguised as a wool buyer. Just prior to shearing time, he asked to be escorted to see the different sheep pasturages and gauge the quality of their wool. At each stop, he discreetly inquired where each sale area would be and the approximate time when the wool would be processed for sale.

When the sale time came, Nahum inspected the perimeter of the grazing areas looking for wool piles in areas that had not been mentioned to him. Within two twelfth- days, he found a pile of wool in a secluded area hidden behind a suspicious mound of dirt. He recognized the seller as a son of Laban's chief administrator. After considerable haggling, he managed to buy four bundles at about half price. He paid for a bill of sale on papyrus, which he volunteered to fill out for the young man who seemed more interested in hawking his goods than recording sales. As Nahum desperately hoped, the young man took his payment, and Nahum walked away with a bill of sale specifying six bundles. The seller never even glanced at the papyrus.

Nahum went back to the roadside hostel where he stayed when he was not camping secretly with Jacob. That evening he started a conversation with some of the merchants at the hostel. He mentioned that he was to receive a wool shipment of six bundles on the morrow, but circumstance had just arisen that required him to head for Nineveh. He would sell the papyrus for three-fourths of the price that he had paid for the wool, which was described on the bill of sale as high grade. The second merchant that Nahum talked to paid him for the goods.

As Nahum expected, the next day, only four bundles were delivered to the merchant, who immediately complained. The young man looked at his records, which specified four bundles, and then at the bill of sale, which specified six.

Nahum had scrambled the writing of the amount so that it could appear to be forged when scrutinized carefully. The young seller asserted that forgery was involved, because his records clearly specified four bundles. Smug in his resolve, he quickly departed before the merchant could complain further.

*   *   *   *   *

Nahum had written the location of sale and the location of the seller on the papyrus in very small script. The merchant proceeded to Laban's home after finishing his morning meal. This necessary and anticipated action fit the plan perfectly. Only Laban and a household servant were at home to greet the merchant, who was promptly escorted to an audience with Laban.

"Master Laban, I have been the victim of a fraud by your sellers. I purchased a bill of sale from another buyer. This bill specified six bundles, but the deliveryman insisted that only four bundles had been sold. I am demanding that this valid contract be fulfilled by delivery of two more bundles from this sale area."

Laban looked at the papyrus and agreed that it appeared valid. After noting the specification of six bundles, he agreed to fulfill the sale and took the merchant to the sale area where the specified quality of wool was being sold. Upon arrival at the site, Laban talked with the lead seller, who looked at the writing and realized that it didn't match his or his assistant's handwriting.

"Master Laban, we did *not* make this sale. This script is not our handwriting."

Laban started to scold and berate his seller, who studied the papyrus while taking the tongue-lashing. As his worry and consternation continued to grow, his mind raced to find a way to prove that he wasn't responsible for this fraud. Just as Laban ordered him back to his residence to await discipline that could be a termination of employment, he noticed the location specified on the bill.

"Master, look—the location specified isn't here, but some distance to the northwest. I ask that we travel there to see if unauthorized sales of stolen merchandise are occurring. I didn't receive the amount of wool that one of the shearers told me to expect."

When Laban started to insist that the seller was stalling for some reason, the merchant spoke. "He is right. The original owner of the bill stated that the sale area specified was where he purchased the wool. He also stated that you were the person to see if any problem arose. I must insist that we do as your seller here suggests."

Laban scowled and called for a mount. Soon all three were headed to the specified spot. When they arrived at the area, nothing but landscape appeared until the merchant heard a camel complaining about its load or something. When they looked over the mound of dirt, only a small amount of inventory remained, but the son of the chief administrator was in the act of selling the last of his stolen wool.

The young man started to flee but halted when a command for a bowshot was threatened by Laban. He readily revealed who the other culprits in the theft of goods were and where the other illegal sale site was. Before sunset the other site was discovered and the seller, a vagabond cousin of the chief administrator, caught. The only other people involved in the thefts were two shearers. A search was made to find the original owner of the bill of sale for a witness, but he was gone, supposedly to Nineveh.

*   *   *   *   *

A few weeks later, Laban met Jacob at the roadside hostel. When Jacob acknowledged that he had heard of the incidents with the thefts, Laban smiled and asked if the original owner of the papyrus were he. Jacob affirmed that he wasn't the wool buyer who disappeared immediately after transfer of the sale. He conceded that he may have seen the buyer, but he suspected that the man had long departed for somewhere else.

Laban continued to express doubt on his face as he looked at Jacob. He reluctantly conceded that Jacob wouldn't admit to any part of the events that had led up to the catching of the thieves among his workers, although he sensed that Jacob had knowledge of the scheme to trap them. The events were so clever that only someone with Jacob's talents could have arranged them. There were no other persons around likely to lay such careful plans. Also Laban could now see that Jacob's talents included many other areas than that of a shepherd. Jacob was, however, too valuable to remove from overseeing his flocks, except at shearing and harvesting seasons. He wanted to arrange duties during those times so that Jacob would be a roving inspector to ensure everything was proper and that no thievery was happening.

*   *   *   *   *

Jacob heartily accepted the assignment of protector of goods. He desperately wanted to recommend Nahum as the new chief administrator, but he knew that was too risky, even though the culprits had all been sent to lands far to the east.

Jacob spent the succeeding moons evaluating the flocks with the help of the shepherds and other workers. He gradually came to the conclusion that carelessness wasn't the only reason that the theft of wool and animals had occurred. Almost no coordination happened between the shepherds and shearers or between the shearers and sellers. Unexpected shortages from predictions were never investigated but considered to be just mistaken predictions. None were curious why the predictions were always higher than the actual goods that came to market.

Jacob started working on an inventory system that required each type of worker to coordinate with the next level. Jacob himself would keep count of his flocks and their condition at all times. When harvest or shearing time approached, he would meet with the production men and sellers to arrive at an expected amount for each commodity going to market.

The servant visiting Jacob for the next annual report on his life in Haran brought some exchange metals and raiment. He began his conversation by telling Jacob that his mother was upset about him being a poor man among plenty; therefore, she had sent some help. He thought Nahum reported that his clothing was beginning to become well-worn. She even asserted that he was undoubtedly the poorest man on earth who was generating so much wealth.

"Abner, it's true that I have little wealth now, but my wages should be excellent when I complete my indenture."

The next topic concerned how the scheme to catch the thieves had turned out. Jacob had sent word with a broker who regularly traveled between Nineveh and Egypt that he was well, but they had no details on how the plan had worked out.

After hearing a pleasant and sometimes jocular explanation from Jacob, Abner laughed heartily and told Jacob that Nahum would really enjoy this news. Nahum had almost been depressed for a while because he had to leave before the outcome of the plan was determined. They would surely have a family celebration over this when he returned. Abner told Jacob that he would have to depart soon thereafter, because he had been instructed by Rebekah to find out everything quickly and get back with the news.

"That's okay with me. As much as I enjoy visitors from home, I am always busy now that I have taken on more duties. I basically oversee all of Laban's business from the field to market, although my title is still that of a lead shepherd. To my liking, he hasn't appointed a chief administrator yet, and I have urged him not to. With my new system where each type of worker cooperates with the levels above and below them in the production of goods, Laban doesn't need anyone administering the business but him. I think the incident with his thieving administrator thoroughly convinced him that he needs to look after his business more closely."

LIKE GRANDFATHER, LIKE GRANDSON

AVING GAINED CONTROL OF Laban's business from the field to the market, Jacob could manage the animals, not just tend to them. His competence also inspired his fellow workers to care more diligently for the flocks. With years still to go on his indenture, Jacob knew that he mustn't revert back to a boring lifestyle as before the thieving incident. Therefore, he decided to keep careful records on the appearance of the offspring of the sires and mothers and the characteristics of those newborns as they matured. His intuitive skills had always worked well in managing a flock, but precise data would help him to enhance the flocks even more. Even though he fully expected to produce healthy flocks in abundance by the end of his seven years of service, he still needed to be skilled in animal husbandry by the end of those seven years. In no way could he expect Laban to give him an ample flock with which to support his wife Rachel. Gaining more knowledge of flock management was absolutely imperative. His father, Isaac, could help if necessary, but Jacob's pride smarted at the idea of asking his father for an advance on his inheritance. He wanted to prosper on his own for those many hoped-for remaining years of his father's life.

Laban gave a party at each anniversary date of his indenture. Pompously, Laban began each year's celebration by explaining that Jacob was so special that he deserved a yearly memorial for his service. Each year Jacob thought, *Would that he reward me properly for service when I marry Rachel.* As with previous parties, Laban continued with a long-winded discourse to various clusters of party members on how well he was prospering. At the sixth-year anniversary, Jacob made several attempts to talk to his uncle about his approaching departure and his marriage to Rachel.

"Uncle, the past six years have been enjoyable. The frustrations and problems of the early years are a distant and vague memory. As this year progresses, I wish to select a modest flock to accompany Rachel and me on our trip back to my home after our marriage. I have learned much about the management of flocks during my stay here. Indeed, I have learned more about how to increase the size of and ensure the health of flocks than I did in all the years I tended my father's flocks. We shouldn't need a significant number of animals for our survival until I receive my inheritance from my father."

A concerned look crossed Laban's face as he told Jacob that he would be happy to talk to him about his departure and wedding when the time neared. Meanwhile, they had a party to enjoy and another year of work to do. He jokingly closed this latest conversation with the statement that he certainly didn't want to think about Jacob's leaving before he had to.

Over the following year, Laban invented excuse after excuse to avoid talking about Rachel's marriage. A few weeks before his seven-year indenture was to end, Jacob asserted his intention to segregate enough animals to support them after their marriage. He planned to move back to Beersheba shortly after the marriage to Rachel. Laban insisted that Jacob postpone the separation process until after the marriage and after he had finished some business matters. When Jacob expressed disappointment at the delay, Laban tried to console him by stressing that it would only be a few weeks of extra time before he could return home. Laban also mentioned that he would have a wife to console him during those extra weeks.

"Uncle, I suppose I am getting too hasty to leave. Rachel may need some time to get accustomed to marriage before leaving home. Of course, if she is anything like her Aunt Rebekah, she will be ready to leave immediately, but a few more weeks shouldn't bother her if she is."

Jacob felt elated that the time of his marriage to Rachel had finally arrived. His happiness to have her as a wife made the extra weeks working for his uncle of no importance.

But Laban had left the conversation with a different resolve in mind.

*   *   *   *   *

Laban had no intention of letting Jacob leave. Nevertheless, he had not been able to think of a good plan to keep him from leaving. Nearly seven years prior, when the contract had been made, he had thought that seven years would be enough to make him wealthy. Over the years, that wealth did increase, but Laban's desire for more wealth also increased proportionally—even exceeding the amount of new possessions. The very idea of Jacob taking his wages with him started to make Laban sick the more he thought about it.

The next morning, Laban left on a "business" trip to Haran. Upon his arrival at the town's center, some old friends greeted him effusively. After explaining why he had been absent from the gossip sessions for so long and catching up on past doings, he broached a problem for which he needed advice. After apologizing for only visiting them when he had a problem to solve, he asserted that he felt no shame in bringing his latest problem to their attention. Most of the group turned their heads to listen to him.

Laban started by mentioning that his seven-year contract with his nephew was expiring. His obligation for settlement included the payment of considerable wages and the giving of his younger daughter in marriage. Because he felt unable to comply with the contract, there had to be some way to void that contract.

Various suggestions followed—but none that would show Laban to be an honest man. While the younger men spoke readily and vainly, an elderly man sat among them, appearing to be asleep. When the chatter started to die down, he asked Laban again if his younger daughter, Rachel, was the betrothed. When Laban nodded, he smiled and cited the custom of many lands around them that no eligible daughter could marry before her older sister or sisters. This custom helped to ensure that the older daughters didn't reach old age without the support of a husband and children.

Laban acknowledged that he was aware of the tradition, but his family didn't always follow tradition. He had secretly hoped to substitute Leah for Rachel, but he was certain that Jacob would reject her in place of Rachel. Also, how did this suggestion help him avoid paying wages to his nephew?

The elderly man taunted Laban for not guessing the solution to his problem. He would have to trick Jacob into consummating marriage with Leah. Once that was accomplished and Jacob discovered that she wasn't Rachel, the man instructed, Laban should propose giving her to Jacob for further service. If he loved Rachel as much as Laban said, he would readily accept a contract for further service.

Laban's countenance brightened as he thought about how to accomplish this chicanery. Because he had forbidden Rachel to associate with Jacob for years, Jacob hadn't seen the face of or touched either Leah or Rachel for several years. He would have Leah disguise herself in some way to make Jacob think she was Rachel.

When Laban apologized for still lacking in understanding of how he would execute this stunt, the elderly man politely told him to give a party before the wedding night. It should be an easy task to convince Jacob to imbibe much wine before access to his bride's room. In the meantime, he must coach Leah in how to act as Rachel. Lastly, he must send Rachel away to some distant relative before that night.

Laban left for home with an elated feeling strangely tinged with uneasiness. This scheme had some potential for failure. He had to persuade Leah to betray her younger sister and hopefully take most of the blame for deceiving Jacob. Leah had always been an obedient child, unlike Rachel, who could act defiantly at times; therefore, he should have no problem convincing Leah to take Rachel's place in the bride's room. His first act in the scheme would be to send Rachel away to a sick cousin's home. He would promise to relieve her duties there before the wedding. He would then tell Jacob that Rachel was too modest to have the marriage consummated during the day. She wanted the marriage to occur at night, during the dark of the moon.

*   *   *   *   *

Jacob worked until the meridian on his wedding day performing some administrative chores, as he had the past few days. It had been years since he had gone so long without the scent of animals on his person. This was to be the most joyous day of his life, and nothing must spoil it. He arrived at the wedding party dressed in a new tunic that his mother had sent to him the past year with orders not to wear it until his wedding day. Both his parents had seen sketches of Rachel taken back to them by the servant who visited yearly. If they objected in any way, they were to send a message of denial for his marriage. No message had been received, so within a short while, Jacob's long servitude would be over.

Over the years, respect for Jacob had grown among Laban's workers. He had persuaded Laban to get rid of not only those thieves but some slackers also. The new workers quickly became his friends. He felt a twinge of regret over the prospect of leaving so many friends—a regret that would have never occurred earlier. As he entered the courtyard, one of his friends greeted him and told him that he looked like royalty, not a rough shepherd. His friend also expressed regret over his leaving them soon, because he had enjoyed working with Jacob for past several years. His departure had been the main gossip for the past few days.

Before Jacob finished talking to this first greeter, Laban handed him a bowl of wine with the admonition to drink up. This was the night that he had been anticipating for all these years, Laban pointed out. Jacob would later reflect that Laban's voice reflected not a hint of guilt for the fraud that he was about to accomplish.

When Jacob tried to stop drinking while insisting that he didn't want to get drunk on his wedding night, his friends told him that the wine had been diluted. Unbeknownst to all of his friends, Laban had instructed the wine servant to put in only half of the sweet cider that was normally used to make seasoned wine. Jacob had never used wine to excess. Accordingly, he used the advice of others on how much he could drink and remain sober. Fortunately, Jacob's tolerance for alcohol was high, because the miscalculation of his friends based on the mistaken strength of the wine only made him happy, not drunk.

After greeting all of his friends and receiving their congratulations, Jacob excused himself and headed for the bride's room. They consummated the marriage without Leah having to speak a word.

When Jacob awoke the next morning, he reached for his wife and asked for her to turn and face him for a kiss. He was so startled to see Leah that he jumped out of bed unclothed. While reaching for his clothes, he exclaimed, "Where is Rachel? Why are you in her bed?"

"Jacob, I must inform you that I, Leah, am now your wife. My father said that it wasn't right for my younger sister to marry before I did. He insisted that I take Rachel's place in the marriage bed. Rachel was sent away to care for a cousin during her illness."

Jacob finished dressing and left the room without saying another word. A servant gave him the directions to where Laban was.

*   *   *   *   *

Before Jacob could utter a word, Laban called out and scorned Jacob for not knowing that he couldn't let Rachel marry before Leah. Leah was now his wife. He almost continued to speak about giving Rachel to him for further servitude, but he decided to hear what Jacob would offer first. Perhaps he could get Jacob to volunteer his services first, thereby assuaging his conscience about selling another child.

Jacob walked up to Laban and shouted in his face, "I worked seven years for Rachel, not Leah. You have committed a fraud against me. I demand that you fulfill your contract by giving Rachel to me as a wife."

Laban just smirked and boldly implied that Jacob should be good at detecting fraud. He reminded Jacob that he had heard of a few instances when Jacob used fraud to further his desires.

Jacob tried to ignore the attempt to deflate his contention, but his firm resolve couldn't get Laban to give Rachel to him. After nearly a twelfth-day of arguing, Jacob said sheepishly, "I would be willing to serve another seven years for her. I deem my life without her to be poor indeed!"

Laban smiled and placed his hands on Jacob's shoulders and pleaded with him not to worry. He knew that Rachel would understand that it was necessary for her sister to marry first. Rachel loved him dearly; therefore, Laban would give Rachel to him for the additional years of service. If Jacob would celebrate Leah's marriage for a week, he would arrange the marriage to Rachel.

* * * * *

Jacob's change to a pleasant disposition started gossip about how he had fully accepted Leah as his wife. His happy mood, however, was inspired by the prospect of his marriage to Rachel. Jacob realized that his half-inebriated state on the night of his marriage to Leah may have caused him not to detect Leah as his marriage partner instead of Rachel and to recall very little about the consummation of the marriage.

Therefore, when the marriage date to Rachel arrived, Jacob drank only a few sips of wine. He must ensure that he both recognized Rachel and remembered the joy of their first night as husband and wife. Consequently, he scarcely bothered with any conversation but soon headed for Rachel's room.

He found Rachel standing by a lamp without a veil over her face. "Look, Jacob, it is Rachel. I wanted you to be sure who you were marrying this time. I can't blame my father for what he did, although I believe it wrong. I wished for you to have just one wife; but if I have to share, I am glad it's my sister."

"Rachel, I am so sorry that I let myself be tricked into marriage with Leah. You are my only true love. I will try to fulfill my conjugal duties to Leah, but I don't love her." Jacob ended his declaration with a kiss.

"Jacob, you mustn't say that. You must love the both of us equally. I know that my father will be very displeased if you favor me."

"Rachel, let's not talk about others. This is our night. The anticipation of this night has made the past seven years pass as no time at all in awaiting your love."

The turmoil and jealousy of divided love between multiple wives had skipped a generation from Abraham to Jacob. This time, the jealousy began to show by the end of Rachel's week. Leah started to pout and become disagreeable with everyone around her.

* * * * *

Laban had had some deep-seated qualms about tricking Jacob into marrying

Leah; therefore, he started watching how the marriages were doing from the morning after the consummation of Rachel's marriage. After a few days, he asked Leah whether there was something disturbing her.

He really didn't need to ask the question, but he waited for her reply.

"No, Father. I am just not feeling well."

Her father mildly rebuked her for trying to hide the obvious and asked her whether he should tell Jacob to show her more love. Leah apprehensively replied, "No, please don't. I could never hide my feelings from you. The trouble is my desire for more attention from my and my sister's husband. Let's not talk to Jacob yet. Perhaps his fascination with Rachel will wane soon, and he will return to me."

Rachel overheard this conversation and reluctantly convinced herself that she should remind Jacob that her sister was also his wife. Nevertheless, she waited until Leah, who had become more pleasant after her talk with her father, started to pout again.

Jacob heeded Rachel's request, but within days found out that Leah was pregnant with her first child from the first week of marriage with him. He immediately used the excuse of pregnancy to avoid intimacy with Leah, which intensified her jealousy toward Rachel even more. Meanwhile, Rachel continued to enjoy the affections of Jacob.

As the time for the deliverance of Leah's child neared, Jacob became more interested in her. At the time of birth, a servant flashed a message by a large obsidian mirror to Jacob, who had spent the last few days working nearby, announcing the birth of a baby boy. Jacob rushed to the birthing room, arriving before the baby had been presented to Leah.

Giving her no time to admire her child, he asked, "Have you decided on a name for him?"

"Jacob, your presence makes me change my mind. I will call him Reuben—behold a child. I think that the name is fitting, considering this scene and the fact that he is our first child." Her emphasis on the word "first" gave Jacob a twinge of shame, but he let the comment pass without reacting.

"Then, Reuben it is! Leah, he is a beautiful baby, and I am proud to be his father. Our yearly messenger should be arriving soon. I will have an artist draw you with the baby. I know my parents will be happy to hear and see the news of his birth."

Within a year, Leah was pregnant again. The beaming, almost smirking, expression on Leah's face changed Rachel's disposition to belligerence, rather than the petulance Leah exhibited when she got jealous. Rachel's actions caused so many complaints that Laban called Jacob in from the field to deal with the problem. Jacob had already had his fill of conflict between the two women and had begun to spend much of his time away from home. Even his love for Rachel couldn't compensate for the bickering.

"Uncle, what can I do to make them quit fighting? I have married two headstrong women. My contemplative life as a boy hasn't stood me well in married life. My brother considered me to be a sissy, and even my father accused me of being suckled by my mother beyond my years. I could use some advice from you."

Laban offered no suggestions, just telling him that he had to learn to deal with the problem sooner or later. Advice by others for squabbles like this often served only to cause the advisor grief and make the situation worse. Jacob had excellent instincts with animals. Hopefully, those instincts would help him solve the trouble with his daughters.

Laban appeared ready to continue his speech but stopped, causing Jacob to wonder, "Do you have anything further that you wish to say?" A shaking of the head by Laban to the question sent Jacob away perplexed. He knew from Laban's expression that his wives' father had had something to say that he thought would upset Jacob. *I suspect that he still thinks that I show too much attention to Rachel, and I have caused her to expect most of my passion.*

When Jacob confronted Rachel about her attitude, she ignored him at first. As he persisted, she almost shouted, "Why haven't you given me any children? My sister is already pregnant with her second child. She boasts that she can have a baby whenever she wants, and that I may have your affections, but she will have your children."

Jacob scolded, "Rachel, what have I not done that could be done? Am I God to intercede in making your womb fertile? I have bestowed much more affection and have done more than my part in trying to provide you with children. Let's plead to God on your behalf for a blessing of a child. I know not what else to do."

The talk with Rachel calmed her disputes with family and servants, but it didn't stop her resentment toward her sister. Her thoughts and scheming against Leah caused another minor problem—absentmindedness—while performing her duties. Then, within a few weeks, Rachel's attentiveness became sharp and her disposition pleasant. This change occurred about the same time that some noticed Jacob attending Rachel's maidservant Bilhah on several occasions. The gossip became so rampant that Laban once again got involved by asking Jacob about her.

Jacob responded with a hint of irritation, "Rachel has gone through anger, pleading, despondency, and other feelings toward me, herself, and others for my failure to provide her with a child. She has just recently insisted that I take Bilhah as a concubine to have a child for her in her stead.

"My remembrance of the trouble that my grandfather had after being persuaded to engender a child for his wife through a concubine made me reluctant to imitate him. Rachel continued to insist, however, to the point of threatening to become celibate if I didn't take Bilhah."

Laban had only heard of Abraham's problem with Hagar and Sarah; therefore, he considered Jacob's reservation about Bilhah as a substitute mother for Rachel as being too doubtful of a good outcome. He urged Jacob not to be concerned, because he was sure that Rachel would be kind to Bilhah's children. Rachel had told him that her pleading with God hadn't given her a child. She felt that God had made her infertile for some reason, and she just couldn't wait for children. She had to stop her sister's boasting now.

*　　*　　*　　*　　*

Within a moon thereafter, Bilhah was pregnant. The announcement from Bilhah filled Rachel with joy. She ran to her sister to proclaim that she would be blessed by heirs through Bilhah. Leah refrained from mocking her about the child being someone else's and not hers. Her restraint came partially from a command from her father not to torment her sister any further. Leah, who was nearing full term, also had other concerns than her sister's argument.

Within a few weeks, Simeon was born. Leah had believed from the moment that she realized she was pregnant again that God had heard her pleas. Her optimism had actually grown from the beginning of Bilhah's pregnancy. This confidence in God's will had helped her to refrain from criticizing Rachel's bragging as much as the command from her father to be quiet.

Jacob again hurried to Leah's room when given the news of the birth. When told the baby's name, he asked, "Why Simeon?" He had heard gossip about several other names but not this one.

"My dear husband, I didn't stop the gossip about the other names because I wanted my confidence in God's blessing of a second child not to be disparaged by those who think that I receive less than my due affection from you. Regardless of what anyone thinks, I have been blessed, despite the deception that my father and I did to you."

Jacob's recent hassles with Rachel had momentarily dulled his affections for Rachel. He gave Leah a genuine kiss and smiled. "Leah, I am sorry for the way I have treated you in the past. I will give you proper attention in the future. But you know that I must still honor Rachel also."

"Jacob, I will be most happy to share you with my sister and her concubine. I only ask for an equal time as Rachel."

Jacob nodded in tacit agreement to her request. "You have another beautiful baby. Is there anything that I need to do for you?" When Leah shook her head no, he kissed her again and told her that he would leave so that she could get some rest.

* * * * *

The birth of Bilhah's first son made Rachel happier than Jacob had ever seen her. When Jacob arrived to see the baby, Rachel was holding the child as if it were her own. "Bilhah and I have decided to call him Dan," Rachel greeted Jacob as he entered the room. "Husband, I know that you are always curious about the names of your children. We called him Dan because he became so noisy immediately after his birth. It almost seemed as if he were trying to order us around. Therefore, we felt that the name would correctly identify a judgmental child. I also feel that God has judged me worthy of an heir through my loyal maidservant."

Jacob had of late shown enough affection to both Rachel and Leah to keep their jealousy subdued. Even the announcement by Leah that she was pregnant with her third child caused little noticeable complaining by Rachel. A few days after the announcement, Jacob's curiosity forced him to try to find out Rachel's true feeling about this latest matter. He had begun to think that the open and friendly girl he once had known had become secretive about her feelings. He carefully broached the subject of Leah's pregnancy, and Rachel immediately expressed her happiness for her sister—to his delight. She continued by expressing her own delight in having Bilhah produce heirs for her, and she also stated that she believed that God would yet produce heirs through her. Jacob went back to work with an inward sigh over the prospect of providing conjugal duties to three women.

* * * * *

Before Leah's next child was born, Bilhah was pregnant again. These pregnancies gave Leah an excuse to demand the main part of Jacob's affection. Jacob's valiant effort to temper Rachel's desires inspired Leah to name her third child Levi. She schemed, *I now have given Jacob three children. My sister has given him none of her own. I should be able to persuade him to accept me as his primary wife. Therefore, my baby's name will give him hint for us to join.*

Rachel and Leah had received enough scolding from both Jacob and their father that they changed from overtly demanding affection to either boasting of their own attractiveness or describing themselves as needy of some attention. Hence, when Leah's purification days were over, she used every opportunity afforded to her to have her children greet or play with their father. She usually took these occasions to mention that she was helping to fulfill the promise made to Abraham of a multitude of descendants. She would also promise him many more children.

*   *   *   *   *

Rachel named Bilhah's second child Naphtali. Because the contest between her and Leah had transitioned to posturing, not sniping, she decided that the child's name would be descriptive of the struggle she had met during her married life.

Leah fulfilled her promise and presented Jacob with a fourth child. When the midwife attending the birth of Leah's fourth child asked her about the boy's name, she replied, "Deborah, I haven't decided yet. Is my husband on his way here yet?"

When the midwife told her that she hadn't heard of his whereabouts, Leah became silent to the extent of ignoring any more questions from the midwife. While awaiting any response from Leah, the midwife cleaned and dressed the baby. Before she had completed these tasks, Leah's face brightened to a smile.

"I will call him Judah. He is surely to be praised, for I now have four sons. I have fulfilled my obligation in giving my husband heirs. Although I am happy to provide Jacob with heirs, surely this is my last child until we have moved back to Beersheba. Oh, how I dread that move, and I certainly don't want it complicated by another pregnancy."

The midwife called to another servant to find Jacob and to bring him to see his latest son. The servant found him talking with Leah's father, Laban. Jacob asked him for permission to resume the conversation after he went to see his latest son.

Leah became upset when Jacob seemed to show muted interest in his newborn son. "Husband, how can you be so unfeeling toward our new son, Judah—a son who I feel will become a very special child?"

"My dear, I am quite happy to see my new son, but I have been involved in an important discussion with your father. We were discussing the matter of our departure to Beersheba. During that discussion, he made an interesting proposal that I am seriously considering. My decision could change our future drastically in a way that will please both you and Rachel."

"What did my father say?"

"He suggested that I become his lead business administrator. I would abandon my servant status and become his top employee. At first, I rejected it, because I fervently desire to see my father and mother once more. Then, when he suggested that I could be spared for a yearly visit to my parents during the post-shearing season, I became interested. I would have an interesting job managing your father's thriving business, and you and Rachel wouldn't have to leave the homeland that you love. I must talk to the two of you about this, because I am willing to accept this offer."

Both Leah and Rachel were pleased with the idea of remaining in their homeland until Jacob mentioned the wages offered to him by their father. Leah voiced a mild complaint, but not Rachel: "Jacob, you can't work for such a low amount of livestock and metals. You are worth three times what my father is offering you. You now have a large family to support, and we need more household servants." Rachel then made a long pause before looking at Leah and saying, "Some of your children need more attention to keep them out of trouble. We must have another child attendant." Leah seemed upset by the stare by Rachel, but said nothing, reluctantly accepting Rachel's implied criticism of her children.

After a lengthy discussion, Jacob left to meet Laban and demand an increase in wages. He asserted that he must have more earnings, or he would return to Beersheba. Laban haggled for three days before getting Jacob to accept a fifty percent increase rather than a doubling of his wages. Once again Jacob departed Laban's presence fully expecting his uncle to keep his word.

REUNION

LTHOUGH DISAPPOINTED WITH THE wage agreement reached by their husband, Rachel and Leah gleefully helped the rest of the family to move into new spacious quarters. Upon completion of the move, Rachel sardonically remarked, "I just hope we can afford this wonderful home."

Leah scolded her, "Quit your complaining! I am sure our father will give us generous raises in the future. Jacob now has an elevated status that demands compensation."

Rachel raised her eyebrows and pursed her lips in a smirk as she walked away.

The mostly delightful feeling surrounding the events before and after Jacob's termination of indenture soon led to further family turmoil, but not immediately. Jacob had become so involved in preparing to leave for Beersheba and then arranging business matters after accepting the job as administrator that he had spent little time attending to the personal needs of his family. Indenture termination, acceptance of Laban's employment, shearing season, and preparation to visit his parents followed in succession, demanding too much of his time to suit his family of wives, concubines, and children.

Leah was the first to complain. "Husband, must you leave to see your family at this time? Shearing season is over, with considerable time until the cool season. Can't you spend a few weeks with us before you go?"

"Leah, this is the best time for me to travel. I must get to my home and back now, because some critical matters will surely arise within a short time. The slack season after shearing doesn't last as long as you think. This is especially true this year because of the late shearing time and the extra time it took to complete the job because of our large flocks."

"All right, why can't you wait to see your parents next year? Maybe Reuben will be old enough to accompany you to see his grandparents next year."

"I have been separated from my parents for over fourteen years. I can't afford to wait any longer to see them. I know that my life has been hectic of late, but my work should become less demanding when I return from Beersheba. I have competent help that should allow for a quick resolution of any problems that arise while I am gone."

Leah continued to argue without persuasion. Jacob finally had an opportunity to see his parents after all these years. His family surely could spare his presence for a short visit with them.

On the day prior to departure, Rachel greeted Jacob while he was bundling some supplies. "Why haven't you assembled the supplies for me and my handmaiden? You seem to be ready to leave, and you haven't asked us what items we will be taking for the trip."

"What? Rachel, only a few close friends and I are making the trip. I am taking the most stalwart, because we intend to travel fast both going and coming. I can't be slowed by someone who is frail."

"We are not frail! My handmaiden and I can keep up with you if you will give us obedient camels."

Rachel smugly asserted that none of Jacob's objections to their traveling with the men were valid. When he realized that he had lost the argument, he offered his final excuse: Leah would be jealous if he didn't take both of them on the trip. Leah couldn't travel, because Judah was still suckling; therefore, it would be inconsiderate to take only one of his wives to see his parents.

Resolutely, Rachel replied, "Yes, Leah can't travel, but why deny introducing me to your parents because she is unable to travel? There is no justification for your argument. I am sure that you can convince even Leah that I should go with you."

Surprisingly, Leah offered no objection to Rachel's traveling to see their father-in-law and mother-in-law. He assuaged Leah's feelings by telling her that she could accompany him next year.

The assembling of Rachel's travel items postponed the trip for one more day. Within a twelfth-day of the group's departure, Jacob became so ebullient and chatty that his companions had troubling getting him to concentrate on the trail. After a few course corrections, Jacob agreed to calm down and to watch where he was going.

Rachel and her handmaid performed according to her promise by coaxing their camels to keep pace.

As Rachel and Jacob prepared for the final day's ride, Rachel chided her husband, "See, I told you all of your objections against my making this trip were wrong. We haven't been a burden at all, and my maidservant has surely provided you and your companions with better meals than you would have had otherwise." Jacob just smiled and nodded his consent.

As they approached the last turn in the road before Beersheba, Jacob signaled for a halt. "I stopped so I can gather an image of what my home should look like. My yearly contacts from home have kept me informed of changes through their drawings. I want to see how accurate their descriptions have been." After a short rest, Jacob led the way around the bend in the trail and uttered a low gasp.

"What a beautiful sight! It is just as the drawings showed it." As Jacob finished his utterance, he espied his favorite servant, who had stopped making the yearly trips. The servant noticed Jacob at about the same time and started to run toward him, but reversed his direction as he ran to get Rebekah, having realized that Jacob should greet his father or mother first.

Rebekah was so startled that the servant had to help her up from the kneeling position she had assumed while stirring the soil in a bed of plants. She and the servant appeared at the entrance of the courtyard as Jacob alighted from his camel.

Jacob and his mother stood looking at each other, not knowing what to say. The servant initiated their contact by taking Rebekah by the arm and leading her to her son. Still silent, they hugged and kissed.

Jacob's first words were, "I told you that I would see you again."

"Jacob, my dear son, how have I fretted over your plight. I am sorry that my brother has treated you so badly, but those days are over. When will you be able to bring your entire family home? I assume that beautiful young woman is Rachel, but where is Leah?"

"Yes, this is Rachel. Leah and my children are still in Haran, where we will be staying. Your brother has treated me better in the past years. I have accepted a position as caretaker of all his business affairs. I am no longer an indentured servant."

Rebekah became upset. "Does this mean that I won't see you again for many years, if ever?"

"Please, don't be so upset. I have an arrangement to visit you each year. Leah couldn't come this year, because she is still suckling your grandson, Judah. Hopefully, she will be able to see you next year. Also, as my children grow, I should be able to bring them to visit you."

Rebekah continued to demand to know how long he planned to stay in Haran, and whether he would ever return to Beersheba to live. Jacob gave her no assurance other than that he would visit yearly. Rebekah followed her questioning with an extended greeting to Rachel before she realized that Jacob still hadn't seen his father.

"Many pardons, but you haven't seen Isaac yet. I know when you departed that he was exceedingly disappointed in you—and me. He has, however, over the years accepted, even nearly forgotten, our actions then. I am sure that he will be glad to see you, and see you he can. His eyesight has improved somewhat from years ago. Nahum, please escort Isaac here."

The meeting of father and son had never been so cordial. Not a hint of animosity showed in either greeting. Jacob even spent more time talking to his father than he had with his mother. At the first pause in conversation, Rebekah told the servants to prepare the quarters for the guests and to start cooking a feast. She then invited everyone into the courtyard for a rest.

Jacob had planned to stay for only three days, but he remained for a whole week. Rachel also persuaded him to take a more leisurely pace back home. As they approached home, Laban surprised Jacob by leading the greeters. He quickly called Jacob aside before he could talk to anyone.

"Uncle, has some tragedy befallen the flocks?"

Laban shook his head before telling Jacob that he had a bigger problem: Leah had become more despondent than ever. She rarely ate. It was good that Judah could eat soft food, or he might have died from malnourishment. The main concern now was getting Leah to eat. Otherwise, the physicians feared for her life. Because the physicians believed that only Jacob's presence would cause her improvement, Laban pleaded for Jacob to stay with her until her spirits improved.

Jacob immediately experienced a feeling of compassion like none before. "Uncle, I am sorry that this has happened. My first thought had been to leave Rachel here, fearing a reaction from Leah. Regrettably, Rachel convinced me that there was no good reason to leave her at home just because Leah couldn't go. Also, Leah seemed to accept Rachel's leaving with us. Therefore, against my better judgment, I took her with me. I will do my best to correct the problem that I have caused, although I certainly didn't think that Leah's reaction would be this severe."

Laban thanked Jacob while asserting that this problem had priority over any problems in the fields or pastures, which his assistants could handle.

Leah began to eat so heartily that her handmaiden Zilpah had to take meal portions to her to keep from overeating. Within less than a moon, Leah's mood and eating habits returned to normal.

The following year brought only pleasantness to Jacob. Leah and Rachel stopped bickering, and Bilhah entered early menopause, relieving Jacob of some conjugal duties. The only conflict to arise was whether Reuben should make the trip to Beersheba after the next shearing season. Leah insisted that she could protect him. "Husband, Reuben is a strong young lad. We can change my riding gear to allow for his safe carriage. The land is peaceful enough that danger from attackers isn't a problem. I know that your parents are anxious to see their grandchildren."

"Leah, I am not worried about his transportation, but about his getting hurt or wandering off when we camp."

She convinced Jacob that Reuben would behave and even talked him into taking Simeon along also. As Leah predicted, the two boys behaved unusually well and were a delight to Isaac and Rebekah.

As the visit progressed, Jacob became perplexed. Rebekah had treated Rachel well on last year's visit, but she became considerably less formal with Leah and seemed to enjoy her company more than she did Rachel's. He thought of asking his mother about her behavior but decided it best to let the matter go unexplained. Before lapsing into sleep on the first night of their return trip, Leah mentioned her mother-in-law's attention: "Your mother treated me more cordially than Rachel said she was treated."

Jacob mused, "I noticed her actions, too. I suspect that she likes you more because you have borne grandchildren for her. Please don't mention this to Rachel. I don't want another fit from her. The two of you have been so civil of late that I have never enjoyed a period as peaceful in my life. My life has been one struggle after another ever since I can remember from my early childhood. Family peace at last is so wonderful."

"What about next year? I heard you tell your mother that you intended to bring both of us for a visit next year. If your mother acts the same way to us, Rachel will truly be upset."

"Leah, let's go to sleep and let next year take care of itself. Maybe my mother will be more circumspect in how she treats the both of you when you are together."

For the second year in a row, no pregnancies arose to concern Jacob, and over the succeeding years, Leah also became barren. Jacob continued to have peace as Leah's barrenness gave Rachel less cause to be jealous.

Jacob should have realized that those peaceful years couldn't continue forever. He didn't, but he probably should have guessed who would cause the next family turmoil.

Rebekah treated both Leah and Rachel with common respect, but her meddlesome attitude finally ignited the family's squabbling. Rebekah proved to be the best person to stop the fighting between Leah's and Bilhah's sons when they visited. Then one year, immediately after stopping some mean wrestling between the boys, she spoke within the hearing range of both Leah and Rachel without contemplating her words. "Jacob, are you going to have any more children? It's good that you have six already, but I want more grandchildren."

Jacob smiled and replied, "Whatever God wills, we will have. Maybe he feels that the six children I already have are all that I can care for."

Rebekah's request for more grandchildren failed to affect the attitude of the childless Rachel. Within six months of her return home, however, Leah became convinced that her barrenness was permanent and began to plead with Jacob to take her handmaiden Zilpah as a concubine. Jacob resolved not to get involved with another concubine, but Leah complained that he treated her differently than Rachel through constantly reminding him about Bilhah. After much disputation, Jacob got her to agree to wait until they could consult his parents the following year.

Both Isaac and Rebekah tacitly approved of Leah's request. During their return trip, Jacob sighed as he informed his two wives that he would take Zilpah as a concubine.

The long-suffering Rachel accepted the decision without comment until they neared Haran. "You can't take Zilpah as a concubine. Leah already has four children, and I may never have any more than the two by Bilhah."

"Rachel, it's most unfortunate that Bilhah can't have another child, but I can't refuse Leah. I am sure that Leah would condemn me to the whole community if I did. I took your handmaiden; she could make a convincing argument that I showed favoritism to you if I refused her handmaiden. Please continue to trust God that he will yet let you have children."

In quick succession, Zilpah became pregnant and presented Jacob with two sons named Gad and Asher.

*   *   *   *   *

Jacob had insisted that all of his shepherds keep the grazing areas clear of poisonous plants. The dangerous mandrake plant had been difficult to eradicate, because wandering bedouin tended to cultivate hidden plants. During the season of Zilpah's second pregnancy, Reuben had discovered some mandrakes among the harvested root crops. Realizing their potential value, he had defied his father's standing order to destroy the plants and tried to hide them for secret sale to dealers in town.

He had nearly covered them when Rachel happened upon his action. "Reuben, what do you have there?"

Reuben mumbled that he was just storing some weeds for mulching.

"I think not. Please remove the cover on those plants, so I can see them." When Reuben failed to obey, Rachel yanked the cover aside to reveal the mandrakes. Indignantly, Rachel exclaimed, "Weeds, you call them!"

By this time, Leah had heard the commotion and joined Reuben and

Rachel, along with some nearby servants. "Son, what are you and your aunt arguing about?"

Reuben embarrassed Leah by blurting out her plan for him to find some mandrakes in the harvested areas and bring them to her without letting Jacob see him. He had found more than his mother needed and was hiding them until he could sell the excess plants.

"Son, your father wouldn't want you to be trafficking in the sale of this dangerous plant. I, however, have a midwife who knows how to brew a safe potion for me, so I will take possession of them."

As Leah started to walk away, Rachel ran after her. "Sister, give me some of your plants. You have more than your midwife needs for a potion."

"No, I won't. You not only command most of my husband's affection, but you want to deny me of a chance to have more children also."

Rachel continued to plead, telling Leah that she soon would have six children while Rachel had only two through Bilhah. At length, Rachel persuaded Leah to give her some of the mandrakes. Rachel had to promise to let Jacob spend the night with Leah after she had drunk a potion from the mandrakes.

Within two days, Jacob returned from an extended inspection of the fields and flocks and headed for Rachel's residence. Before he could enter, Leah intercepted him. "Jacob, you must stay with me tonight. Rachel promised you to me tonight for a portion of the mandrakes that Reuben found in the fields."

Jacob winced as his anger arose over Reuben's defying his rule about destroying the mandrakes. He remained silent, however, as he realized why his wives had also defied his rule by using them. The midwives knew how to prepare safe potions from the roots, and he didn't want to enter into an argument about the supposed fertility benefits of mandrake tea. He mentally resolved to renew his efforts to eliminate the plants from the fields and to give Reuben a good scolding.

Within a moon, Leah realized she was pregnant again after several years of childlessness. She attributed her good fortune to the use of the mandrakes and would never the abandon the belief, although the remedy didn't work for Rachel.

Shortly after Issachar's birth, Leah became pregnant with Zebulun. After the birth of the latter child, the focus of both wives seemed to change from squabbling over Jacob's affections to concern over their husband's low wages. Jacob fought every year for the full payment of his wages, and nearly every year, Laban found some way to be deficient in enough assets to meet his bargain. Mindful of his eventual inheritance from Isaac and the perceived constant need to settle family quarrels, Jacob always failed to collect the growing debt owed to him.

On the day following Zebulun's birth, Jacob informed Leah that he had to see Laban for some wages-in-kind of wool. Although still weak from giving birth, she spoke loudly: "Don't let my father postpone payment, as he has done in the past. You now have ten sons, and we have a greater need for clothing than in the past. Should we have a cold winter, our family could suffer from lack of warm clothing."

Despite the dire warning, Jacob once again allowed Laban to renege on part of the promise. His uncle feigned shame over allowing the wool brokers to sell too much wool and promised to give Jacob extra wool next season. Only judicious use of the actual wool received and careful repairing of old clothing kept the family warm the following winter.

Jacob continued to listen to but fail to act on the demands of his wives for him to force their father to pay proper wages to the family. They tried to shame Jacob by showing him that their children were poor in the midst of plenty, but it took a miracle to spur Jacob to action and formulate a plan to exact the payment of the back debt to him.

In recent years, Rachel had occasionally failed to experience her regular monthly cycle. Her first proof of pregnancy came from repeated spells of vomiting in the morning. When the daily examination by the physicians confirmed her pregnancy, the whole community became so preoccupied with the news that Rachel had to beg for everyone to let her get some rest.

Meanwhile, Jacob resolved from the day of the announced pregnancy to acquire the wealth due him. Nevertheless, he realized that he could never expect Laban to honor any of his contracts. He must come up with a scheme that Laban couldn't thwart. Given Laban's record of successful deflection of wage demands, only the cleverest of plans would have any hope of succeeding.

Considering Rachel's sometimes frail health, Jacob didn't want to move until after the birth of her child. Therefore, he had enough time to hatch several schemes in his mind and to review the pitfalls of each. He must fool his uncle in some way that wouldn't involve outright fraud, for the rules of local tribal law would subject him to serious retribution.

As the days of Rachel's giving birth approached, Jacob became more apprehensive. He still didn't have a workable plan in mind, and the days when he could travel were near. During the time spent celebrating his new son Joseph's birth, a precise plan for collecting his wages suddenly came to Jacob's mind. Before telling his wives of the plan, he thought it best to get Laban's sworn approval, but first he must review his flocks once more.

Jacob longed to return home to be nearer his parents. His visits home had become infrequent in recent years because of his duties to work and family. This desire to leave had also been enhanced by both his wives becoming less reluctant to leave their father's home.

With high expectations, Jacob approached Laban. "Uncle, I have discussed our return to Canaan with Leah and Rachel. They are sad to leave home but believe that our large family demands I must seek my fortune as a herder. I have served you well for the fourteen years of indenture and the past twenty as your administrator. It's now time for me to return home."

Laban showed immediate distress over Jacob's decision to leave. He did compliment Jacob for the blessing of wealth that he had received; therefore, he hated to send Jacob away. Laban barely managed to form the words asking him what he deemed his stake for the years of servitude to be.

Jacob opened his mouth to complain about the unpaid wages of the past twenty years, but he instantly decided not to be confrontational. He had spent many years with the flocks and had noticed that certain traits were often passed on by the sires of sheep and goats. Instead of stating a precise number that might lead his scheming uncle to reduce the agreed-upon compensation, Jacob would propose a plan that would likely provide him even more animals and allow him to get even with his greedy uncle. Thus he would receive just payment for his years of service, and he would get Laban to agree to a division that would seem highly advantageous to his uncle but would prove otherwise.

Jacob's request for a week to write his request for wages clearly pleased Laban. He told Jacob to take as much time as he wished in making his decision, likely hoping for more time to hatch a scheme to thwart Jacob.

Jacob spent most of the next week revisiting his herds and inspecting the sires and mothers and their offspring carefully. He noticed that certain plain white sheep and goats tended to produce speckled or mottled young. He would propose a plan where he would take all of the current speckled animals, which were a small part of the flock—the speckled animals were never retained for wool or breeding. He would then agree to accept only the speckled or streaked offspring from the plain white animals; Laban would get all of the plain offspring. He was sure that Laban would readily accept the deal, because he would assume that the solid white animals would produce few speckled cattle, goats, or sheep. Laban would fail to notice that some of the solid white animals had faint coloring in places not usually visible when looking straight at them. These animals had a propensity to produce offspring that showed visible streaks in their hair or wool.

Within the week, Jacob presented his proposal to Laban, who asked him if he were certain this was the way that he wanted to procure his starter herd. Jacob assured him that he didn't desire any agreement that his uncle would find unwarranted. He would let the chances of nature determine how much his wages would be. Laban's expression became skeptical as they bargained, and he asked for another week to consult his friends.

*   *   *   *   *

The next day, Laban headed for the bazaar area of Haran, where he found some animal buyers, to whom he told Jacob's wage proposal. Most of the older buyers seemed perplexed, except for one who advised in a firm voice for Laban to accept the deal immediately before his nephew changed his mind. He believed that Jacob felt that his work wasn't worthy of a great reward. Laban should still have most of his flock after giving Jacob the few mottled animals that would be produced.

One of the younger buyers shook his head in disagreement. He had heard of this Jacob and had friends who knew him rather well. He was *not* a person devoid of a desire for wealth. Although the deal appeared to hurt him, a plot of some sort must be afoot. Otherwise, why hadn't Jacob set a certain high figure and bargain down to an acceptable level? If Laban took this deal, the man said, he might live to regret it. The man was rather sure that Jacob expected to profit.

A couple more buyers tended to agree, but the rest thought that Jacob was gambling for a big return he was unlikely to receive. The odds were heavily in favor of Laban. He had a choice of paying a set number of animals to Jacob and losing a goodly portion of his flock, or accepting the proposal with a nearly certain chance of retaining most of his animals.

Laban thanked the buyers for the good advice as he left. He had grown wealthy because of Jacob and feared that his increases in riches would lessen with Jacob's departure. The chances of retaining that wealth was worth the risk of any scheme his nephew had planned. Also, if things went as they should, he might be able to persuade Jacob to stay for more compensation. When they saw the meager flock that Jacob would have, Laban knew, his daughters wouldn't leave their surroundings for a poor sojourn in the dire land of Canaan.

Laban returned home with high spirits. He wanted to call Jacob immediately and accept the deal. As he started out to contact Jacob, however, he realized that acceptance of the agreement so soon might cause Jacob to reconsider the proposal. A hasty acceptance was more likely to cause Jacob to decline his proposal. Hence, at the end of the week, Laban met Jacob with the agreement detailed on two pieces of papyrus. One of these witnessed copies was given to Jacob, after which both parties departed with a kiss.

*   *   *   *   *

When Jacob told his wives that they wouldn't be leaving their home for a few years, both seemed relieved. Conversely, Jacob couldn't relax. He had a lot of work to do if his plan were to pay out. He had to keep the flocks segregated enough to permit conditions whereby the sires capable of producing mottled offspring were more likely to breed. When the healthier females came to drink water, he would lay down lines of saplings stripped of their bark. The animals would refuse to cross over the saplings, giving the sires capable of producing mottled offspring a chance to sire. When the weaker females drank, he would remove the saplings to allow the sires likely to produce plain animals to breed.

The first year produced few additional mottled animals, somewhat to Jacob's consternation. Nonetheless, he wasn't discouraged; he was confident of his plan, and he trusted God to correct any unlikely mistakes made in judgment.

Shortly after the first anniversary of Jacob's contract, Leah became pregnant with her last child before menopause. The birth of his first daughter pleasantly surprised the entire community, prompting a lengthy celebration that gave Jacob a break from the overseeing of the flocks that took nearly all of his waking hours.

About two years into Jacob's contract, Laban and one of his sons rode into Jacob's field camp. Laban began with an alleged complaint from his daughters that Jacob was devoting so much of his time in helping him gain wealth that he was neglecting them.

The absurdity of the statement caused a set of emotions to race rapidly through Jacob's mind, with the final one being comic disbelief, which he suppressed into a faint smile. He knew that his wives no longer confided in their father because of his often ridiculous meddling. Jacob offered only a greeting signifying his regard for the question as rhetorical. Laban's next questions revealed what he was after. The use of the stripped saplings was his main concern.

Jacob had known from the beginning of his plan that sooner or later he would have to answer about the saplings. He replied without any hint of deceit, "I use the saplings to control access of the animals to the watering troughs. The saplings help to ensure that the weaker animals get the water they need to grow and improve in health."

The statement, while true, gave no information about Jacob's real motive for their use. Continuing his air of confidence in his actions, Jacob invited

Laban to review the flocks. He took care to show Laban how the plain white animals were more numerous than the mottled ones. Cleverly, he also stressed that a few strong animals were being born that weren't plain, and that he would have a good breeding flock with which to depart for Canaan, while avoiding any indication of the size of the flock.

Laban and his son rode away with congratulations for Jacob's good shepherding.

*   *   *   *   *

When they were out of sight, Laban and his son waved their arms in glee. Laban started to boast about how they had outsmarted Jacob once again. The few mottled animals that Jacob had couldn't possibly produce any considerable amount of animals for his wages. Laban now must find a way to encourage his daughters to refuse to leave with the rather meager holdings that Jacob would have by the time that he would want to leave, which could only be a few years away.

Laban's son suggested that he act on his father's behalf in trying to persuade his sisters to stay, because his daughters had lost their esteem for Laban in the years subsequent to their marriage. He, however, had always been able to influence Leah whenever he wanted to. Rachel was unruly, but if he could persuade Leah to stay, Jacob wouldn't leave without her and her children despite his only true love, Rachel.

*   *   *   *   *

Laban was so confident of his bounty that he stopped his close observation of the increasing mottled and speckled flock that Jacob continued to breed. The early slow production of animals for Jacob's flock rapidly changed to a large percentage for him in the succeeding few years. Jacob hid his animals by keeping the plain animals toward the outside and mixing the slightly mottled ones with the highly mottled ones.

This deception worked far longer than Jacob could have expected, until another son of Laban finally noticed the state of the flock; there was no hiding the results to a discerning eye that had not been fooled by an earlier assumption. The son was so aghast that he almost fell off his horse before asking Jacob what he had done with his father's flock. He accused Jacob of selling most of the flock and demanded the money Jacob had received for the sale. If Jacob didn't hand over the proceeds immediately, he would be punished for theft.

Jacob, emboldened by his good fortune and his firm conviction that this was now the time to leave for his parents' home, laughed at the accusations. "I have stolen nothing. God has blessed me with many spotted animals since your father last inspected the flocks. The overall size of the flocks that you see here is proof that I haven't stolen any animals. Your father entered into an agreement that he thought would deprive me of a just wage, but God has blessed me abundantly. Your father let his greed cloud his mind to the dangers of his contract. He took a chance, although he probably thought that there was none, so now he must pay the price of his agreement."

The son mocked Jacob for accusing his father of greed when Jacob was also guilty of the same. Jacob had acquired much wealth at his father's expense; there must be some other more equitable division of these animals, the son suggested.

"You say that I am greedy. The circumstances, however, speak differently. My flock is indeed large, but I have served and prospered your father for lo these many years. I have endured cold, wet, and even danger from wild animals. My increase is not only a blessing from God but also a just payment for my labor."

As he left, the son angrily declared that his father would refuse to honor Jacob's contract from the moment that he heard about this situation.

Jacob's first thought was to gather up his wives, children, and flocks and to flee immediately. He resisted the thought nevertheless, because he doubted his wives would leave until he had talked to their father. Knowing Laban's character, Jacob started to segregate his animals immediately. It was virtually certain that Laban wouldn't keep his agreement; hence, Jacob must be ready to go once he had made the supposedly obligatory talk with Laban.

Laban rode hastily into Jacob's camp the same day, scattering some of Jacob's sheep before he halted. He sneeringly remarked about his agreement turning out to his hurt. Laban incredulously accused Jacob of bringing evil into his home by contacting evil gods; otherwise, there could be no explanation for Jacob's good fortune.

"I have no contact with evil spirits, but I have been blessed by the true God with a just return for my years working for and enriching you. The blessing I have received is from the God who upholds heaven and earth. You took a chance—a foolish chance, as it turns out—that has resulted in far less livestock than you expected. You changed my administrator wages many times, never wanting to pay a full salary. The speckled, streaked, and mottled animals you see before you are the just wages that you have denied me until now. Had you paid me through the years, you wouldn't be shocked as you are now."

Jacob stood almost aghast at the expression on his uncle's face and immediately surmised, *I cannot be surprised at this. I surely could have guessed that he would act this way. I must act quickly, if I am ever to see my parents again.* Jacob left a fuming and angry Laban to talk with his wives about fleeing. He must get their consent and ensure their readiness to leave before he finished separating the animals.

Both Leah and Rachel listened intently to Jacob as he told them about the anger that his uncle was showing. He feared that Laban would follow his son's suggestion and accuse him of theft. Laban had many "friends" enjoying his wealth. Those friends were likely to join, even encourage, him in punishing the nephew who had done him wrong. Jacob advised his family that they must hasten to assemble all of their household goods and the belongings as stealthily as possible.

Both wives agreed to comply, with Leah exclaiming, "Our father treats us worse than most of his few friends—who have helped him squander much of his wealth that you have acquired for him. Both Rachel and I are sad to leave our father in this state, but he will never learn. He has also corrupted my brothers so that they act and do almost as he does. There often comes a time in one's life when that person must leave the family to its own doings. I agree that we must act quickly. My father will pout for a few days, and then he will act on anything that his fawning associates say. I say 'associates' because he has no true friends."

Both maidservants were at the meeting also. Jacob's departing words were, "Please contact some trusted servants to help you to assemble the household possessions. We must be ready to leave by tomorrow night. I am also sad to leave at this time, but I am afraid that we must move now or wind up as virtual slaves in your father's house for the rest of our lives. I even wonder if my life wouldn't soon be taken if I stay."

Jacob's bounty was so large that he left behind not only the plain white animals but also all animals that had only a hint of color in their coat. Only prominently speckled, streaked, or mottled livestock were driven away. The industrious work of his wives, maidservants, and other trusted servants enabled Jacob's family and flocks to depart on the second night after his talk with Laban.

*   *   *   *   *

The relief and freedom felt by everyone in the entourage leaving Haran was destined to be replaced by mourning in the years hence in the land of Canaan. Jacob's knowledge of God consisted mostly of wonder and acceptance. He knew essentially nothing of the jealousy of the true God against idols and rituals of worship that didn't exemplify the dignity of the Creator. Hence, he made no effort to prevent his wives and maidservants from following pagan forms of worship. The corrupting pagan influence from Laban had grown over the years.

As Jacob increased Laban's wealth, the latter became more and more protective of the wealth—from thieves and robbers, that is, not feigned friends who helped him disperse it. In an effort to ward off danger from those who would plunder and steal, he regularly purchased household gods over the years. While Leah and the servants were busy with packing the family's goods, Rachel had sneaked into a treasury room of her father's and stole some of his household idols. She accomplished this feat by fooling the servant assigned to guard the room with a story about some dangerous animals prowling nearby. She took no precious metals but only the household gods.

This act and Jacob's incredulity toward her committing such an act led to her death. The rashness and naïveté of her beloved husband would be the cause of her death.

*   *   *   *   *

Laban's concern over a significant reduction in wealth had to be delayed while he directed sheep-shearing activities for his still considerable flock. A servant who had seen Jacob's family leave thought that Laban would return from the shearing the next day. When he failed to return as expected, the servant rushed to tell him of Jacob's departure.

The servant had scarcely finished his first sentence before Laban's face darkened from intense anger. He wanted to know what his nephew had done and if he had taken his daughters with him. Upon hearing the full story, he remarked that this act of cowardice had to be dealt with. Laban seemed particularly upset when told that his daughters also took a large amount of household goods.

Laban blustered that he couldn't abide this insult to his authority. Jacob had to feel guilty of fraud toward him, or he wouldn't have left without several long days of feasting. They must gather a troop to overtake them and bring them back with what had been stolen.

When Laban returned home to assemble the necessary goods and camels for the chase, he noticed that a treasury box was slightly open. The guard who had abandoned his post of guarding the treasury when Rachel distracted him hadn't looked closely into the tent. He had no reason to suspect that any treasury had been taken because of all the activity by Jacob's family nearby.

In fact, Rachel had promised to guard the tent while he was gone looking for the nonexistent wild animals.

Laban's first glance into the box revealed no loss of precious metals. As he knelt by the box, he continued to wonder why it had been opened. He knew that neither he nor anyone authorized by him had touched it since he had last closed it. Then he noticed that the cloth covering the household gods looked as if it had been disturbed, and the outline of the cloth was also different than he recalled when he had added to his store of gods on the day he left for the shearing of the sheep. When he pulled back the covering, he found rocks in place of the household idols. The only conclusion he could draw was that one of the guards or someone in Jacob's family had taken them.

When a thorough search of the tents of the guards revealed no theft and he had obtained their solemn oaths of innocence, Laban knew where the idols must be. He wailed aloud as to why he had let that thief into his house and had given his daughters to him in marriage. Jacob had stolen his animals, his daughters, and now his sacred gods. Jacob was a nephew, but he had none of the restraint that Laban's beloved sister Rebekah, his mother, had.

Laban rushed outside to force all of his servants to drop all of their chores until they had helped outfit the camels for travel. He didn't wait for the next morning but started to chase Jacob's family late that day.

*   *   *   *   *

Jacob had pastured all of his animals well in the moons previous to his departure. Hence, they were all strong and capable of a rapid pace. He knew of the fertile pastures to the west, near Mt. Gilead, and decided to try to reach them quickly, thereby setting a safe distance between him and his uncle. If he could get away far from Haran, Laban should become discouraged and give up any chase he might mount. The animals could stand the fast pace for a few days until they could stop at Gilead for a long rest and recuperation.

The rest started for the animals before it did for Jacob. He had scarcely reached a pasture area before a troop of fast-paced camels approached. At first he thought that the riders were a group of bandits, but then he recognized his uncle. His original fear became somewhat muted, because he was sure that Laban wouldn't cause him serious harm in front of his daughters.

Stunned by the unanticipated meeting with his uncle, Jacob didn't know what to say. Laban, however, began to shout before halting his camel. He first assailed Jacob's ingratitude toward him by leaving without notice. Laban was saddened at not being able to send his daughters off after days of feasting.

Their departure for the cursed land of Canaan merited a long and pleasant farewell.

"Uncle, both my wives and I were concerned that you wouldn't let us all depart together. We are family that needs to become independent of a benefactor."

Laban promptly eased Jacob's fear and curiosity by explaining his conciliatory attitude. God had appeared to him in a dream two nights ago. God bade him to do Jacob no harm. Reluctantly, Laban must accept the division of the animals as Jacob's wage. He then begged for forgiveness for past actions and the harm he had threatened when he had discovered that his household gods were stolen, but those idols were definitely not part of any agreement that he and Jacob had ever reached. Also, thorough search and inspection of his servants' tents proved someone in Jacob's family took them on the day that he fled from Haran.

Jacob showed anger but controlled it to reply calmly, "I am certain that none of my family would steal your idols. You may search all of our tents if you wish."

*   *   *   *   *

Laban's men started a thorough search of everyone's goods. Their upturning of belongings and goods upset several in Jacob's group, but he told them that they must cooperate, so Laban would be satisfied that the idols weren't with them. Laban's men searched from tent to tent until they came to Rachel's tent, where they also found no idols.

The fruitlessness of the search put a scowl on Laban's face as he started to leave Rachel's tent. Not knowing what to do, he thought, *The idols must be here, but where could they be? We have searched everyplace.* When Laban realized that Rachel was sitting upon her riding furniture, he asked her to allow his inspection of the riding stuff.

"Father, the time of the moon is with me. Please don't require me to rise."

Laban scowled even more when he realized that his younger daughter had stolen from him, and there was nothing that he could do about retrieving his idols. He greeted Rachel again just before uttering a sigh and leaving the tent. Rather than subject himself to great embarrassment, he would purchase new gods.

Jacob accosted him as he left Rachel's tent about his arrogance in assuming that any of his family would steal his idols. Jacob's anger flared so intensely that he uttered the rashest oath of his life: "We didn't steal your gods. If any here are guilty of this deed that you so senselessly accuse, let that person's life not be spared. We have given our sacred oath upon condition of death if any of us are guilty."

When that confrontation ended, Laban and Jacob retired to their separate camps. The following morning, Laban informed his head servant that they would remain in Gilead for a few days. He wanted to give Jacob time to calm his anger, and then he would propose the feasting denied him in Haran. After a couple of days, a servant was sent to ask Jacob if they could join his group in several days of celebration in honor of the new life that his master's daughters were commencing. The servant told Jacob that Laban had given his solemn oath that he wouldn't argue over possessions again.

After a week of parties, day and night, Laban embraced Jacob and offered a proposal to set up a boundary marker at their current location to define the limits of occupancy by their families. He wouldn't encroach upon Jacob's land; nor would Jacob possess lands to the east of the marker.

*   *   *   *   *

Just prior to their departure, Laban asked Jacob for a final promise. Jacob swore that he would be faithful to Laban's daughters and take no other wives. Laban also invoked God as witness against Jacob if he mistreated Leah or Rachel in any way. Jacob felt a slight offense at having to take the oath because of Laban's continuing protectiveness, but he issued it nevertheless.

By accepting the oath, Jacob reasoned, he should finally get rid of his meddling uncle and father-in-law, and the promise was nothing more than his duty toward his wives anyway.

FREEDOM

I N THE SUCCEEDING DAYS, Jacob settled into a pleasant life in Gilead. Before he could be conditioned to stay there, however, Jacob had an encounter with some angels of God who gave him an upsetting command, telling him that he must move on. Jacob was near the land inhabited by his brother, Esau. The last time Jacob had heard about his brother, the news included a threat of harm toward him. After pondering what to do, he decided to send a servant to Esau with the news of his service to Laban for the past decades. He authorized the servant to promise many animals as a gift to Esau and to ask him permission to travel through his land.

The servant, who decided not to approach Esau, returned with distressing news: Esau was approaching with a band of four hundred men. Jacob held his composure while he thanked the servant for the information. Jacob immediately returned to his tent and asked not to be disturbed. There he implored God to save them from his brother's horde, while reminding God that this return to Canaan had been an order from him.

After a long and pleading prayer, Jacob decided to divide his family and animals into two groups. Thus, if they received no protection from God, one group should be able to escape. Then he sent a servant ahead with a drove of animals to offer to Esau as a gift. Jacob's group followed after the servant to the brook of Jabbok, where Jacob tarried while all of the others moved on.

Immediately upon deciding to cross the stream to catch up with his family, Jacob was met and assaulted by a strong, handsome man. As he strove with the man, he began to realize that this man wasn't any ordinary person; but as he continued to wrestle with him, he reached a strange realization that this man posed no threat to him or his family. The stature, visage, and voice of his attacker were familiar. This man was the being who appeared to him in his dreams as God.

This full realization that he was fighting with God caused a momentary relaxation by Jacob. To Jacob's surprise, God in the form of a man didn't relent but almost threw him into a pool of water in the brook. At that instance, Jacob resolved to wrestle; he wouldn't give up, although he fought with God.

The striving went on all through the night. Jacob was determined not to be the one who relented. God had started this match, and he had to be the one who ended it. With the approach of dawn, the man apparently decided not to remain visible to potential passersby and asked Jacob to let him go.

Jacob refused. "I'll not let you go unless you bless me." Jacob felt no presumptiveness by the request. If God would presume to wrestle with him for much of the night, he surely was familiar enough to accept a request to bless him

The man looked directly at Jacob without any apparent emotion showing on his face and asked, "What is your name?"

"My name is Jacob."

"You have been more than a worthy opponent. Your name shall no more be Jacob but Israel. You are a soldier of God."

Being a complex man, Jacob often seemed timid, but in this wrestling match, the exceedingly bold and tenacious side of Jacob had shown itself. If he could fight with God, he could also ask him his name. "And what is your name?" The question was uttered almost before he had mustered the courage to ask it.

After a pause that began to cause fear in Jacob, the man replied, "Why do you ask my name?" Jacob made no reply, because the sternness of the voice indicated no answer was expected. The man then stretched his right hand toward Jacob and blessed him, after which he turned and walked away before disappearing.

Jacob stood nearly motionless for a long time. Ordinarily he would have been to the point of complete exhaustion, but he felt energetic as he continued to stand. The realization that he had touched the face of God and lived, however, suddenly drained all of his energy, causing him to fall to his knees. He soon regained his strength and realized he must catch up with his family, who had failed to divide into two groups as instructed. They surely must be worried about him by now. Also, he didn't know how close Esau was, and he must be with them for the meeting with his brother. As he crossed the brook and hobbled toward the camp of his family, he paused to name the place The Face of God.

The first person to greet him was one of the servants sent to find him.

As he saw Jacob approach, he ran to meet him. Because of Jacob's limp, the servant feared that his master was injured.

Jacob smiled and told the servant that his long night of struggle with a man at the brook had caused him to strain his lower back as he ended the fight. He also immediately added that the man had been alone and had left the area, thus posing no threat to them.

The servant's concern was eased, and he tried to console Jacob with the fact that a physician was traveling with them; he should be able to treat the injury. The servant then wrapped one of Jacob's arms around his shoulder to assist him to camp.

"Thanks, but I don't need any help. I am awake and well, except for the problem with my back, which seems to improve with movement. I should be able to heal by walking, the only activity that helps the pain."

When Jacob reached the camp, the physician inspected him before directing him to a travois upon which he could lean for support. This arrangement allowed him to rest in a nearly upright position and provided a means for him to stretch his legs occasionally.

By the next day, Jacob wanted to continue the family's journey to Canaan. As preparations for the day's travel commenced, Jacob saw a dark cloud in the distance, except that this cloud continued to hug the ground and not rise in the sky. *This must be Esau's army,* he thought. He hurriedly told the maidservants and their children to lead the procession, followed by Leah and her children, and then Rachel and Joseph.

As he raced to the front of the train to greet his brother, Esau, Jacob hoped that the servants leading the main part of his animals were ready to take evasive action if necessary. As Esau halted his horde that was threatening by its sheer size, Jacob knelt in respect to him. Esau promptly dismounted and ran to embrace his brother. They spent much of a twelfth-day in kissing, hugging, and weeping.

Esau eventually took critical notice of Jacob's family standing in the distance. "Jacob, who are these people accompanying you?"

"I am happy to say that they are my wives and children that God gave to me while I lived in Haran, serving my uncle. Please let me introduce them. Except for the servants, each one is either a cousin or nephew, and Dinah is a niece."

After the procession of family members was over, Esau turned his attention to the large flock of animals surrounding them. When Jacob told him that this bunch was a gift to him, Esau refused to take them.

"My dear brother, please accept this livestock from me. God has prospered me in these past years. He has also inspired me to be generous with my bounty. I beg of you to honor both God and myself by accepting them. We do, however, have many more animals that must pass through here. We have hurried on our departure from my uncle. Therefore, both my animals and children are still somewhat exhausted. We would appreciate the permission to proceed slowly on our way to Canaan."

"You may do as you request. I will also accept your gift. Please accept my gratitude for it. If your flock and people are as tired as you say, I will assign some of my men to accompany you for a distance, so your herders can get some extra rest." Jacob refused the help at first but relented when he noticed that Esau wasn't pleased with his refusal.

Jacob turned south and traveled down the east side of Jordan to a place that would become known as Succoth. It was located near a fording place on the Jordan nearly opposite the town of Shechem, where Jacob hoped eventually to reside. Not being certain of the conditions in Canaan, however, he decided to settle for a while. After building some temporary shelters or booths—hence Succoth—for his animals and family, he finally had time to relax for a few days.

His relaxation soon became boring, and he decided now was the time to visit his parents in Beersheba. One day after morning chores, he called to his head servant, "Please arrange for a trip to my father's home in Beersheba. We will be staying here for a considerable time. We need some time to search out Canaan for a place to settle permanently. I doubt that my father's land would support both of our flocks. I have a desire to settle in Shechem, but I can't wait until we find whether we can move there before I talk to my parents about our move."

*   *   *   *   *

News of Jacob's settlement in Succoth had reached his parents just recently. The anticipation that Jacob might visit anytime caused Rebekah constantly to scan the horizon. A younger servant working alongside her had adopted her habit of looking into the distance frequently and was the first one to spot Jacob's band. Rebekah's eyesight, like her husband's, had started to fail, putting her at a disadvantage in seeing distant objects clearly.

Surprisingly, when told of Jacob's approach, Rebekah didn't run to meet him. Her first words were, "How do I look? Please help me to be properly groomed for my son. He mustn't see his mother looking like an old hag." She then called to her husband about their son's visit.

*   *   *   *   *

"Mother, I am so glad to see you. Where is Father? I hope that he is well." When Rebekah pointed to Isaac's approach, Jacob waited until they were both together and proceeded to hug them both at the same time. He then gave his father a kiss, followed by a kiss for his mother.

Rebekah chided him for kissing his father first. Jacob told her half in jest that it was time for him to quit being a pet of his mother. Isaac smiled as he spoke. "You must tell us about your life in more detail. The few yearly visits from you didn't give us the whole story of your life. We have heard that you are not yet dwelling in Canaan, but have stopped on the other side of the Jordan. When are you moving here?"

"Father, I have vast flocks that couldn't be supported here. I know that the last visiting servant couldn't have known how my recent good fortune happened. Also, I have stopped opposite Canaan to survey the land for a place to settle. Right now I am about ready to end my search until I hear from a servant I have dispatched to Shechem. I sent him there to bid on some land. I have my heart set on that place and believe that God will bless my servant's endeavor to purchase some land there."

Isaac replied with elation, "Please let me know when you move. Should you settle in Shechem, I will move back to Hebron, where your grandfather Abraham dwelled for a time—also, that is the place where your grandmother Sarah died. Then we should be close enough for you to visit often."

"I would be pleased with your move to Hebron, and I promise to bring my family for a visit if I get to Shechem. I did bring the latest drawings of all my wives and children with me. My artist has produced astonishing likenesses of them. Interestingly, his name is Hebron; he was named after the land of my grandfather, who still is an honored man."

Jacob and his companions were accompanied to quarters where they could bathe and rest. Over a late morning meal the next day, Jacob began his tale about his "escape" from Laban. The narrative took on a sense of comedy, danger, tragedy, and pathos. After nearly a twelfth-day of talking, Jacob finally noticed that his mother was becoming upset. He paused to ask a response from her, but she motioned for him to continue. He concluded that his mother didn't like what he was saying about her brother. To ease her feelings, he decided to continue with the rest of the story at the evening meal, when he would lessen his criticism of Laban.

As they left for their daily duties, Rebekah asked Jacob to accompany her. "I would like to show you our entire household and work areas." Rebekah spent the rest of the morning showing Jacob around the household areas, gardens, and orchards. At the end of the tour, she motioned for a rest stop and asked, "Is it true what you say about my brother?"

"Mother, I sensed that you were upset about what you heard, but you shouldn't have been. His actions have been told to you over the years. My uncle acted as one could have expected him to act. He even accused us of stealing his household gods; it shocks me to think that any of my people would do such a thing. By his very words, his plans to essentially enslave us, or even take my life, were only thwarted by a directive from God, who told him to leave us alone and do us no harm."

"It's difficult to believe that my brother would act this way. I knew that he was bossy—and, I suppose, greedy. I thought, however, that he would have treated my son better. Maybe you shouldn't have entered into that contract that had a chance to produce so few animals for him."

"Mother! I knew from the constant changing of my wages over the years of administrative service that I had to risk a small return if I were to get a fair wage. True, I felt that God would permit the results that I got. I have noticed over the years certain patterns of offspring from animals with different shadings of coat. I was confident that unless God intervened against me, I would have a large herd of my own within several years. God allowed the blessing, and I had a right to take the animals that I did."

When Rebekah still worried about what her brother might do, Jacob reminded her of Laban's fear to act counter to the directive from God and of the boundary marker between them. "No. I believe that I have finally seen the last of my uncle. I am sorry to say that it is unlikely that you will ever see him again. He indicated that he was returning to Haran for the rest of his life, and he gave me a vague warning to stay away from Haran also."

After another three days, Jacob gathered his companions and camels to leave for home. "Father, Mother, I must be on my way home. You seem to have adequate help here, making it unnecessary for us to give you any assistance. I need to be ready to act on any agreement my servant reaches about Shechem. Wherever we eventually settle, I will send servants to tell you about our surroundings. I do hope to bring my family for a visit again within a few moons."

*   *   *   *   *

As his group approached Succoth, Jacob could see that everything appeared to be normal. The workers were busy, and the animals could be seen peacefully grazing in the distance. As they drew closer, he could see the servant he had sent to Shechem waving something held in his right hand. Jacob's heart seemed to skip a beat from joy, because he knew what the item in the servant's hand was. It had to be an agreement on Shechem.

"Master Jacob, I contracted for a goodly parcel of land in Shechem. The seller is here to close the deal."

"Where is he? I am ready to agree to the contract now. You did get an agreement for the price that I suggested, didn't you?"

"Master, I am sorry, but he demanded a fourth part more. The lay of the land and the watering places presented too much temptation for me not to agree to his higher price. I tried to get him to reduce the amount, but he would not move from his sales figure. You still can refuse the deal with only a twentieth-part penalty on my original proposal, but I believe the higher price is a worthy purchase."

"You have done well, my good servant. I became worried on the way home that you might not purchase the land if the asking price was more than I had approved. I trust your judgment; I will agree to the new asking price without bargaining."

Once the contract was signed, Jacob recounted a historic remembrance passed down to him by a servant, now dead, who had known his grandfather's chief assistant. "Eliezer loved the land of Shechem and wished that it would have been the place they could have settled when they entered the land. I believe my grandfather liked it also. At last the desires of our forefathers can be fulfilled."

Jacob told the seller that he wanted to move to Shechem immediately.

No special preparation would be necessary for this trip, because it wouldn't be lengthy. There would be no fatting of the sheep and cattle beyond normal. A leisurely trek would get them to their new home soon enough.

Upon arrival in Shechem, the joyous anticipation turned into realized contentment. Jacob had suppressed the urge to get to his destination rapidly. The slow pace had provided healthy flocks at the end of the journey that seemed to express enjoyment over their new grazing grounds. Within a few days, Jacob determined that the new grazing area would soon be too small for a large increase in his flocks. He must find more land within a couple of years. The land here would be ideal as a base for his breeding flocks for the rest of his life, or so he hoped, but marketing animals would have to be moved elsewhere. After proper construction had begun to progress sufficiently, he would take his family to see his parents while surveying the land for expanded pastures along the way.

On the day after the celebration of their first year in Shechem, Jacob started preparing his family for a trip to Hebron, where his parents now dwelled. Word of their visit had been sent by three different messengers to ensure that Rebekah would have lodging and food available for the group upon its arrival.

When Jacob had finished the long introduction, Rebekah beamed at his family, "I am so pleased to see you have so many children. For much of my married life, I despaired that your father and you wouldn't fulfill the promises received by your grandfather Abraham of a sea of descendants. First was my barrenness, and then the lateness of your marriage, but God has blossomed our family suddenly. Now your father and I can go to our sleep with confidence that we have done our part in the plan through such wonderful grandchildren."

Rebekah started to dote over Dinah, who appeared to be sick from the trip. Before Leah could determine how to treat her, Rebekah's nurse grabbed the child and started soothing her. Without being asked, she prepared a tonic and looked for a soft pallet on which to place the child. The nurse reckoned that Dinah's stomach was upset from the bouncing she had received during the trip. A night's rest in the nursery should make her better, the nurse said.

Leah opened her mouth to complain, but Rebekah pursed her lips, signaling for Leah to be quiet. "Deborah, will you look in on the child tonight—or better yet, will you sleep next to her bed?" The nurse nodded assent and headed for the nursery with Dinah.

The concern over the sick child and talks with the adults distracted Rebekah enough that she didn't notice or chose to ignore the bickering and fighting among the eleven male grandchildren around her.

Cutting, even cruel, remarks against the children of Bilhah, Rachel's maidservant, had been uttered for some time, especially since Jacob had adopted faithfulness to Leah and Rachel. Both Dan and Naphtali were hot-tempered and returned their insults. The fracases had been well controlled before now, because none were allowed to associate with the two boys unless they acted civilly. But their living space at their grandparents' put all of the boys close together. After a subdued first day, the quarrelling and fighting broke out. Naphtali, who had been a stout boy from the toddler stage, had heard all of the insults from Reuben that he could take. A quick blow when Reuben was looking away caused a bloody nose. Reuben immediately ran to his mother, accusing Naphtali of trying to kill him.

A suppressed dislike had existed in Leah and her maidservant Zilpah toward Bilhah since the latter had become a concubine of Jacob. All of those pent-up emotions finally burst forth over this childish incident. Instead of two "children" to separate and reprimand, there now were four who needed correction, because Bilhah and Leah starting exchanging accusations. Nearby servants disagreed on whether it was after the third or fourth exchange of insults that the screaming, scratching, and pulling of hair started.

After Jacob had reconciled the two women, including consoling Leah over the mussing of her latest hairdo, he turned his attention to the two boys.

"All right, I assume some major problem started this fight. Let's hear your reason for this fight."

Naphtali was still pouting and reluctant to speak. He clearly felt justified in what he had done and was ready to accept any punishment he had to endure.

Reuben, who had growing sociopathic tendencies, believed that anything he desired should be his. He also held no regard for how his comments affected others, especially those whom he disliked. He promptly accused Naphtali of attacking him without provocation and hurting him seriously.

Jacob looked at Reuben with skepticism and then turned to Naphtali. "Is this true? Did you seriously hurt him?"

Naphtali continued to pout but had to speak because Jacob's eyes stayed fixed on him. "Reuben has insulted me for over a year now. He has started accusing me of being the child of harlot, because my mother has no husband. I have tried to reason with him time after time, but he never shuts up. I thought maybe a bloody nose would take his mind off me for a while." At first, Jacob smiled inside himself until he realized that this was a serious problem that was going to be difficult to explain to his children, not just the two fighting boys.

Servants took the young men aside to watch them while Jacob went to talk with his wives and concubines. "This may be a rare occasion to have all four of you in one place, but I need to stop some gossiping that probably was started by one or more of you. When I promised Laban that I would be faithful to Leah and Rachel only, it didn't make the children of Bilhah, or Zilpah also, suddenly to have been born without a legal father. Reuben didn't pick up his accusation on his own; he heard it from an older adult. That adult was one of you or some servant. Regardless of who started this vain and hurtful accusation, it must stop. If Reuben has heard it, I am sure nearly everyone has. I am directing you, Leah, and you, Rachel, to put forth an effort to stop it. Whether or not either of you are involved, it has become your responsibility to end it."

Leah started to protest, but Jacob repeated his command. He wasn't interested in assigning blame, nor did he even desire to know who had started the gossip. A proper corrective action should help the culprit or culprits to assign their own blame. "Reuben, your accusation comes from overhearing others, I am sure. Naphtali, you have acted in an understandable manner. Therefore, I will not punish either of you, but you must listen to both your mothers, who will explain that the accusation is wrong and must stop. When that is accomplished, I expect the two of you to treat each other with kindness; else a strong punishment will be given to both of you."

The rest of the visit went well—everyone was at least civil. The quick recovery of Dinah and the quiet, albeit sulking, mood of some of the boys allowed the adults to complete the visit in peace.

On the day before their return to Shechem, Rebekah called Jacob aside. "Your family isn't happy. I have been cheerful, because it is a great blessing to see my son's family. They are the only grandchildren I have seen for years; Esau never comes by to see us. Now I have seen twelve grandchildren. You must, however, do something about the ill feeling that your sons have for one another. I even see a jealousy among the sons of Leah, not to consider how they feel about the children of the maidservants."

"Mother, I have made a poor decision in accepting the maidservants as substitute mothers. Your brother's fraud started this string of events. But had he not acted falsely, I would now have only one son. I guess the blessing of many children requires more care than I have given them."

"Son, you have a problem that can't be solved just by spending time with the family. I believe that Leah and Rachel are beginning to be concerned about what their sons will inherit. Their quarreling over the prospective inheritance is affecting the attitude of the children. The best advice I can give you is to talk with your wives and get this resolved. Also, don't forget to include Dinah in your promises."

As Jacob began to ride away the next day with his family, he dismounted and returned to tell his mother that he appreciated her advice and thanked her for the hospitality of the past few days. He reasoned that the trip had been especially valuable in highlighting some family problems that needed his attention.

Jacob's increasing flocks at Shechem soon forced him to seek the expanded pastures that he had surmised he would need at his arrival there. He wanted to expand toward his father to the south, but he found bargain land to the north, near Dothan. Within time, he even outgrew those fields and then reached an agreement with his father to combine some of their flocks at Hebron, making better use of Isaac's ample grazing land. His parents encouraged Jacob to move not only some of his animals but also his family to Hebron, but his love for Shechem prevailed. He did, however, spend many days with his parents overseeing the branding of the new lambs and other cattle each summer.

The expansion of his flocks allowed Jacob to assign his sons to different places, keeping antagonists separate most of the time. Jacob was truly happy again. His wealth was secure, and he had none to assault him, as Esau had in Jacob's youth, or to force him to work as a virtual slave, as he had for fourteen years in adulthood.

Jacob's pleasant life in Shechem became even more joyous when Rachel announced that she was pregnant after many years of barrenness. Within the week, the joy became somewhat muted when he got a command from

God to move, with Bethel as his first stop. He was being forced to leave his beautiful home.

Although Jacob had traveled past Bethel on trips to see his parents, he hadn't stopped there overnight since his trip decades before to find a job with his uncle. Before he started to build a new altar at Bethel, he searched for the one built by his grandfather and the one he had constructed on his trip to Haran so many years ago. Abraham's altar was still remarkably preserved, possibly because of protection from overgrowth. Jacob's altar had suffered from disturbance by animals.

Before starting to build a new and more sturdy altar, he inspected all of his family and servants again to ensure that they had complied with an edict from God to put away all of their idols, which were buried at Shechem. Jacob issued a sigh of relief when Rachel failed to hand him any household idols, and none were found among her personal possessions. Nevertheless, he did have a brief uneasy feeling when he noticed that some of the items buried looked like household gods that he had seen at his uncle's place in Haran. Because he couldn't be certain that they were the same idols, he convinced himself that they weren't Laban's.

*   *   *   *   *

When hearing about their son's arrival in Bethel, Isaac and Rebekah decided to join him for a stay. They were close enough now for a comfortable transportation arrangement to his camp. Several days after their meeting with their son at Bethel, Rebekah's nurse became violently ill and died the same day.

Rebekah sobbed, "I have lost a dear friend. I can't believe that she is dead. She seemed so strong. The joy of our living with our son has been saddened."

Jacob soothed her, "I am sure that the trip wasn't responsible for her death. She seemed vigorous and healthy as late as yesterday. Our family physician will be arriving any day now. He will find another nurse for you, although I am sure that none else can ever replace Deborah. Shall we bury her here?"

"Yes, son. We have no suitable burial ground near enough."

*   *   *   *   *

As Rachel drew near the time for her delivery, Jacob doted upon her to an excess, making sure everything was perfect. Only a complaint by the new family nurse to the resident physician about Jacob's care, which had become meddlesome and annoying, caused the physician to beg Jacob to quit trying to guide affairs that had already been properly handled.

Just when some peace had returned to the nurse's life, an upset but anxious Jacob disturbed her daily routine again. He exclaimed with a sound of regret, "I have been given a directive from God to move to Ephrath. Knowing Rachel's condition, I pleaded with him as to why now. He assured me that now was the time to leave. Can you prepare a safe conveyance for Rachel?"

The nurse looked at Jacob in disbelief but reluctantly stated that she had helped move women in late-term pregnancy before. She would oversee the assembling of a safe and proper conveyance for Rachel. While travel definitely was not advisable, the trip shouldn't place Rachel in any serious danger. Hopefully, they would reach Ephrath before the child was born.

Jacob rode next to Rachel to steady her and to be instantly present for any problems that might arise. As they drew near their destination one evening, Jacob decided to halt for the night. "We are close to our destination, but the remaining distance is a bit far to reach today. Let's have a good night's rest before proceeding. A leisurely pace tomorrow should get us there before Rachel's delivery."

Jacob suppressed his desire to celebrate their good fortune so far, because a small distance remained before he could once again relax. He was the last person, except for sentries, to prepare for sleep. Shortly before the night meridian, he made a last check on Rachel and then retired for the night. Just as he was entering sleep, he and several others were awakened by a loud scream. Rachel had gone into birth labor, which rapidly became severe.

*   *   *   *   *

By morning light, Rachel had started to despair that she would live long enough for the baby to be born. By early post meridian, she was becoming quite weak, but she managed one last strong push to allow the midwife to remove the child from the birth canal.

The midwife caressed her forehead and told her, "You have borne a son."

Rachel smiled weakly as she was dying. "Please call him Ben-oni, son of my sorrow. I …"

Jacob, who had held her hand for most of the day, shook his head as tears streamed down his face. "I have allowed my wives to name their children if they wished. I cannot, however, honor this most precious dying request of my beloved wife. The name would remind me of her death every time I called him. I must accept her death, but I cannot accept a constant reminder of it. That's more than I can endure. I will call him Benjamin, son of the south—all his brothers were born in Aram, north of here."

*   *   *   *   *

As the mourning lessened, some of the servants began to congratulate Jacob on his twelfth male heir. Jacob offered faint thanks in return because of the price he had had to pay to have that son. In a moment of reflection, after yet another congratulation, he wondered: what had caused Rachel's death? Then a horrific thought crossed his mind: had she stolen her father's household gods? *I never found any of them on her person, but she could have given them to others.*

He called a meeting of all the servants for the next day at a common morning meal. Most of the servants were apprehensive as they gathered around the food-laden table. None could remember a meeting of all the servants at once.

Jacob arrived after everyone had started their meal. "Friends, I have called you here to find out some information that you may consider of no consequence. But please believe me that I am serious about what I am requesting when I tell you that it is important that I know if Rachel gave you any idols before we left Shechem."

A long period of silence ensued as none indicated that they had anything to say. Indeed, many were incredulous that he would call a meeting for such an inquiry. Did it matter who had the gods? They were all buried and soon to be forgotten. Was Jacob becoming disabled with grief?

Jacob continued to look over his audience. He tried to raise his hopes that their silence meant a negative answer to his inquiry. Then he noticed the look on Bilhah's face. He knew his former concubine intimately; she could never hide her feelings from showing on her face. He would wait awhile longer before leaving his servants to finish their meal. When Bilhah continued to look down, trying to shield her face, he thanked all of them and left after inviting them to enjoy the rest of their meal.

As he suspected, Bilhah rushed out of the dining area as soon as he departed. He had stopped nearby so he could catch up with her before she ran away someplace to hide from him. "Bilhah, I can tell from the expression on your face that you knew something about this. I suspect that Rachel gave you some household gods, and those gods were gods that she stole from her father."

Bilhah expressed doubt about his being able to know what she was thinking just from the look on her face.

"I have been around you for many years. Not only I but others have said, 'You can always know what Bilhah is thinking about by studying her face.'"

Bilhah sighed in resignation, acknowledging the futility of trying to deceive the man who was the father of her two children. She gave a detailed account of how Rachel had stolen and hidden the gods not only from Jacob but also her father on the day of his search. Rachel had only taken fertility gods, which her father didn't need. Why should he have such gods? She had expressed her confidence to Bilhah that her father wouldn't replace them after he had a chance to review his inventory of the gods that she left.

Jacob could scarcely hold back the tears as he thanked and excused Bilhah. He hurried to the privacy of his tent, where he spent the rest of the morning sobbing. Around the meridian, he arose, washed his face, and hastened to see his mother, whom he called aside for a private talk.

"Mother, I have been responsible for Rachel's death."

"Son, don't speak so foolishly. I have been hearing talk among the servants that grief is driving you toward a dangerous mental state."

Jacob excitedly motioned for his mother to let him speak. "I know what I did in calling a meeting of all the servants to ask about any idols that Rachel may have possessed—looked foolish or worse. Please believe me when I say that I had a good reason for my actions. When I left your brother's place, he thought someone in our group had stolen some of his household gods. He demanded a search of all our goods when he overtook us. I was quite offended by the accusation that any of us would or even could have taken any of his gods. The accusation was totally absurd. I then made the most foolish statement of my life—not only foolish, but so irresponsible that I doubt any have ever acted more stupidly. I swore that any of us who would have dared to take his gods was worthy of death. For all the grief that this unbelievable oath has brought me, I am thankful that God didn't exact the penalty for several years, and he permitted me to have a twelfth male heir. By obtaining the information that I did, I now know that it wasn't the birth of Benjamin specifically that caused her death. God chose that occasion to teach me an awful and terrible lesson."

"Jacob, Jacob, I have no words to say. I don't understand. I am sure that others have offered similar oaths without having to pay the penalty."

FOURTEEN

SIBLING RIVALRY

AFTER THE DAYS OF mourning were over and a memorial had been
set up at Rachel's grave, Jacob decided to move away far enough not
to be reminded of her grave. With no other directive from God, he
settled in Edar, close to a watchtower.

Isaac became despondent from seeing the grief of his son and finally
concluded it was time to get back to Hebron. He winced when Rebekah tried
to persuade Jacob to move with them and felt relieved when Jacob declined to
move. Rebekah's insistence, however, reminded him that he and Jacob should
finish mixing their flocks; therefore, he also tried to persuade Jacob to move
but only mildly. To Isaac's delight, Jacob agreed to a temporary trip, sending
his father and mother to Hebron with a promise to follow within two or three
days. There were no extensive parting rituals, because all should be together
in Hebron within the week.

Jacob worked nearly day and night, with only a short daily nap, while
helping to segregate the flocks. He was ready to return to Edar after a
week at Hebron. His father noticed that work kept Jacob's sadness hidden.
Because there would be plenty of work to do in Hebron, he changed his
mind and asked Jacob to move there. "Please move next to us. My days
draw near an end. I would like to spend as many days with you as possible
before I die."

"Father, these days with you have been precious, but I believe that God
wants me to tarry at Edar yet. I sense a mystical quality to the area. You
know that it isn't far from where Melchizedek had an altar in the days of my
grandfather. I do believe I will get to come to Hebron before you must go
to your sleep. Also, depending on how long I must tarry there, I will make
occasional trips to see you."

*   *   *   *   *

Try as he might, Jacob couldn't show Bilhah any warmth of interaction. No one around him had ever seen him so critical of a servant. In the past, any servant who had offended him was treated coolly but without unnecessary reprisal. The old feud between Reuben and Bilhah's children had been resolved by keeping the three boys or young men apart. Jacob was never able to find out what caused a horrific escalation of Reuben's hatred toward his former concubine and her sons, but he knew that his own actions toward her undoubtedly triggered the act of sexual intercourse with Bilhah by Reuben.

Jacob didn't immediately accost his son when he got news of the gross impropriety by his oldest son. Instead, he went to the privacy of his tent to plead for his own forgiveness. The concept of doubt entered Jacob's mind for the first time. He acknowledged his own wrongdoing in this incident, because he had secretly blamed Bilhah in his heart for Rachel's death; if she would have told him of Rachel's theft at the beginning, he could have returned the household gods to Laban and begged his forgiveness. Yet he knew it was really his rashness in making the oath that eventually caused Rachel's death. He passionately pleaded with God to absolve him of his gross error in judgment.

He continued to wait for a few more days to let his remorse, anger, and other assorted emotions subside. He had planned to severely punish Reuben for the gross effrontery to him but decided to talk to a servant who worked extensively with his oldest son. All of his servants were outwardly—and, he believed, actually—loyal to him regardless of their close work associations with Reuben. He was certain that the servant would give him a proper insight into the appropriate reprimand for Reuben.

Jacob was surprised when he was told none. The servant stated that Reuben would cite that Jacob had put Bilhah away; therefore, she was no longer Jacob's wife. Before Jacob would be able to bring up that the act was still a forbidden custom, Reuben would mention that Jacob himself wasn't one to let custom stand in his way in getting what he wanted. Reuben's first argument would probably be that Jacob had gone against custom by trying to marry Rachel instead of his mother, Leah. The haughtiness of Reuben's demeanor indicated that Jacob couldn't shame him, the servant explained, because he would be resolute in believing that he had done no wrong.

"What you said is interesting. He has done this deed primarily to diminish or deprive Bilhah's children of an inheritance. He probably would do the same to Zilpah's children, except he would catch some grief from his mother, Leah."

After the additional exchange of ideas, Jacob decided upon a plan. He would say nothing to Reuben, because Bilhah, being the older adult, should have resisted his attention. Few effective actions existed to help either of the offending individuals. He could, however, show his disdain for their act by putting Naphtali and Dan in charge of his breeding herd at Shechem. This assignment would demonstrate that he still had high regard for the two sons who were receiving scorn not only from Reuben but others in camp also.

While the elevation of the status of the sons of Bilhah showed a desire for equitable treatment for all of his children, Jacob wasn't entirely successful in avoiding playing favorites among his sons. He began to dote upon the pleasantness and the abilities of Rachel's oldest son, Joseph, and show little attention to the baby son, Benjamin. As he couldn't effectively divide his love between his wives, he failed to divide the love between his sons. Soon the brothers' envy and hatred for Naphtali and Dan began to be expressed toward Joseph also. This resentment was further inflamed by the tendency of Joseph to scheme for favors from his father. Whereas Naphtali and Dan had one primary antagonist, Joseph had ten—all of his brothers, except Benjamin.

The growing dislikes among the eleven oldest boys faded in expression for a while. Just as Jacob was gaining some contentment, a servant arrived with the dreaded news that his mother, Rebekah, was gravely ill. He promptly decided that he would not only go see his mother immediately, but he would direct members of his household to follow him to Hebron in a permanent move. He would now spend the last days with his parents. Hopefully, his mother would recover, so he would yet have some time to visit with her.

Remarkably, the joy of hearing of her son's decision to move to Hebron revived Rebekah to a state of seeming health, which lasted for less than a year before the sad event of her death occurred. She was buried in the family plot with Abraham and Sarah without the attendance of her son, Esau, whose estrangement remained. Esau's relative civility toward his father, Isaac, didn't extend to his mother.

With his beloved wife Rachel and his mother now dead and a growing wealth that required only easy administrative duties, Jacob had for the first time a chance to attend primarily to family matters, which mostly consisted of trying to keep peace among the quarreling sons.

The incident with Bilhah changed the relationship between Reuben and his father considerably. Hence, no more demands for special favors came from the offending son. But those demands were soon replaced by similar ones from Joseph, who sensed that he was his father's favorite son. Joseph's alleged superior moral conduct merited more favors than the rest of his brothers, or so he told his father.

Joseph was so successful in selling himself that his father put up little to no resistance to Joseph's request to have an expensive and regal-looking tunic of many colors woven for him. Much of the wool was imported from other lands, including the highland home of their ancestor Abraham.

Leah objected to the exclusivity of the favor and requested tunics of comparable quality for her sons. Jacob refused by justifying the expense as an act of kindness toward Joseph to help console him over the death of his mother. The coat would lift the spirits of the mourning son. Leah looked at Jacob in disbelief, but gave up the argument at the obvious delusion of her husband. It was useless to condemn his treatment of Joseph in any way. It seemed nothing was too good for Joseph, who could do no wrong.

*   *   *   *   *

The gift of the regal tunic to Joseph caused the envy of Judah and Dinah to flare up. Both of these children had been more docile and compliant than the other siblings, but this favoritism was more than they could take. As the only daughter, Dinah received very little attention after she had outgrown her babyhood. Judah's neglect probably resulted from his not being a problem child. Now both of these children expressed their rebellion by forbidden association with the children of some of the surrounding tribes whenever they could slip away from the scrutiny of their parents.

*   *   *   *   *

Meanwhile, Jacob had convinced Zilpah's children, Gad and Asher, that it was best for them if they joined Bilhah's children at Shechem to help maintain his prime flocks there and in Dothan. He would shelter Joseph, and Benjamin was too young to cause jealousy. These arrangements divided his children and reduced the bickering to a manageable level—though even Leah's older children had squabbles among one another.

Feeling confident that Joseph was old enough to handle inspection of his flocks and herds, Jacob sent him to Shechem to appraise the progress of his breeding flocks there. Joseph brought back a report of carelessness in caring for the animals. The report of the loss of some of the prize animals upset Jacob to the extent that he sent another servant to verify the report. While the report had been basically true, the problems had been overstated. Some of the losses were older animals who had been culled out for slaughter and given reduced protection. All but one of his very best breeders was still alive and healthy. Some of the reported carelessness probably stemmed from the rather relaxed manner of administering care, not from actual neglect. Jacob was relieved but said nothing to Joseph, considering his biased report to be a result of Joseph's lack of experience.

After some months, Jacob decided to give some credence to Joseph's report by demoting the children of his concubines to looking after his local flocks and sent Leah's children to tend the flocks at Shechem. The delayed timing of the change did little to stem the rage of the demoted children.

This move of separation brought a period of peace in the family, giving Jacob a false sense of having finally solved his family problems. The lull in his life allowed him to start spending many pleasant days with his aging father, who became closely reconciled to this son. No longer did Esau seem to be the center of his thoughts. In fact, Isaac ceased mentioning Esau's name.

Jacob continued to use Joseph as a direct assistant in his business affairs, which included continued inspection of the flocks that were spread out over the land of Canaan. Since his first inspection tour, Joseph had become more circumspect in his criticism, but he upset his brothers with his continued reports of minor incidents that they deemed trivial. To their dismay, Jacob seemed to accept everything that this pompous braggart said.

It was a dream, however, that led to action by the brothers against Joseph, not his petty complaints. Arrogantly, Joseph proclaimed that he had a dream indicating that he would rule over all of his brothers, and his father and stepmother also. The presumptive telling of the dream showed such lack of concern for the feelings of others that it prompted an extremely rare reprimand from Jacob, but the scolding didn't noticeably affect Joseph's attitude.

Unfortunately for Joseph, the time for a regular inspection of the flocks in Shechem came due within weeks after he had described his dream to his entire family. Jacob would later condemn himself for sending Joseph on this inspection trip. He had other capable servants who would have gladly assumed the duty. He had even suggested to Joseph that maybe a servant should go in his stead—probably from a premonition caused by the recent bragging by Joseph or by the fact that Joseph seemed unusually eager to leave. Nevertheless, the ever persistent Joseph persuaded his father to send him.

When Jacob had contracted for the weaving of the multicolored tunic, he instructed Joseph to wear it only when he was not doing field duties, but Joseph insisted on wearing it on the inspection trips. He argued that the coat increased his authority, especially with his older brothers. Again Jacob acquiesced, contrary to his better judgment.

When Joseph arrived in Shechem, his brothers couldn't be found anywhere in the pastures. While wandering in the fields, Joseph came upon a man who appeared to be attending his father's flocks.

"Sire, who are you?" When the man identified himself as a hired man of a fellow named Reuben, Joseph quickly inquired about the whereabouts of his brothers.

The hired shepherd wasn't sure but thought that the brothers had some business in Dothan. He was a new shepherd, replacing a cousin who had worked for Joseph's family for many years; hence, he wasn't yet familiar with all their activities.

The normally reserved Joseph asked almost petulantly, "Why did all of them depart for Dothan at the same time?"

The shepherd did recall them talking with the lead shepherd before they left. From the tone of their voices, he got the general impression that they had some urgent business there. The lead shepherd was now on a perimeter tour, but should be back soon, the shepherd explained. Joseph might be able to find out about their reasons for leaving from him.

Joseph, still acting as a wronged child, asked, "Do they run off together very often?"

The shepherd reasserted that he knew nothing of their plans, which finally convinced Joseph that the employee had no further important information. Because it was late in the day, Joseph waited for the lead shepherd to return and asked him for sleeping quarters for the night. He would go Dothan the next day.

*   *   *   *   *

From afar, Simeon identified Joseph as one of the approaching riders, and he could tell that Joseph was angry from his hunched-forward riding position on the camel. He could also see that Joseph was trying to get the even-paced camel to increase his speed. His silhouette was exactly opposite the absolutely erect posture and the restriction on the reins of his normal approach.

Simeon immediately alerted his brothers that Joseph was approaching and appeared to be angry. He quipped that they must do something about *the* dreamer, or he would enslave them. Joseph's bearing and demands were becoming like those of the fabled Assurites. Levi suggested that they take his coat from him and spread his blood upon it to make it look as if a beast had torn him. Reuben countered by suggesting that they throw him into an animal pit; in time a ravenous beast should fall into it and do the job for them. It would be quite difficult to tear a coat to look as if it were torn by a wild beast.

The same resentment that Simeon, Levi, and Judah felt toward Joseph was also felt toward Reuben to a lesser extent. He had somewhat the same regal and condescending manner in dealing with them. That resentment, however, had become almost completely subdued because of the growing intense dislike for Joseph. Hence, the other three reluctantly accepted Reuben's plan without dispute, partially because Joseph was so near that they had to step aside for fear of being trampled by his camel.

Joseph dismounted his camel so quickly that he almost fell flat on his face—a stance lacking in regal bearing. He righted himself while assuming an imperious pose. "It is unforgivable for all four of you to leave my father's breeding herd in charge of servants. My father will certainly hear of your carelessness … or is it thievery? Have you segregated a portion of the flock in a hidden spot for thieves to pick up? If you are away from the herds, you can't be held directly liable for any loss, thereby concealing your theft."

Joseph's accusation was unfounded, because almost the opposite was true. There had been recent trouble with losses in the flocks at Dothan. Suspecting collusion by some of the shepherds there, the four brothers decided that all of them were needed to inspect the perimeter at Dothan and possibly set a trap for the thieves. Because they couldn't determine the loyalty of every servant, it wouldn't be safe to pick any for the entrapment plan.

This effrontery was all that Simeon could take. He instantly concluded that no reasonable explanation would satisfy Joseph. Therefore, he immediately grabbed him and easily wrestled the unsuspecting Joseph to the ground. Simeon was joined by Levi and Judah, who stripped the tunic from their accuser and bound him with leather thongs.

After a short ride to the pit, they inspected it to ensure that there was no way for Joseph to crawl out, whereupon they removed some of the covering and lowered him to the dry bottom. After using some of the branches to tear Joseph's tunic, the brothers carefully replaced the covering to camouflage the pit from warning any wild prey. They then left, ostensibly to return periodically until they found his torn body and to wipe his tunic with his bloody remains.

*   *   *   *   *

Unbeknownst to Simeon and Levi, his other two brothers had other plans for Joseph than killing him. Reuben intended to return to the pit and lift him out so that he could return to his father. As for Judah, he knew that it was about time for some caravans to be passing nearby. He would return to the pit, wait for a caravan train to appear, and sell Joseph to a member or members of the caravan after hailing the riders to the site.

Reuben pretended that he needed to inspect some areas north of Dothan for possible theft action. He would be careful not to get caught by any thieving bands and report back within a few days.

The other three brothers had ridden only a short distance farther before Judah spotted some wandering Ishmaelites. His immediate thought was to switch prospective buyers. The Ishmaelites were known to be involved in the growing slave trade in the area. Families had to take care to protect their children at all times—especially young, nubile daughters. If Judah sold Joseph to a caravan member, his owner might keep him in Canaan, where Jacob might learn his identity sooner or later, whereas the Ishmaelites would surely take him to Egypt to be sold as a slave and never be seen again.

Judah called out to the other two brothers, "Halt! I see a band of Ishmaelites in the distance. Why kill him when we can sell him as a slave for a good price? They will certainly take him to Egypt, where he will be out of our sight forever. We don't have to become killers to get rid of a tyrant."

Simeon complained that they wouldn't fool their father with a torn coat and animal blood. He reminded them of Reuben's comment about trying to fool him that way.

Judah continued to insist that they could fake the animal attack against Joseph. After an extended back-and-forth argument, Judah finally persuaded his two brothers to sell Joseph into slavery.

They backtracked to the pit only to find it empty.

Judah was furious. "See what you have done! While we talked, the Ishmaelites must have taken him away. You know how stingy our father is with our pay. Some servants live better than we do! A slave of Joseph's bearing would have brought a big price in Egypt. They would have paid us half of the sale price for him in Egypt. We have just forfeited many nights of merriment by losing him to them."

*   *   *   *   *

Judah was actually mistaken about who had removed Joseph from the pit. Joseph had started to yell when he thought his brothers were gone. Meanwhile, Judah had stopped scanning the landscape when he saw the Ishmaelites. A band of Midianites were closer to the pit but still obscured from view all during the time that Judah was on lookout. The Midianites heard Joseph's scream and rescued him from the pit. Their leader was originally inclined to let him go free until Joseph's boasting incensed him to cause him to change his mind when he spotted the Ishmaelites in the distance. He immediately hailed them to join his band.

The two leaders discussed what should be done with Joseph. The Midianite leader remained torn between selling Joseph to the Ishmaelites and escorting him to a safe place where he could escape to his freedom. The demands and complaints continued to sound from Joseph, despite the overwhelming numbers of antagonists surrounding him. In a fit of anger, the Midianite leader released Joseph into the custody of the Ishmaelites for half of the price Joseph would bring in Egypt. The rescuing leader had heard enough complaining from Joseph and wanted to be rid of him. His last words to the Ishmaelite leader were, "Get this insolent son of an ass out of here. Take him to the border of Egypt to our cousins, who will see that he stays out of our country."

The Ishmaelites, who would be reimbursed for their payment when they reached the border of Egypt, turned Joseph over to the cousins of the Midianite leader, who controlled most of the commerce coming into Egypt. The Egyptians hated so-called "sand eaters," such as the Ishmaelites, and would only deal with people coming from a "nobler" society, such as the Midianites.

*　　*　　*　　*　　*

Reuben had taken a lengthy route from and to the pit. The time required to cover the distance traveled had prevented him from seeing any of the happenings at the pit after the brothers had initially placed Joseph in it.

When Reuben looked into the pit, he lost his composure and nearly fainted from the shock. As he gradually recovered his senses, he remained transfixed, staring at the bottom of the empty pit. After a long time, he looked up, but he still had trouble getting his mind to contemplate what had happened or what he should do next. Had he closely scrutinized the state of the covering or the numerous camel tracks around the pit, he could have surmised that Joseph had been taken away by a group of people, possibly slave traders. Instead he abruptly left in his state of shock and raced back to his brothers, clueless to why Joseph wasn't in the pit.

Judah raised his hands at Reuben's first exclamation of wonder. "Reuben, he has been taken by some Ishmaelites. I had persuaded my brothers that we should sell him to a member of a passing caravan, but a band of Ishmaelites beat us to the pit and took him."

Reuben breathed a sigh of relief. His momentary joy in knowing that Joseph was alive was interrupted by a comment from Simeon that they still had a problem. They couldn't tell their father that he had been captured, because he would wonder why some of his other sons hadn't been taken also. Joseph wasn't inclined to wander off by himself where he could be abducted. The safest ruse would be to go with earlier thought of telling Jacob that he had been killed by a wild beast. Should Jacob ever want to see his body, they would say that the beast dragged him away, and they couldn't find his body.

After a long discussion, they had to agree that they were forced to adopt Levi's original suggestion. As Reuben left to kill a kid, he asked his brothers to bring him the tunic, so that he could sprinkle its blood on the coat.

The four brothers left their most trusted servant in charge of the flocks and brought the bloody tunic to Jacob. All of the four had reviewed the account of Joseph's demise several times and vowed to one another to abide by the story, regardless of what their father said or demanded.

Reuben had been chosen as the spokesman. He extended the torn and bloody tunic to his father and spoke with a convincing show of feigned ignorance. "We found this tunic in the field on the perimeter of our grazing area. Does this belong to Joseph?"

Jacob looked in stunned silence as he fingered the coat and turned it inside out and back again. "Yes, this is my son's tunic. I even remember the distinctive weave from the day that I took delivery of it."

The four had also agreed on telling their father as little as possible. They hoped that the act of appearing before him at once and the hint of innocence at the presenting of the tunic would lead their father to his own conclusion.

$$*\qquad*\qquad*\qquad*\qquad*$$

Jacob looked at his four sons, standing in a row before him, from left to right and back for three or four times. As the four later discovered, they didn't fool him for more than an instant. He could see that the tearing wasn't done by a claw, and his time spent as a shepherd enabled him to tell with virtual certainty the difference in texture between dried animal blood and dried human blood. In fact, he was rather sure that the blood on the tunic was from a goat. Nevertheless, the stoic looks of his sons also indicated that they wouldn't tell him anything about what had really happened to his beloved son.

The four sons continued to wait for a response from their father. Reuben broke the silence by offering him condolences for the loss and expressing sorrow that they hadn't taken care to be with him. They hadn't deemed accompaniment necessary, Reuben explained, because no fierce animals had been spotted near their pastures for over two years.

Realizing that the truth of the matter wouldn't be forthcoming, Jacob went along with the charade and spoke. "I have lost a son to a ravenous beast. I would ask for you to take me to the spot, but I couldn't bear seeing his remains. Perhaps we can send some servants to try to find his body." *I doubt that there is a body anywhere, but what have they done with him?* Jacob thought.

Reuben then assured him that the four of them had done a thorough search for Joseph's body. It would only endanger more lives to conduct a continued search that was almost certain to produce no findings. For the protection of the shepherds and animals, they had removed the flocks from the area where the tunic had been found. The flocks had indeed been moved, should Jacob question any of the shepherds about the incident.

Jacob held a memorial meeting for Joseph. After receiving deepest sympathies from family and servants, he started a period of mourning in sackcloth and ashes. The end of the official mourning didn't end Jacob's expression of grief. Hardly a day went by without a comment from Jacob bemoaning the loss of Joseph.

*   *   *   *   *

Jacob's constant harping on the loss of Joseph started to depress his children, who used every excuse they could find to get away from him. Judah became so upset from a combination of guilt and disgust at the harping that he left the family and went to work for a Canaanite ruler.

Meanwhile, Dinah chose to spend most of her time in Shechem, away from her quarrelling parents. Leah had also become upset because Jacob spent most of his days moaning. Not only did he neglect his conjugal duties, but he also made unpleasant company. Fortunately, the loss of Judah and the effective loss of Jacob caused few problems with operations. Jacob had gained a cadre of loyal and competent servants who performed all necessary duties well, even correcting misdirection from Jacob.

Dinah found a freedom in Shechem that seemed to be a turning point in the dull life she had bemoaned. This turning point would bring yet more grief to Jacob. Without her parents around, her brothers were lenient, even neglectful, in guiding her conduct. She purposely associated with the daughters of the surrounding tribes rather than those of the servants. After several weeks of Dinah's lack of apparent guidance and her blatant disregard of instructions given by her parents, a servant sent a detailed message to Leah describing Dinah's wild and careless behavior. The message prompted no response from Leah, whose despondency undoubtedly caused her to fail to understand the significance of the message. She even retained the papyrus without showing it to Jacob.

Dinah ranged farther and farther from the shepherd community in Shechem, spending most of her time with the children of the Hivites in the far northern part of Canaan. As the weeks of her nearly constant sojourn in the camp of the Hivites passed, the son of a tribe ruler gained a rapid infatuation for her. He soon sought methods to contact Dinah and her friends, gradually forcing Dinah's female companions to leave while he communed with Dinah.

As his communing changed more from talk to sensual gestures and advances, Dinah started to resist. She tried to get her friends to help her by complaining to the prince in question, who was named Shechem, after the popular place. Her companions, however, didn't care or were afraid to criticize the prince and said nothing. Meanwhile, Dinah continued to tease the prince with seductive poses, contradicting her rejection statements. The prince soon played his most effective proposal by saying that it was improper for a woman to deny the desires of a prince.

Whether this persuasion from Shechem or her own lust caused Dinah to acquiesce, none ever knew. She shunned her father and actually never spoke to him for the rest of her life, as events would soon dictate. She did mention the coercive statements made by the prince to her Hivite female companions, but didn't indicate whether it had caused her acceptance of intercourse.

*   *   *   *   *

Shechem didn't wait for enough time to pass to determine if Dinah were pregnant before he petitioned his father, Hamor, to obtain Jacob's consent to marry his daughter. His father looked at him almost in disbelief while telling him that he couldn't make such a request. The children of Jacob were forbidden even to associate with them, stemming from an edict that went back to Abraham, Dinah's great-grandfather.

Assuming such an edict, Shechem wondered why Dinah had associated with his friends and cousins. Maybe the restriction no longer applied because her brothers knew of her associations. He begged his father to talk Jacob because he loved Dinah very much. His soul desired her love to the extent that his stomach would scarcely hold down the food that he ate.

Hamor reluctantly agreed to his son's request to talk with Jacob. Shechem's initial proposal for marriage was firmly denied. But when intercourse between Shechem and Dinah was mentioned, Jacob indicated that he might agree to the marriage. He advised Hamor that he must talk with his sons about the suggestion first.

*   *   *   *   *

The idea of Dinah's marriage to a Hivite instantly brought rejection from all of Jacob's sons, but the announcement of Dinah's loss of virginity caused a sudden silence to the loud and interruptive conversations. This gave Jacob a chance to collect his thoughts and formulate a persuasive argument that the circumstance rather dictated the need for marriage. Although society accepted and even expected men to be promiscuous, it maintained an illogical moral standard for women compared to men. A violated woman had meager prospects for a good life and could even face starvation. Sometimes their only means of life resulted in harlotry.

*   *   *   *   *

While Jacob was pleading, Simeon and Levi were secretly conspiring. They allowed the discussion of their father's proposal to follow. When it seemed not to convince their other brothers, who reckoned that Dinah could live with members of her family as a spinster if necessary, they put forth a plan for acceptance of the marriage.

Simeon repeated one of the main objections raised to their father's proposal, which was the lack of circumcision among the Hivites. He believed one of the comments was, "We can't allow our sister to marry someone who is uncircumcised." They should propose that all of the men of Hamor be circumcised before the wedding was allowed. Once the circumcision was finished, they could verify the circumcision and let the marriage proceed.

*   *   *   *   *

The ruler, Hamor, and his son, Shechem, agreed to be circumcised after a short talk with each other. When they spoke to their citizens, however, a pronounced murmur arose. One of the older men in the group complained that circumcision was an unreasonable request. Even the people who practiced the ritual took great care to perform the cutting while the male child was still a baby. He believed that something was amiss. An even older and feebler man struggled to his feet to contradict the complainer. It was true that circumcision is only performed on the very young, but according to the traditional story, the noble Abraham and his grown male servants had been circumcised when they first came into Canaan. He certainly dreaded the pain, but he felt that they should comply.

Hamor smiled broadly as he recalled that the families of Isaac and Jacob had been good neighbors. While they had a considerable number of animals, the land was able to support Jacob's flocks and theirs. If the Hivites agreed with the demand, they would be allowed to marry into Jacob's family. Within a number of years, the Hivites should come to possess most of Jacob's flocks through dowry payments. Hamor knew that it was offensive to accept circumcision, but acceptance would provide great future wealth. Therefore, he was ordering all of them to see the physician to have the cutting done. For a little pain, they would acquire much wealth.

*   *   *   *   *

Jacob hadn't actually agreed to ongoing intermarriage, just the marriage of Dinah to Shechem. Hamor had misunderstood his vague reply when asked for continuing intermarriage between their families. Jacob wanted to get Dinah married without risking dispute or rejection from Hamor. He spent several nights in fitful sleep from concern over how Hamor would react to his denial when he came to realize that there would be no further marriages. He was rather sure that Hamor had interpreted his actual refusal as acceptance of future marriages.

Because Simeon and Levi had been the ones to suggest the condition of circumcision, Jacob allowed them to handle the setting of the time and place, and the assigning of physicians to perform the ritual. The brothers' first action was to convince the camp physician that he would be needed elsewhere on the day of circumcision. Hence, he would have to appoint assistants who were less skilled to perform the painful operation. These assistants would likely do more damage to the flesh, making for a more painful recovery.

After the circumcision was over, Simeon and Levi posted servants to watch the activity in Hamor's camp. The daily activity decreased by day two and seemed to stop completely on the third day. Simeon and Levi stealthily approached the camp during the twilight of the third day and went from tent to tent, slaying the moaning and incapacitated men, who were unable to defend themselves. Once all of the men were slain, Reuben and some of the servants joined them in robbing the camp of valuables and animals.

*　　*　　*　　*　　*

The brothers brought Dinah back with them to Hebron. They excitedly approached their father while bragging about how they had avenged the defilement of their sister. Before Simeon could utter another word, all got the scolding of their lives—even more castigating than the incident with Joseph.

"You fools! Do you have any idea what you have done? You don't have to answer that question, because the circumstances prove that any member of this family who had taken even a moment to think would never have done this. We are a small family with few protectors to defend us. You have given all of the tribes around us a reason to annihilate us."

Simeon showed no remorse by shouting that Shechem had defiled their sister. He further asserted that the family would have no standing among the tribes if they let this offense pass. The Hivites had gotten what they deserved for protecting the prince instead of delivering Shechem to them for punishment.

Jacob wasn't fazed in the slightest by their excuse. "Who gave you the right to administer punishment? I just recently read a report by a servant that said you allowed Dinah to associate with the cousins of Shechem in a manner unbecoming to a virtuous woman. As I see it, much of the blame for her defilement belongs on your heads. You were to care for your younger sister, and you failed to do so. Your disregard for my ban on close association with the tribes around you went unheeded, and we reaped a reward for your neglect or lack of concern for Dinah. I charge you with greed. You could have guessed that she would do what she did, giving you a chance to retaliate and acquire wealth of your own."

Simeon and Levi became so enraged that they started to attack their father, but were restrained by the servants protecting Jacob. Jacob had known that his sons were unlikely to accept the reprimand, so he brought along extra servants to protect him.

After his sons had been restrained for some time, Jacob spoke in a calmer voice. "Because you are my sons and your deed has validity in tradition, I will not punish you. You may live to see the effects of what you have done. Nevertheless, I must ask what we have to do should some of the surrounding tribes insist that I administer punishment, even death, to you."

Simeon and Levi both became composed at the reality of the question. Their reply, however, showed not the slightest hint of regret. They argued that tradition indeed required their slaying of Shechem and all of his supporters.

The defilement also merited compensation in valuables and animals. In fact, it was their desire that the proceeds of their spoils go to Dinah.

Reuben also interrupted to state that many of the tribes near them hated the family of Hamor. Undoubtedly, many of them were secretly pleased with the brothers' ridding the land of an oppressor. He cited a rumor circulating in the northern areas of Canaan that accused Hamor of getting much of his wealth through controlled stealing of animals. He never took enough animals to cause herders to be sure of the stealing; it was, however, strange that nearly all of the missing animals were prize stock.

Jacob made his summation of the matter. "I will leave it to God to deal with any punishment that you may or may not deserve. I recommend, because I am sure that I can't force you, to remain in Hebron and stay away from the surrounding tribes. I will contact the neighboring Perizzites and other tribes and tell them the reason for this action. I will try to persuade them that we are *not* out to conquer the land or harm anymore of the inhabitants."

*   *   *   *   *

While Jacob was trying to assuage any anger felt by the other Canaanite tribes, Dinah began planning her future in seclusion. She had established contacts not only with Canaanite people, but with people to the east who often frequented hostels along the caravan route. One of her contacts was a descendant of a son of Keturah, Abraham's wife.

He gained knowledge of the turmoil recently experienced by Dinah and resolved to help her. He accurately surmised that she would eventually be treated harshly by her family, possibly being ostracized. It was highly unlikely that she would ever lead a pleasant life with her family, and prospects for marriage would be bleak. He loved his cousin and decided to contact Dinah's servant with a plan to escort Dinah away from her family in secret. He doubted that Jacob or her brothers would allow him to marry her, and now was the time for her elopement before her activities came under closer scrutiny.

*   *   *   *   *

Dinah's servant requested a trip for her to Bethel, so she could perform a series of spiritual contemplations of remorse. Dinah spent a week in Bethel attending the altar that Abraham had built. The long years of overgrowth had recently been cleared, revealing an altar that had finally begun to crumble.

The community had decided to honor their ancestor by preserving it as is and not restoring it.

Early in the second week of Dinah's stay, servants of her cousin sneaked in under cover of deep twilight and led her away. Her two attending servants also left with her.

*　　*　　*　　*　　*

Because of Dinah's habit of rising late in the morning, her disappearance wasn't discovered until almost the meridian of the next day. The search party sent to find her was uncertain about what had happened to her. Another servant who had contact with her during her stay professed no knowledge of significant despondency by her. Really, she had seemed to become happier every day of her stay. After a wide perimeter search for her body, they were rather certain that she hadn't committed suicide. They concluded that she had been abducted. The leader of the Bethel community sent a preliminary report of their completed actions and conclusions along with an outline of further actions they would take in trying to find her.

Before the Bethel community got a response from Hebron, a messenger arrived at Bethel with a document signed by Dinah. She gave a description of how she had eloped and was now married. She gave no indication of her exact location and advised her family not to look for her. She was sorry for her actions in betraying her family, but she was beginning a new life with people who loved her. She wanted no contact with her former family and pleaded with them to disown her while once again stressing that they were to avoid contacting her.

*　　*　　*　　*　　*

Her message was forwarded to Jacob in Hebron. When he read the message, he almost smiled. *Dinah has made a wise decision in marrying now. Also, knowing my presumptuous sons, her life here would soon have become miserable. Daughter, I should have loved you more, but you have more sense than all of my sons.*

Jacob decided to wait and see if her brothers would even miss their sister. Their probably feigned offense over what happened to her would likely be forgotten, as her person would also.

Unexpectedly, Simeon inquired about Dinah's whereabouts in less than a moon from her leaving for Bethel.

After listening to Jacob's reciting of Dinah's message, Simeon became visibly upset but only grumbled a few indistinguishable words. Jacob assumed his reaction meant that he was up to no good.

Jacob exclaimed in a loud voice, "This day I pronounce a curse upon anyone who tries to find Dinah and interfere with her wishes. She has chosen her future well, and I don't want anyone depriving her of it, whether from an intent to help or harm. Everyone failed her. Let someone who truly loves her enrich her life."

Both Simeon and Levi went away sulking, while Reuben seemed to accept the command readily. After all, he had his own world to manage, and Dinah never listened to or liked him anyway.

*   *   *   *   *

As all of this was happening, Judah steadily grew in his sympathy and actions toward the pagan ways of his benefactor. Jacob's consolation in the fortunate outcome in Dinah's life was offset by the knowledge that Judah had become pagan and was engendering children by a pagan wife.

FIFTEEN

REGATHERING OF FAMILY

THE UNEASY PEACE THAT Jacob was able to establish between his family and the Canaanites brought calm to his family once again. As it continued to prevail, he was able to spend more time visiting his father. Isaac had become a pitiful sight: almost blind, barely able to stand, and almost completely deaf. Jacob did nearly all of the talking during these visits. His father had obviously become tired of trying to make an effort to hear; his replies were always a positive response. None of the children were permitted to speak with him unless an adult was present, because they made fun of Isaac by asking sets of questions demanding alternating positive and negative responses and laughing at the incongruity of his answers. Nevertheless, his attending nurse had noticed how much happier Isaac's expression was whenever someone talked to him. Therefore, Jacob would keep his father company by discussing the affairs of the day without a pause for any response.

The breeding stock in Shechem had diminished in quality for the past two years. A rally in Jacob's father's spirits coincided with the time for the selection of the breeding animals. Jacob left for Shechem concluding that he would be able to oversee the selection process and be back in Hebron before his father died. He was finishing his duties in Shechem and preparing to return to Hebron within a couple of days when a messenger arrived with the news that his father was dead. Jacob asked the messenger to wait while he drafted instructions for a memorial service for his father. After the instructions were written, he attached a list of invitees. He was sure that Esau would want to attend his father's service, even though Esau had disregarded that of his mother.

Because he couldn't be present for the burial and the memorial was days away, Jacob remained at Shechem for another week, mostly contemplating his father's life and what he would say at the memorial.

The servants riding back to Shechem with him had never seen Jacob so reflective and introverted. Despite their best efforts, he talked about nothing but the happenings around him at the moment. On the morning of their arrival in Hebron, a servant mentioned how Jacob's many days of service to Isaac had blessed him.

Jacob couldn't suppress tears as he finally spoke about his father: "Yes, he has been a blessing to many of the people around him. He experienced setbacks, but every one of those setbacks seemed to be replaced with a great blessing. Until the last several years, I was never as comfortable with my father as I was with my mother. Nonetheless, our closeness in the recent years didn't bring a sense of deep, forgiving empathy from him as I had from my mother. I do mourn the death of my father, but I will let Esau have the honor of addressing the final praises to my father. He had a relationship with my father during his early years that I never had. Although Esau became alienated from him for the past several years, his passing will surely help my brother to recall the pleasant times he spent in youthful days with him."

The servant praised Jacob for the noble thing he was doing by extending an unwarranted forgiveness to Esau. The mention of forgiveness stung Jacob to the extent that he let the conversation end until they reached home. Esau had acted harshly with him as a child, and Esau had long neglected his father, but Jacob had deprived him of both his birthright and the main blessing from his father. Now, in reflection, the torment that he had received from Esau was small compared to what he received from the birthright and the blessing. And yet he, too, had paid a high price for these two benefactions. His life, starting with his father's blessing, had been one great struggle tinged with sorrow. The promise of the birthright to be fulfilled through his children brought seemingly constant family problems, and the wealth had been a burden to acquire.

Upon arrival at home, Jacob found high activity that immediately alleviated his despondency, as his sadness was replaced with the busyness of coordinating the chaos around him. Surprisingly, several leaders of the surrounding tribes had arrived—even uninvited ones—to pay homage to Isaac, and his servants weren't prepared to provide them lodging or care for their animals. The problem had been made worse because some servants had been sent to invite distant friends and relatives. Fortunately, the members of Jacob's entourage were well rested from the previous night and immediately helped correct the situation upon alighting from their camels.

Esau arrived the next day to a tearful reunion with his brother. After a brief review of their recent past, Jacob asked Esau to give the final blessing at the service for their father. "Brother, you had a close association with our father in your younger days. Don't you want to give your last regards for the good things that he did for you? I have reconciled to him for the last many years, but the closeness that you had with him, I never experienced. Please honor him and even me by giving the final words of praise."

Esau thoughtfully considered Jacob's suggestion and agreed. His speech extolled the virtues of his father, not mentioning any of the family problems. After the ceremony was over, the two brothers knelt in front of their father's grave while bowing their heads and hugging each other.

The years immediately following Isaac's death were exceptionally prosperous. Even as Jacob prospered and turned much of his wealth into exchange metals, he felt unease, almost an impending doom. The traumas of the past few years and the evident prosperity helped to direct his sons away from concern over their inheritance. The sadness over what had happened to their sister, Dinah, and the death of their grandfather also helped them to focus on other things in life besides wealth, because the abundance of their father's wealth allayed any fears of poverty.

Even Judah began to spend more time with his brothers, even expressing a desire to work for his father. When Judah asked permission for his children to associate with the children of his brothers, Jacob readily agreed. "Judah, I have never forbidden your family any association with us. Your alienation from me and your brothers was your doing and not ours."

"Father, you forbade us to marry into the other tribes. When I took Shuah for a wife, how could I not stay away?"

"Son, you are absolutely right in that I didn't want any marriage with the pagans around us, but once you disobeyed and the marriage was consummated, my command was irrelevant. In fact, I strongly desire your family's association with us, so we can win you over from paganism. Please return to your family."

*   *   *   *   *

Meanwhile, Jacob's son, Joseph, for whom he still silently mourned, had ascended to the office of a secondary pharaoh in Egypt. Egypt, like Canaan, was in the midst of a prosperity boom. Like his father, Joseph felt uneasy over the burgeoning wealth of his land. Unlike his father, however, Joseph knew for certain that the prosperity wouldn't last. God had appeared to him in a dream, which revealed a seven-year abundance of crops to be followed with seven of famine.

Being forewarned, Joseph instantly petitioned the lead pharaoh to avert a disaster that would certainly befall his land in the near future. Through an edict of seemingly illogical rationing of food during a period of abundant crops, Joseph oversaw the accumulation of immense amounts of grain and foodstuffs to be used when the famine struck. His efforts would prove to save not only his new country, but his family in Canaan also. Additionally, the stored wealth of Egypt would lead to the fulfillment of the dream of Joseph's youth that had led to his brothers causing his capture by slave traders. That dream foretold his rulership over his family, including his father.

*　　*　　*　　*　　*

Judah tried to persuade his sons to visit their cousins without much success. The sons not only thought that their cousins were boring, but they also spent much of their time together fighting. He soon withdrew from his family again. Judah had hoped that the meeting with his cousins would influence his oldest son to give up association with the local warlocks and witches.

Because the attempt to influence his son Er toward humane behavior failed, Judah tried a last resort by procuring a wife for his oldest son. For a few days after his marriage, Er seemed to enjoy marriage and forget witchcraft and necromancy. By the end of the first moon after the marriage date, he had reverted to immersion in the rituals of witchcraft. He not only completely neglected his conjugal duties, but was constantly too inebriated to work. Just as Judah despaired of what to do, Er left home in a drunken state for another ritual observance. Before he got more than fifty steps from home, he fell to the ground, writhing. His wife, Tamar, who had sadly watched him leave, ran to his side only to have him die in her arms as she tried to control his convulsions.

Judah dispensed with a mourning period for his son and buried him in an unmarked grave. The shock of Er's death at such a young age by means other than an accident disturbed Judah's family. Whether this death caused the second son, Onan, to act foolishly years later was never determined. When Onan came of age to marry, Judah pleaded with him to fulfill tradition and marry his older brother's childless wife, Tamar. Judah began to fear for his second son's life also. Despite having his mind clouded with pagan superstitions, he knew enough of the life of his immediate ancestors to understand that a superior being could guide events in the world. He sensed in some way that this being had been displeased with his oldest son and had taken his life.

Before despair could set in, however, Onan agreed to marry Tamar. Less than two weeks after the marriage, Judah was awakened by the frantic cries of his daughter-in-law, proclaiming that his second son was dead. He couldn't believe the news and rushed to Onan's bedroom, fully expecting to have to wake him from a drunken stupor. Unfortunately, Onan's stupor was more permanent than lethargy brought on by too much alcohol. He was dead.

Tamar's description of Onan's conduct toward her during their intimate encounters left Judah aghast. Every time Onan had engaged in coitus with his wife, he arose from the marriage bed before he could deposit his seed and let it spill on the ground. Tamar was rather sure that she would not have been impregnated during any of those encounters. Judah denied the account in his mind until Tamar was able to show evidence on the rug near the bed from the last sexual activity. Judah went away in sorrow to bury his second son, whom he placed in a marked grave.

As she expected, Tamar remained childless. When she asked her father-in-law what she should do about marrying, he promised that he would give her his third son, Shelah, when he reached the proper age. Tamar was pleased with the promise and agreed to wait for Shelah. Judah's offer of his third son in marriage came more from shame than a desire to fulfill the tradition of having younger brothers marry the childless widow of an older brother. His secret desire was to delay the giving of his third son in marriage long enough to cause Tamar to remarry someone else or engage in an act of harlotry.

The succeeding years brought famine to Egypt and decreased rainfall in Canaan. Jacob had been through a drought period many years before and recognized the signs of an increasing dryness. Accordingly, he began to decrease his herd size, expressing his hope that he would be able to survive this one without a great loss of wealth. While he had wisely converted a considerable amount of his wealth to exchange items and jewelry, he knew that ultimate wealth was created by ownership of flocks.

Shortly after the death of his second son, Onan, Judah resumed contact with his family that eventually led to complete reconciliation with his family. The event that drove him to this reconciliation arose from his resolve to avoid fulfilling his agreement with Tamar about giving Shelah to her in marriage. As time passed after the death of his first two sons, he searched for a reason for their deaths that didn't include any blame upon him or his sons. He quickly went from blaming himself or his sons to considering Tamar to be an evil woman who caused the death of his children.

*   *   *   *   *

Shelah matured at an early age, causing Tamar to ask her father-in-law almost incessantly for his marriage to her. At first Judah was able to dissuade her by claiming that Shelah was still too young. When it became obvious that Judah wouldn't allow the marriage, Tamar decided upon drastic measures to settle the inheritance issue.

She knew that Judah had frequented harlots since the death of his wife. Therefore, she dressed up as one and waited by the roadside on a route that he took to visit the shearers during this shearing season.

Late in the afternoon of that day, Judah decided to return home. Tamar's position by the road was close by to a hostel but hidden from view of the proprietors. Judah ogled her as he passed but walked on by; however, his burning lust must have overcome him, because he retraced his steps and asked her to join him for a night of passion at the hostel.

After Judah had satisfied his lust and lay back to relax, Tamar gave an excuse that she needed to see other clients yet and asked for payment for services rendered. Her real reason was that she wanted to be gone before morning to ensure that she wouldn't be discovered. She had worn a veil until the dark of the night, but she was afraid that he would see her without it on before she could leave in the morning.

Judah hadn't expected to encounter a harlot on his trip back and forth from home. Consequently, he didn't have enough exchange metals to pay for the room and Tamar's services. He gave her some expensive jewelry to hold as a surety. He would return within two days with the payment and reclaim his goods.

*   *   *   *   *

Two days later, Judah walked up to the hostel owner and asked, "Where's your harlot? I must pay her for her services of two days ago."

"Sire, there *is* no harlot here. I run a responsible lodging place. Harlots attract too many people of low class." Judah blanched at the comment but decided to let it pass, because he was intent on reacquiring his jewelry. He listened as the owner continued, "We are careful to run all such women off our premises. The more stubborn ones sometimes have to be threatened by being reported to the authorities. I wasn't here two days ago, but my son was. I will get him for you. I am sure that he can support my word that there was no harlot here on that day."

The son verified the owner's assertion. "Father, this man rented lodging with his elegantly dressed wife. She and the wife of a traveling trader were the only women to stay at our hostel that night."

Judah started to bluster just as the trader and his wife entered the hostel on their return trip and also stated that they had seen Judah and his wife on the night in question. Judah had to accept that he had essentially been robbed by someone who knew his habits and life's actions well. Inquiries, some discreet and some not, over the succeeding days failed to reveal who the harlot could have been. After a few days, he decided that the effort to recover his jewelry wasn't warranted by the amount of the loss.

Within three months, one of attendants realized that Tamar was pregnant and told Judah about it. Because Tamar had no husband, the logical conclusion was that she had committed fornication. When questioned by Judah, she readily admitted to her pregnancy. But before she had a chance to tell him that he was the father of what proved to be twin boys, Judah angrily demanded that she be put to death for the harlotry that she had committed while a member of his family.

The servants next to Judah looked at him with a mixture of wonder, doubt, fear, anger, and humor. Here was a sensual man driven by various carnal urges—the chief one being sexual desire—condemning another of falling prey to his main weakness. Judah stared at his servants, who remained transfixed to the spots where they stood. When he saw that they weren't obeying his command, he lunged toward Tamar and grasped her by the shoulders.

Despite her pregnant condition, Tamar was still quite lithe and strong. She instantly raised her arms and made a sideways chopping motion against his arms, easily deflecting his grasp. She spun away and reached into a pouch by her wardrobe, extracting some jewelry that registered recognition by him.

"Master Judah, I believe these pieces of jewelry are the items that you pledged to me for the night of passion that I gave you, which now has me pregnant with what I believe are twins."

One of the servants lowered her head and ran from the room, barely suppressing her laughter until she was outside. She actually had no need to worry about embarrassing herself or her master, because Judah stood motionless while staring at the jewelry in disbelief. His senses were so focused on what Tamar held in her hand that he couldn't have noticed what anyone else around him was doing.

The shock of the moment seemed to remove all sensation from his body. He probably would have collapsed, had Tamar's voice not restored some sensation to his body. "I am returning these items to you now ... although, as an official concubine, I feel that I deserve possession of them. I will, however, return them to you if you wish. As regarding tradition, you have now provided me with children. My childless state should be over within a few more moons. I should but have yet to feel remorse over what I have done and caused you to do. I acted improperly, but you must let me live. I carry your children—boys, I am sure."

Judah regained his voice, which still sounded hollow and unreal to him. "Tamar, you will indeed live and bear my sons—or daughters, in case you are wrong. I must talk with you alone, but before anyone leaves, I wish to make a confession to all. I have these many years carried myself in rebellion against my family with an unrealistic self-appraisal of my own worth. I can't remember a time when I didn't feel that I was superior to all around me. You just saw how that feeling of self-importance resulted in my belief that I have the right to proclaim who lives and who dies."

Judah walked over to Tamar and took a bracelet from her hand before continuing. "Also, this bracelet proves that I can devalue the morals and status of another individual for deeds that I allow myself to do without the slightest feeling of guilt. Within these last few moments, I have come to realize that I hold the regard of my own person to be far greater than those who are nobler than I am."

With those words, Judah stopped talking. The attendants seemed to sense that he was through speaking to them and wanted to talk to Tamar. After everyone else had departed, Tamar politely nodded to him to speak. She directed her attention to him and seemed to listen carefully, although she probably could have guessed what he would say. "Tamar, I guess you know that we can't live as husband and wife, and you should remain unmarried for the rest of your life. Do not despair, for I will treat you as a wife in all respects, except for conjugal duties. Although I am to blame, your actions have changed our lives in an unpleasant way."

For the first time, Tamar addressed him as Lord and agreed with his condition for her life. She ended her talk with a promise to be a good mother to his boys, because she still insisted that they would be twins.

Judah contacted his father within a week of the incident with Tamar. He begged forgiveness from his father and asked to move closer to Jacob.

"Son, I do forgive you for your ill feelings toward me and my family. We do, however, have a greater problem than your move. We are nearly out of grains for the sustenance of both us and our animals. I have reduced our herds to a bare minimum. These few animals are the best breeding stock and must be maintained if we are to live as shepherds in the future. Most of the tribes around here are doing better than we are, because they have gone to Egypt to buy grain. Please go to Egypt with all of your brothers and buy the grain we need to sustain us. This drought is now upon all our surrounding country and will not be gone soon."

All of the brothers gathered for the trip to Egypt except Benjamin. When Jacob's youngest son started preparation for the trip, he was ordered to quit packing his belongings, because he was not leaving with his brothers. Benjamin objected strongly but wasn't able to change his father's mind.

"Benjamin, you are the only child by your mother, Rachel, that I have left. As you know, she gave her life giving birth to you. She was also my special love. I won't let you put your life in danger by going on this trip. Your ten brothers should be able to handle the transportation of the grains. Consequently, I am sending only four servants with them. Fourteen men should be enough."

* * * * *

Even a contingent the size of Jacob's sons drew the attention of Egyptian officials as they entered the country. When Joseph heard their description of the purpose of the visit, he suspected who they were. His dream of many years prior came vividly back to his mind. The inspiration of his dream about to be fulfilled and the joy over getting to see his brothers again filled him with mixed emotions. He almost decided to run out and greet everyone with a hug, but he changed his mind and instead disguised himself until he knew their plight in Canaan.

As he ascended his throne, Joseph congratulated himself for deciding on the disguise, because he only saw his ten half-brothers standing in front of him. An urge to ease his mind over the whereabouts of his younger brother, Benjamin—even his existence—was suppressed as he allowed the men identify themselves.

After a detailed description of their home of origin and purpose for visiting Egypt, Joseph accused them of being spies. This ruse was partly a plan of punishment for what they had done to him and partly a means by which to get to see his younger brother. He suspected that his father would never let Benjamin out of his sight after losing Joseph. He also knew that his father disliked Egypt and might even refuse to travel to see him even if he knew Joseph were alive. Also, the knowledge of his being a ruler in this hated country could keep him away. His father surely would remember the dream that Joseph had related to him years ago. Being an independent and self-sufficient man, his father probably couldn't stand to be ruled over by his son and would nearly starve before he would move to Egypt with Benjamin.

* * * * *

Joseph's brothers vehemently protested the charge of espionage. Their denials, however, seemed to fall on deaf ears as Joseph soon placed them under arrest. By the second day of detention, they began to accuse one another of being responsible for their plight through some alleged impropriety committed during the past or present.

On the morning of the fourth day, the lead ward keeper informed them that they would be released, but they must see the pharaoh again to agree to the conditions for their freedom. The revived mood of the brothers became quickly deflated when they learned that they must leave one of them behind as surety and bring Benjamin to Egypt to redeem the one left behind.

To avoid offending the pharaoh with an outright refusal of his request, they feigned a need for time to determine who would stay. They had to come up with a proposal that wouldn't require Benjamin to come to Egypt, because his father would never allow it. Reuben stared intensely at Simeon before criticizing him for what he had caused. The God that their fathers worshipped must have brought this retribution upon them because of what they had done to Joseph. He had told him not to harm Joseph, but he had to fulfill his spite.

Simeon appeared scarcely able to contain himself from striking his older brother before scorning the accusation as ridiculous. It was evident that Joseph had been taken into slavery by some bedouin. Someone as elegant as Joseph would have brought a goodly price in the slave market. Likely, Joseph was some ruler's head valet in this very land, Simeon argued as he rejected Reuben's stupid remarks. Simeon threatened that unless Reuben retracted what he had just said, he would bloody his nose.

Reuben advised him against such action. First, they had enough trouble without giving their captors an excuse to throw them into some more loathsome prison. Second, was Simeon sure that he was strong enough not to receive severe punishment in return?

The belligerence soon subsided, and the brothers spent more than a twelfth-day trying to come up with a counter-proposal. As the ward keepers approached, Simeon agreed with unusual contrition that Reuben was right. He was the leader in getting them into this situation. Were Joseph with them, their father would certainly have let all twelve of them make this trip. Arguably, had Joseph been with them, he would have talked the pharaoh out of half of Goshen by now. Yes, it was his duty to volunteer to be their hostage. He believed that this pharaoh would treat him well as a slave. He bade them to take good care of his family, because he was sure that their father would never risk sending Benjamin to Egypt to redeem him.

Before the ward keepers could lead the brothers away to the pharaoh, which none of them suspected to be Joseph, Simeon asked to say good-bye to his brothers. He further requested enough time to hug and kiss each of his brothers. Simeon tactfully added, without revealing his doubts of ever being free again, that he had no assurances of ever seeing them again.

*　　*　　*　　*　　*

By the time the ward keeper imprisoned Simeon, the wagons and animals were laden. Despite the sorrow from starting home without the missing brother, Reuben set a fast pace toward home. When the others complained about the strain on the heavily laden animals, Reuben told them that they would slow down after they were beyond the sight of the pharaoh's compound. They must get out of sight before the pharaoh placed some other restriction upon them.

About midway home, Reuben decided to give the animals a day of rest and to stop at an inn. While rewarding their animals with some of the grain from their sacks, the brothers discovered all of the exchange metals that they had given to the Egyptian treasurer. Reuben once again expressed his chagrin by asking how they were going to explain this to their father. They couldn't retrace their steps back to Egypt, because the animals would be tired just by the completion of the rest of their trip. Also, the officials probably hadn't noticed the missing money, or they would have already overtaken them. He accused Judah of taking the metals. Where money was concerned, Judah was usually involved.

Judah flushed with anger and then burst out with incredulous laughter, "Brother, I am not responsible for this. I am just as surprised as you are about why the metals are in our sacks. Besides, when did I ever have an opportunity to steal the metals and place them in all of these sacks? You are a fool! And since when are you concerned over what our father thinks? You haven't been very accommodating to his wishes for a long time. I heard about some of your antics even while I was living with the Philistines. Our father will survive this tragedy, as he has many others. I know of no other man who faces the terrible events of life as he does. Don't worry; I am sure that I can assuage his grief and yet another disappointment from the vain actions of his sons."

A moody, depressed group of nine brothers rode into camp. Judah didn't have time to mention the absence of Simeon before Jacob asked, "Where is Simeon? Has death befallen our family again?" When Judah finished telling him about all that happened in Egypt, Jacob wailed loudly, "I now have lost two sons, because I cannot allow Benjamin to go to Egypt in hope of rescuing Simeon from slavery. There's no guarantee that the pharaoh will keep his word. It seems that he dealt with you capriciously. I hate to imagine what the rulers of that dark land might do to the tender young Benjamin."

A long and heated argument followed over why the brothers had told the pharaoh about Benjamin's existence and about their robbing the pharaoh of payment for his grain. Jacob finally held up his hands to demand their attention.

"All right, what you have done can't be changed. If none of you will admit theft, I must forget the matter. As sad as I am about losing Simeon, there's nothing that I can do about it either. I just hope that each of you will finally learn some lessons from what you did. God is punishing us with drought, and you sometimes act worse than the thieving bedouin around us. May God yet bless us with rain, so we never have to seek grain again."

*   *   *   *   *

The unanswered prayer for rain showers caused the supply of grain gradually to dwindle, even with further reduction in herd sizes. Amid the gloom over losing Simeon and the stress of deciding how to support a large community during a severe drought, even more distressing news tormented Jacob. Leah had been ailing for the past few moons after having suddenly taken ill from a state of seemingly vibrant health. Within a week of learning of Simeon's confinement, the physician left her quarantine tent and told Jacob that she likely wouldn't live until sunset.

Although he had expected this news at almost any time, Jacob still spoke from shock. "How can this be? She is still young. What has she done to shorten her life?"

The physician reminded Jacob how they had talked about the declining life span of humans. Leah had never been as healthy as she seemed. She had always been a determined woman bent on getting the most out of life. People often considered such persons to be strong because they masked their illnesses and weaknesses. He had known her for many years and was a bit surprised that she had lived this long.

"Why haven't you mentioned this to me before?"

He explained that as a physician, it was his duty to keep any speculations about the people that he attended secret. If he didn't know their quality of health for sure, it was wrong for him to tell others. One reason for his secrecy was that his speculations were often wrong. Unfortunately, in Leah's case, they appeared not to have been.

After the physician nodded yes to Jacob's request to see her, the latter walked toward her tent. Leah was awake with her head elevated by pillows sheathed in brilliant colors, which seemed to give her an almost healthy glow.

Jacob stood silent for a long time until Leah spoke. "The physician reluctantly answered my question about how long I have to live. Husband, I have had a good life despite many disappointments, but the only really sad thing about dying is not knowing the fate of our son Simeon. Please do all that you can to rescue him. I know there are mercenaries who secretly remove prisoners or escaped wrongdoers from Egypt. Please consider contracting one or more of them to bring Simeon back home. That is my only request. Otherwise, my life has been fulfilled beyond what I could have ever dreamed of as a young girl."

After another long pause, Jacob scarcely could speak through tears. "Leah, I am truly thankful for your acceptance of me as your husband. There's nothing that I can do to undo the slights and neglects of the past. Nevertheless, you faithfully stood by me all of these years. I promise to do all within my powers to find Simeon. Also, all of your sons will receive a just share of my wealth. I have wisely sold most of my animals at a time when they brought a goodly price. Assuming God blesses us with rain soon, I should have a considerable estate to give to them."

Leah smiled and drifted off to sleep from which she aroused for brief periods. About a twelfth-day before sunset, she slowly exhaled her last breath. Leah was buried in Machpelah next to Jacob's mother, Rebekah. After a short grieving period, Jacob asked his sons to return to Egypt for more feed and food.

As all of the sons stood, clearly not knowing how to respond, Judah hesitantly replied, "Father, we can't return to Egypt. You won't let us take Benjamin, and the pharaoh sternly forbade us to enter Egypt without him."

"Are you sure that you understood him correctly? Why would the ruler of an imposing land like Egypt be interested in the youngest son of a shepherd? You are speaking foolishly again."

Several exchanges of denials, including supporting arguments from all of Judah's brothers, finally got Jacob to relent. "All right, if we must, take Benjamin. The drought has become so severe that I have no choice but to risk his life. Prepare to leave on the day after tomorrow; we will need all of tomorrow to pack the payment and provisions for your trip." Jacob walked away murmuring about the stupidity of his sons for mentioning the existence of Benjamin to the pharaoh.

Jacob supervised the assembling of goods the following morning, ensuring that exchange metals for the prior provisions received were included with the current payment. His pleasant demeanor became dour when Reuben complained about the inclusion of a generous amount of balm from Gilead in the payment sack.

"Son, I know that the price of balm has become exorbitant, even if you can find it. I also know that our wives and physicians won't like reducing our inventory of it, but I must. Many Egyptians love our balm above any product that these lands produce. My generous accommodation to their likes will help ensure Benjamin's safety. Your description of the pharaoh indicates a man who can be influenced by respect shown to him."

*   *   *   *   *

Meanwhile, the mood of the two brothers in Egypt followed strangely divergent paths. Simeon resolved from the outset that he would never see his family again. The respect for the God of his fathers—a God he didn't understand—prevented him from becoming deeply despondent and committing suicide. This servitude was his punishment for his vile action toward his brother Joseph. He even felt a bit of gratitude toward his masters, because only light work duties were given him. He did fear, however, that as the years wore on, he would be assigned onerous duties.

Conversely, Joseph, the master, suffered more consternation than Simeon did. He became apprehensive that his father would rely on the prospect for rains that wouldn't come in time to save them from death by sickness from poor nutrition, or from servitude by being too weak to defend against a foe. He just hoped that his father wouldn't try to beat the unbeatable foe: drought. The concern for his father and brothers changed Joseph's countenance so much that one of his aides sent a message to the lead pharaoh of the land about his condition. Joseph's reputation as an administrator above all others mustn't be allowed to wane for any reason. The head ruler of Egypt immediately dispatched his two leading consultants to see about Joseph's unhappiness.

*   *   *   *   *

Not wishing to alarm Joseph by their sudden appearance, the aides notified him of their arrival by a message requesting that he accommodate them with a review of feedstock storage and security procedures. They hoped that this ruse would allow them to determine his problem during their talks. Given Joseph's reluctance to reveal his personal feelings, they knew better than to confront him about his gloomy countenance.

By the late morning of the second day, they had no reason for further inquiry. Just before the day's meridian, a courtier entered with news that ten brothers from Canaan were in the visitor's area, waiting to see him and hoping to redeem their brother Simeon. Joseph's countenance abruptly shone through a broad smile, and he arose as he informed the courtier to bring the brothers to the ruler's bench. The perplexed aides to the lead pharaoh said nothing when Joseph excused himself, but followed him to greet the visitors.

*   *   *   *   *

Before stepping from behind the curtains, Joseph paused to look at his brothers, especially Benjamin. He remained silent and motionless for a long time, overcome with emotion at the sight of his full brother, Benjamin. When an accompanying assistant motioned for him to proceed, he shook his head and replied, "No, I have changed my mind. I will not see them now, but greet them at a banquet. Please tell the food preparers to cook a large feast for me and my visitors. Also, have the guards bring the prisoner Simeon to my dining area when the meal is ready to serve."

The assistant looked at him incredulously; Egyptian rulers didn't eat with shepherds. But he said nothing when he noticed the two high-level officials standing behind Joseph. He indicated his understanding of the instructions and left to get the meal preparation started.

*   *   *   *   *

Meanwhile, Joseph's brothers waited in apprehension for their appearance at the pharaoh's quarters. The general consensus arose among them that he planned some particularly cruel fate for them. Exactly what they should say to assuage the wrath of the pharaoh soon became the topic of concern.

Only Judah framed a positive response about their fate. He scolded his brothers for their depressive mood. "In recent months, I have started to understand the God of our fathers. Although most of my life has been spent following my own will, the incident with Tamar caused me to change my attitude toward the way I conduct my life. This God promised a family of nations to descend from our grandfather Isaac. That promise could never be fulfilled if we were to die; Dinah's descendants would be counted through that of her husband. For at least this time, place some trust in that God to see us through this meeting. Contrary to all of you, I feel confident that good results will come from this meeting."

Judah's brothers still didn't believe him, but his argument was so forceful that they nodded and quit making negative speculation. Judah smiled as he noticed that the doubt on their faces countered their tacit agreement.

As the brothers were being escorted by the steward of Joseph's house, several of them began to speak at once. Reuben quickly motioned for silence.

Because Judah had been the most positive among them, he was asked to speak for them.

Judah spoke in a firm voice. "Sir, we earnestly beg your forgiveness for failing to pay for the provisions provided to us on our first trip. We didn't notice that we still had the money with us until we were too far away to return for payment. We now have a double payment for the additional provisions that we must buy. We have also brought a special gift for the pharaoh. We hope that this action will atone for the injustice that we committed on our last trip."

The steward laughed loudly. He explained that he had known that they were departing with the money and that there had been no false dealing by them. As an honor to the God of their father and grandfather, he had the money returned. Also, he noticed that they had brought Benjamin with them. Therefore, the pharaoh would honor his pledge by returning their brother Simeon from detention. He had been treated well during their absence.

A collective sigh emanated from the brothers before an extended round of hugs and kisses were given to Simeon. As Reuben started to ask the first question about what happened to him during his imprisonment, Joseph appeared with the steward by his side.

By the time Joseph had finished asking several questions about their father, Jacob, and giving a special salutation to their youngest brother, Benjamin, the brothers were making questioning glances at each other. Furthermore, when Joseph ordered for the brothers to be seated according to the order of their birth and had an elaborate fare of food placed in front of Benjamin, they were even more perplexed. Stunned by the events of the day and unsure what they should say in the presence of the pharaoh and his aides, who ate at a separate table, the diners enjoyed their meal mostly in silence.

*   *   *   *   *

After the meal, the brothers were shown to spacious living quarters normally reserved for visiting dignitaries. The Egyptian escorts promptly left, giving the brothers ease to speak. Reuben turned to Simeon to get an explanation for the strange events they had just experienced. The only thing that made any sense had been the pharaoh and his aides eating at a separate table. He didn't understand the pharaoh's familiarity with a group of despised shepherds.

Simeon shrugged as he told Reuben that his suppositions were as good as his. He had expected to do heavy labor during imprisonment. Instead, he was given light duties around the court area, although he was never allowed into the pharaoh's inner court. Their fate in Egypt had been both strange and pleasant.

All of the brothers arose very early, because their hosts had scheduled their departure within a twelfth-day after sunrise. They gave one another short but cheerful greetings and then hurried their preparations to leave. Not until they were under way did they have a chance to ask Simeon to give an account of how he felt about going home. The elated Simeon became verbose in expressing his joy. He especially stressed how he intended to change his ways out of gratitude to the God who must have saved him.

The conversation had just turned to others when the brothers were overtaken by an Egyptian troop led by the steward who had just overseen their departure. Not without considerable frustration did they pause with more than one uttering something to the effect, "What now?"

The steward spoke in a manner that was loud and convincing. At his request, each of the brothers dismounted. He continued, "What an outrage you have committed against our realm. You have stolen the silver chalice of our pharaoh, making me appear incompetent in his eyes. I reward you good things, and you treat me and especially our pharaoh with disdain. I suppose that you intend to display the chalice to your associates to prove how vulnerable our land is to thieving shepherds? We must punish the one responsible, and because I don't know what the pharaoh will want to do with the rest of you, all must return to court."

Reuben again motioned for Judah to speak. "Lord High Servant of Mizraim, I am sure that none of us is guilty of this theft. Why can't you inspect our goods here? Then you can let us be on our way after it's proven that we don't have your chalice. I am so sure that none committed this act that I pledged to allow you to put to death whoever did this, and the rest of us will be your servants."

Grudgingly, the steward motioned for his aides to start the search with Reuben's provisions. Joseph had been so generous with the provisions that the inspection seemed to last interminably. When the process reached the provisions of the youngest brother Benjamin, Judah breathed a sigh of relief and signaled to his brothers to prepare to remount. Some had turned their mounts in the direction toward home when the steward almost screamed a deafening order to halt in Judah's ear.

He continued in a calmer voice, "What is this?"

Judah stood with his mouth agape as he looked at the chalice held aloft by the steward. As the realization that the impossible had occurred settled into his mind, he resigned himself and his brothers to a life of servitude. Yet he recalled how only yesterday, he had extolled how they must be blessed because of the promises made by God to Abraham, Isaac, and their father,

Jacob. Maybe God would somehow still rescue them, or maybe they would engender descendants who could later gain their freedom. Nevertheless, there was an even worse problem to solve: Judah had promised the execution of the actual thief. That couldn't be allowed to happen; somehow a way must be found to cause the pharaoh to spare Benjamin's life.

All signaled their surrender by rending their cloaks before turning their mounts toward Egypt. Because they had been intercepted by a rather large contingent of armed men, they quickly concluded that it was futile to fight their way free, especially given their laden animals.

The steward and his troops immediately escorted the brothers before the pharaoh. The steward's pompous accusations had both shocked and cleared Judah's mind. As he spoke, Judah's fear and apprehension waned, allowing ideas for their defense to come to mind. The first thought: *How could the theft of a valuable chalice by a young impressionable lad merit the death penalty?* Then a number of worthy punishments followed in succession. The most desirable punishment would be for them to pay a large fine for the freedom for all. He would even propose that his youngest brother considered the chalice to be a memento of a memorable trip—just compensation for the generous gifts given to the pharaoh. He concluded, however, that such a demand for leniency accompanied by rather implausible excuses would offend the pharaoh, although he sensed a level of compassion unusual in a ruler of this stature. Hence, before the steward finished his condemnation, Judah concluded that he must offer himself up to slavery to save Benjamin's life and gain the freedom of all his brothers.

A prolonged hush followed the steward's blustering. Judah started to speak but decided proper decorum dictated waiting for the pharaoh to ask for a plea. As he and his brothers stood looking at the pharaoh, he thought he saw the pharaoh purse his lips to suppress a smile. *Can anything get any stranger?* he wondered.

Finally, the pharaoh's voice stopped his fidgeting. "This theft grieves me greatly. I deemed you to be nobler than the other shepherds. What have you to say?"

"My Lord Pharaoh, we have no defense for the actions of our youngest brother. While he is sometimes rash and childish, he still knows it is wrong to steal. As you have been tolerant of us in the past, we ask your forbearance by sparing the life of our brother, although I foolishly pledged his death. I could not believe that any of us could or would steal a valuable item from the pharaoh's court. In exchange for Benjamin's life and the freedom of all my brothers, I volunteer to be your slave. Indeed, I deserve this servitude for making such a rash promise as death for a theft."

Judah had scarcely finished his impassioned plea when tears appeared in the pharaoh's eyes. The pharaoh spoke haltingly, "Your servitude won't be required, and none will lose his life. I had my steward put the chalice in Benjamin's provisions. I am your brother Joseph, whom you allowed to be sold into slavery. God has turned your dislike and unseemly act toward me to the advantage of our entire family. I am sure that you were allowed to express your anger toward me in a manner that resulted in my enslavement here in Egypt. Out of enslavement, God directed my actions to allow me to impress my masters. And finally, I was blessed with a promotion to rulership in this land that disdains shepherds like me. These unlikely and even unbelievable events now put me in place to save my entire family from destitution and death."

Even before Joseph had finished his latest discourse, all of the brothers walked backward in fear. Was this some final cruel playacting that would end in their slaughter? Or was this just another prank to torment them?

Joseph smiled and paused, speaking as he tried to think of a way to prove his identity. Not wishing to remind them further of the fateful day of his capture, he began to speak of several childhood pranks made by both him and his brothers. He soon convinced them that he indeed was Joseph.

*   *   *   *   *

The weeping and shouting that followed alerted most of the attendees to court. The lead administrator dispatched the news of the tearful meeting to the lead pharaoh, who happened to be on tour of his realm and close by. Within about a twelfth-day, the supreme ruler appeared at Joseph's house. He alighted from his chariot and raced to greet Joseph and his brothers without formal introduction. "Joseph, so this is your family?" Sensing that the pharaoh wished to continue without interruption, Joseph only nodded. "This occasion would normally call for an extended period of feasting, but my aide tells me that your brothers must return to their home promptly. Given these circumstances, I have ordered my helpers to prepare additional wagons laden with provisions for you. These extra provisions should sustain your flocks until they can be moved to our land. They must leave Canaan if they are to survive."

The brothers bowed and gave their thanks while promising to convey the invitation to their father. The lead pharaoh left as quickly as he had arrived.

*   *   *   *   *

At last Judah could broach the subject of the family moving to Egypt. He looked at Joseph and spoke with frustration in his voice, "How are we to handle this problem? I am certain that our father will *not* want to move to Egypt. How will your superior ruler react? His invitation seemed to be a command."

"You must convince our father to leave home. There will be five more years of this drought. As the pharaoh said, you can't survive where you are. Tell him that I desperately want to see him. As you know, he possessed a special love for me when I was a child. In fact, it was that love that drove you to jealousy toward me. If you tell him that I can't leave Egypt because I am a ruler of the country, I believe that his yearning to see me will make it impossible for him to resist coming here."

SIXTEEN

TO SLAVERY

ECAUSE THE BROTHERS HAD taken longer than expected to return, Jacob became excessively despondent. His close friends and aides almost constantly reminded him that some minor adversity had likely delayed them. They asserted that a band as large as that of the brothers could protect themselves against any likely foes. The advanced news of their arrival improved Jacob's spirit somewhat, but the sight of the many animals laden with provisions caused him to shout for joy.

While Jacob directed the storage and protection of the goods, the brothers whispered among themselves about how to tell their father of Joseph and their invitation to move to Egypt. They again chose Judah to reveal the news.

As the last sack of grain was stowed away, Judah approached his father. "Father, I have more good tidings." He tried to speak calmly, because he wished to reduce the shock of Joseph's being alive. "You may have worried about us because we took so long to complete this trip, but the delay couldn't be avoided. The pharaoh made sport of us by placing his silver chalice in Benjamin's provisions. His steward overtook us and forced us to return to Egypt while making threats of severe punishment. Our fears soon turned to joy, however. After a few dark words from the pharaoh, tears started to flow from his eyes. Father, the next thing that I wish to tell you requires you to be calm."

When Judah paused, Jacob exclaimed, "How can I be calm when I see that you are excited? And how do you expect anyone to be calm by telling them to be?"

Judah breathed a deep sigh before continuing, "You are right. There's no calm way to tell you this, but believe what I say is true, however unbelievable. The pharaoh identified himself as your son and our brother Joseph."

Not unexpectedly, Jacob burst forth with a loud complaint about being tormented again over his terrible loss of the past and expressed disgust over their mentioning Joseph's demise at this difficult time. After letting him rant for a brief time, Judah approached his father and grasped him by the shoulders and shook him. When his father stopped talking, Judah again emphasized that Joseph was alive. He followed with an account of most of the childhood events—a few were still embarrassing to tell—that Joseph recalled. There was no way that anyone but Joseph could have known any of these deeds of youth.

Jacob still wasn't convinced that Joseph was alive. "Please tell me how someone torn by animals as you described could wind up alive in Egypt?"

Judah looked at his brothers and spoke firmly. "You may yet wish to keep Joseph's disappearance secret, but the time has come to let our father know what really happened. As you probably already realize, he expects that Joseph wasn't attacked by an animal."

He then turned to his father and gave him the complete story of everything that had happened with proof of Joseph's abduction by some roving band—a slave-trading band, as they had guessed at the time.

Jacob lost some composure while trying to determine whether he should scold or console his sons. He finally decided to forget their transgression. After all, he had suspected from the beginning something similar to what Judah had just told him. He spoke with a voice still breaking because of joyful emotions. "Judah, I am pleased that you admit your wrongdoings. I also forgive you for all the grief you have given me over the supposed loss of my son. I am so overjoyed from the news about Joseph that I cannot let any negative thoughts diminish my happiness."

Jacob saw Judah's continuing anxiousness and nodded for him to continue. "Joseph told us that God permitted his enslavement to save his family from this current crisis. He asserted several times that we must move to Egypt if we want to survive, because this drought will last for another five years. He had a dream many years ago. The being told him that there would be seven years of plenty followed by seven years of famine. During the seven plenteous years, a vast amount of excess food and feed was stored in government warehouses all over the land. We are now two years into the years of famine. Egypt has the food available for our survival."

As Judah continued, Jacob responded loudly, "All right, I will move to Egypt. I have resisted the idea until now because of a saying presumably uttered by our grandfather Abraham. He is supposed to have said that his descendants would spend over four hundred years of servitude in Egypt. Given that Joseph is a ruler in the land, we should be able to spend a few years there and return after the drought is over. I foresee no likelihood of any indentured service for the present age, at least. Without Joseph to help us, I would fear the move."

Judah gave little thought to the possibility of servitude in Egypt, but he suddenly worried about some of the hardier Amorite warriors usurping the family's land during their absence. Jacob scorned him, "Haven't we chased the Amorites from some of our land already? We may have to hire some mercenaries temporarily when we return, but the necessity of retaking any land will be far easier than surviving this drought. I have trusted Joseph in the past, and I believe he has properly assessed the danger of this drought. Anyway, I must risk some future problems, because I must see my son."

Given the abundant supplies brought back on the past two trips to Egypt, the family was able to plan the move at leisure. Jacob spent several days culling the herds for only the prime breeding stock. Unfortunately, Jacob had built herds of mostly prized animals, and despite warning by his sons to cull even more animals, he kept too many livestock. This error in judgment would later prove disastrous in Egypt.

*   *   *   *   *

After about two weeks, the procession of animals and wagons laden with household goods started the trek toward Egypt. On the morning of the first day, Dan rode up to his half brother Judah to note the irony of everyone's mood. "We thought our father would be hard to convince to make this trip. Now he is the only one wholeheartedly behind it. Perhaps we can yet persuade him to sell some of these herds. It's difficult to believe that the government won't demand a large payment for the necessary feed. Joseph has been generous until now, but I don't trust him to remain so. His acts of torment during our two trips indicate to me that he stills harbors resentment against us. Our father remains unconvinced of his resentment—not only of us but of him also. This trip, which a moon ago seemed so desirable, fills me with apprehension. I just hope that my fears aren't realized."

Judah's first impulse was to reprimand Dan for being so negative, but he returned only a mild suggestion about having a positive attitude. As the significance of Dan's feeling settled into his mind, he, too, became apprehensive about their future. As unofficial spokesman for his brothers, he must find a way to make his father properly evaluate Joseph's deceitfulness, especially if Dan's fears came true. While uttering a sigh, he resolved to see what awaited them in Egypt first. He hoped that Joseph would deal with them justly. Almost certainly any hope of fair dealing from Joseph was vain, but Judah had more immediate concerns. *Today's problems must be considered before tomorrow's.*

The jubilation expressed by Jacob increased daily until the sight of a large escort procession at the border of Egypt caused a level of exultation never before seen by his sons. The entire entourage of people, animals, and laden wagons were motioned across the border without stopping for inspection. When some of the spirited goats butted over a guard station, hilarious laughter erupted.

Joseph's head steward rode up to Jacob once the procession had stabilized into an orderly and nondestructive flow. "Let me welcome you to Mizraim in the name of our assistant pharaoh and your son Joseph. We will take you directly to his house. After you have had time to enjoy a reunion with the son whom you feared dead, the head pharaoh of our land will give you an official state welcome."

Jacob and Benjamin were escorted to Joseph's quarters while the rest of the family settled into temporary guest rooms.

*   *   *   *   *

When Jacob entered the spacious living room where Joseph sat to greet him, he almost fainted. Unlike his sons, who had not been able to identify Joseph in his Egyptian garb, Jacob recognized him at once. Jacob could barely resist the urge to run and hug his long-lost son, but his sense of decorum prevailed over his emotions.

After an awkward pause during which neither father nor son knew what to do, Joseph ran to his father and gave him an extended hug before speaking. "Father, how I have longed to see you since my brothers first arrived. The awful events following my capture removed any hope of ever seeing you again. Even my rise from prisoner to pharaoh failed to revive any hope of seeing you again. Then, out of distress of drought, a seeming miracle occurred: my brothers came to Mizraim. Please forgive me if the making sport of my brothers along with the request to bring Benjamin here caused you any grief."

Jacob immediately extended his forgiveness, but he felt a twinge of disappointment when Joseph offered no reason for his actions. The hurt feeling soon passed as they continued the conversation. They talked well into the night before retiring with a promise for a week of festivities.

As the days of feasting neared an end, Joseph sent a request to the head pharaoh to make an official invitation to his family. He also called a meeting with his father and his four oldest brothers on the post meridian of the day before the audience with the pharaoh.

Feeling a renewed familiarity with his son, Jacob spoke first. "Why are we meeting now? Your steward told us that we would meet the head pharaoh tomorrow. Have we done something to offend you or some official?"

Joseph's smile seemed forced as he spoke. "No, but I feel that this meeting was needful to remind you of what to say to our supreme ruler. I don't wish for him to get a wrong impression of you. Above all, you mustn't try to hide the fact that you are shepherds. To do otherwise would only bring you distress one way or another. Because you are my father and brothers, all rulers in the land, including the supreme ruler, will esteem you well. Also, shepherds are allowed to stay in the land of Goshen, which is the most fertile and enjoyable place to live in Mizraim. I know that the pest problem can be annoying there, but the other benefits are worth it."

When Joseph added no further instructions, Jacob replied almost petulantly, "You called us here just to remind us about who we are? Do you think us to be too simple to comport ourselves well in front of the pharaoh? Aren't there some more obscure ritual procedures that you need to tell us to observe?"

Joseph shrugged as he answered, "Just act politely, as you have done with all the other officials so far. I called you here because I wanted to make certain that you understand the gravity of having an audience with the supreme ruler of this land. Now I am certain that you understand how to act and what to say, I have no further instructions. I do want to tell you, however, that the five of you will represent the entire family before the pharaoh. The supreme ruler doesn't usually like to address a large number of people, so only you five have been chosen to meet with him."

*   *   *   *   *

As Jacob left the meeting with the supreme ruler, he spoke to his sons. "I feel so relieved. I not only have all my children back, but we have a prosperous place in which to reside. At last I can end my life in peace, knowing that my family is in the care of a ruler of a prosperous land—a ruler who is my son."

Those words sent a shudder through Judah, who looked at his brother Dan and shook his head. Over the next several days, neither Judah nor Dan could convince any of the other brothers to confront the blind faith that their father had in Joseph. To Judah's surprise, the first payment for food and fodder seemed reasonable. Assuming the prices didn't increase substantially, they should be able to end the remaining five years of drought with adequate resources to support a large family back in Canaan. They wouldn't be wealthy, but they would still have enough animals and exchange metals to rebuild their wealth.

The days of inflation arrived with the second purchase of goods. The price for the same provisions jumped by twenty percent. When Jacob authorized the payment without the slightest concern, Judah could hardly suppress a complaint, but he decided to wait for one more round of purchase before accosting his father.

Yet another price hike with the next purchase caused Judah and Dan to beg their father to petition for redress to a higher court for easement. When Jacob refused to act, Dan scolded his brothers, "You are wiling to allow this usury to continue. Persistent rumors abound even here in Goshen that the stores held by the government are more than adequate to last. Rumors also claim that the high prices are nothing more than a ruse to make all citizens of the land poor and dependent on the government for sustenance. The fear of universal slavery is felt by nearly everyone but the corrupt priests who use religion as an excuse for their luxurious—and some say licentious—life. I can almost assure you that slavery awaits us as shepherds, if it awaits most of the other citizenry. We can*not* continue to obtain the same prices for our exchange goods and pay these prices for our provisions without depleting our coffers and flocks. Our wealth will never last until the end of the drought."

Dan's pleading failed to persuade his brothers, except Judah. Out of frustration, he and Judah decided to let the situation continue until their resources declined to a point where their father would surely respond.

*   *   *   *   *

Over the following two years, an alarming number of Egyptians spent their possessions, had to sell their land to the pharaoh, and became sharecroppers on the land that their families had owned for generations. These events finally alarmed Jacob, causing him to petition his son Joseph, whom he had seldom seen since the early days of their residence, for redress. In keeping with his neglect of his family, Joseph refused to see his father for almost three moons.

The long-awaited opportunity to see and talk to his son momentarily removed worry and concern from Jacob's mind. He nervously waited for the introductions to end before he was given a chance to speak. Addressing his son formally, he pleaded, "Lord Pharaoh, I earnestly request that the prices for provisions be reduced. We produce considerably more goods than we need for family use. The high prices and low credit for our substantial goods threaten to deplete completely the wealth with which we entered Mizraim.

You have ample stores; in fact, it's reported that your bins have increased in the past two years except for fodder and grain, and even those items are in ample supply to last the rest of the drought. Surely, you wish for us to have adequate animals to return to Canaan when the drought is over." Jacob could barely suppress the urge to declare that if they became indigent, they would have to stay in Goshen, thereby making the rulers of the land deal with even more hated shepherds.

Joseph smiled and addressed his father familiarly. "My dear father, I am sorry your resources have declined. I am, however, unable to reduce your payments. The price for commodities is approved by a committee chosen by the Lord High Overseer; I have no authority to change those prices. Nevertheless, you shouldn't despair; even if you become sharecroppers, the fertile land of Goshen will allow you to prosper above the pharaoh's charge for usage of his land. Father, you should recover enough wealth soon enough to see your homeland again."

*   *   *   *   *

When Jacob told his sons of Joseph's denial of cheaper provisions, most of his sons applauded the statement about being able to recover their wealth—except Dan, who despaired over the verdict. In his powerlessness to change his family's descent into poverty, Dan became more and more despondent during the following days until he became almost mechanical in his movements. After several weeks, Judah concluded that more was bothering his brother than the frustration that he himself felt; it was time to find what was causing Dan's gloomy countenance.

At the next opportunity to speak to Dan alone, Judah asked, "Why are you moping? I know the rest of us were disappointed in the response from Joseph, but you must take a brighter approach. It's truly sad that we will become wards of Egypt, but the years of drought have made nearly everyone poor. Sadly, it has even caused the loss of many lives. At least we will live and be able to recover—indeed, even prosper again."

Dan had often replied with sarcastic laughter to comments and questions from his brothers, but the laughter seemed quite sinister this time. An appeal for an oral response drew only another smirk.

Undaunted, Judah persisted until Dan burst forth with vitriol: "I am too sick to abide the stupidity of my family. How can we resign ourselves to becoming paupers? Once we do, there will be no escaping Egypt. Our father has sold all of his children, maybe for generations, into slavery. This avowed generosity from the pharaoh is false. This government is oppressing its people with usury in bad times; it will never relinquish its yoke in good times. After some number of decades, the populace will grow to accept slavery as a way of life. Oh, where is the promise of greatness for this family?"

Judah looked at Dan with feigned disdain. He didn't want to believe what he had just heard, but suddenly everything that Dan said made sense. Still unwilling to accept the blunt truth, he scolded Dan, "Where is your faith? The God of our fathers has preserved us with our lives and blessed us with the lifting of Joseph to rulership in the only country that could spare our lives."

Dan shouted back, "You wonder why I am despondent? I am despondent because the only ally—you—that I had has been deluded by the master liar, Joseph. I will grant you that he is more sophisticated than any tyrant I have ever heard of. Most of his actions as a young man caused our gullible father to believe he was just and pure. Then we meet him in this depressing land under dire circumstances, and he is still the same Joseph we knew many years ago. Our forefathers tried to dispel tyrants and their tyranny from the world only to produce a tyrant within their own descendants."

With these words, Judah signaled his acceptance of Dan's lament by hugging him tightly. As he released his grasp, Judah tried to console Dan. "There's another reason that I have seemingly accepted our plight, and it doesn't involve faith. You have heard the folklore that our forefather Abraham's descendants through our grandfather and father will someday spend over four hundred years as slaves in Egypt. None of us believed those years would start now. I suspect that we two are the only ones who fear that they are just about to begin." Judah closed his comments with a sardonic statement. "As our father says, how could we be in trouble when we have such a righteous benefactor as our brother Joseph?"

Neither Dan nor Judah spoke further for almost a twelfth-day as each looked out over their dwindling flocks. In another setting and time, the scenery would have been pleasing to almost any shepherd, but the knowledge of where they were and where they were going drove any pleasantness from view.

*　　*　　*　　*　　*

As the moons passed, Jacob would gain frequent audiences with his son Joseph. He would leave for the meetings in a rather blue mood, but he always returned in good spirits.

A constant string of promises came from these meetings, but Judah had now given up any hope of saving his family from slavery. By the end of the drought, the family had meager amounts of exchange metals and barely enough animals to sustain their lives. Abraham's large estate had disappeared.

Just two days before the seventh anniversary of the first signs of drought, flooding rains occurred over the northern portions of Egypt, and within weeks, the Nile turned from a nearly dry wadi to a daily increased flow. The land was once again being restored by rains in both upper and lower Egypt.

The rejoicing over the return to bountiful harvests soon turned to subdued gloom. The government started to restrict the amount of land each farmer could manage. This action, along with offers for better working conditions on construction projects, led many farmers to abandon their way of making their living from the land to live in government housing at construction sites. As a result, the remaining farmers could produce barely enough food to satisfy the needs of the populace. As the old stores finally depleted and the government demanded large amounts of food for its workers, Jacob's family and the other farmers failed to prosper.

*   *   *   *   *

As the years passed, Jacob's health started to wane. During one sick spell, he called Judah and Dan to his bedside. When his sons suggested various things they could do for him, he spoke in a surprisingly strong voice. "Stop! The physician is attending to my needs quite well. He is also certain that this is just another spell that will pass; my end is not yet. I wish, however, to permanently relinquish some of my daily activities. I hate to become, in effect, a burden to my family, but the physician says that I must."

Judah interrupted. "Father, all of your children know that it's time for you to rest. You shouldn't speak so foolishly." Judah had chosen his words carefully. He didn't wish to disrespect his father, but he also felt that his father could have helped them avoid the significant poverty they now faced.

His father must have sensed the dilemma being experienced by his two sons. He looked down while addressing them. "The two of you were the only ones to warn me of what would happen to us. To my great shame, I placed an undoubting trust in Joseph. I have only recently come to understand what caused you to put him in that pit. You did wrong, but his cleverly disguised contempt for the rest of his brothers, especially those of my concubines, was wrong also. There is no foreseeable way that this family will ever escape Egypt. I can hardly abide the fact that I have lost the great wealth our grandfather Abraham built for us, and that I am the one who led his descendants into slavery. Amid all of this woe, yet another irony stands out: while my family was looking elsewhere to thwart tyrants, one of our own lineage managed to become a tyrant in an enemy land."

Dan had been experiencing a confusing array of emotions. He was grateful that his father at last understood the devious nature of Joseph. Yet he could scarcely forgive him for his blindness to Joseph's motives, both during his youth and in recent years. It seemed as if his father had been willingly ignorant of Joseph's nature and had exalted him regardless of the facts of his actions. By the time that Judah had finished his talk, an acceptance of his father's remorse filled Dan. Other than also admonishing his father to rest, he added nothing to the conversation.

Upon the two brothers' telling their father that they should go, he called to them to wait. "There's one more thing that I must mention. Although I am confident I will arise from this bed, I am also certain that my remaining years are few. I have been promised by God that I will know the time when I must give my final instructions to my children. I will call all of you together for my final words. Some of those words will sound harsh to a few, and it may perplex you that Joseph will get by far the largest share of my blessing. I will not do this out of favoritism to him, but because I have been instructed by God to do this. I don't completely understand God's plan for this blessing, but I can only guess that the reason has something to do with the great abilities possessed by Joseph. I also admit that I favored him much more than my other sons, because I saw in him an ability to accomplish."

Jacob tired from speaking and stopped talking. Both Dan's anger and curiosity became aroused. "But why did you have to favor him if his abilities were so great? Couldn't he accomplish his deeds on his own? Your extra help should not have been needed."

Jacob seemed to be deep in thought as he spoke. "I feel that God sees in Joseph a man who will engender children who will someday be leaders in a government that will permit God's word to flourish. Joseph's tendency toward control of people, which you view as tyranny, does allow them to have free will in their individual lives. True, he has taken our wealth, but we still have our own lives much as before. He is a tool for God, although we and others may chafe under his rulership."

Judah turned to voice a parting consideration. "Father, your children, including myself, have done much to aggrieve you, and I am sure God also. I more than my brothers have seen the error of my rebellious ways. Perhaps God has sent this bondage, as I view it, upon us to teach us a lesson. Assuming that you are right, and I do, I am most happy that some of my future descendants will have a chance to live free."

Jacob nodded and said, "Judah, you are the only child who seems to understand the true will of God. As such, you will get a special blessing that in some ways is superior to Joseph's."

After they were out their father's earshot, Dan began to grumble again. Judah, however, felt a peace of mind that he didn't want distracted by any talk, negative or not. Therefore, he waved to his brother and walked away without another word. All that had happened in his life—his youthful rebellion in leaving home; his loss of two evil sons; his promiscuity; his arrogance toward the prostitute Tamar, who bore his twins; and his loss of wealth—were no longer a factor in his life. He must now live an exemplary life while helping Tamar's sons to pass on descendants that would one day do God's will. Their plight in Egypt must be borne.

*   *   *   *   *

As Jacob had predicted, a feebleness that signaled his imminent death overtook him within a short time. He immediately sent word to Joseph's court with a request for a final audience. At first Joseph was dismissive of the need to see his father, but the grave expression on the messenger's face convinced him that he must let the affairs of state wait until he had seen his father.

He hastened to his father's bedside, taking his two sons along for their first visit with their grandfather. After a brief conversation about the past, Jacob motioned to speak. "I must ask you to listen to me, for I don't have much time left. Your brothers will be here soon, but I wanted to talk to you before they arrived. I don't want you to be surprised by the blessing I will give to you. God has chosen to bless your descendants materially far beyond that of your brothers. I can't understand why, but you should be grateful that he has chosen to bless them so abundantly. This blessing should be an incentive for you and your sons to worship the true God."

The mention of his sons reminded Joseph to introduce his sons to their grandfather. Joseph was almost startled when his father extended his arms to bless his sons instead of him. Also, when Jacob crossed his arms to place his right hand on the younger son, Ephraim, Joseph grasped his arms to switch them, but before he could move them, Jacob complained, while insisting that the older son, Manasseh, would indeed receive a great blessing, but the younger would receive an even greater one.

Jacob seemed to sense that Joseph still didn't comprehend the significance of the blessings. Upon finishing the blessing of his grandchildren, Jacob admonished, "Son, don't doubt my word; the descendants of your sons will surely leave this land and dwell in Canaan at some far future date."

By the time all of his sons had gathered by his bedside, Jacob had become quite weak. As they all stood in hushed quiet, he began his final instructions. "Please listen carefully, for I am near death, and I must tell each of you what awaits your descendants. You must accept these words, because they come from God. I assure you I didn't choose these words, but God did."

All through Jacob's discourse, the twelve brothers maintained a stoic look, even when he pronounced a much greater blessing on Joseph. Whether from being inured by recent adversities, or out of reverence for their father, none complained. Even the youngest, Benjamin, whose blessing seemed to be nothing more than a harsh afterthought, showed no contention.

Giving the brothers scarce time to contemplate what he had just said, Jacob made an effort to rise and speak passionately to evoke a promise to take his remains back to Machpelah for burial with his wife Leah and his forebearers, Abraham, Sarah, Isaac, and Rebekah.

A unanimous reply had barely been given when Jacob slumped back into bed and drifted off to sleep—a sleep from which he would not awaken.

*   *   *   *   *

Shortly after sunset, the attending physician thought he saw a heaving of Jacob's chest as he breathed his last breath. The physician turned to the assisting nurse to comment about the history of this family. He lingered on how it had been both a tragedy and an irony that Jacob died in a land that he hated.

*   *   *   *   *

The physician summoned the embalmers after extensive tests for death. When Judah saw their approach, he furtively looked for Joseph, who had departed. Judah then quickly turned to plead with the embalmers to leave the body intact and only apply spices until he could talk to Joseph.

After several entreaties, the lead embalmer told Judah to cease speaking. Pharaoh Joseph had given specific instructions that their father must receive embalming rites. He must be transported back to Canaan within three moons. Only embalming methods would preserve his body for the trip. The lead embalmer apologized for his inability to fulfill Judah's wishes.

Judah promptly left to accost his brothers and ask them to help him search for Joseph, hoping to persuade him to change his embalming command. None of the brothers, however, would accompany him on the search.

The forty-day period of embalming rituals caused more sadness from the brothers' having to accept the desecration of their father's body than did his death. The forty days were immediately followed by thirty days of formal mourning.

On the morning following the ten-week ordeal, the eleven brothers were told that Joseph had received permission to move their father's body to Canaan. Judah breathed a sigh of relief at the news. "Some may not agree, but it is good that we can finally move our father's body from this land." All adults and teenagers rapidly prepared for the trip. Only the young children were left with servants.

The day of departure brought irritating news. The provision leader took one look at the procession and informed the eleven brothers that their packed provisions could prove to be inadequate for the round-trip. Judah looked puzzled as he replied, "The distance to Machpelah isn't that far. Grazing should be good for our mounts, and we have ample dried foods for the few days involved with the trip."

The provision leader wondered why they hadn't been told that the trip would be much longer, because citizens of Mizraim avoided travel through Canaan. Pharaoh Joseph didn't want the mutual disdain felt between citizens of Mizraim and Canaanites to mar the solemn ritual of their father's burial. Hence, the trip would take them beyond Jordan to an oasis east of Jericho, from where the family must proceed to Machpelah. Their escorts would wait there for their return from the burial rites. Also, Pharaoh Joseph had requested an extended mourning period at the oasis after the burial.

*   *   *   *   *

Within a twelfth-day of encampment at the oasis, Joseph emerged from his tent. The captain of the guard stood aghast before asking him why he was dressed in shepherd's clothing.

"Captain, I must attend my father's burial, and it would be unsafe for me to dress as an official of Mizraim in Canaan."

The captain expressed concern whether it was safe for Joseph to enter Canaan even in disguise. He should let his brothers conduct the burial while he mourned there with them.

"Captain, I will be safe! Mourning, I will do after I have buried my father."

Before the burial procession had finished crossing the Jordan, Joseph's steward scolded the guard captain, wondering why he was allowing their lord to cross the river. Should evil befall him, they would lose their positions, if not their lives.

The captain explained to him that the pharaoh couldn't be dissuaded by any means appropriate for a person of his rank. The captain was confident that he could defend his conduct to their overlords. Besides, the pharaoh was well disguised, and the captain was sure that a burial procession for the noble Jacob wouldn't be bothered by the Canaanites.

The steward was more concerned about what Joseph's brothers might do to him than the Canaanites. The captain probably hadn't heard about some of the ill feelings that some of his brothers had toward the pharaoh, the steward explained. They left him in an animal pit during his youth. This trip again gave them an opportunity to kill him. He wouldn't have any slave traders to rescue him this time.

The captain respectfully disagreed. He pointed out that the brothers' young children were still in Mizraim. Assuredly, they wouldn't act untowardly because of concern for the safety of the children.

*   *   *   *   *

As Jacob's body was placed next to that of his mother, a daughter of Levi sang a lament for her departed grandfather. At the sealing of the tomb, Joseph addressed his brethren, "My compatriots wish to commemorate the passing of our father and grandfather. Let us return to our camp for a period of mourning."

The mourning rituals became a spectacle accompanied with the wailing of professional Egyptian mourners. The sound of their cries drew the attention of the residents for long distances from the oasis. Many of the Canaanites passed by to view the activities, but none crossed the Jordan to interfere in any way. A local chieftain was so impressed, however, that he named the oasis Abel-Mizraim—that is, mourning of the Egyptians.

On the morning before the crossing into Egypt, Judah and Dan met for one last look toward the land of Canaan. Both remarked on how a calm and peaceful acceptance of their fate had settled over all of the family. A healthy resolve to live their lives as well as possible had replaced all recriminations and remorse over what might have been.

That evening, as they crossed the border, Dan rode to the end of the procession and dismounted before bowing on one knee and giving a farewell salute to the land of his youth.